The Mountain

ALSO BY HELEN BRYAN

The Valley
The Sisterhood
War Brides
Martha Washington: First Lady of Liberty
Planning Applications and Appeals

The Mountain

Book Two of the Valley Trilogy

HELEN BRYAN

Published by Lake Union Publishing, Seattle

www.apub.com

Amazon, the Amazon logo, and Lake Union Publishing are trademarks of Amazon.com, Inc., or its affiliates.

ISBN-13: 9781503941045
ISBN-10: 1503941043

Cover design by Shasti O'Leary Soudant

Printed in the United States of America

For my grandchildren, Bo Hackworthy Bates
Bryan-Low, Poppy Anne Helen Bryan-Low, Jake Leo
Orlando Horsman, and Heath Rudy Otto Horsman
For their parents, Michelle Hackworthy and Niels
Bryan-Low and Cassell Bryan-Low and
Jonathan Horsman
And for my husband, Roger Low, always

PROLOGUE

The Chiaramonte homestead, June 1783

Stefania Albanisi opened her eyes and saw the morning star shining through a large gap between the logs. The chinking had come away in many places, and it was always chilly early in the morning, even in summer. Drowsily, she hugged her quilt over her shoulders, prolonging the moment before she had to get up and start her morning chores. Suddenly she remembered what day it was and sat up, rubbing her eyes. Her friend Magdalena de Marechal was getting married. She had to hurry—Peach Hanover and Little Molly Drumheller would be waiting. The three of them were going up to Wildwood, to help prepare for the wedding.

There'd be breakfast first, Magdalena had promised. Stefania and her mother usually had only a bite of cold corn pone and some sumac tea in the mornings, but at Wildwood, breakfast meant bacon and coffee, perhaps even pie. Stefania was almost always hungry, and at the moment the prospect of breakfast was more exciting than her friend's wedding or the fact that she had a new gown for the first time in her life.

She threw back her quilt and rose from the corn-husk mattress. She splashed cold water from a bucket into a cracked basin and washed her face, then pulled on her patched homespun dress. She gave it a tug—she'd grown much taller in the months since she turned thirteen, and her dress felt shorter by the day. Hastily she braided her hair into a single pigtail down her back and, barefoot, slipped out of the cabin.

She dragged open the sagging door of the small barn and milked the two old cows. They didn't give much. Then she hurried the cows out to the small fenced-off pasture to graze. The cows lowed in protest at being driven outside so early. In the next field, horses whinnied and came toward the fence.

Unbolting the door to the chicken house, she wrinkled her nose at the smell—it needed cleaning. She'd do it tomorrow. Hens penned up since nightfall for safety against foxes and mountain lions came out clucking, while the rooster flapped his wings and crowed halfheartedly. They pecked around her bare feet for stray grains as she filled a bucket from the nearly empty corncrib for the horses—poor horses, they looked skinny. The field wasn't really big enough to allow them as much grass as they needed, but she and her mother had to eke out the corn until they could harvest the crop in their small cornfield.

She sympathized with the hungry animals. Her own middle felt hollow. She patted her stomach as if to reassure it. There'd be breakfast up at Wildwood, then wedding food later. *Syllabub and cake,* she thought greedily. *And perhaps Magdalena's sister Kitty will make a trifle.*

She searched for eggs, happy to find half a dozen. She took them in with the milk and found her mother awake and a pot of tea waiting on the hearth. Rosalia was sewing, trimming her least shabby gown with scraps of fabric too small to work into a quilt. She'd fashioned them into tiny flowers and was now stitching them onto the bodice. "This will do for the wedding, won't it?" Rosalia held the gown up and considered it hopefully. Just thirty years old and having borne but one child, she looked much younger than most of the women in Grafton.

She'd kept her good looks, her graceful walk, a full head of dark hair, and nearly all her teeth, though closer inspection revealed the fine lines care had worn in her pretty face. She did her best, but she hadn't been raised to manage a homestead, and it was a daily struggle to maintain the dilapidated smallholding, upon which she'd grandly bestowed the only legacy of her aristocratic Sicilian family, their distinctive name, Chiaramonte. It was difficult to prioritize the most urgent tasks when practically everything that needed doing was pressing. Still, hardship had not extinguished her capacity for moments of joy, and the prospect of a wedding lifted her heart. She was fond of Magdalena, and above all it promised to be a happy day for Stefania.

"Is that your old black gown? How pretty it looks now, Mother!" Stefania exclaimed.

Rosalia smiled with pleasure at her handiwork. "Thank you, *cara*." She hugged Stefania. "You should go. I'll finish your chores and come along later. They'll have a great deal to do at Wildwood. Mind you have a wash before you put on your new dress."

"I will!" Stefania cried happily. She kissed her mother and ran down to the river. Her bare feet squished in the mud on the riverbank, causing a frog to croak and leap out of her way. She reached the post where three canoes, one half-sunk, were tied up, gently bumping into each other. She left the best canoe, the one that didn't leak, for her mother and untied the third. A little water sloshed in its bottom as she crouched, grabbing the gunwales, and her long legs quickly launched her into the middle so the canoe barely rocked with her weight. She used her paddle to push away from the bank and out onto the Bowjay River's deceptively glassy surface. Shivering slightly, she swung the canoe in the direction of the trading-post jetty on the opposite bank, feeling the pull of the current grow stronger.

At first the only sound was the quiet swish of her paddle, dipping in and out of the water. By the middle of the river, she could hear the rhythmic sound of the mill wheel turning behind the trading post. Here and there a rooster crowed up and down the valley, and as she pulled closer to the jetty, the sun was turning the east sky pink beyond Frog Mountain. She caught a whiff of wood smoke on the morning air as people in the homesteads fanned up the fires they'd banked overnight.

As she drew closer to the trading-post landing, Peach and Little Molly walked out onto the jetty, calling their hellos and waving. Stefania used her paddle to swing the bow around next to the jetty post. Peach caught the rope Stefania threw her and tied up the canoe as Stefania clambered up the ladder.

"Look, Stefania! Our gowns!" cried Little Molly joyfully, her arms full of frothy printed muslin. They had new dresses because they were to "stand up" with fourteen-year-old Magdalena when she married Robert Walker, just as they'd stood up with fourteen-year-old Annie Vann on Twelfth Night, five months earlier, when she'd married Magdalena's older brother George. The three of them had worn their everyday patched homespun without a second thought then. Only Annie, the bride, had had a new dress, and it was the one her mother had made her to wear for the Blackberry Picnic that autumn when she and George became engaged, and Magdalena had been forced by her older sister Kitty into one of Kitty's dresses that was too big for Magdalena and had to be hastily stitched in round the middle. Stefania hadn't been so tall then and hadn't minded whether she looked shabby or not.

But Annie's mother, Caitlin, claimed she'd been the matchmaker, because Magdalena had met Robert Walker under her roof. Caitlin had approved and even urged Magdalena to marry him. Once the wedding was decided upon, Caitlin declared she would make new dresses for Magdalena's friends to stand up with her when she got married. Knowing Rosalia would reject any offer of charity, Caitlin told the three girls to select material from the bolts of fabric at the trading post. During the agonizing process of choosing, each girl changed her mind several times before a final selection was made. Caitlin had promptly begun cutting and basting and pinning. By the time Rosalia had learned of

Caitlin's intention, Stefania's new dress was half-made and even Rosalia couldn't refuse it, much to Stefania's relief. She'd never had a new dress before and thought about hers every night before she went to sleep.

So Stefania was almost breathless with pleasure as Peach laid the finished dress across her outstretched arm and then took her own from Little Molly. They held their dresses up and admired each other's choice, each privately thinking hers the loveliest. Peach had a sprightly lavender-and-green flowered muslin because her black skin could carry off bright colors. Little Molly had chosen blue-and-white striped cotton that set off her blue eyes and fair coloring. Stefania, after agonizing deliberations, had chosen the pink flowery muslin the others insisted became her olive complexion and dark hair.

"And there's another surprise. Look! Aunt Caitlin gave us these." Peach distributed three snowy-white muslin kerchiefs they hadn't noticed at first.

"Ruffles! Look, on the trim!" exclaimed Little Molly. "Ruffles!"

"How fine we'll be!" Stefania whispered.

"Hold everything up so it doesn't get wet!" ordered Peach.

The long grass in the orchard was still wet with dew, and they held their new clothes high and skirted the cemetery on the lower slope of Frog Mountain, chatting like magpies about whether Magdalena ought to put her hair in curl papers like Annie had before her wedding and how marriage would transform Magdalena into a housewife. Magdalena was careless, even slovenly by nature, famous for leaving her chores half-done to wander off and fish or hunt for birds' nests or follow bees to see if they were swarming near a hollow tree.

"When she married she can't go off climbin' trees and fishin' and wanderin' off the ways she likes to do," said Peach. "Mama says a man spects his wife to tend to the house, tend to his dinner."

"Tend to the children too. She'll have babies," said Little Molly knowingly.

Stefania was so caught up in the excitement of her friend getting married and her new dress that she hadn't given much thought to what came after. She tried to imagine Magdalena in an apron going about her housework with children underfoot. It didn't seem at all like Magdalena. Her enthusiasm for the wedding dampened slightly.

Not long ago Stefania, Peach, Little Molly, Magdalena, and Annie had been inseparable, despite the difference in their ages. Peach, as the eldest, was the bossiest, the effect of growing up with five robust older sisters and an outspoken mother. Neat, efficient Annie took after her Welsh mother, Caitlin, and could be counted on to deal calmly with emergencies like wasp stings and always carried a handkerchief and snakeroot in her pocket as an antidote, because rattlesnakes and copper snakes were everywhere. Magdalena, who people said was the image of her dead mother, Sophia, was acknowledged to be the prettiest. She had large brown eyes, a tumbling mass of brown curls, her mother's fine features and graceful, slender figure, and a sweet nature. Until Robert came, she hadn't bothered at all about her appearance. She'd rarely combed or braided her tangled hair or washed her face, and she preferred George's cast-off breeches and shirts to dresses. Caitlin once laughingly asked her if she'd put on her clothes with a pitchfork. It exasperated her elder sister Kitty.

Little Molly was pretty too but so willful and clever and curious about everything that as soon as she opened her mouth, people noticed that more than her looks. "Sharp as a new knife," according to her proud grandfather Rufus. She avoided household chores when she could, not because she was lazy, like Magdalena, but because they bored her. Little Molly had learned to read at an early age, had read every book in Grafton, including Caitlin Vann's Bible, and could figure sums faster than her grandfather. This tickled Rufus, who swore she took after him and spoiled her to the extent that he'd indulged her wish to have a "school." He'd built an additional room on the back of Little Molly's parents' cabin, where she could teach her younger brothers and sisters.

Since the days when Sophia de Marechal had ceased to teach the children of Grafton in her kitchen, after her favorite child was kidnapped by Indians, there'd been no school. Children were taught at home by their mothers when the mothers could find the time, or not at all, so it wasn't long before other Grafton parents inquired if their own children could attend Little Molly's school. Rufus, never one to miss an opportunity for profitable enterprise, had been quick to agree and negotiate payment in chickens, hams, and vegetables for Little Molly's teaching.

Stefania was the poorest of the girls, but she had an interesting and exotic mother from Sicily who was kind and pretty and could sometimes be persuaded to perform Gypsy dances for them or make delicious little Sicilian cakes from nuts or wild grapes and honey, if she happened to have any.

The five girls had shared their first lessons at each other's kitchen tables, stitched samplers together, helped each find livestock that had wandered off, played games, shared sorghum candy when they were lucky enough to have some, stood together against the boys' teasing at Blackberry Picnics, and attended midweek hymn singings at Brother Merriman's church, where they whispered secrets between hymns and got the giggles mimicking Mattie Merriman's facial expressions as she led the singing.

But first Peach, then Annie had developed a "shape" under their dresses and aprons. Annie became particular about washing her face and hair in rainwater, to the scorn of Magdalena, who barely washed at all, and Peach persuaded her mother to make up some sweet oil scented with flowers, which she and Annie rubbed on their hands. Peach paired off with Bryn Vann while George de Marechal continued to tease Annie as he'd always done; he also never left her side if he could help it. Stefania was astonished to see Annie look down shyly and blush in George's company.

"Why is she doing that!" she demanded of Peach. "It's silly! It's only George! Last summer she pushed him in the river because he said he'd kiss her whether she wanted him to or not. Now she's doing this!" Stefania made a face, crossing her eyes and batting her eyelids in imitation of Annie.

"Something's afoot between them," said Peach in the superior, knowingly older-girl kind of voice she had begun to use more and more often. Stefania hated that voice because it made it clear Peach knew something Stefania didn't. "What?" Stefania had demanded, but got no answer.

Caitlin had made Annie a new dress for the last Blackberry Picnic. Annie had spent a long time putting up her hair with the help of a paper of hairpins from the trading post, and by the time she was dressed, Annie had looked different and older. She'd walked sedately up the path to the clearing on Frog Mountain where the picnic was held, instead of scampering over the rocks and boulders as she usually did, and spent the picnic talking with George and surreptitiously holding his hand instead of picking berries or playing games. As the picnic ended, Gideon Vann had announced Annie and George were getting married.

Once married and living at Wildwood, Annie had become very much like her mother, Caitlin, passing her days in a flurry of domestic activity, churning and washing and scrubbing and baking. Her father-in-law, Henri, was fond of her and gave her a free hand, and Magdalena, who wasn't at all proprietorial about her home and was lackadaisical about housekeeping herself, had been happy to let Annie do whatever she liked. Annie reveled in the importance of being in charge of the large cabin at Wildwood.

Magdalena, however, had been quickly disabused of the notion it would be fun to have her friend living in the same house. Though she was only a few months older than Magdalena, once in command, Annie began to give orders, insisting Magdalena do her share of chores and do them right. Annie and Magdalena were often out of sorts with each other now.

"Tell you a secret," said Peach, "Annie's expecting a baby. Mama told me."

Stefania sighed. Worse and worse. Of course marriage meant babies. She'd helped with mares foaling, and like all country children, she'd learned how animals reproduced, but she'd gleaned there was more to having babies than that. It required a girl and a man "liking" each other in a way that Stefania didn't understand but Peach and Little Molly seemed to, because they irritated her by hinting and giggling about it incessantly. As if they knew a secret she didn't.

"Why do people always act like a baby coming's good news? Birthing hurts, and you bleed, and the mothers and babies die sometimes" was Little Molly's response to the news.

Peach nodded. Two of Peach's older sisters had both been so ill after having babies that their mother, Venus, feared they'd die. "Nearly bled to death," a subdued Peach had said. Peach had passed on the graphic details of the births, which she knew because her mother and Annie's mother, Caitlin, were usually the ones called to help when a baby was coming to any household in the valley.

And all the children knew it wasn't unusual for a flatboat to pull in to Grafton with the body of a woman who'd died giving birth on the journey, and often the body of her infant as well because there'd been no one to feed it. Husbands and families tried to carry the bodies, if they could, as far as Grafton so they could have a decent Christian burial in the cemetery below the orchard, with a psalm read and a prayer said over them by Brother Merriman and a grave marker placed. Fathers of these bereaved traveling families would tell their sad-eyed children that Mother—and maybe the little brother or sister—was safe now, in the company of the other women and babies buried there.

The three girls thought of this as they skirted the part of the cemetery where these women were buried. There were stones carved with a woman's name and dates of her life, sometimes a Bible verse or a "Rest in Jesus." There was one that just said, in uneven letters, "Lizbeth an hir babby," as well as the nameless graves marked only by a wooden cross, or even two crosses, one large and one small. These crosses grew weathered, then leaned until they fell over. A few graves were marked only by stones laid in a rectangle.

"I'm glad I'm not Magdalena. I don't want to get married and work like Annie all day and have babies," Little Molly whispered to Stefania. "I'd rather have a school. A big one, with lots of books I can read any time I want without bothering about chores. Where I'd be in charge and everyone had to do what I say."

"Don't you wish Robert had gone to Kentuckee some other way?" asked Stefania. "I do. If he had, Magdalena wouldn't have met him."

"But he didn't and she did," sighed Little Molly.

Little Molly, Stefania, and Peach stopped by a low stone wall that had been begun and then forgotten about long ago and separated the orchard from the cemetery below it. It was overgrown with honeysuckle in bloom, and whenever they passed it they could never resist pausing to pick a few blossoms to suck the sweetness out of the ends. They talked about how Magdalena had decided to marry Robert. Peach thought it was sweet, and Little Molly was skeptical. How could you know that fast if you wanted to marry someone?

They debated whether Robert was handsome or not.

"Magdalena thinks so," said Peach.

Robert Walker had been passing through Grafton late in November. He'd stopped at the trading post to buy buttermilk, if Caitlin had any to spare. And a blanket, he'd added, and Caitlin had seen the man was shaking with chills. She'd exclaimed that he was sick, and he'd said he was a doctor, he'd had these fevers since the war, and the attack would go as it came. She told him to stay at the trading post until he was better; he wasn't the first ailing veteran to use the pallet there.

He shook his head, politely declining to inconvenience her, and then collapsed.

Caitlin and Gideon Vann half carried, half dragged him to the storeroom. He mumbled there was a supply of Jesuit bark in his saddlebag. For nearly two months Robert lay ill with what Stefania's mother called *mal aria*. In his feverish nightmares he saw blood-soaked battlefields strewn with bodies and shredded clothing, dead horses and mules, churned-up earth. His dreams echoed with the thunder of cannons, the screams of the wounded and dying, their cries for help, when all the help he could give was the terrible rum issued for amputations or a drink of dirty water to ease their final moments.

Nursing him, Caitlin learned he was a widower, that his wife had died in childbirth along with the baby during his absence. The Pennsylvania farm he'd left in the charge of his younger brother was burned by the British, who shot his brother. He hoped to make a new start in Kentuckee.

Magdalena had gone down to the trading post to help prepare for Annie's wedding. Caitlin had sent her into the storeroom to fetch something, and she'd stepped over to see the war veteran Annie had said Caitlin was nursing back to health. This one seemed to have all his arms and legs, and no crutch propped against the wall. He was sleeping, so Magdalena crept closer to see what he looked like.

Robert awoke from his nightmare to see a pretty girl with a candle, soft brown eyes, and a curious expression bending over him, like an angel from heaven, if angels wore shabby old men's coats and had tangled hair. Magdalena asked, "Would you like a drink? Shall I fetch you a dipper of water?"

"Please," he croaked.

Magdalena had fetched the water bucket and a dipper, helped him drink and wash his face and hands.

"Don't leave," he said.

Helen Bryan

"There's going to be a wedding and I must," she said. "My friend Annie is marrying my brother. Aunt Caitlin says I have to look presentable, and she intends to see to it. I think that means a bath after Annie has one. And she'll take a comb to my hair. I hate that. But there'll be syllabub later, it does you good if you're poorly. I'll bring you some."

Afterward he drifted between sleep and wakefulness, listening to the wedding. He heard bursts of laughter, then someone fiddling, calling the steps of a round dance. He imagined the girl dancing in his arms. He fell asleep and woke tasting cream and sweetness as Magdalena, looking prettier than ever with hair combed and clean, and dressed for the wedding in her borrowed frock, held a spoon to his lips.

"Syllabub, nice, isn't it?"

He nodded, swallowing.

"I didn't tell you. My name is Magdalena," she'd said.

"Yes. Marry me," he'd said, desperate not to lose his chance.

Magdalena had been surprised but decided she would if Robert was willing to stay at Wildwood and help George. She didn't want to go to Kentuckee, and George needed another pair of hands.

"Grandmother Patience said Magdalena's too young to get married, that it was shocking that Aunt Caitlin left her alone with a strange man, and she disapproves of girls marrying in a hurry," said Little Molly. "She always says things lots of times, like she's hammering it into your ears."

"Your grandma disapproves of everything," said Peach, biting the end off another blossom. "Always talkin' about what folks do in Massachusetts, how she got courted through a speakin' tube sittin' in the parlor with her parents. Imagine!" She snickered. "Her fellow pick up the tube and say, 'Ooooh! Miss Patience, I love you, give me a kiss.' Bryn try that in front of Mama. You know who do all the shoutin' down the tube? Mama, that's who. I wouldn't get a word in. Kiss neither."

"Aunt Caitlin says Magdalena's not too young—she'll be fifteen soon. Aunt Caitlin was fifteen when she married Gideon. And Annie was fourteen when she married George. And look how Magdalena

12

perked up after she met Robert. Less *gloomy*, you know how Magdalena can be," said Little Molly. She sighed. "So perhaps she'll be happy."

"I think that's what made Magdalena say she'd marry him," said Peach. "He was poorly and she made him better."

"Wonder if Kitty gone be rude to Brother Merriman like usual," said Peach.

"It's Magdalena's day, perhaps she'll keep quiet," said Little Molly. "Otherwise he'll get offended and just walk off if Kitty aggravates him too much. Won't be any wedding."

"Oh no! Then Magdalena's dress would be wasted!" Stefania was aghast.

To all three, Magdalena's wedding dress was a matter of greater interest than the groom. It was the loveliest thing the girls had ever seen, yellow-and-white sprigged lawn with rows of lace at the sleeves and bodice. Magdalena had found it folded beneath some paper in the bottom of the old trunk her mother had brought from England, where it had lain forgotten for years. Caitlin had cut away some of the volume of the skirt so it would fit Magdalena. She'd fashioned a nightshift for Magdalena from the excess material.

"So she'll look pretty for Robert on her bridal night," Little Molly pronounced. "Oh please, Peach, I want to know what happens on a bridal night. Do you and Bryn . . . ?"

"Why do you want to know! I thought you wanted to teach school, not get married!" Stefania said, crabby now with hunger. "Come along! I want my breakfast!" Honeysuckle wasn't all that filling.

"I'll race you to Wildwood," Peach cried, and set off running up the orchard path.

Little Molly sprinted off after her, shouting, "You didn't answer my question, Peach!"

Stefania didn't bother to run. Little Molly, who had longer legs, would overtake Peach and win. The only one who could outrun Little Molly was Magdalena. Peach claimed that was only because it was easier to run in breeches. Aunt Caitlin had said Magdalena must stop wearing breeches now.

Up ahead, Little Molly reached Wildwood first, and Stefania heard a chorus of excited hellos. Fresh from a bath, Magdalena sat on the porch, looking unlike herself in her new shift, with Annie behind her, combing Magdalena's wet hair dry in the sun. Annie waved the comb, and Magdalena cried, "Stefania!"

Stefania walked slowly toward them, hugging her new dress and wondering grumpily why Magdalena was wearing a nightshift in the morning.

Annie put down the comb and patted her stomach. On her girlish figure, her apron was hitched up over her swollen waist, and she was letting Peach and Little Molly feel the bump. Magdalena stood and shook her hair back and, holding out her arms, twirled round in a billow of yellow lawn like a ray of sunlight on bare feet, smiling as the fabric swished around her. "Come along, Stefania. Breakfast's ready. Annie's made green tomato pie and fried apples!" Magdalena called before the girls disappeared inside.

I don't like weddings, Stefania thought. *Annie's different now. Magdalena's different, and she's not even married yet. And Peach, what if she marries Bryn? Then there'll just be Little Molly and me.* The tantalizing smell of frying bacon reached her, but even that failed to lift her spirits. She wasn't hungry after all. She wanted to turn and run away. But she couldn't let Magdalena down. She trudged reluctantly toward the cabin.

CHAPTER 1

STEFANO

New Orleans, summer 1783

America! The stooped gray-haired man walked slowly down the gang-plank, taking in the sights, sounds, and smells of New Orleans—the quay and the warehouses and slaves calling to each other in some incomprehensible tongue. Above all it was hot. The sultry air that engulfed him was heavy with smells of the Pontchartrain Basin—sweat, rotting vegetation, manure, all overlaid with a waft of some sickly scented flower. Stefano Albanisi drew out a linen handkerchief and wiped his brow, and reminded himself that after more than a decade in the Inquisition prison in Palermo, he could survive America.

He was less certain he could withstand happiness. When he tried to contemplate the possibility, it was as sharp as the torturer's instruments. But more ephemeral.

He'd smuggled a message out of prison to his pregnant young wife awaiting the birth of their baby at her father's summer villa in the mountains, unaware that her father had been responsible for his arrest. He'd told her to leave at once and go to America, to an Albanisi cousin in New Orleans, where he would follow her when his family had paid enough to negotiate his release. Through the terrible years in prison, he'd been kept alive by his faith that Rosalia and his child, if, please God, it had lived, were waiting for him in New Orleans.

It had cost his wealthy merchant family a fortune in bribes, but at last he was here to rejoin his wife and child and rebuild their lives. The Albanisis had commissioned him to establish a branch of the family's trading house in America and provided him with the name of a New Orleans agent connected to the Albanisis' agent in Naples and a letter of credit he could draw on. The sense of purpose revived him. The thought of commerce was less painful, less unbearably sweet than thinking of Rosalia.

He concentrated on that. He would make his fortune anew in America.

He summoned one of the conveyances for hire, had his luggage loaded on, and gave the address. Would Rosalia recognize him? Had the child lived? A son? A daughter? He must prepare himself to find no child, only let him find Rosalia. He had sent a letter, but perhaps it had not reached her. How ought he to announce his arrival? Best to ask for his cousin first, he decided.

Reaching his destination, Stefano stood for a few minutes, brushing off the dust from his coat and settling his cravat. He looked up at the grand house with its tall shutters and wrought-iron balcony that ran the length of the second story. His cousin had been a kind man, and it was a comfort to know Rosalia and his child would have been well treated and secure with him. He rang the bell with a shaking hand and asked the liveried slave for the master.

A few moments later he collapsed in shock. His inquiry for the master brought the news that his cousin had died many years earlier.

"What of Signora Albanisi?" he inquired faintly. Did anyone know what had become of Signora Albanisi? The liveried slave shook his head.

A young Negro maid was sent to fetch a cordial. She must have told her story of the strange visitor in the kitchen, because she returned with an old slave who'd been kept by the new owners of the house. He recalled that years ago, just after the old master had died, a young lady had come to the house, claiming the old master was a relative and she'd expected to stay with him until her husband joined her. She'd given the slave money with a message that if her husband should come, tell him that she and her child had left New Orleans with an older couple who'd befriended her. There'd been some mention of horses, but the old slave couldn't remember what horses had to do with it. They were bound for Williamsburg, in Virginia, and traveling overland through the mountains. Perhaps that woman had been Signora Albanisi?

"Of course," muttered Stefano. The hope that had sustained him through years of hell evaporated. Stefano stumbled away and wandered blindly into a tavern. He sank onto a chair and ordered a glass of brandy, then another. He'd drink enough to drown out the city, the steamy heat and the stench of rotting vegetation, the mosquitoes and the rowdy party of merchants and fur traders sitting nearby, talking loudly about a horse race and spitting odorous brown gobs that spattered his boots. It didn't matter. He drank steadily. When he was drunk enough, he would throw himself into the lake.

One word penetrated his fevered brain and changed his mind.

Chiaramonte. A fur trader was claiming he'd never raced a better horse than the one he bought from the old Gypsy at Chiaramonte, years back. Stefano leaped from his chair like a madman, clutched the startled fur trader's coat, and demanded to know where this Chiaramonte was and who lived there.

He narrowly escaped being shot by the fur trader's companion as a dangerous lunatic before he could make himself understood, and eventually he learned that the Chiaramonte horses were to be found in the

Bowjay Valley, that Chiaramonte was the name of the homestead near the Grafton settlement on the river.

"Was there a woman there? A young woman? A child?" he demanded.

The fur traders looked at each other and shrugged. It had been some time ago . . . "Didn't the trader have a grown daughter?" asked one. Another recalled a little girl had trailed after the Gypsy.

How could he reach it? he cried.

They told him there was a regular packet that went upriver to a trading post near Chiaramonte. Vann Station, it was called, in Grafton.

Stefano just had time to call on the New Orleans agent to introduce himself, present the letter confirming his line of credit, and declare he would make his fortune in the New World, before the packet departed.

CHAPTER 2

STEFANIA

Grafton, October 1790

In the sitting room, her parents were speaking Italian. Her mother laughed at something her father said. Stefania calculated that if she left now, while they were taking their coffee and, as was their Sicilian custom, the customary small glass of cordial or Madeira after their two o'clock dinner, she could row across to Grafton and see if her friends were safe, then be back before dark. When she returned, her father was sure to deliver a lecture about the folly of crossing the river alone at this time of year, but Stefania had gone about as she pleased until Stefano arrived in Grafton—and by then her independent frontier habits were too ingrained to be easily curtailed by an anxious Sicilian father determined to guard his only child from every imaginable danger.

She took the shopping basket from the kitchen. Into the housewife at her waist, she had tucked a list of supplies her mother had wanted from the trading post for weeks. Rosalia worried less than Stefano did, would be pleased to have the supplies, and would calm her husband down later. By teatime the storm would have blown over. Stefania snatched the old bonnet she wore for gardening from its peg by the side door, slipped out, and hurried down the path to the river.

She needed to know whether Magdalena, Peach, Little Molly, and Annie were safe. There had never been trouble on the Chiaramonte side of the river, but October was a dangerous time in the valley. The Cherokee believed the world had been created in the autumn, and as the Great New Moon Festival that signaled the start of the new year approached, tensions flared between the Indians and the settlers. Braves hunting game for the ceremonial feasts ignored settlers' claims of ownership, their boundaries and fences. The valley's fragile trappings of white civilization—the wooden church, the trading post, the log cabins and barns and foundry and paddle mill—were disregarded. This land had been their hunting grounds since the Great Buzzard flapped his wings and carved it between the mountains. Who could own it?

But the settlers had caused damage. Game was no longer abundant. Trappers and long hunters had killed the buffalo and bears beyond their own need for meat or skins, selling their pelts in great piles to the fur traders who came to Grafton and shipped them downriver. Up and down the valley, settlers had changed the landscape—felled trees, plowed fields, and put up fences—until the remaining game went deeper and deeper into the mountains.

The marsh that drew the deer and buffalo had also provided the tribes with salt to keep food through the winter, but now Little Molly's grandfather Rufus Drumheller claimed the salt marsh as his property. He and his sons patrolled the marsh, on the lookout for telltale smoke from the fires the women and girls still furtively lit to boil the brackish water and extract the salt. The men would smash the pots, put out the fires, and drive the women away with whips. Still they reappeared year after year.

Indians raided homesteads for cattle and geese, burned cabins and barns, stole horses. In settlers' cabins, through the night, men and boys strained their eyes for any movement in the surrounding darkness, alert for any disturbance among the animals, listening for the call of a night bird that was no night bird but a signal to attack, watching for a sudden red glow of a flaming arrow.

Settler women and children snatched a few hours of sleep, buckets of water and dirt on hand to extinguish the flames before fire drove them out of the cabin. If that happened, they'd be taken prisoner, perhaps tortured, perhaps enslaved by their captors, perhaps sold to other tribes. But if the braves found the whiskey or spirits distilled by most households, they would scalp or massacre entire families. The army retaliated by destroying Indian towns that had no defenders with the warriors gone. They burned huts, council chambers, winter stores of dried corn and fish and beans; killed livestock; and scattered old people, women, and children.

Indians would retaliate.

Hostilities would subside only when the feasting began, allowing both sides to bury their dead and plot revenge. Uneasy, volatile truces between the Indians and the army were negotiated but could not be relied on.

Tucking her skirts up, Stefania grabbed the canoe by the gunwales. Leaping nimbly in, she took the paddle and pushed off into the river, hoping her parents wouldn't happen to look out of the sitting room window and see her. Stefano would rush out and order her back. Well, if he did, she'd pretend she hadn't heard him. Stefania had to know if her friends were safe.

When he'd arrived in Grafton seven years earlier, her father's joy at finding his unknown child alive had soon been eclipsed by fears for her safety in this wild place. He was horrified to learn his precious daughter was in the habit of rowing herself back and forth across the river alone and roaming Grafton and Frog Mountain at will. He promptly tried to forbid what struck him as dangerous for a girl. This was practically everything Stefania was accustomed to doing, such as hunting with a rifle, climbing Frog Mountain alone to visit her friends at Wildwood, or saddling one of the horses and riding up to the Drumhellers'.

Knowing very well that her ability to shoot carrier pigeons and wild turkeys and catch fish in a net the Indian way had been necessary if she and her mother were to eat, Stefania had at first been incredulous, then rebelled against his restrictions. In the tempestuous early days after Stefano's arrival, Rosalia acted as intermediary between them, explaining to Stefano that girls brought up in the wilderness had to be hardy and self-sufficient in ways that were unthinkable for well-brought-up girls in Sicily.

Rosalia explained to Stefania that in Sicily, fathers expected to rule their families as they pleased and be deferred to. They must give Stefano time to accustom himself to American ways.

"Stefania must learn to conduct herself with the dignity of an Albanisi!" Stefano pronounced, as if this were the final word on the matter.

Rosalia sighed.

"Mother! This isn't Sicily!" expostulated Stefania.

"I know, Stefania, but remember what your father endured in prison. We must allow him some authority at home now, let him know that we respect his wishes."

But Stefania's habit of independence was as strongly ingrained as were her father's ideas of his paternal responsibilities. She perfected ways of getting round Stefano, which mostly involved agreeing, "Of course, Papa," very sweetly, before doing as she pleased and then claiming to be surprised and dismayed by his disapproval later.

There were many clashes. Stefania and Rosalia were relieved when Stefano's new projects and enterprises gradually began to divert his attention.

Stefano had taken stock of the decaying homestead, his wife and daughter reduced to poverty and nearly given way to despair. But an entrepreneurial sixth sense saved him. The merchant house of the Albanisi family, trading in wine and spices, had flourished for generations. Trade was in his blood. In spite of everything, his interest in life revived as he considered things from an entrepreneurial perspective. There must be business opportunities—there were always business opportunities if one looked for them. He was not without resources; he had a line of credit . . . Perhaps, he decided, it was possible to make his fortune here after all.

Observing passing shipments of lumber on the river prompted him to buy a large stretch of wooded property from the de Marechals and negotiate the building of a sawmill with Rufus Drumheller near the river so Chiaramonte lumber could be conveniently shipped from Vann Station to New Orleans and Natchez. He contracted with Jack Drumheller to oversee it.

And Rosalia had inherited some horses from the Gypsy Tamás Morgades, who'd brought her and Stefania to Grafton. Tamás had been a successful horse trader, but after his death Rosalia had struggled to feed them and had sold several but was cheated on the price. Stefano admitted all he knew of horses was that they were saddled by servants, ridden by gentlemen, and raced by rogues. "But they say the Gypsies know their horses," he mused, thinking there must be money in them. Stefania suggested young Henry Stuart knew more about horses than most people, because he'd learned from his French grandfather, Henri de Marechal, who'd been something of a cavalier in his day. Stefano thought it unlikely anyone so young would have the necessary expertise, but Stefania persuaded him to ask Henry's advice on feeding, grooming, and breeding. Stefano conceded Henry knew more than he did and gave the boy a job.

Henry was in his element and quickly took over responsibility for the stud. Word spread among the river travelers that there were Chiaramonte horses for sale again.

Within a few years the timber and horse businesses were thriving. Stefano spared no effort to make the lives of his wife and daughter comfortable, and the poverty and privations Stefania and her mother had endured after Tamás's death were a distant memory now. Rosalia was happy. Stefania struggled with a twinge of guilt, knowing how Stefano would worry until she was home again.

Sunlight danced on the ripples made by her paddle—the river was running calm on this hot autumn day. Around her the Bowjay Valley and the mountains, dotted with homesteads and log cabins, were a blaze of color, the changing leaves turning everything russet and gold in the sunshine. Rowing, she looked back at Chiaramonte, thinking as she always did how handsome their old homestead looked now.

The homestead had been a moneymaking scheme of Henri de Marechal. He'd been anxious to raise money to return to France and had conceived a scheme to sell plots of cleared land with a cabin as ready-made homesteads to passing settlers. He'd been in a hurry and built the cabin with unseasoned wood. Not long after Tamás bought it, the logs shifted and the chinking began to fall out. In winter, draughts blew through gaps between the logs, and Rosalia had developed a permanent cough.

The first thing Stefano did was demolish the cabin and rebuild it. He drew up plans and sent them to his agent in New Orleans for a skilled builder, a carpenter, a team of Irish workmen, and shipments of bricks. "Papa says one room is to be just for *sitting*!" Stefania had reported to her friends. "And there's to be a fireplace in *every room*!" They all agreed that the first sounded odd and the second was unimaginable.

In place of the old cabin and the sagging structure that passed for a barn stood a handsome brick house with black shutters. Beyond it were outbuildings, fenced pastures where sleek horses grazed, and fields stretching in every direction striped with harvested rows of corn and wheat.

Stefano had at first been at a loss for laborers for his fields, lumber mill, and stud farm. In Sicily there had been peasants, a fact he'd casually mentioned on the riverboat that brought him to Grafton. His first lesson in the ways of American democracy came from his fellow travelers, who were quick to inform him there were no peasants in America, that Americans were as good as anybody; indeed, liberty-enjoying Americans were superior to inhabitants of backward European countries with their kings. Slaves were the thing, they'd assured Stefano.

Stefano found there were no slaves to be had in Grafton, and Rosalia had an unexpected reaction when Stefano announced he would return to New Orleans to buy some to work for him. He assured Rosalia he'd buy a cook and a chambermaid while he was at it.

"No! We will not have slaves at Chiaramonte!" said Rosalia so passionately that Stefano was taken aback. Rosalia, normally so yielding, had a fierce look in her eyes that he'd never seen before.

"Don't be foolish, Rosalia! Slaves are necessary to make the place pay. I'll see they're well treated, my dear," he said indulgently.

"No, Stefano! No slaves. If you bring slaves here, I will leave you and Chiaramonte and take Stefania with me."

"*What?*" Stefano roared, suddenly reverting to his role as a Sicilian paterfamilias who, however indulgent, did not expect to have his authority questioned.

"Do not misjudge me, Stefano! I have crossed the ocean alone and have endured many hardships here. There is little I fear now. Either promise you will not return with slaves or I swear on my mother's memory to leave." He was outraged, but Rosalia, his sweet Rosalia, had an obstinate expression and refused to speak to him. For days the atmosphere simmered; then Stefano capitulated and promised he would buy no slaves. Stefania had been relieved. How could she have explained slaves to Peach, Venus, and the Hanover women?

Stefano resolved the problem by following the example of the de Marechals and the Drumhellers, who hired passing war veterans heading south and west in search of land. Many of them were taking their families west, complaining there was no good land left for homesteaders in Maryland or Virginia or Pennsylvania. A lack of ready money was a common factor. Some had been impoverished by the war against the British, while others grumbled they'd never received their promised bonus for their army service. Some were willing to stay and work, and Stefano usually had a dozen or more hired men working for him at any one time. This afternoon she could see Stefano's workforce busy in the fields, baling hay.

Beyond Chiaramonte, smoke rose from the fieldstone chimney of the small cabin where the itinerant portrait painter Secondus Conway and his Hessian wife, Anna, lived. The badly built two-room cabin was one of Henri de Marechal's projects to raise cash. It was surrounded by a small yard of bare earth and a fenced vegetable garden where Anna, with no assistance from Secondus, labored to feed them. Beyond the cabin Henri's half-hearted efforts to clear the land had been swallowed up again in the encroaching wilderness. Rosalia had bought the place from Henri with the last of the money left to her by Tamás, thinking she could lease it to a settler who'd pay rent in food to support her and Stefania. Her father's peasants in Sicily had been obliged to supply food from their land in the same way. It had been the only plan she could think of.

Secondus, however, had come to live there following an unfortunate incident with the de Marechal family, and in a cloud of misunderstanding about paying Rosalia anything in any form for the use of the property. He'd been unwell at the time and only too willing to live on charity. Rosalia was too softhearted to turn him out.

Stefania dragged her paddle to swing her canoe next to the trading post's jetty ladder. She tied the canoe up and, gathering her skirts out of the way, climbed nimbly onto the dock. She raised a hand to shade her eyes under the rim of her bonnet and anxiously scanned her surroundings for signs of an attack.

Vann Station and the Vann family's large cabin were unscathed.

The Drumhellers' cluster of cabins above the forge on Little Frog Mountain looked intact, and the only smoke to be seen was rising sedately from the chimneys. She swung her gaze to the east. In the orchard on Frog Mountain, she could see Annie's children gathering windfalls into baskets, so the Walkers and de Marechals up at Wildwood must be safe.

Wildwood was probably the least likely homestead to be attacked. Annie's father, Gideon Vann, a half-blood and "beloved man" of his tribe, had said tribes mostly avoided Frog Mountain. They believed it contained a sacred place, where spirits of the dead could be summoned to advise the living, provided the right offerings were made. When fog shrouded the top of the mountain, it was visited by the higher beings. No one liked to disturb the spirits' gathering place.

But Stefania remembered a terrible night when the Cherokees forgot the spirits. It was during the war against the British. Stefania and Magdalena had been children, and Rosalia had invited all the settlers to celebrate Assumption Day at Chiaramonte. Magdalena, her father, and her sister Kitty had come without Sophia, who was waiting at home for Magdalena's brothers to return from the fields.

They'd been dancing to Tamás's fiddle, Magdalena and Stefania whirling with joined hands, when someone screamed that there was a fire on Frog Mountain. The music had stopped, and they saw Wildwood was ablaze. At Wildwood, Sophia and her son Francis were found in a pool of blood, and George lay wounded in the yard. George had recovered, but Sophia and Francis died the next day.

It was Gideon who discovered the Americans were responsible. They were hunting down real and imagined Tory sympathizers and were certain the English heiress Sophia de Marechal, whose two sons had not volunteered to fight the British, was aiding the redcoats. The Americans had a pact with their Cherokee allies to attack each other's enemies. The Americans provided rum and guns, and the Cherokees had done the rest.

It added to the tragedy that Gideon's elder daughter, Rhiannon, was married to Two Bears, the brave who had led the attack. Caitlin, who'd had a troubled relationship with Rhiannon ever since Rhiannon had fiercely adopted Indian ways as a girl, had declared her daughter was now dead to her.

It was rumored that afterward Gideon had killed and buried four braves in a standing position to the south, north, east, and west of Wildwood and, using his powers as a beloved man, cast a spell to prevent the dead going to the Darkening Land to be reunited with their ancestors; instead their spirits must guard Wildwood from further Indian attacks forever. While no one knew whether the story of the dead braves was true, it had kept the Indians away. Long hunters and trappers who were often attacked in the wilderness breathed easier when they reached Frog Mountain.

Stefania had never again looked up at Wildwood without remembering that night and the look of anguish on Magdalena's face.

But all seemed to be well in Grafton. Stefania breathed a sigh of relief. She felt in the housewife at her waist for the list and walked briskly to the trading post. "Hello, Aunt Caitlin," she said, tripping up the porch steps. "I've come to be sure everyone's safe."

"Stefania, dear!" cried Caitlin, looking just a little bit too much to the left of where Stefania was standing, a sign that her eyesight was failing. "No trouble here, thank the Lord, though there was news with the last packet boat that downriver the army had to bury a farmer and his two boys who were killed. Surprised in the cornfield, they say. But Bryn said he had to chance a trip to the mill today, the mill wheel's stuck. The two older boys took their rifles and went with him, and I'll be glad when they get home. The children are all well enough to wear out their clothes faster than I can mend them." She gestured to the overflowing basket at her feet. "And your parents? Is your mother over her cough?"

"They're well, thank you. Papa's busy, as usual. Mother's cough is tiresome. It goes, and then when we think it's gone for good, it comes back. It tires her. Papa insisted on arranging for Anna Conway to come every day to help her in the house so she can rest. Mother agreed only because Anna and Secondus need what Papa pays Anna."

"It will help poor Anna. Things are hard with them." Caitlin shook her head. "Peach will be happy to see you. There's so little news—you know how nobody goes about at this time of year. Peach," she called, "we have a visitor."

Peach was bustling inside, wrapped in a big apron as usual, busy making room for a shipment they were expecting when the afternoon packet arrived. She came to the open door and smiled to see her friend. "Step in, step in! Wish they'd start the festival so we could go around without looking over our shoulders. Keeps us all cooped up at home like chickens. Now Bryn's gone off with the boys, and I'll be worried sick till they get back. Does your mother want anything today?"

Stefania began ticking her mother's order on her fingers. Peach measured out wheat flour from a barrel, filled a homespun sack with it, dusted her hands on her apron, and then unwrapped a hard gray cone of sugar from its covering of newspaper. "How much your mother wantin' again?"

"Two pounds. It's a great deal, I know, but Papa has a sweet tooth, and Mother's making his favorite pastries, with ground hickory nuts because she forgot to order almonds."

Peach shook her head and began whacking off rock-hard chunks of sugar with her hammer. Mostly settlers made do with sorghum, or honey if they could find it.

Stefania knew what Peach was thinking. Extravagance! She still felt apologetic placing orders for luxuries like sugar, nutmegs, coffee, almonds, and lemons, things that Rosalia said were household essentials in Sicily. But Peach couldn't deny it had been good for business at the trading post. Vann Station had expanded and now stocked whatever Stefano and Rosalia fancied. In addition to sugar and tea, there were raisins and dried figs, casks of wine, and Madeira sent upriver from New Orleans and Natchez. The new storeroom had bolts of fine wool and muslin, ribbons and shawls, sewing boxes, shoes, and ladies' walking boots alongside the rolls of homespun and iron cooking pots, barrel staves, and nails from the Drumheller forge at Rattlesnake Springs.

"That's a pretty new gown you wearin'," said Peach, packing Stefania's purchases into the shopping basket. "It's India cotton, isn't it? The pink is becoming." It was. Self-conscious of the fact she was wearing a new dress on an ordinary occasion, Stefania flushed. Like her friends, she usually wore homespun. But recently Stefano had taken it into his head that Stefania should have some new clothes, from a dressmaker his agent in New Orleans had recommended. Stefano often took it into his head to order some pretty thing for his wife and daughter. Rosalia had taken and sent Stefania's measurements, and weeks later a box from the dressmaker had arrived, packed with new clothes for Stefania: half a dozen dresses, a new riding habit, fine cotton stockings, and some lace-trimmed shifts. Stefania admired them but said they were too pretty to be practical except for special occasions. But to Stefania's astonishment, Rosalia cut up the old homespun dresses, saying they were old and shabby and the chickens could use the remnants for their nests.

Stefania sighed. Her parents meant well. "Thank you. Mother sent for it. The dressmaker called it a morning dress. Do you suppose there are ladies who have dresses just for wearing in the morning?"

Peach smiled good-naturedly. "Need a morning dress to sit in your sitting room, I reckon. But step lively in that dress if you're passing men from Susan and Isaac's tavern or you'll have tobacco juice all over it. Susan put cuspidors everywhere, but she says most men couldn't hit one if she tied it under their chins. Mother Vann and I step behind the counter every time they come in. Your pa expecting anything special today on the packet?"

"I believe he's ordered a French clock that chimes," said Stefania.

"A *what*?" Peach demanded. They looked at each other for a moment and then burst into laughter. In Grafton a chiming clock was as absurd as sitting rooms and morning gowns.

"I hear two more of your horses got sold," Peach remarked, still chuckling as she measured spices—a piece of ginger, a nut of mace, and a piece of cinnamon bark.

"Yes, the two yearlings. Some timber merchants came to see Papa, and Henry exercised them outside Papa's study. Papa couldn't make the merchants concentrate; they kept looking out the window. They finished the timber business in a hurry and went out to examine the horses, asking if they were for sale. Henry said they weren't before Papa could say they were, but kept leading them up and down, saying he was just cooling them off, saying Papa wouldn't take anything for them, he planned to race them. He did all the talking, wouldn't let Papa get a word in. Finally Henry let the merchants buy them for three times the price they'd offered at first. It made Mother laugh till she had one of her coughing fits."

"Henry's a nice boy."

"He's a big help to Papa. The men he hires don't stay long. I wish I had a brother. Papa never says so, but I'm sure he wishes he had a son. Not instead of me, of course. But he often talks about his family back in Sicily, how all the men are involved in the business, how convenient to have so many uncles and cousins, there's always someone to fill any vacancy. Cousins often marry each other. He says he needs an assistant and I need a husband and he's going to write and inquire if a spare cousin can come to America to help him and marry me while he's about it."

31

Peach rolled her eyes.

"Papa's teasing. At least, I think he's teasing."

"Maybe not. Your papa likes making everybody do what he say. There's some news about Magdalena you won't have heard yet," said Peach. "She's expectin' at last. Seven years it took her! Nothin' like me, is it?"

"You were quick—four months after the wedding." Stefania giggled, and Peach shrugged, looking proud. "I hope she'll have an easy time. And, Peach, Secondus's wife, Anna, is expecting too."

"No!" Peach exclaimed. "You'd never think to look at him that he could . . ."

"I know, but he must have, and she's terribly sick, poor thing. I hope it lives. Well, I must take my basket and get home before Mother misses me and Papa is cross with me for not telling him I intended to visit you so he could forbid it because it might be dangerous." Stefania lowered her voice. "But, Peach, before I go, has Aunt Caitlin had any word from Gideon?"

"No." Peach lowered her own voice and shook her head. "He goes off when he's a mind to. He left for a clan gathering, Mother Vann worried he's been gone so long, took it into her head he's stayed away because of Rhiannon. I overheard Gideon tell Bryn his sister was expecting again—she's had a dozen or so, and Bryn said her last two died. Bryn said Gideon had a dream something bad would happen, and he must fetch this baby to its mother's people. That's the custom with Cherokees, but I don't know Mother Vann would have it . . ."

They were interrupted by shouts from the jetty. "Wonder who'll come today?" Stefania wandered to the door and watched as the packet tied up and disgorged its passengers. "Mother likes to know what the ladies are wearing. There seems to be a new fashion for short jackets."

But today no females emerged from the ladies' compartment. The passengers were all men—two middle-aged merchants with polished boots, gold watch chains, and coats stretched tight over well-fed stomachs, the rest shabbier travelers who might have been tinkers or wilderness guides or merchants hoping to supply the trading post with calico or rum or bargain for a consignment of Rattlesnake Springs iron goods to supply settlers passing their own trading posts.

They were rumpled and bleary after several nights of the kind of camaraderie men establish over cards and whiskey, boots stained from tobacco spit. She watched them take a hearty leave of each other as they disembarked. The Ozments' tavern would profit tonight.

She sighed and was turning back to go inside when the last passenger came striding down the gangplank to catch her eye.

"There's a nice-looking gentleman, Aunt Caitlin. He still looks fresh and neat. Not like the others." Caitlin's eyesight was failing, but she sewed so efficiently and neatly by touch, just as she felt her way through other household tasks, that everyone forgot she couldn't see well. Obligingly Caitlin raised her head and pretended to look.

"Who, dear?"

"That tall man, in a blue coat. He looks . . . official."

CHAPTER 3

COLONEL CHARBONNEAU

Peach snatched up the loaded basket and hurried onto the porch. "Official? Is it that sheriff, come back?" she demanded. She shaded her eyes with her hand and peered anxiously at the newcomers. "Or a justice of the peace?" she faltered.

"He doesn't look as rough a character as you described the sheriff," Stefania conceded. There was a quick intake of breath from Peach.

One day late in spring, she had been alone in the trading post, arranging some brooms and woven baskets, when three strange men rode up leading a packhorse loaded with ropes, chains, and manacles. The hard-faced man who strode in ahead of the others said his name was Jonas Tyree. He owned a plantation at the foot of the Alleghenies, and he'd been appointed sheriff, and the men with him were deputies. He was based in a parish south of Roanoke, and from now on would be making regular visits to faraway settlements and homesteads to remind people they were within his jurisdiction and subject to the laws of the commonwealth, which he intended to see were enforced. He'd scared Peach. She knew he'd meant to. Her mother had been a slave.

Peach had silently thanked God her children were out of sight, up at the Drumhellers' in Little Molly's school. They rarely saw anyone official in Grafton other than soldiers on the packet boats, an occasional military detachment passing through to a stockade deeper in Indian country, or, most recently, the men who'd come to take the first United States census, going from homestead to cabin to list the heads of households and the free white males, females, and children living in them, together with their "taxable," or slaves. The census takers had been taken aback to find there were no taxables in any household and that the Negroes in Grafton were all free.

They'd included the free black households in the census, saying they had to be counted along with the rest but commenting how unusual it was.

"Looks like you've been left in charge," the sheriff said to Peach, leaning on the counter. "Folks own you mus' trust you with their money."

"Oh, sir," Peach had said in a sweet, soft, artificial voice nothing like her usual commanding one. "My husband's family own Vann Station. Gideon and Caitlin Vann."

"*You're* married to Bryn Vann?" exclaimed one of the deputies. "Against the law for a nigger to marry a white man!"

"Bryn's a half-blood," said the other. Bryn wasn't a half-blood, he was three-quarters white, but Peach knew better than to correct him.

"Yes, sir."

"Hmm," said the sheriff. "If he's a half-blood, no law against your bein' married long as he ain't white if you're really free."

"Yes, sir, I am. The marshals noted that when they come and took the census, that we free in my family. They noted down my parents were both free. Venus and Seth Hanover. If Mama was free when my sisters and I born, we free too. They say that's the law. Mama showed her free paper, and all us six Hanover girls are married, but we keep our free name."

"What your husbands say to that?" asked the sheriff, smirking.

"Our husbands say that's what we must do, so there's no mistake 'bout bein' Mama's daughters. Otherwise they's people think we ain't free." She managed not to say this in a sassy way.

"Keepin' your folks' name like that, they's people think you ain't married," sniggered a deputy, and all the men laughed. "Just fornicatin'."

Aching to slap him, Peach said, "I hope not, sir. We married, got the license from Brother Merriman."

"A license! Next you be tellin' me you can read it!" They laughed again.

Peach bit back a retort, managed a self-deprecating shrug, and struggled to arrange her expression to suggest that as a Negro female naturally she could not read. It made her face ache, but no good would come of irritating the deputy or saying anything about learning to read and write at Sophia de Marechal's school.

She listened politely as the sheriff talked a lot more, saying what a fine day it was and Grafton was bigger than it had been, riverboats must be good for the trading post, and were Brother Merriman's sermons as long and powerful as folks said. All during this rambling talk, he looked at Peach like he meant something else.

What did he really want, she wondered uneasily.

"They say he can preach the Devil under the table," the sheriff remarked, "under the table and out the door."

"He can," Peach agreed, eyes downcast. She smoothed damp palms over her apron. "He a powerful voice for the Lord, every Sunday we go to his church. Devil don't dare look in."

The sheriff didn't seem like the type of man who'd enjoy passing the time of day with a woman going on about her work or churchgoing habits. What was his purpose? What did he want from her? Had Brother Merriman done something wrong?

The sheriff's voice was suddenly cold, his eyes hard. "That's good. Because the Devil looked in on some slaves in Montgomery County last month. They got hold of guns, shot their owner and his whole family— wife and five children—set everything on fire, ran away. We caught all but four, but we're after 'em now, and it looks like they came this way. Either they got them a canoe and took to the river or they headed up Frog Mountain. You see any runaways passing, go that way?"

"Runaways? No, sir."

"We'll catch 'em eventually. We hung the ringleaders, fixed some of the others so they won't run anywhere again. Considering how we got 'em to confess, I b'lieve the ones we hung were the lucky ones, glad to die by the time we did it. Worth remembering, anybody helps runaways, likely to be hung too."

"Sir, we haven't seen none." Peach tried to keep the sob out of her voice.

"You keep an eye on your mother's freedom paper, girl. Never know when it might be needed, 'specially when there's been slave trouble. That gets folks lookin' at free niggers, thinkin' maybe they causin' the problem. Some folks will go to the magistrate and claim freedom papers is forged. Magistrate will take a look then, investigate, who knows what he'll decide, especially when he wants to keep the peace, stop troublemakin' before it start. And slavers don't care about the difference between free niggers and slaves, even if the magistrate does. Snatch you away, sell you fast as they'd sell a black wasn't free. So any runaways or strange niggers come through here, don't you go helpin'."

He and the deputies turned to leave. Then the sheriff turned back and leaned over the counter again toward Peach. "Free niggers ain't the only ones causin' problems. They say it was some white men stirring up the slaves. Quaker troublemakers. Preachin' abolition."

"Hasn't been no troublemakers here, sir," said Peach, struggling not to betray her nervousness, praying her mother's boarder Iddo Fox, who was a Quaker, wouldn't choose that moment to come through the door, crying, "Good day to thee, Friend Peach!" She also prayed that Bryn wouldn't come home just then. Bryn was listed as Cherokee in the census, but in looks he took after his mother, Caitlin, and looked white. That would start the sheriff asking questions again.

"You see any slaves being walked down to be sold in Louisiana and Mississippi on the river trail?"

Peach shook her head. Why on earth would she have seen such a thing?

"You're likely to, 'fore long. And I'm warning you, if you see 'em coming, tell your free nigger friends to stay low and keep quiet. Not cause trouble, not give 'em ideas 'bout getting free like you are, you understand me?" he said. She dropped her eyes and busied herself with a roll of muslin. *Don't say nothin',* she told herself. *Won't do no good, don't make it worse.* She bit her tongue hard.

The sheriff didn't seem to notice, because he carried on talking. "We're travelin' regularly now, like a circuit preacher does, visitin' the settlements, makin' sure everybody keeps the peace, don't break the law, and runaway slaves is a danger to the peace. Any felons or runaways, we take 'em back to be dealt with by the justice of the peace. Runaway slaves, they get a good whippin' 'fore they's returned to their owners. What owners do after that is up to them. Grafton doesn't have a jail yet. I plan to talk to your husband and the Drumhellers and the de Marechals about building one soon. Meanwhile, you see any strange niggers tryin' to go by river or over Frog Mountain, get somebody to take word to the county seat so we can go after them. You do that, girl, your free people do that, and perhaps a magistrate won't need to come and look close at free papers or who married who around here."

"Yes, sir," murmured Peach, keeping her eyes down until she heard him outside telling the deputies to mount up. She walked to the open door and watched them prepare to leave. All three men had chains and fetters looped over the back of their saddles, and they rattled as the men mounted.

Chains. Her mother, Venus, and her father, Seth, who'd run away from their owner, had told their girls about some things. How her father had been shackled in the field to another slave. How the child of a slave woman was a slave even if its father was white. How when runaways were caught, they were chained by their wrists and ankles and pulled along behind the horses. Back to their owners and punishment. Seth had claimed he heard the rattle of chains in his sleep. He'd had nightmares of whippings and a cage being soldered on his head and of something happening to a woman—"Don't hurt her, don't hurt her!" he'd woken the household shouting many times, and his terrified daughters had held their breath until Venus's sleepy soothing voice told him over and over he was safe, they were all safe now.

She'd known all this, but she'd never seen chains and manacles. Now she imagined cold steel snapping closed on her wrists and ankles . . . and oh God, on her children too. How safe were she and the children really? Her sisters? Her mother? She suddenly realized they were all only as safe as the law allowed, as safe as the sheriff allowed, as safe as a magistrate allowed, as safe as all the white people allowed and no more. For a long moment she couldn't breathe. It felt like the sheriff and his men had sucked away all the air in the valley.

CHAPTER 4

PEACH

In the weeks and months following the sheriff's visit, Peach lay awake at night worrying about what the sheriff would find out if he came sniffing around.

Peach's eldest sister, Susan, was married to Isaac Ozment, a long hunter who might or might not have been a half-blood, he wasn't sure. But Magdalena's older sister Kitty de Marechal, who was the image of her English mother and clearly white, had married Cully Stuart, whose mother, Saskia, had been born a slave. Cully was clearly a mulatto. If it weren't for Saskia's free papers, Peach understood, Cully would be a slave too. He and Kitty had a brood of children whose dusky-white skin showed they'd definitely broken the law—marriage between whites and mulattoes was as much a crime as between whites and Negroes.

The first Grafton settlers had ignored that law. Sophia and Henri de Marechal had brought escaped slaves when they came to take possession of the patent of land Sophia had inherited, and had promised land to any who would stay. It was such a struggle to survive that every pair of hands mattered, and it didn't matter that Kitty and Cully got married, followed by Susan and Isaac. At the time, the little Grafton settlement was buried in the wilderness and remote from the authorities. The slave laws and the prohibition against intermarriage had been irrelevant, so far as the de Marechals, Drumhellers, and Vanns were concerned.

But now settlers from slave-owning Maryland and Virginia and Georgia were coming through Grafton, stopping at the trading post to stock up on what they needed before heading west. They were always shocked to find not only so many free blacks in the Grafton settlement but also that one of them was openly married to the trading post's white owner. And no slaves at all in Grafton. Not one. Word of this must have got back to the sheriff.

Free blacks made whites uneasy. It was one thing if they were old slaves who'd been freed and lived on charity. But in Grafton there was a large community of free blacks who were significant landowners or, like Peach and Susan Hanover, had a prosperous business with their husbands. Free blacks were likely to help, even arm, runaway slaves, encourage them to revolt. Free blacks were dangerous.

Peach had seen slaves in Grafton, but not many. Rarely, a passing settler had a slave or two in tow. Sometimes a successful merchant who came for fur or timber or the iron goods from Rattlesnake Springs was accompanied by a body servant. A few Cherokee traders and home-steaders scattered across the valleys owned a slave or two they'd bought or kidnapped, and sometimes these slaves accompanied their masters when they came to the trading post. According to Gideon, slaves could be adopted into a clan. Peach asked if that made them free in the eyes of the law. Gideon didn't know, but he was not excessively concerned by white men's laws.

Peach had told Little Molly and Stefania that when a slave came through Grafton, her chest got tight so she couldn't breathe, and she never let her eyes meet those of the slaves. Her friends' responses didn't reassure her. "But you're free, Peach. And no one's ever seen runaways in Grafton, have they? The sheriff won't take you or the children."

Peach knew better than not to worry, but all she could do, she decided, was hope slavery would, mostly, stay out of Grafton like it always had.

But she lay sleepless with worry through many long nights. The more she thought on it, the more frightened she became. If a magistrate came, would he take a close look at her parents' freedom papers? Just to be sure? According to her mother, Venus, Sophia de Marechal had written them after they'd reached Grafton, when Venus and Seth had taken their free name, Hanover, to go on the papers giving them land.

Peach had always suspected there was some irregularity in the free papers and the homestead deeds, because Venus always refused to be specific about their origins. Sophia and Henri de Marechal had helped six slaves—Venus; Seth; Saskia and her boy, Cully; Meshack; and Nott—run away from a cruel owner. That much Venus had told her. Venus was also adamant Sophia and Henri had never owned a slave themselves, yet Sophia had written the papers claiming the escaped slaves were free. But how could Sophia give free papers to the runaways if she didn't own them in the first place? Were the free papers not real? Could the sheriff or a magistrate tell?

But when Peach tried to get to the bottom of it, Venus just said Sophia de Marechal had always done just as she pleased, not bothering with whether or not it was the law if it didn't suit her. She was white, and high-handed, that was just how she acted, said Venus, that was how white folks did things. They could; they were in charge of the law. Sophia had brushed aside any mention of the law that she felt was inconvenient with a wave of her hand. Poof! Saskia refused to elaborate further, and Peach's fears about the freedom papers increased.

And there was something else. Susan was much lighter than her five sisters, and though this was another thing Venus would never discuss, Peach guessed Susan's father must have been the white owner who Venus still hated after all these years. In fact, Susan bore a close resemblance to Cully Stuart, who everyone knew had been fathered by Venus and Saskia's owner. Venus said the old owner was dead, had died shortly after they'd run away.

All Venus would say was that Susan had been born on the road after her escape, months before they reached Grafton. Sophia had told all the slaves they were free but hadn't actually written the official freedom papers until they'd reached the valley. Piecing this information together, Peach was fairly certain a justice of the peace would say that according to the law, Susan was the child of a slave at the time she was born and that was enough to make Susan a slave even now.

And if a magistrate ruled Susan wasn't free because her mother had been a slave when she was born, her other sisters, Patsy, Polly, Pearlie, and Pen, would be looked at too.

Though surely no one could know if the Hanover freedom papers weren't good, not so long afterward?

Would they go looking at everybody in Grafton then? The children . . . Kitty and Cully had five. Her sisters were strung out along the valley with their families on the homesteads Seth had bought for his daughters. Some had white husbands. Could they pass the children off as half-bloods rather than mulattoes? What would happen to them all?

So, months later, when Stefania stood on the trading-post porch, observing the travelers and remarking the newcomer in the blue coat looked official, Peach was in a state.

She hadn't told Bryn or her mother or Susan or her friends, but if she hadn't seen runaways before the sheriff's visit, she had now. There'd been stowaways on the last packet boat. It docked at dusk, and in the melee of passengers and things being unloaded, she'd watched two dark figures slip ashore and run, crouching, toward her and Bryn's cabin behind the trading post. In the blink of an eye, they'd disappeared into the space under the porch. When it got dark, something compelled her to leave a plate of food and a blanket there.

She'd regretted it almost at once. She'd lain awake all night straining to hear noises under the porch. She'd crept outside before the morning star appeared and Bryn and the children woke. The plate was scraped clean; there was no one in the space. The blanket was gone.

Relief fluttered like a nervous butterfly in her stomach. No one would ever know what she'd done. Peach wondered if the runaways had heard about free blacks in Grafton and come thinking they'd get help. But what if the runaways were caught and confessed she'd helped them? She regretted she'd done anything so rash.

"He does look like an official somebody," muttered Peach, eyeing the newcomer. "And those men with him, in black dresses. They his clerks?"

"No, I think they're Catholic priests," said Stefania. "Papa says there are many in New Orleans."

"Just priests?" Peach let out a sigh of relief and pressed her hands under her heart to calm its racing. "Still wish I knew for sure about that man," she murmured.

CHAPTER 5

STEFANIA

Stefania and Peach considered the stranger. The object of their scrutiny was tall, with a military bearing and graying hair tied back in a queue with a black ribbon. He paced back and forth on the landing as if he were waiting. "He doesn't look like a trader or a merchant or a preacher, does he?" said Peach.

The man was joined by a lanky young Creole who had a whip coiled on his shoulder, in charge of a pack of large, unruly dogs whose coats were a mixture of black, white, and brown. The dogs whined and yelped, straining at their leads. The man stood talking to the priests, waiting while an entourage consisting of a light-skinned manservant, two slave grooms leading six laden pack mules roped together, and some horses came down the gangplank.

Seeing the dogs, Peach moaned. Slave catchers and patrollers used dogs to hunt down runaways.

Stefania laid her hand on Peach's arm. "I'll discover his purpose," she declared. She smoothed her skirts and retied her bonnet. The bonnet was faded and fraying, but Rosalia had made it from strips of a colorful old dress she'd danced in once, and it was Stefania's favorite. Stefania had sewn on new ribbons and decided it would do. She pinched her cheeks to make them pink, then took her basket back. "If he's anybody official, I'll come back and warn you. Otherwise I'll just go on home. Papa and Mother will be in a state."

While the grooms saddled the horses and the young Creole strode around, cracking his whip and shouting in patois to the dogs, the man in the blue coat looked about him, as if to get his bearings, then walked toward the trading post. Stefania took her heavy basket and hastened down the trading-post steps, eyes intent on her basket as if its contents were a source of fascination that blinded her to anyone who might be in her path. Her mother had shown Stefania how in her dancing days she'd made her skirts sway enticingly with little obvious hip movement. Stefania made her skirts sway now.

The man intercepted her, removed his hat, and bowed.

"Madam, good day." This saved Stefania from having to bump into him while looking at her basket.

"Oh!" She gave an artless start of surprise.

"Forgive my addressing you on no acquaintance, but can you tell me, does a gentleman named Henri de Marechal still live here? Is he alive?"

She raised her head and watched his expression change as she opened her eyes wide. "What is your purpose in asking, sir?" she asked sweetly. As far as she could judge from her reflection in the looking glass, Stefania privately thought she did rather well. She had dark eyes and brows, a smooth olive complexion set off by even white teeth, and dark hair that framed her face with stray wisps. But there were almost no pleasant men to notice, so his reaction was gratifying.

"I . . . er . . . an old acquaintance," he stammered.

Stefania fluttered her eyelashes. "Of course. You'll find him up at Wildwood." She set down her basket and pointed. "It's up there, about halfway up Frog Mountain. You go past the burying ground, there, then up through the orchard. There's a path. I expect his daughters will be pleased he has a visitor," she added encouragingly. "Have you traveled far, sir?"

"Yes, from France . . . How the apple trees have grown, of course, after so many years," the stranger murmured, looking up the mountain. Stefania wondered why he was suddenly interested in apple trees and waited for him to turn his attention back to her. She tapped her toe impatiently, needing to engage him a little longer and discover whether Peach's fears were justified, but he was looking around, saying something about the trading post, the buildings, and the orchard, as if he recognized them. And he'd forgotten her! Tiresome man! After a moment she bent to lift her basket, muttering an oath in Italian at its heaviness.

"Allow me," he said, turning back to smile at her while lifting it from her hands. "Where are you going?"

She pointed across the river. "My home, Chiaramonte, is there, on the opposite bank. Perhaps you've heard of the Chiaramonte horses? They've become rather famous, many people know the name. Have you come to buy some? If so, my father would be delighted to see you if you choose to call." The man looked pensive, as if he was trying to decide that very question. As if he didn't know whether or not he'd come to buy horses, thought Stefania, exasperated.

"*Are* you here to buy horses?" she demanded.

"Chiaramonte!" he exclaimed. "I certainly know that name! It's Sicilian, is it not?"

She nodded, surprised he knew that.

"An old title," he said, musing. "The family were Christian, had a stronghold in the mountains, held out against the Moors . . ."

Stefania sighed and quickly recited what she knew. "Indeed, such a curious name, Chiaramonte. My father says the sense of it is 'mountain light.' Like a beacon, you know, shining in the mountains . . ." This was tedious. She needed to find out about him, not discuss Moors and Sicilian topography. "How I rattle on! Are your dogs good travelers, sir?"

He nodded. "Yes, the dogs are French, a new hunting breed. My intention is to buy land and breed them for sale. Americans are as fond of good hunting dogs as of fast horses. But I fear I'm detaining you, madam."

They'd reached the far end of the jetty. "Surely there's a ferry to fetch you home."

Stefania decided not to waste more time trying to charm information out of him. Peach needn't worry. For all his fine coat and his air of distinction, he hadn't turned out to be a magistrate but an old Frenchman who fancied himself a gallant come to visit Henri de Marechal, not to cause trouble for the Hanovers.

"How obliging of you to carry my basket so far, sir. There's no ferry. My canoe's tied just here, below the jetty. I enjoy rowing myself across." She gathered her skirts, mischievously high enough to allow him a sight of her slender ankles and calves, then climbed in nimbly to settle herself in an unsteady Indian canoe before the man could offer his hand to help. He handed her the heavy basket, and she braced it in the gunwales.

He stepped back, saying, "I neglected to introduce myself. Colonel Thierry Charbonneau, at your service."

She untied the rope with one pull and shoved the canoe away with her oar. "I am Stefania Albanisi, at yours. *Au revoir,* Colonel," she cried, swinging the bow of her canoe round.

"Albanisi?" she heard the colonel exclaim, staring after her.

"Do you know that name as well, Colonel?" Stefania called.

"Albanisi is well . . ." But she was out of hearing. She gave a quick wave and dipped her oar into the water. At least he hadn't spat tobacco juice on her new gown.

She cast a look over her shoulder and saw him rejoin his companions. The young man with the dogs was staring after her; then he turned to Thierry and laughingly said something that made Thierry turn away abruptly. The young Creole shrugged. He swung his whip, and Stefania heard him shout commands in French until the jostling hounds were brought to order behind the riders. Then he turned back to cast a last long look at her over his shoulder. He kissed his fingers in her direction and turned away.

How impertinent!

CHAPTER 6

Up at Wildwood the de Marechals were taking advantage of the fine afternoon and preparing for winter. The men were cutting logs and stacking kindling. On a bonfire the sharp, sour smell of apples stewing rose from a large iron cauldron. Baskets of windfalls were being cut up by a host of barefoot children and tossed into the pot to make jelly.

Magdalena liked the jelly. It was tart, one of the few things she could bear to eat now that she was pregnant, but Annie had been very cross when she'd eaten an entire pot of it.

Now Magdalena was obliged to leave the apple jelly to the children and help with the soap. She, Annie, and Kitty were standing over a second bonfire, faces red from the heat. Sleeves rolled up and skirts hitched up behind them, the women were waiting for an egg to float in the boiling lye they'd made from ashes and water. The last egg sank and disappeared. Magdalena was thinking another minute and she'd be sick into the cauldron. It smelled disgusting, and the thought of an egg made Magdalena's stomach turn. She wanted to lie down, she felt constantly sleepy, and the only food besides apple jelly that appealed to her was the tart juice she siphoned off from the sauerkraut barrel behind the house.

Robert was solicitous and told her not to lift heavy things and to rest when she was tired, but Annie, who'd had five children and claimed never to have felt too sleepy or sick to manage her housekeeping when *she* was pregnant, wasn't at all sympathetic.

"Do you suppose we'll have good luck with the soap this year?" Magdalena said as Annie dropped another egg in. It bobbled dizzily until Magdalena had to look away. Women always talked about having "luck" with their soap if it set. Magdalena didn't actually care. She hated soap making at the best of times, but she was trying to sound housewifely and ingratiate herself with Annie, to prove she was just as competent as her sister-in-law now that she was finally going to be a mother.

"I hope so! Oh, good!" Annie exclaimed, as the egg came bobbing back up to float. Now the lye was strong enough to be mixed with grease and boiled into soap. Annie poured a summer's worth of rancid cooking grease into the lye and shoved more wood onto the fire beneath the cauldron, frowning with concentration as the thick mess boiled. Magdalena's stomach heaved, and she tasted bile. She bent over and retched, avoiding the basket of lavender at her feet. Before she straightened up, she rubbed a spray between her fingers and inhaled the fragrance gratefully.

Sophia had taught her daughters to scent soap with herbs or flowers, just as she'd learned to do in England when she was a girl. That was another thing about being pregnant—she found herself wanting her mother. Magdalena felt tears well up. She didn't remember Sophia very well, but she missed her, just as she missed her older sister Charlotte, who'd been kidnapped when Magdalena was small. She couldn't remember her very well either, just the pain of her absence. Magdalena wished they were both here now!

But they weren't. She swiped her hand quickly across her eyes and tossed the basket of dried lavender into the boiling mixture. Too late she remembered she'd neglected to separate the flowers from their stalks, had just given the lavender clippings a hasty chop, and now the boiling mess looked as if hay had fallen into it.

Magdalena saw Annie wince with irritation as she pointed out crossly that the *right* way to perfume the soap was to wait until it was done, then scrape some off and melt it before mixing in the spirits of lavender she'd made in the summer—following the recipe of *her* mother, Caitlin, not Magdalena's mother's recipe—and some fresh lard.

Magdalena resolved to chop the lavender up with a long knife later, when Annie wasn't looking. Annie went about the soap making as if life itself depended on it, the same way she went about boiling and scrubbing and scouring. Her Welsh mother had waged a constant battle for order and cleanliness against wilderness dirt, mud, and men who marked their presence with jets of tobacco juice. Annie was just the same.

Magdalena sighed and, when Annie's back was turned, picked up a stick and gave the lye and grease a surreptitious stir to push the lavender out of sight.

Annie caught her and snatched the stirring stick out of her hand. "You must stir soap only *one* way, *this* way, Magdalena, if it's to set right! You stirred it the other!"

Behind Annie's back, Magdalena's older sister Kitty crossed her eyes in sympathy and mouthed, "Cross to bear," pointing at Annie. "I'll fetch some fresh lard," Kitty said, and disappeared into the cabin.

"Look," called one of the children. "Someone comin' up through the orchard."

The arrival of a man on horseback interrupted everyone's work. The women hastily let down their skirts.

Kitty's husband, Cully Stuart, stepped forward from the kindling pile he was building.

The stranger swept off his hat and bowed to the ladies from his saddle. "Good day. Colonel Thierry Charbonneau, at your service. Is Henri de Marechal still alive? Your master, I suppose."

Cully's expression hardened. "My wife's father," he said coldly.

"Henri's daughter married a Negro?" exclaimed Thierry. "Impossible!"

The man turned in his saddle, looked around at the silent, now-hostile family. He adopted a conciliatory tone now. "Allow me to explain. I was with your father and mother the first time we saw this valley, from that big rock ledge." He pointed up the mountain to the jutting rock shaped like a man's head that they called the Old Man of the Mountain. "It made me think of a big wild boar wallow—I called it *une bauge*. It was a joke, but no sooner had I said it than a boar with her litter came out of the forest, and the sow charged me, as if to confirm I was correct. Now this is the Bowjay River, the Bowjay Valley . . . all from my joke."

He waited.

"Come, shake hands. I misspoke. We French are no friends of English slavery. Please, have the goodness to tell Henri I've come. May we dismount?" He gestured to the Jesuits who'd ridden up behind him.

Cully hesitated and then shook Thierry's hand. "Yes. But Pa may not remember so well as you. He forgets who people are, knows them one minute and forgets the next."

"Pa?" Cully called through the door. "There's someone asking for you." An old man with white hair shuffled out.

"Henri?" said the stranger. "Don't you know me?"

Henri peered at the stranger. "My sight isn't what it was. Who are you?"

"Don't you recognize me, old friend? It's Thierry. On the day your daughter Kitty was born, I left. I wanted to return to France but you preferred to stay. I promised I would be back. And now after many years, I have kept my promise."

"Eh?" said Henri. "Did you go to France?"

"Henri, do you remember me?"

"What?"

"It's Thierry! Surely you've not forgotten me! We were like brothers once."

"Who?"

"Thierry! We last saw each other the morning your daughter was born. I'd despaired of going back to France with you, and left. It's been a long time."

"Eh?" Henri's mouth dropped open, and he rubbed his hand across his eyes. "Kitty?"

Kitty stepped forward. "Papa, your visitor is Thierry Charbonneau!" she said loudly. "You've spoken of him often."

"Oh dear, Papa doesn't remember," Magdalena murmured to Annie, but then there was a cry.

"Non! Thierry? C'est vraiment toi?" Henri opened his arms. *"Vraiment toi?"*

"Thank God, Henri! I find you still alive!" The two men embraced a long time. Then Thierry clapped his friend on the shoulder. "So much time, so much time. And now, this is your family. Eh?"

Sweating from his wood chopping, George stepped forward, offering his hand. "I've heard my parents speak of you, of course, Colonel. You are welcome at Wildwood, sir! I'm Henri's son, George de Marechal. There is my sister Magdalena; her husband, Dr. Robert Walker; my other sister, Kitty, Cully's wife. This is my wife, Annie, and these . . . our various children. Too many to name." George smiled, sweeping a hand at the gawking children.

"And Sophia? I hope she is well?"

"My mother died," Magdalena told him in a strained voice. "Papa took it hard. We all did, but Papa hasn't been the same since, doesn't always remember she's gone. Kitty looks like her; he often thinks Kitty *is* Mother. He has good days when he seems his old self, and bad days when he's a stranger."

"It was Injins kilt her," piped up one of the children. "Kilt her and Uncle Francis too. They's buried down yonder." He pointed toward the orchard.

"You can see the blood still in the floor. Ma put a rug over it," said Annie's eldest.

Magdalena watched as the blank look settled on Henri's face. It always happened when they spoke of Sophia, as if someone had blown out a candle. Robert had told her he'd seen it happen to soldiers, when they couldn't bear a memory of something. Henri turned to go back inside the cabin, as if he'd forgotten the visitors and something was waiting for him there. Kitty took his arm and said firmly, "Papa, there is company, we must invite them in."

"Naturally, *chérie*. We must. Of course. As you say. Invite the company . . ." Henri seemed to come back to himself. He patted Kitty's hand. Then there was a chorus of barking, and everyone turned to see the young Creole and the pack of hounds emerge from the orchard.

Henri raised his head. "Dogs?"

"They're big as donkeys," Annie gasped.

Thierry threw an arm around Henri's shoulders. "French hunting dogs. A new breed, the finest in the world, and you shall have a pair, *mon ami*." Thierry walked to the pack and dragged one large squirming animal forward. "You won't have seen a dog like this before. Look at those hindquarters, those jaws, eh? And their coats, black, brown, and white, *tricolores*. They can bring down a stag. Even a bear, I imagine.

"This young man Gustine, from the Jesuits' orphanage, is the *maître de chenil*. He's the only one they obey. We'll hunt the dogs together, and you'll see their worth. I brought them to breed and sell in America. We can discuss later if you perhaps have some land you're willing to sell me. But there's another reason I've come, the Jesuits are here to . . ."

Henri wasn't listening, on his knees, absorbed by the hounds until Magdalena gently tugged him up. "Papa, invite our guests in," she reminded him. Henri put an arm round Kitty's shoulders and led the way in. Magdalena sighed and calculated as people crowded into the cabin. How were they to feed eight extra people? Even Annie could only stretch a half-eaten cold ham so far.

Just then the frisky hounds were turned loose for exercise by Gustine. Barking furiously, they raced around the clearing and then bounded into the cabin, large paws thudding on the pine boards, making an instant enemy of Annie as they overturned furniture, smashed crockery, and leaped on the table to fight over the remains of the ham.

Chased by Gustine shouting, *"Allez, allez,"* brandishing his whip, followed by Annie and Magdalena wielding brooms, they upended a churn that Magdalena had left full of buttermilk, ripped up a feather mattress with their teeth, and lifted their legs or squatted at will. Driven outside at last, the hounds spotted Magdalena's chickens pecking peacefully through the vegetable garden and pounced. There was a cacophony of terrified squawking and fierce barking before Gustine finally managed to catch and restrain the hounds with choke leads. The cabin stank. Outside there were mutilated chickens and feathers everywhere. Annie swung her broom and whacked the nearest dog with all her might. It yelped and dropped a dead chicken.

Kitty grimly fetched hot water and lye soap. A nerve quivered angrily in Annie's cheek as she retrieved broken crockery before she and Kitty set to scrubbing, while Magdalena gathered up the mutilated corpses of her chickens with barely suppressed fury.

Annie prided herself on being equal to any domestic emergency, but today she pulled her sister-in-law aside. "Kitty, I don't know how we're to feed everyone. With the soap making, I haven't anything for dinner but corn pone and dried beans soaking for soup, and since the dogs took the ham, there's no bone to cook them with! Of all days for company! Go home and fetch whatever food you have. We mustn't disgrace George," she begged.

"Or Papa," added Magdalena. "Especially Papa. It's his house, his company," she added pointedly.

Leaving the soap to bubble on the bonfire, Kitty set off with Cully. Back at their cabin, the Stuarts' eldest child, Henry, was repairing a chicken coop, and the younger children were collecting beans and tomatoes that had dried on a platform in the sun or stuffing dried ears of corn into sacks for the winter. Kitty told them to hurry, Granpapa had visitors and they were all going to Wildwood for supper. She surveyed her own supplies and hastily made an apple pie in her largest dish and stirred up an Indian pudding. Cully and Henry finished milking and feeding the animals and hitched mules to the wagon.

She'd been looking her worst when the colonel came, and there was something about him that, old as he was, made Kitty wish she could make a better impression. Telling herself she owed it to her father to look her best to entertain his friend, she swiftly combed and rebraided her hair and donned a fresh kerchief. Would he notice the improvement? When they were preparing to leave, she grabbed each protesting child to scrub their face and hands with a wet rag before they climbed into the wagon.

The children's bare feet dangled, swinging over the side. Cully drove and Kitty wedged the Indian pudding under her feet and held the warm pie on her lap, not trusting either near her hungry brood.

The children were curious what company at Wildwood could be important enough to drag them from their chores.

Cully said, "There's a colonel, from France."

"France!" The children gasped with delight. The French were heroes. General Lafayette was as famous as General George Washington and General Nathanael Greene. As they reached Wildwood, Kitty turned round and warned her children to remember their manners; Colonel Charbonneau was Granpapa's oldest friend, and they mustn't disgrace Granpapa.

At Wildwood, Annie's biggest iron pot simmered on the hearth. "Chicken fricassee!" crowed Henry. "Colonel Charbonneau must be important if Aunt Magdalena killed so many chickens!" Henry

60

surreptitiously snatched a handful of dried tomatoes from a string by the big fireplace.

"I daresay," murmured Kitty, putting down her apple pie. Annie hadn't let the dead chickens go to waste.

Henri was animatedly telling a story, and there was a roar of laughter from the men gathered round the fireplace. "It was worth the chickens. Talking to the colonel, Papa seems like his old self," whispered Kitty to Magdalena, who was still cross about the chickens and had a face like thunder. "Papa could charm everyone; Mother, us children, all the neighbors."

"Could he?" the usually placid Magdalena snapped. People always said Henri had been charming, but she could scarcely remember what her father had been like before her mother died. At dinner the boisterous children were mesmerized into silence by their grandfather's stories as he and his guest reminisced about their adventures, how they'd been French spies in Virginia, when France and England were at war over land on the Ohio River, and had slipped away from Williamsburg to avoid being captured and hanged, how they'd set out for New Orleans with no idea where it was, how they'd fallen ill and spent the winter in an Indian hut, how they'd followed a river trail looking for Sophia's patent of land.

Henri asked Thierry how he'd made his way back to France when they'd parted company.

"The Jesuits in La Nouvelle-Orléans felt obliged to assist me since I was a cardinal's son. But when France entered the war, I was appointed an aide-de-camp to General Lafayette."

"How?"

"Because I was one of the few men in France with any experience of the American wilderness—with you."

Henri roared with laughter.

"General Lafayette!" The children were awed.

"And did you meet General Washington?" asked young Henry breathlessly. "The hero? They say he's taller than other men and can't be killed with bullets."

"But of course I knew him! He was our commander. General Lafayette and I were always with him in camp. Yes, he is tall, and there is something about him . . . It's true his old Indian enemies believed bullets couldn't touch him. He was never shot or wounded, though horses died under him and his jackets had bullet holes. But it is well he lived, no? We must call him President Washington now."

"Henry wants to be a soldier," said Cully, clapping his son on the back.

"And your family, Colonel?" asked George.

"I've never married. On my return, my father arranged for me to manage some of the church's estates. When he learned the Marquis de Lafayette required an aide in the American colonies, he put my name forward. After Yorktown, General Lafayette hastened back to France on family business, and I accompanied him. Lafayette had negotiated a stipend from the king to be paid to me and several other officers for our service, and he advised us not to wait but to return and claim it at once. I purchased a *manoir* on the Loire where we hunted as boys, Henri— just as we once planned to spend the royal reward for our spying."

"Ah yes. We dreamed of an easy life then . . . wed to heiresses." Henri shrugged.

"Yes, we imagined we'd live like princes, but it was not so easy as we thought, and I put off marrying. The only estate I could afford was neglected and decaying, uninhabited for many years. And making land productive is hard."

There was a murmur of assent around the table.

"The peasants belonging to the *manoir* had no master for many years. They were lazy and came and went as they pleased. I introduced a system to make them work, turning off the land those who would not. After an example was made of the most troublesome, the rest grumbled but worked harder. Crops grew where no crops had been harvested in years, a vineyard was planted, and there was enough money to restore the house.

"But the situation now in France . . ." He shook his head. "There are angry mobs in Paris, everywhere, peasants and tradesmen; they say it is the fault of the Austrian witch, Marie Antoinette, that they pay so much in rent to their landowners that their children starve, while she and her ladies shut themselves away at her little chateau, Petit Trianon, to play at being milkmaids. They began by hating the queen, but now they hate the king and all his family too. Everywhere mobs gather, they cry, 'Down with aristocrats, down with the church.' They are madmen, savages, and they cannot be controlled, even by the soldiers. I don't know what will happen.

"The madness spread to my own peasants. They were surly and pilfered openly. Then one night I woke to find my bed curtains alight. If my manservant had not braved the inferno with a wet sheet and dragged me out, I should have burned to death. We took such money and valuables we could carry, saddled my two best horses, and escaped as the *manoir* burned. It was a night I cannot forget, the sound of the peasants cheering as they hurled stones and smashed windows as the flames leaped up.

"Later, I understood. God was angry with me. I'd neglected to honor the vow I made long ago."

"What vow?" Henri looked confused again.

"Have you forgotten the winter we came? We nearly starved, we'd eaten one of the horses, and there was no food. There was no game at all, and I rode down into the next valley, determined to die. I sat under a tree to wait for Death and was saying the rosary when the Virgin showed me a field of unharvested Indian corn and we were saved. I vowed to return here with some holy relic and dedicate a shrine to her in thanksgiving."

"A holy relic," Henri muttered scornfully. "Like the splinters of the true cross and vials of saints' breath sold to gullible pilgrims in Rome?"

"No, Henri, by the grace of God I possessed one and managed to save it the night my *manoir* was burned. During the restoration, I found the ruins of a chapel, and I sifted through the debris to see if anything could be salvaged and used. Next to the remains of the altar, I found an alcove containing a small metal casket with broken hinges. Inside. Lying on a dusty cushion was—"

"The crown of thorns!" Henri laughed at his own joke. "Ha-ha-ha!" The Jesuits frowned.

"Papa!" hissed Kitty reprovingly.

"No!" said Thierry solemnly. "Listen! It looked like a piece of bone. The casket proved to be gilt, with a Latin inscription saying it contained a piece of bone from the thigh of St. Eustace. St. Eustace, Henri, the protector of hunters! I knew at once it belonged to the shrine I'd vowed to make in America. And when my *manoir* burned, it was God's way of telling me to delay no longer. That's why the Jesuits are here. They will say Mass and bless the shrine. And I must stay in America and make my fortune anew."

"Who was St. Eustace?" piped up a child.

"He was a pagan hunting in the forest when he saw a stag with a cross between its antlers," said Henri. "The only saint I remember."

"In France?"

"Of course! Have you ever heard of a saint in America?"

"What's a pagan?" demanded another child.

"What's the Virgin?"

"What's Mass?"

"What's a cross? An Indian spell?"

"Er . . . Hmmm," temporized Henri.

Thierry was shocked. "Henri, your grandchildren are heathens! You were baptized a Catholic, you have a duty to baptize the children at once."

The Jesuits leaned over to agree. "Pah!" exclaimed Henri, waving a dismissive hand.

"Let's go poke sticks in the jelly and lick them," whispered one of the boys, and the children melted away. The Jesuits withdrew to the porch to say their evening prayers.

Thierry turned to Magdalena. "Today I met a young woman, Madame Albanisi. She pointed out her homestead across the river, called it Chiaramonte. Curious, I thought, since the Chiaramontes are a Sicilian noble family."

"Ah yes, Rosalia Albanisi was a close friend of my mother's," said Magdalena. "Yes, she's from Sicily."

"No, her name was Stefania."

"Oh, that's Rosalia's daughter, we grew up together," said Magdalena. "Rosalia was a Chiaramonte when she married Stefano Albanisi."

"That's another prominent name in Sicily. Strange to find it coupled with Chiaramonte here. I assumed Albanisi was Stefania's husband."

"Oh no. Stefania's not married," interjected Kitty.

"Is she not?" said Thierry thoughtfully.

Henri slapped Thierry on the back. "Stefano Albanisi is a wealthy man, brought family money with him and turned a homestead I sold Rosalia into a handsome property with a horse farm. Has a lumber business too. Stefania's his only child. Time to go courting, *mon ami*. I'd call on them tomorrow."

"Papa!" This time Magdalena was reproving. Stefania wouldn't be interested in an old man.

One of the girls popped her head round the door to say the boys had dropped so many sticks in the apple jelly it had boiled over. Annie hurried out to reprimand the children, save the jelly, and check the soap hadn't boiled over as well.

Looking pensive, Thierry excused himself, telling Magdalena he'd go make sure the dogs were securely penned.

The women shook out straw pallets for the guests to sleep on, and Magdalena fetched an armful of quilts. Henri disappeared briefly, to return with the jug of Meshack Tudor's good whiskey. Magdalena signaled urgently to Robert, who tried to take it from him. Henri wouldn't relinquish it.

"Henri, be moderate," cautioned Robert.

"Bah. Doctors!" Henri snorted into his whiskey.

Thierry insisted Henri must go along to the ceremony of the shrine. Mass would be said. Henri had not been to confession or taken the Sacrament in many years. He brushed aside Robert's protests that despite tonight's merry mood, Henri was stiff and unsteady in the saddle, that he complained of dizzy spells, sometimes confused Kitty and Magdalena with each other and both of them with their mother.

Thierry toasted, *"Demain!"* Tomorrow.

"Demain," echoed Henri enthusiastically, fired with whiskey and French memories. *"Demain! Oui!"*

The whiskey jug emptied, Thierry and Henri fell asleep sprawled in their chairs by the dying fire. When Robert finally came to bed, Magdalena crept out and hid her father's boots.

The whiskey consumption had its effect the next morning. Henri woke a different person than he'd seemed the night before. His head ached badly. Finding his boots had disappeared made him roar with fury at Magdalena, who burst into tears, and swear to shoot the dog that'd broken in and taken them. He grew so agitated that Robert finally told Magdalena the safest thing to do was return the boots, saddle the plodding old workhorse, and let him go. Mounted, Henri was impatient to set off, though there'd been no breakfast. Because they were to take communion later, Thierry chided.

They set out after dawn with a pack mule laden with the things for the ceremony. Henri startled Thierry by asking irritably where the hounds were and why they'd begun before a huntsman had blown the horn. Though Henri wanted to gallop, the mules were slow, and it took a long time to reach their destination. His head ached worse than before, and he was hungry.

When they reached the next valley, they meandered here and there until Thierry located the stream and grove of trees where he had tied his horse and settled to say the rosary before he gave in and died, when he'd been roused by the sound of dried cornstalks, heavy with unharvested ears, rattling in the wind.

"It sounded like the sea," Thierry said.

What did the sea have to do with the hunt? wondered Henri. He looked around. There was no sea. He dismounted and sat down. The Jesuits and Thierry set to work. An altar was erected in the grove, between two low rocks, and the Jesuits set out incense and holy water, communion wafers and wine, then finally, a small statue of the Madonna and the silver box. Off to the side a priest heard confessions. By the time it was Henri's turn, and Thierry was pulling him up, the excitement of the day had paled, he was cold and stiff and light-headed from hunger, and he'd forgotten why they'd come.

The priest had to prompt Henri with questions, to which Henri from force of old habit answered absently, "Yes, I sinned in that way, mea culpa." He had immediately forgotten the penance prescribed. There was an interminable Mass, a murmur of Latin chanting, monotonous like the hum of bees. By Thierry's side Henri automatically mumbled half-forgotten responses. Rosaries were said—Henri found one had been put into his hands. He shut his eyes . . .

A sudden whiff of incense stung his nostrils. Shaken awake by Thierry, he was cold and disoriented, looking around for his chair by the fire. Annie hadn't made the fire. The Jesuits were placing something in a pile of rocks beneath a tree. There were more prayers and incense. His knees hurt. He was tired. The hunt had left him cold and very hungry. His head hurt. Had they raised a stag? He couldn't remember.

Back to Chambord and dinner now. A good fire and a plump peasant girl to serve him at table and in bed. He closed his eyes and woke as something thin and dry was thrust into his mouth.

There was a silver box. Body of Christ . . . He tried to open his mouth. Someone called his name . . . Had the hunt begun? A distant horn sounded, the notes signaling the quarry was spotted. Ahead there was a tantalizing movement, a glimpse of hindquarters, some large animal? A stag. In the distance the hounds were baying, giving chase. Ha! He kicked his horse on, harder and harder. Ha-ha-ha! He'd outrace Thierry this time. François too . . . be there when the hounds brought the stag down. He was flying, shouting with the thrill of the hunt.

He felt his horse sway under him. Then the ground tilted, and a mighty blow knocked his breath away. There was another blow, and something was heavy, heavy, heavy . . . "God be praised, he just took the Sacrament," a voice said. A girl in a blue gown watched . . . He couldn't remember her name. He tried to brush her aside . . .

"*Est morte?*" a voice whispered.

"Henri!" a faraway voice cried.

Henri tried to explain that the stag had a cross in its antlers. The girl in the blue dress was riding on the stag's back. She turned around, beckoned him on. He felt lighter; his horse was up. They were galloping again. The voices behind him grew fainter, then faded away altogether as he chased the stag and the girl into the silent trees and was swallowed up by darkness.

CHAPTER 7

A FUNERAL

When they carried Henri's corpse in, Magdalena fainted. Annie had the men drag the long wooden table onto the porch to lay Henri out there, where it was cooler than in the kitchen. Annie burned a feather under Magdalena's nose to revive her, then sat with her head in her hands, thinking what must be done before people started arriving.

Robert sat up with his distraught wife all night and at first light went to spread the news. Annie asked him to fetch her mother.

"They'll be here soon," said Annie as day broke, bringing Magdalena a tumbler of tea, "all the women." Children wandered in and out, rubbing their eyes and staring at Granpapa lying on the porch. Annie distractedly attempted to feed them breakfast while saying they must get everything ready for the funeral. Magdalena nodded and tried to think what needed doing first but found it was difficult to think of anything. She went outside and threw up the tea.

Stefania and Little Molly arrived to find Annie trying to attend to a dozen tasks at once without accomplishing anything. Annie tried to check her exasperation that Magdalena was no help, saying she hoped the shock wouldn't make Magdalena miscarry.

Magdalena was incoherent with exhaustion and grief, her eyes ringed with dark circles. "Poor Papa! He was so happy to see the colonel . . . I tried to stop him. So angry! Robert said let him go . . . If you'd seen how he looked when they brought him . . . Annie laid him out . . . before Kitty could see . . . She's tried to make him look better, but Kitty will feel it worst. She was Papa's favorite! He always loved her best!"

"Shh," said Little Molly, hugging her. "Shh." She patted Magdalena's shoulders. Quick footsteps mounted the porch, and Kitty burst in, followed by her eldest daughter, Mariah. "What's happened? We heard Papa was hurt! I came as quick as I could! Where is he?"

"Papa's . . . oh, Kitty, he's . . . it's terrible. Papa's dead!"

The color drained from Kitty's face. "What?"

"He died—in the next valley . . . The colonel and the priests were with him. He had a turn during the ceremony . . ."

"No!" Kitty whispered. "No! Not Papa! Dear God, not Papa!" she cried and covered her face with her hands.

Robert returned with Caitlin and a hastily made pine coffin. With her usual efficiency, Caitlin set about bringing order to the grief-stricken household, making sumac tea for Magdalena, telling her daughter Annie to lie down for a minute, feeding the children cold corn bread spread with preserves she'd brought with her before sending them about their morning chores feeding the livestock, milking the cows, and gathering eggs. She made coffee and told Stefania to take it to the men keeping watch outside by the coffin.

Stefania went out to the porch at the back of the cabin. George and the colonel she'd met two days earlier were seated on chairs bedside the open coffin. Henri had been a handsome man, and charming to women and children, even in his later years. Now he looked terrible, his features pinched and gray, his mouth in a rictus. Stefania couldn't bring herself to utter homilies about God's will or the hand of Providence. She handed around beakers of coffee and murmured, "Oh, George! How terrible for you all, we're so sorry!" She laid a hand on each man's back as they started to rise from their chairs. "No, don't get up."

Thierry started at her touch and looked up. "I am responsible. God forgive me, I killed my friend." His face was twisted with sorrow, and she patted his shoulder, then instinctively hugged him the way Rosalia hugged her when she needed comforting. His shoulders were hard and unyielding, but then he reached for her hand and held it.

"But he was in a state of grace," a Jesuit said. "A good death . . ."

Stefania looked up, caught their gazes. Ravens in their black robes. Her parents hated priests.

The young Creole Gustine walked out to the porch, nodded to the others. By her other side, he knelt by the coffin, crossed himself, and then rose and stood looking down at Henri, silently paying his respects. He was so close to Stefania that their arms touched, and she was acutely aware of his physical presence. He had polished his boots, she noticed, and his hair was wet, as if he'd held his head under the pump. He was head and shoulders taller than she was. There was something intimate about the way his side pressed against hers, the way he seemed to engulf her in his physical aura. As if he'd cast a spell . . . She remembered how he had kissed his fingers to her . . . Stefania told herself sternly that this was no time to be fanciful. Inside the cabin there was a subdued murmur of women's voices, the swish of a broom, and the scrape of furniture being shifted. Stefania extricated her hand from the colonel's grasp and detached herself from Gustine's side. "I'll fetch more coffee," she said, and went to join the women.

By the time Stefania and Little Molly untied the aprons they'd borrowed from Annie and joined the other women going down through the orchard, it was twilight. Wildwood was tidy and swept, a fire laid, water fetched, animals fed, supper prepared for the family, best clothes laid out for the children to wear the next day, furniture pushed back against the walls to make room for the mourners, and sewing and household clutter cleared to make room for the food people would bring.

Magdalena had joined the vigil on the porch and fallen asleep in her chair.

The following morning, people assembled at the foot of Frog Mountain, discussing Henri's death and who was to blame. Some thought the de Marechals were at fault for letting him go; some thought Robert Walker ought to have stopped it; most blamed the French visitor. Gradually the men and women and children separated, women leading the way, carrying food and talking among themselves, men behind, looking grave, and children everywhere.

Little Molly lagged behind the women with her bonnet askew and a grumpy expression. Since leaving Magdalena the previous evening, she'd developed a toothache, but her mother, Malinda, had been too busy to make her a poultice for it, and she didn't feel like talking to anyone. Every time her top and bottom teeth touched, an excruciating pain shot through her head. She wouldn't be able to eat any of the funeral food. She cast a morose eye around to see what she'd be missing. There were chicken and dumplings, brawn, Indian pudding, batter bread, persimmon pudding, baskets of beaten biscuits with slivers of fried bacon, apple fritters, and crocks of boiled custard.

Rosalia had a Sicilian dish of sweet-and-sour vegetables and dried grapes that plumped again in the cooking. Stefania had small cakes made with ground nuts and soaked with honey. The Hanover women, who all had a sweet tooth, carried pies, cakes, and preserves, and cordials made from the blackberries gathered that autumn.

Ungainly Anna Conway had rowed across with a pot of cabbage cooked with apples and vinegar, causing a stir among the women because she was obviously pregnant under her apron. Anna caught the looks directed her way. Nervously she patted her swollen stomach and gave a tentative, gap-toothed smile. "*Ja!* Is baby." She shrank back as Toby Drumheller spat in her direction, cursing the Hessian bastards who'd cost him a leg at Kings Mountain.

Brother Merriman's prim wife, Mattie, carried the scripture cake she always brought to funerals, to remind those who ate it of the word of God. It tended to be dry and was always the last thing on the funeral board to be eaten. Little Molly's mother, Malinda, who carried a basket of dried peach fritters, cast a scornful, sidelong glance at the scripture cake. It looked lopsided.

Mattie kept her ten-year-old twin boys, Mortify and Endurance, by her side, separate from the other children, who, Mattie thought, were undisciplined, rowdy, and a bad influence. Especially Little Molly's younger brothers and sisters. So many of them and all brought up in such a lax way by their mother, Malinda, so they might be happy.

Mattie struggled constantly with the question of why God had seen fit to bless the Drumhellers with a large family of hearty children and laid such a heavy hand on the godly Merrimans. Mattie had suffered a succession of stillbirths before finally giving birth to the twins, and her husband had wondered aloud if this was God's punishment for his decision, years ago, to stay in Grafton instead of going to Kentuckee to preach the Gospel as he'd set out to do.

Thinking this way had hardened Brother Merriman's temperament. Over the years his judgment of his neighbors grew harsher and his sermons fiercer. He accused the settlers of every sin in his repertoire, of wallowing in their lusts, their pride, and their greed, doomed to everlasting torment and hellfire. He described what awaited them in apocalyptic metaphors that transfixed his congregation, who were mainly women and children. Men were less susceptible to his oratory and preferred to while away the hours of church talking horses and crops outside. But funerals were an opportunity to address a captive audience, and he felt called to make the most of them. Afterward at funeral meals, he always said a long admonitory grace before being first to help himself to food. He partook lugubriously but plentifully, to restore his strength.

Mattie and her cake were left to the company of Patience Drumheller, Rufus Drumheller's second wife, and her grumbling teenage son, Zebulon. Zebulon reluctantly carried his mother's offering to the funeral dinner, a pot of dried beans that had simmered overnight in the embers, with salt pork and molasses. According to Patience, beans prepared this way were eaten at supper every Saturday by every godly household in her home state of Massachusetts. The same custom had now been imposed on the Drumhellers. Zebulon detested the beans, hated being forced to walk with his mother and Mattie and the twins instead of with the men at the back. If he could escape his mother, his father would give him a tot of liquor.

At the rear of the procession, Toby swung a large jug of Drumheller apple brandy in one hand as he swung his crutch in the other, while behind him Cully Stuart led a mule ridden by old Meshack Tudor, a former slave. Meshack had a jug too. The Drumhellers and he had engaged for years in an alcohol war, competing to sell to thirsty long hunters, fur traders, and settlers.

Rufus's apple brandy was a rough-and-ready throat-grabbing liquor. Apples mashed up, worms and all, and aged, it was said, by the addition of lye and throwing in a rat to drown in every batch.

Meshack was precise and particular about everything he made; was careful with his distilling, his filtering, and the wood used to make the barrels for his whiskey; and was scornful of the Drumhellers' liquor. He charged more than the Drumhellers did, but his product was in demand among the fur and timber merchants who could afford it, and Meshack was believed to have saved a small fortune over the years from his inventions and his whiskey. It was generally believed that Meshack had buried his money somewhere on his land. Meshack, when he heard this, would grin and say, "Might have, I might have!"

Now he talked loudly to Cully, who was leading the mule.

"Henri always say Virginia liquor taste like rat pee, all 'cept mine. 'Your whiskey like good wine, Meshack,' he say, 'good French wine,' knew to drink it slow, taste it all the way down, not like a horse suckin' water at the trough, way mos' men do. Knew better'n to take it raw and too new. Never drink it till he had to either fight somebody or fall down either. I'se sorry Henri dead. Ain't many white men I sorry to see die. But weren't for Henri and Miss Sophia, wouldn't be livin' in my fine cabin I built, have my fields, sell my whiskey an' put some money by. Us'ta think on buyin' my chillun back someday . . ." His voice sank to a mumble. "Niggers kin dream. I had me a good life here, only wish I coulda saved my chillun, find where they taken and buy them back was my plan but ain't never been possible. Couldn't do it. Otherwise what I gone do with money?"

"What?" said Cully. Meshack often talked to himself. When asked what his ramblings meant, Meshack always denied he'd said anything— it was just his thinking people heard.

"I said, where's Little Molly?" Meshack said louder. "Why she walkin' by herself?"

"Says she's got the toothache."

"We'll see about that. Tell her step back here and say hello!" Little Molly had always been Meshack's favorite among Malinda's children.

Little Molly heard him and dropped back. She pointed to her jaw and muttered that it hurt. "Poor chile," said Meshack. He pulled a small, finely carved wooden cup from his pocket and told Cully to stop the mule. He pulled the corncob from his jug and poured a drink of whiskey. "This fix a tooth. Fix anything. Swish it roun' yo' mouf good and then swallow." Little Molly shook her head. "Go on!"

She took a tentative sip. It tasted very strong and sort of burned the place where her tooth hurt, but she swished and drank it down. For a moment her mouth was on fire and her tooth hurt worse, and then it felt a little better. She drank again until the cup was empty and she felt a warm glow. "Thank you, Meshack." She smiled. "I'm drunk now."

Meshack laughed. "Tooth better?"

Little Molly moved her jaw this way and that. "I believe it is."

Meshack leaned over and muttered, "Tell your mama save me some peach fritters."

Little Molly nodded. "Of course she will. She always does, Meshack. Oh Lord!"

Up ahead she saw Zebulon stop, making a show of shifting the pot of beans, looking around until he caught Little Molly's eye. His mother and Mattie were too deep in conversation to notice and walked on ahead. He waited until she and Meshack reached him, said, "Wait!" and fell in step. Cully gave the mule a switch to hurry it on ahead, leaving Little Molly with Zebulon. Meshack's opinion of Zebulon, which he wasn't slow to voice, was that he was nothin' but a big, fat baby.

Little Molly found him insufferable and spoiled at the best of times, but now Zebulon was sweet on Kitty's pretty daughter Mariah. At fifteen, Mariah was the oldest girl pupil at Little Molly's school. A clever girl and a sort of assistant teacher, Mariah didn't care for Zebulon. Few people did.

But Patience had convinced him he was a catch for any girl.

"It's Mariah," began Zebulon, as he fell in step with Little Molly, complaining she didn't want to sit with him or dance with him and had slapped his face when he'd kissed her after the last hymn singing. Mariah was a silly fool, he grumbled, didn't know what was good for her or she'd be nicer to him. He had a big inheritance coming, and she'd be sorry if he married someone else. "Can you have a word with her?" he wheedled, accidentally banging the bean pot against Little Molly's shin.

Little Molly wanted to slap him herself. She shook her head earnestly, determined to do no such thing, but he was oblivious, droning on about all the money and land his father, Rufus, owned, which Zebulon was going to inherit.

Little Molly murmured, "Is that so?" and listened instead to the conversation behind her, where Bryn had his mother, Caitlin, on one arm and stout Venus Hanover on the other. Both were discussing the priests from New Orleans. Caitlin, whose family had been firm Dissenters, disapproved of papists on principle.

Venus agreed. "Iddo don't like them, say they is Roman priests and he don't like priests, I don't understand why 'cept it something to do with all that religion. I'm sick to death of religion! Brother Merriman preach you half to death 'bout sin, how everybody evil, got to despair, woein' up and down, gon' burn in hell. My girls like it, say way he preach, give them a bit of excitement, but my ears just gets tired, by the time he finish my heart feel heavy like when Seth died, just want to go lie down in the corner. Feel like he talkin' about Seth burning, hurts my ears to hear that. Quakers good at bein' quiet. They thinkin' 'bout good, pray quiet, got their inward light, that quiet too. No shoutin'. No slaves neither, Iddo say Quakers don't hold with slaves."

Bryn steered his mother and Venus over some tree roots. "French don't either," he said. "I read about it in one of the newspapers Little Molly got. They might make it unlawful."

Venus halted in her tracks. "They's white people sayin' they don't want slavery?" She was incredulous.

"That's what the paper said," Bryn assured her.

"Hunh!" Venus snorted as they followed Little Molly and Zebulon up the steps at Wildwood. "Don't believe *that*! Hunh!"

The cabin was already crowded, and Zebulon abandoned Little Molly to go in search of Mariah. A wan, red-eyed Kitty was going distractedly from one unfinished task to another, hugging women, accepting condolences, laying out the food for after the burial, and directing mourners to the porch to view Henri's body. Mariah was busily shooing away hungry children hovering like locusts over the pots and plates and baskets of food, trying to snatch a bite or two before the funeral meal, and she ignored Zebulon, who was trying to crowd up against her.

Magdalena explained over and over how Colonel Charbonneau and Papa had come to Virginia Colony together, and Annie explained that the awful howling in the barn was dogs the colonel had brought from France.

"Colonel!" muttered Venus in disbelief, rolling her eyes. "I knew him when he was complainin' every step we took. Henri had to jolly him on. His dogs mighty loud."

Annie glared in the direction of the barn. "Aren't they a trial! They got loose in the house the first day and tore it up. They howl all night. But George keeps asking that boy Gustine questions about training the two the colonel gave Papa. I can see George won't give them back. Do you suppose I'm mean enough to poison them?"

"Maybe," said Venus, patting her hand. "I would be, honey, if I had to put up with that noise."

People crowded in, setting down dishes and crocks of food, wandering out to the side porch to view the body and pay their respects. A sheet had been pulled up tight to Henri's neck, and his head above it was at an odd angle. He'd been a handsome man once, a swaggering charmer in his younger years and a gallant, if sometimes confused, older man.

Kitty couldn't bear to look at the body but was unable to stay away.

Caitlin finally told Kitty and Magdalena they had to get down to the graveyard if they didn't want to bury Henri in the dark. The days were short this time of year. From the porch there was a melancholy banging as George and Cully nailed the coffin shut. Kitty stopped her nervous bustling and burst into tears again at the sound.

George, Cully, Robert, and Thierry heaved the coffin to their shoulders to lead the funeral procession down through the orchard to the little cemetery at the bottom. Most of the original Grafton settlers were buried there now, along with stillborn infants and children who had died of fever or snakebite. Meshack Tudor had carved wooden grave markers until his hands grew too crippled with arthritis.

Off to one side was a large plot containing the nameless graves of settlers massacred and scalped by Indians during an earlier period of hostilities. One day years ago, Caitlin had watched as a flatboat drifted into the trading-post jetty, piled with bodies of men, women, and children, arrows stuck here and there. No one knew their names. They had plain grave markers, noting whether it was a man, woman, child, or infant and "Killed by Indians in 1768."

An open grave waited by the side of Sophia de Marechal's, whose headstone read:

SOPHIA GRAFTON DE MARECHAL
DAUGHTER OF PEREGRINE GRAFTON, VISCOUNT
CONSORT OF HENRI DE MARECHAL
BORN LONDON, ENGLAND, SEPTEMBER 1735
DIED GRAFTON, VIRGINIA, 1779, KILLED BY INDIANS
REST IN JESUS

The procession halted, and the coffin was lowered into the grave. It was quiet except for Magdalena sniffling and Kitty choking behind the handkerchief she held to her mouth. Everyone looked around expectantly. "Brother Merriman isn't here." Stefania whispered the obvious to Little Molly.

"Annie's the only one of the family to set foot in his church, but she didn't want to listen to him go on about the de Marechals, so she just told Mattie, and Mattie promised to tell him," Little Molly whispered back. "But he's taking a long time to get here. Probably late on purpose?"

"My husband forgets time when the Spirit's upon him with inspiration," Mattie leaned forward to say primly. "People would do better to attend to what he has to say rather than finding fault."

Little Molly sniffed and raised her eyebrows at Stefania.

The mourners shifted from foot to foot.

Everyone knew the de Marechals had never taken to Brother Merriman. He'd inherited an unbending priggish righteousness from his peasant Puritan forebears and imbibed their historic resentment of the ruling classes. Sophia's father had been a wealthy viscount and a hereditary landowner. This, unfortunately, inspired him to assert a spiritual authority and humble her. This had brought out Sophia's imperious aristocratic side, and she'd made it clear that she thought him an oaf.

When Sophia's little daughter Charlotte was kidnapped by Indians, Brother Merriman had waded in clumsily, advising it was her Christian duty to bear the affliction God had laid on her, without repining. "Rejoice in the temper of holy Job," he'd admonished her. "'Whom the Lord loveth he chasteneth.' The Lord chastises the pride of those that hold themselves mighty on earth, and took your little one for the good of your soul. Bow, bow to the yoke laid upon you and repent of your . . ."

Knowing her favorite child was in the hands of savages, bewildered and frightened and crying desperately for her mother, had nearly cost Sophia her reason. She had turned on him, white lipped with fury. "Be silent! Sanctimonious fool! How you must irritate God! Get out of my sight!" she'd hissed.

Kitty and Magdalena, themselves grieving for their sister and frightened by the way their mother had retreated into herself, loyally sided with Sophia and were as rude as they dared be to him.

It was galling to feel himself the butt of the sallies of two young girls, and Kitty could be particularly sharp. Brother Merriman retaliated from his pulpit as far as he dared, denouncing high Anglicans, though Sophia had ceased to have Anglican views or any faith in anything. He made no secret of the fact he thought the de Marechals deserved their lesson in humility. Not quite daring to confront them directly, he referred in his sermons to the unrighteous who "dwelled on the mountain of pride"—here he would fling an arm up to point toward Frog Mountain—"only to fall from a greater height into the everlasting pit where hellfire burned."

Brother Merriman was emboldened by the fact that aside from Annie there were no de Marechals present to hear his sermons, and he trusted gossip would carry the import of what he had said back to them.

But the most deeply felt humiliation at the hands of the de Marechals was that Henri had befriended Brother Merriman's archenemy, Iddo Fox, the Quaker abolitionist. Iddo, who lodged with Venus, had got in the habit of going up to Wildwood to share a companionable pipe at "Friend Henri's" fireside.

Brother Merriman loathed Quakers with all the vehemence of his Puritan forebears. Quakers were a troublesome, godless sect who disdained ceremonious attendance at church and "talking God and godliness," the very bedrock of the Puritan way, in favor of what they called real religion. Quakers dwelled on their inner light rather than their vileness before God. Brother Merriman was proud that his Puritan ancestors had been active in whipping Quakers out of Massachusetts towns on many occasions. He longed to drive Iddo Fox back into the wilderness by the same method, but sensed his own position in Grafton was not quite established enough to allow him to do so.

But Brother Merriman had always conducted funerals, except when Sophia and her son Francis were buried, and it wasn't like him not to be waiting at the graveside, grim of face and Bible in hand, for the mourners to assemble.

The sun went behind a cloud, and the mourners began to feel cold. The silence was broken by a murmur of conversation. Mattie confided to Patience that her husband meant to smite the de Marechals with a sermon that proved Henri was going to hell.

Patience nodded approvingly. Those who overheard muttered that the de Marechals wouldn't endure *that* meekly, and there was a ripple of interest because there was bound to be trouble. People craned their necks to see if he was coming yet.

"Seth and Saskia and Nott dead, Miss Sophy dead, now Henri. Not much longer, I be gone too," said Venus mournfully.

"Don't talk like that, praise the Lord, you still here, still with us, Mama," murmured her six daughters, patting Venus's shoulders, surrounding her with their families like a fortress around a queen. The daughters, an independent and forceful group of women of whom Peach was the youngest, had taken to Brother Merriman. His alarming sermons perked them up and, like him, they disapproved of Iddo Fox boarding with their mother.

That spring the widowed Venus had taken Iddo in after learning he'd been driven out of one town after another across Virginia for preaching against slavery. Iddo did gardening and odd jobs in return for room and board. Venus and Iddo were both elderly; Venus liked having a man to feed, and both took pleasure in the other's company. But the innocent arrangement that suited them both scandalized Brother Merriman. He refused to believe that fornication, his favorite sin, was not taking place, especially given their plentiful intemperate diet, something he strove to discourage as being a kind of wallowing in voluptuousness, dangerously akin to fornication. Venus, who was a good cook, prepared stews and pies and light bread with fresh butter with a lavish hand until they both grew rather stout. It further stoked Brother Merriman's ire that Venus's table contrasted unfavorably with that of the Merriman household, where Mattie excelled in boiled dinners featuring meat and cabbage cooked for hours into stringy messes.

He persuaded the Hanover daughters, who all attended his church regularly, that it was a scandal and a sin that their mother had a strange man under her roof. Now the Hanover daughters muttered to each other so Venus could hear, "Praise the Lord." Peach said pointedly, "Take warnin' from Henri's death! Still time for you to repent, Mama. Accept you got a sinful nature and send Iddo to stay at the tavern where he belong, and Susan can keep an eye on him. Ask divine forgiveness, 'cause you don't, the Devil standin' ready."

"Oh, be quiet, Peach!" Already depressed by this funeral, Venus felt her heart sink at the prospect of the long, shouty, doom-laden funeral oration along these lines that Brother Merriman would certainly deliver when he finally came. She had felt so bad when she lost Seth she could hardly get her head off her pillow, just wanted to die herself right then and there. Iddo cheered her up. He was soothing company, and everything felt better when he was around. The more her daughters went on about sin, the more they urged her to send Iddo away and to join the church, the more she approved of the Quakers, their abolition, their inner light, and their silence.

Curiously, considering his antipathy to Quakers, Brother Merriman called on Iddo often to warn him of the error of his ways. Iddo remained provokingly calm and mild in his demeanor, calling Brother Merriman "Friend Cotton Mather" while Brother Merriman grew red in the face from exhortations. And when Brother Merriman paused to draw breath, Iddo would take out a tract written by his distant relation, the Quaker preacher George Fox, "The Mighty Day of the Lord Is Come, and Coming, Who Dwells Not in Temples Made with Hands, nor Is He Worshipped with Men's Hands, but in the Spirit, from Whom the Scripture Was Given." It was a title that rolled mellifluously off Iddo's tongue.

Brother Merriman would bang his walking stick on the floor, shake his fist at Iddo, and stamp home in a rage to tell Mattie that Iddo Fox was destined for hell and the sooner he went the better. But after a few days' wrestling with his conscience, Brother Merriman would reason he mustn't shrink from creating obstacles in the path of Satan's envoy. He would put his personal repugnance aside and set forth in yet another attempt to lead Iddo Fox to acknowledge his evil nature and get him out of Venus's house. An example had to be set for the young people of Grafton.

"Henri didn't repent, did he, when he still had a chance?" murmured one Hanover daughter. "Give too much of his ear to Iddo when he should have listened to Brother Merriman talkin' on the true word. Brother Merriman says the Lord don't make allowances if you don't take salvation when you got the chance." The others shook their heads.

"I wish the Lord make allowances for folks' feelin's, send Brother Merriman do his work somewheres else!" Venus snapped. "An' you can't say you know what God gon' do. You think God waitin' on your opinion?"

Susan looked up, exclaiming, "Finally! Here come Brother Merriman and . . . Oh dear! Thought we'd left those priests in black dresses on the porch, but they back by the trees, this whole time, look like they and the colonel doing some religion off by theyselves with those strings of beads they prayin' on. Brother Merriman see that, he'll be mad, 'cause papists instruments of the Devil and . . . Oh dear, Mama! Here come Friend Fox from the other way, lookin' like his inward light done caught fire and he gon' speak a revelation. I thought you said he stayin' home! But no, they both hurryin' 'long like they on the path of the sanctified, tryin' to get to the grave first and take charge. Which one did the family ask, Mama?"

Venus raised her head to look. "Annie prob'ly ask Brother Merriman, 'cause she like him. Kitty and Magdalena wouldn't have, 'cause they don't, but they in a state, might not think to ask Iddo. Maybe Robert thought if anybody ask Henri befo' he die, he'd said Iddo. And somebody got to do the buryin'. Let me see can I stop trouble 'fore it take hold."

Venus extricated herself from her daughters, and with a quick step for so large a woman, she moved to intercept the two holy warriors.

"Goodwife!" said Brother Merriman sternly, acknowledging Venus. "Brother Fox, stand aside."

"Friend Merriman, good day to thee," said Iddo, standing in the middle of the path with his hat firmly on.

Brother Merriman glowered at his enemy.

"Ain't a good day! Henri lyin' dead, Kitty broke down, Magdalena in the family way lookin' terrible, folks have to leave soon to do the milkin', and everybody hungry. And nobody doing any funeral! Which of you the family ask to lead the buryin'?" hissed Venus.

The adversaries glared at each other. "The ordained minister is the emissary of Christ and needn't wait to be *asked*! I must turn the other cheek and ignore trifling slights by the family, because it's my awful privilege to remind the de Marechals they were born in iniquity and doomed by their willful wickedness to the everlasting wrath of God. My sermon will bring . . ."

Venus drew herself up. "Never min' that sermon! It'll be too long an' wear everybody out! You ain't distressin' the family any more than they already distress. You hear me? No arguin', no hell, no everlasting wrath, especially no mention of Henri burnin' in the eternal flames. They all takin' it hard. Don't need more misery!"

Brother Merriman drew himself up indignantly and snapped, "*Misery?* Goody Hanover, a sinner must not presume to instruct the emissary of . . ."

Venus ignored him. "And you, Iddo, you been asked?" Venus demanded.

Iddo Fox shook his head. "It was unnecessary. I felt a sudden conviction Henri would want a Friends' observance to comfort his family, so I hastened here."

The mourners had all turned to stare at them, anxious to get Henri decently buried. Iddo Fox and Brother Merriman glared at each other. Brother Merriman tore off his coat and put up his fists. Iddo smirked and bowed his head.

Venus stood her ground and sniffed with irritation. "So! Nobody been *asked*, and whatever *conviction* somebody felt didn't poke its head out until the last minute. You got to take turns. Day be over soon, not time for much. Both a you pray a little, then you each lead some singin', two hymns each, no more, and then, stop! Any more singin' an' prayin', not to mention a long sermon, those girls can't stand it, get worked up all over again."

Now both men turned to Venus, equally annoyed. Brother Merriman drew himself up to take charge. "'Suffer not a woman to teach,'" he quoted sanctimoniously. "'Let her remain silent.'" But Venus, not the kind of woman to be silent, simply raised her voice, which could be louder than anyone's when it needed to be.

"It gettin' late, be dark soon. Can't have no buryin' in the dark when the Devil can creep up an' grab the spirit 'fore the body sets in the grave. Let's make a bargain. You always sayin' ought to be a mission school for the Indian chirrun. Do what I say, and I give that nice piece of land at the end of the valley, at Slipping Creek, so's you can have one. Seth bought from Henri 'fore he died, and I was thinkin' to give that land to Susan when the other girls got married and she didn't, then Susan go and marry Isaac and now they got that tavern behind the trading post, they busy an' got no time for farmin'. If they want land, they can get it theyselves."

"A mission school?"

"Beg pardon, Goody Hanover? A mission school?"

The need for a mission school was the only thing the two men had ever agreed on. At once Venus had their full attention. The elders of Brother Merriman's church in Massachusetts had written, exhorting him to thrust forward with mission work in Indian territory. Iddo Fox's Pennsylvania meeting had urged the same thing. Both believed that a mission school was God's purpose to reconcile whites and Indians, bring salvation to the heathens, teach a generation of Indian children white ways, and make them Christian and peaceable.

"That piece of land, they's trees on it, for building. Got springs. You even got a teacher to hand. Little Molly been teachin' for years. You get the fathers to cut the logs and raise the building, soon's the school's built, she can step right in and start. She bring all the chillun she teachin' now at home an' send word Injin chillun can come too. Get some started comin', rest follow."

Venus was way ahead of them. The two men were astonished by her forward planning. "But you got to have that school together. You commence to squabblin', I take it back, sell the land to Stefano Albanisi. He always askin' do I want to sell it 'cause of the lumber. He give me a good price too. But it's a good place for a school, seems to me, down at the end of Frog Mountain like it is, Injin chirrun and Grafton chirrun there, an' their folks got to have peace."

The two enemies looked warily at each other. This offer was too momentous to be refused.

"I knows it like tellin' a rabbit an' a rattlesnake to make friends, you ain't gon' agree 'bout religion, but you got to find some way teach the chirrun about good. Not go talking an' whispering behind the other one's back how he wrong, settin' a bad example till the chillun confuse, and they parents say this religion sounds like a bad idea."

"Yes . . . well . . . But how would we outfit a school, Goody Hanover?"

"We'd require materials, books, slates, Bibles."

"Primers."

"I see what I can do. Might be Rufus Drumheller'll give something 'ccount of Little Molly. Rich old man actin' like he ain't, but he think the sun shines out of Little Molly's eyes, says she takes after him, startin' her school up at their place till all the fam'lies barterin' for their chillun to go to it. She have a bigger school, he'll like that an' think of some way it can make her or him money. And Meshack." Venus's late husband, Seth, had always thought Meshack had a stash of money somewhere. "I'll see about Meshack. I'll ask other folks too. But you got to start the good work right away, don't keep the Lord waitin'."

Both men nodded, calculating. Each of them was determined to have the school in accordance with his own convictions. Each of them was already framing a request to send north for teaching missionaries.

"Remember, start arguin', I takes the land back." Venus glared at them. "Shake hands."

There was a pause. Then Iddo Fox stuck out his hand. He would work with Brother Merriman so far as needful. No more. "Peace be with you, Brother Merriman."

Cotton Mather Merriman took a deep breath and looked at Iddo Fox with loathing. "By the grace of God, let there be peace between us, Friend Fox." He held out his own hand, then put his coat back on.

"Now, do this funeral," ordered Venus, wondering if the truce would hold long enough for the two enemies to get the school built.

Brother Merriman turned and strode purposefully toward the grave, not exactly breaking into a run, but a determined step ahead of the Quaker. He reached the coffin ahead of Iddo and cried the first lines of his laboriously composed and lengthy sermon. "Hallelujah, let us pray and be humbled before Death's terrible face."

Here Magdalena wailed, and Robert Walker said, "For God's sake, man, if you'd seen Henri's face . . . ," with Iddo spluttering beside him that they must have a hymn first.

Seeing that something was happening at the graveside, the cluster of Jesuits who'd been standing apart looked up from their rosaries. A priest grabbed Thierry's arm and said something urgent. Thierry led him forward through the mourners and shoved Iddo and Brother Merriman aside.

"Father Xavier is right. Henri must be buried as a Catholic." He beckoned the Jesuits forward. One lit a censer, and as incense wafted across the mourners, another one held up the crucifix he had carried and followed him to the graveside.

"Papists! Stink from the bowels of Satan! Abomination before the Lord!" shouted Brother Merriman, shaking his fist. "Be gone!"

Kitty raised her swollen, tearstained face. "Be quiet, Brother Merriman! We've been waiting long enough. Let them bury Papa! The colonel's right. Papa *was* a Catholic, in France. He always wanted to go back, go home, but he never got the chance, because of me. Now he'll be buried the French way, though. It's fitting," she said fiercely.

Annie gasped, but Magdalena put her arm around Kitty and said, "I agree. Bury Papa like he was in France."

Robert nodded, and George turned to say, "If you please, Father Xavier."

Brother Merriman scowled and weighed up his obligations as Christ's emissary versus Kitty de Marechal Stuart's sharp tongue. He'd come off the worse in front of everyone if there was a confrontation. He grimaced and gave way, comforted by the knowledge the whole stiff-necked, unregenerate de Marechal clan would join Henri in the hellfire.

Father Xavier raised his hand and intoned, *"In nomine Patris et Filii et Spiritus Sancti."*

People looked around uncertainly. Some bowed their heads. A few shrugged. Stefano and Rosalia Albanisi looked straight ahead. But from the back of the crowd, there was a cry, half joy, half sob. *"Ein Priester!"* People turned to see Anna Conway sink to her knees, crossing herself. *"Ein Priester! Ein Priester! Grüß Gott!"*

CHAPTER 8

February 1791

At Chiaramonte, Stefania was frequently woken at night by the irritating sound of the new French clock striking the hour. One night she put a pillow over her head as it began chiming midnight—one, two, three, four—when it was drowned out by a loud banging at the door and frantic cries of "The mistress! Call the mistress! It's Anna! Her travail is upon her!"

She heard Rosalia cry, "We're coming, Secondus."

Stefania threw back her quilt and dressed as the banging grew more frantic. In the passage Rosalia was buttoning her bodice. "Mother, where's the bundle you prepared?"

"Under the stairs." Rosalia hurried downstairs to let in a shivering, terrified Secondus, moaning piteously about his wife.

Secondus clutched Rosalia's arm. "Hurry, it's terrible! Terrible! Don't let her die, mistress, I pray you won't let her die!"

"We'll see to her, don't worry, Secondus," said Rosalia. Stefania was uncomfortably aware neither she nor her mother had ever helped at a birthing, and she wished Caitlin and Venus and Susan, who had, weren't across the river. But the river was running fast and high, swollen by a thaw that melted a heavy snowfall. It was too dangerous to cross in daylight, let alone in the dark. She and Rosalia would have to manage.

Caitlin had told Stefania what to do. Caitlin had delivered many babies and made it sound manageable. Now in the dark and urgent night, Stefania was frightened by her lack of experience, which was limited to helping Tamás when the mares were foaling. But Anna wasn't a horse.

Rosalia's nervousness was palpable. "Goddess of Many Crowns, let all go well with the birth . . . ," she whispered, hurrying off to the kitchen to pack a basket with a loaf of bread, eggs, and a pot of fruit marmalade said to be good for restoring women after childbirth.

"What did you say, Mother?" asked Stefania, lighting two lanterns, then flinging her own cloak over her shoulders and grasping a large bundle. "It sounded like you said *goddess* . . ."

"Just an old Sicilian prayer."

Secondus scurried and stumbled ahead of them, urging, "Hurry, hurry!"

Holding up their lanterns, the two women went after the agitated little man, their cloaks swirling behind them. The screams reached them before they got to Secondus's cabin. *"Gott! Gott hilf mir!"*

Stefania handed her lantern to Secondus and ran ahead. The door was ajar, letting in the cold night air, and she cried, "We're come, Anna!" She sent a trembling Secondus to fetch water and wood, told him to make up the fire. By the light of the lanterns, she and Rosalia managed to help the woman onto the straw pallet covered with sacking. Anna gasped and shouted in German.

While Rosalia tried to soothe Anna, Stefania unpacked her bundle and laid on the table what Caitlin had said they'd need. Linen for swaddling, a small quilt, two baby's caps and dresses her mother had embroidered, a knife, folded linen squares to wipe the suffering woman's forehead, bandages, salve, a goose-down pillow.

Anna screamed louder. Secondus cowered by the fire, his hands over his ears, crying that he sensed Death waiting to snatch his own infant and Anna too. Secondus rocked back and forth, moaning in time to Anna's cries.

Through the long night, Stefania was constantly ordering him to put more wood on the fire to keep Anna warm. Secondus would totter to the woodpile, fetch a few pieces of kindling, then forget what he was about and collapse into his seat by the fire, whimpering, "What shall I do if Anna dies? Who'll look after me then?"

"Who indeed," muttered Rosalia, wiping Anna's brow.

The oiled cloth at the windows let in a dim morning light. Anna's screams had been replaced by a gasping, animallike grunt. Then a baby's wail. Secondus dozed, slumped on his stool. Rosalia took the small swaddled bundle from Stefania. "I'll do it. He's more afraid of me."

"Secondus!" Rosalia was standing by his side in a blood-spattered apron, shaking him awake. "Secondus."

He shook his head. "No!"

"Secondus!" Sharper this time. As if she wanted to slap him. He twisted his head sideways and peered up. Rosalia's hair had come undone and was hanging in her eyes, and she looked exhausted, but she held a bundle. "Look, you have a fine son."

Secondus's hands dropped from his ears. Anna wasn't screaming any longer. Stefania was calmly doing something for her with a cloth and basin of water, making soothing noises. He heard Anna's guttural tones. She sounded tired, but she wasn't dead.

Secondus cast a frightened peek at this child of his. It was very red and looked angry, with a tuft of black hair. "It's the image of my mother!"

"It's a boy."

"A boy? Are you sure?" He quavered, "Considering the resemblance to my mother."

"Quite sure."

"Anna wants to know what his name is to be," said Stefania from the bedside.

"Name? Must I name it?"

"A father's privilege, to name his son," said Rosalia firmly. "Anna is a Catholic and wants to baptize him at once. For that, the baby must have a name."

"A baptismal name! A responsibility, to be sure! . . . Well . . . he must have an artist's name. Not all of it, just the first part. With the Conway at the end, of course."

"Naturally," said Rosalia tiredly.

"Perhaps . . . Leonardo? Leonardo Conway? Or Raphael? Raphael Conway?"

Stefania looked up at her mother and rolled her eyes.

"No, perhaps . . . Rembrandt! Rembrandt Conway! Let's see if that fits him," said Secondus, peering at the baby. He considered. "Yes! Rembrandt Conway, that's the one. Rembrandt, Anna. It shall be called Rembrandt. How's that for a fine name, eh? And now that's settled, mistress, is there any hope of a bit of breakfast?"

Drained with exhaustion and deeply relieved she and Stefania had managed to deliver the baby, Rosalia went home to Stefano, but Stefania lingered in the cramped little cabin to help Anna, who had no family other than Secondus. It was obvious Secondus couldn't look after her or Rembrandt. He was like a demanding baby himself. Anna's terrible sojourn in the mountains following the deaths of her husband and children had taken its toll. The birth had been hard on her as well, and afterward she suffered first from a fever and then her leg swelled up so badly she couldn't put it to the floor.

Annie de Marechal paid a visit, bringing a boiled fowl in its broth with dumplings. "Anna mustn't dare get up until the swelling subsides," she said firmly. Stefania sighed and resigned herself to a longer sojourn with the Conways.

Other women heard the news from Annie and crossed the river, bringing soup, clabber, Indian pudding, and cabbage-leaf poultices for the leg. When visitors were present, Secondus strutted and mentioned Rembrandt Conway with every breath he uttered.

Magdalena came with a baby quilt and surprised Stefania by efficiently boiling the Conway laundry. Under her apron Magdalena's belly was swelling.

Malinda brought baby's caps and swaddling her own children had worn. Little Molly accompanied her, bringing the cradle Meshack Tudor had made when Little Molly was born. All of Malinda's children had slept in it.

Anna wept with gratitude and promised to give the cradle back when Little Molly had a baby of her own.

"That's unlikely to happen soon! I'm too busy with the mission school and making everything there work as it should," Little Molly told Stefania. "The main building is finished, and there's a dormitory for the girls and one for the boys to board, with a wing for the women teachers on the girls' and one for the men teachers attached to the boys'. I'm to live there during the school term because it's too far to ride back and forth to Little Frog Mountain. Granpapa wasn't pleased, but then Patience got on her high horse about how improper and shocking it was for single girls to live alone without a chaperone—it was a mark of loose ways, and who knew what we'd be doing. She certainly hoped we didn't expect to be comfortable, and she told Granpapa to make certain our quarters were as small and plain as possible."

Little Molly giggled. "So Granpapa gave money to the school for books, provided Brother Merriman and Iddo Fox agreed to my having a room of my very own because I'm in charge of the lady teachers. He's had them lay a stone fireplace and build bookshelves just for me. We've had a shipment of primers and Bibles, material for their clothes and boots—we decided it's best if the children are dressed alike. There's the kitchen to be arranged and beds and . . . so many things. The children will start in September, after the Blackberry Picnic, and will board until they go home at Christmas, then. It's grand, Stefania! I'm in no hurry to have babies!"

"After seeing what Anna's suffered, I'm in no hurry either," said Stefania.

"Magdalena's near her lying-in. I hope she doesn't brood about Robert's first wife dying with the baby."

"Poor Magdalena!" said Stefania feelingly.

It was spring, and the leaves were coming out before Stefania thought it safe to leave. "*Gott* to me a new life has given," said Anna, finally well enough to rise up from bed and care for her husband and child. Stefania could finally go home.

The next day as Stefania bundled up her things, Rosalia came bringing a syllabub to build up Anna's strength. Stefania gave Rembrandt a last cuddle and promised to come see him soon. He was filling out and plump now, and she was certain he'd smiled at her. She felt strangely sorry to be leaving him and promised Anna she'd ride over to visit him often.

Walking back to Chiaramonte with Rosalia, she saw that her mother's step was uncharacteristically slow and that she kept coughing into her handkerchief.

"Mother, your cough is worse."

"It was only the going about in the cold night air, *cara*, when we had to reach poor Anna quickly."

"That was two months ago!"

Rosalia shrugged and made one of her Sicilian hand gestures that meant *What can one do?*

Stefania looked at Rosalia closely. "Your cheeks are very red, Mother."

"The heat. Let's sit here under this tree for a moment, and I'll tell you our news." Rosalia sank to the ground, settled her skirts around her. "You'll find changes at home."

"What's Papa built now?"

"A kennel and a dog run. A big one. Because of the hunting dogs. They've decided to raise them at Chiaramonte." Rosalia sighed.

"I thought the colonel bought land from George to raise them. He was building a cabin."

"Yes, well, he has a cabin there now, but Gustine persuaded your father it was better to have the kennels at Chiaramonte," said Rosalia dryly. "That way anyone buying horses or contracting for a shipment of lumber might buy a French hunting dog too. Or the other way round, if someone wants dogs for hunting, they might also want a good horse. Stefano loves such thinking. And since they need Gustine to manage the animals, your father agreed he could build himself a cabin behind the kennels."

"Gustine lived in the barn at Wildwood. Magdalena said he'd hung a quilt in the corner of the barn and slept there. And now he has his own cabin at Chiaramonte?"

"You'd mind if he wasn't there. The dogs howl all night, unless Gustine comes to quiet them. Thierry's bred a new litter, and Gustine and your father and the colonel talk of nothing else but the price they'll fetch when they're trained. Though even with training, those dogs are exceptionally disobedient.

"With more orders for timber from New Orleans and Natchez, the horses, and now the dogs, your father's busier than ever. He hired a new fellow, Will Pine, to look after the land and crops. He's a farmer and was taking his family to Kentuckee when they were attacked by Indians. They killed the oxen pulling their wagon before Will drove them off. He and his wife and children reached Grafton with only what they could carry, and needing work. Your father told Will he could build a cabin and have a piece of land if Will would agree to stay and work for him.

One boy is Zebulon's age, another is a little older, and they and Will work in the fields and look after the stable and kennels."

"Mercy!" Stefania laughed. "Papa's schemes are wonderful! He likes fitting people into the places that suit him."

"He's fit two more in. Anna's in no condition to come back to work in the house, but Will's wife and daughter have been hired in her place. The wife, Jane, is cook and housekeeper, and their daughter, Linney, is our washerwoman. Jane is a hard worker and most efficient. But Linney—" Rosalia paused. "One mustn't be unkind to servants, but for all she's a good laundress, I don't find Linney congenial. There's something sly about her. Jane watches her too, never lets Linney out of sight for long. Perhaps it's just . . . as a mother Jane thinks . . . it's necessary to be watchful. There are so many men working at Chiaramonte who don't stay long. And I must say, Linney has the countenance of a girl hoping to be taken advantage of."

"Mother!"

"Well, there's just something about her that invites their attention. Though lately I notice she likes Gustine. Whenever he comes to the house, Linney puts herself in his way, even hovers in the next room pretending to sweep."

"Does Gustine like Linney? It might be a good match."

"It's difficult to tell—Gustine doesn't say much, though somehow one is always aware he's there. I suppose he's rather handsome . . ."

"Is he?" Stefania held out her hand and pulled Rosalia to her feet, determined not to recall how his presence by her side had affected her so powerfully at Henri's funeral. "Since Papa agreed not to buy slaves, we must put up with the Pines, whatever their peculiarities. Let's go home. I'm anxious to see Papa. Has he missed me?"

"He has. As for Papa and his schemes for people . . ." Rosalia fell silent.

Stefania laughed. "Has he another? Perhaps he'll tell me about it over supper."

CHAPTER 9

GARETH

September 1791

On Saturday afternoons, there was a half holiday from lessons at the school when the children had allotted chores, such as cleaning the buildings and weeding the vegetable garden. Little Molly was released from her teaching duties and always rode home to spend Saturday night and Sunday with her family.

Passing the jetty on her way home one Saturday afternoon, she met Stefania coming out of the trading post, who told her that Annie had given birth to a son a month sooner than she'd expected to. Since Caitlin could no longer see well, Venus had gone up to help at the birth, and Peach had told Stefania that it hadn't gone well and both Annie and the baby were poorly.

"We should go up and see her. Come on, you can ride behind me," said Little Molly, giving Stefania a hand up.

At Wildwood they were shocked to see how dangerously pale and weak their friend looked. Robert had ordered her to stay in bed, and

Magdalena was in charge of all the children. The household was chaotic. Magdalena whispered that the baby wasn't interested in suckling, no matter how often Annie put it to the breast. "He hardly cries," Magdalena confided.

The baby was tightly swaddled, very small with a head of fine dark hair and long eyelashes closed tight. "The quietest thing in the house," Annie whispered, looking down at the sleeping infant in her arms with a strained smile. She didn't like to put him down in his cradle.

"What's his name?" asked Little Molly.

"Gareth. Mother says it's a good, strong Welsh name," said Annie. "Maybe that will help." A tear slid down her cheek.

Stefania and Little Molly did what they could to bring order and make Annie comfortable. They swept and scrubbed and tidied, made a pot of stew and corn pone, and fed the children. Annie dozed off, and they took the baby gently from her arms. Gareth made a faint mewing noise and seemed to go back to sleep. His eyelids were blueish.

Afterward they stopped at the trading post to see Peach and give her the latest news of Annie and Gareth. "Poor little thing," said Stefania.

"Mama say if he live, it'll be a miracle," said Peach, shaking her head. "Poor Annie."

Little Molly left, and Stefania began reciting the list of things Rosalia wanted.

"Linney and her mama was in yesterday." Peach frowned. "That girl reminds me of a she cat, lookin' for a tom."

"Peach!" Stefania remonstrated. "But Mother said much the same thing. I've seen her follow Gustine into the barn. I don't dare tell Mother in case she makes Papa send Gustine away to protect Linney's virtue. Papa says he'd never manage without Gustine now, said he thinks like an Albanisi. But he relies on the Pines too. Says he's deeded them land so they'll stay. They've built a nice cabin on it."

"Well, Jane lookin' at Linney real sharp, like she think Linney up to mischief. Maybe that keep Linney out of trouble."

"I hope so." Little Molly and Magdalena and even Annie agreed with Peach that Gustine was nice-looking—dark haired and fine featured and lithe. But he had little to say to anyone except Stefano. He had a disconcerting habit of sliding his eyes sideways, and Stefania caught him watching her intently from half-closed lids, his lips almost smiling. As if he knew some secret she didn't. And the air always seemed charged when he was around.

Since her return from the Conways, Stefania found that every time she stepped outside, Gustine was there. He'd ask if she wanted him to saddle her horse or row her across the river. She had the odd feeling he meant something else. She always thanked him but refused.

"Linney was telling her mother Gustine was your admirer, not hers. Sulky, like. Say he always hangin' round you."

"Oh no, it's just that Papa was used to servants in Sicily, and he told Gustine to saddle my horse whenever I want to visit the Conways and see Rembrandt. So Gustine's careful to do what Papa wants. Though it does seem that every time I step outside . . ." She considered for a moment. "Actually, the way he half closes his eyes puts me in mind of a lizard, waiting for a fly. I half expect his tongue to flick in and out." Peach laughed. "He just watches me, but says hardly anything. Yet he's *there*. It makes me uncomfortable, especially since I know he and Linney . . . But I mustn't say anything to Papa."

But there was something she didn't tell Peach.

Days earlier she'd evaded Gustine and his offers of help, saddled her horse herself, and gone to the Conways with a basket of things for Rembrandt. Returning, she was gathering her skirt to dismount in her usual quick jump when Gustine appeared, startling her, and reached up to catch her. He'd taken her by surprise, and she instinctively placed her hands on his shoulders for balance. She felt his strength as he set her down and didn't let go. He slid his hands slowly up over her bodice. She gasped. She both did and didn't like the sensation. He didn't let go but pulled her to him. He bent to kiss her. She felt his breath as he said, "There's nobody here to see." It was intoxicating . . .

"No!" Instinctively she struggled and tried to pull away, but he was too strong for her.

Then, after a minute, as if to prove he could hold her there if he wanted, he let her go, looking down at her with a self-satisfied half smile. "But you want me to," he said.

"What were *you* thinking?" Stefania retorted, backing away. Then she told herself it didn't matter what he was thinking. He was presumptuous. Her heart beating very fast, she turned and stalked off, resolving not to be alone with him again. Ever.

She didn't notice Linney Pine quietly hanging out washing. From behind a wet sheet, Linney watched the little scene, eyes narrowed to angry slits. She ran her hands over her own bodice, looked back to where Jane was hard at work beating a stiff biscuit dough with a paddle, then ducked behind the hung sheet and ran toward the stable.

Stefania began to regret that the dog breeding was a successful business. Gustine's presence was a constant irritation now, and Linney seemed to be watching them both. But many of those doing business with Stefano left with a young *tricolore*, sometimes even a pair, just as Gustine predicted. Stefania replayed the scene outside the stable over and over. She wondered how it would have felt to stay in his arms, to go into the barn. Where Linney or her mother might have caught them, she thought wryly. If only Gustine and Linney would get married. That would put an end to her fantasizing.

It was a welcome distraction whenever Stefano invited Thierry to stay to dinner. He was good company, entertaining Rosalia and Stefania with stories about his days in the Continental Army; how officers' wives, like Lady Washington, as George Washington's wife was known, braved the dangers of kidnapping and came to join their husbands in camp during the winter, where they sewed and knitted for the soldiers by day and contrived music and balls to keep up morale at night. He described how General Greene's pretty young wife, Caty, had been the toast of the camps and had once spent an entire night dancing with General Washington to see who would tire first; how Lady Washington had named her tomcat Alexander Hamilton because of the disgraceful behavior of General Hamilton himself; and how the same General Hamilton's romance with a pretty heiress had ended in his marriage, much to Lady Washington's satisfaction.

After one pleasant evening, Stefania remarked innocently to Rosalia that the colonel wasn't as old and dull as he'd seemed at first. "Mmm," murmured Rosalia in agreement, her mouth full of hairpins. Rosalia was concentrating on putting up Stefania's dark hair to show off some pretty tortoiseshell combs that had arrived in a recent order.

Rosalia had begun to take an interest in Stefania's toilette. Fashion papers with the latest styles worn in Paris appeared at Chiaramonte. New gowns for Stefania arrived from the New Orleans dressmaker, not simply cut as before, but made, according to the dressmaker's note, in the latest high-waisted style, which emphasized the bosom and exposed the ankles. Although there were petticoats, Stefania complained to Rosalia that they felt flimsy, too diaphanous. She was used to voluminous skirts. "Nonsense," said Rosalia briskly. "This new fashion suits a womanly form."

Stefania was certain the last thing she ought to display was a womanly form if Gustine was about, but she couldn't say so. And Gustine seemed to be in the house more often than before. Thierry was as well. She wore two shifts under her new dresses and wrapped her top half in a shawl.

Between her mother's sudden interest in her toilette and her father's frequent commendation of something either Gustine or Thierry had done—he seemed to praise them both, constantly—Stefania began to feel there was something odd in the atmosphere. "Mother, I feel like a horse that's just scented smoke in the barn. Only I don't know which corner of the barn's on fire. Why are you and Papa behaving so oddly?"

"*Cara*, you are old enough to be married."

Stefania laughed. "All that's required is a man to court me, Mother, but I don't know of any suitable . . ."

"The colonel has made your father an offer for your hand."

"*What?* The colonel! But he's said nothing to me that could be described as courting!"

"Of course not. He spoke to your father, who promised to give the proposal serious consideration."

"*Papa* promised to give it consideration! What about me? Papa isn't going to marry him! I'm not going to marry him! He's old!"

"Yes, he is older than we might wish your husband to be. But there's another suitor."

"Pray, Mother, who?"

"Gustine."

Stefania was speechless.

"Your father likes Gustine, very much. If your objection to the colonel is age, that cannot be an objection in Gustine's case."

"No! No! No!" Stefania protested.

Rosalia ignored her. "Your father has considered the matter carefully and persuaded me either man would make you an acceptable husband. He wishes only to know which you prefer, and then he'll allow him to—"

Before she could finish, Stefania stormed into Stefano's study to repeat what her mother had just said.

"Papa, how could you! I wouldn't marry either of them. The colonel is agreeable company, he's had an interesting life, but he's old enough to be my grandfather! And I know you rely on Gustine, he's become like a son to you, but he's . . . rather odd." She hesitated. *I don't even like or trust Gustine,* she almost said. *He would have had me in the barn if I'd let him, just like Linney.* "He's just not . . . not someone I could think of marrying, Papa. I haven't the slightest feeling of love for either of them."

"Love, pah! It's a father's duty to decide who is a suitable husband. A girl is not expected to have a view, she has not the experience to judge. It's enough if she finds a man agreeable. I've observed both men admiring you, and both seem as agreeable as necessary. Better still, both understand Chiaramonte and all its concerns. I told them I would put the case before you and you must have some time to consider your feelings . . ."

"Papa! I can't speak more plainly! I refuse! I won't marry either one!"

Stefano spoke sternly. "And I will speak equally plainly. It's your duty to obey your father in this matter even if you have not done so in others. I shall not give way this time, miss, not when I have your good at heart. What will become of you when I am gone? You'll need a husband to manage the estate to deal with Rufus Drumheller. Especially to deal with Rufus. Life was hard for your mother and you when Tamás died, I won't leave you in such a situation.

"And a girl your age ought to be married, you ought to have children of your own. In Sicily a suitable match would have been arranged by now, but where is a suitable match here? Passing veterans, like Magdalena's husband? He at least is a physician, but most looking for homesteads beyond the Mississippi have already had a hard life, their women look worn and tired and frightened already. That is not a life for you. Otherwise there are only those oafish long hunters or merchants who call on me with their cheeks full of tobacco."

"Ugh! Certainly not!"

"Is there any other young man to like? Henry?"

"Henry? Papa, he's a mere boy!"

"Exactly. You are clever, my dear, and though your mother had few means to educate you, she's done her best. You have a good mind, a sound understanding, and a true heart, but if you do not marry a man who is educated, you will be miserable, and educated men are rarely met with in this part of the world. At the same time, you need a husband capable of making a success of the business when I'm gone. Gustine could do that. He's quiet, but clever. He learns quickly, has a deferential manner with the merchants but misses nothing. He is eager to establish himself in the world. He would normally have few prospects in life, but the Jesuits have taught him well. He is quick and ambitious and has absorbed the Jesuits' polish and manners. If he was not born a gentleman, he gives the impression that he was, and that will suffice here. He'll be very successful and rich one day. And your mother seems to think he's handsome enough."

"Does she indeed," muttered Stefania.

"Now, the colonel is older, I grant you, and as I dislike the church, it's against him that his father was a cardinal . . . but that's no matter, his father is not here. He may be a Catholic, but he will be content that you are not. In his favor, he was educated at the French court with Henri de Marechal, *is* a gentleman and a landowner in France."

"Not any longer, Papa. His peasants tried to kill him . . ."

"Yes, well . . . but he has experience of large estates, that is the thing, like Gustine he has worked with me. Both, as far as I can tell, are, er . . . abstemious as to . . . that is, they're free of vice, and er . . . the pox . . ."

"Papa! I won't . . ."

"It's a father's duty to decide what's best, Stefania. But since I've observed it's the custom here, ill-judged though it is, for girls to decide for themselves, you may choose between them. I have stipulated neither is to court you openly or make declarations of love until you decide which it's to be."

"Oh, Papa! No! You didn't say that! How awful, how very awkward this is!"

"It is the only way to avoid open competition between them, Stefania. I need them both. Make up your mind. Forbidden to address you, they're growing antagonistic toward each other, like fighting cocks, and it will affect the business before long. Resolve it by choosing one and leaving the other free to marry another girl. I want to see you settled before I die."

"Oh, Papa, please don't speak of dying. Don't be precipitate!"

"*Cara*, I am not as well as I could wish—prison takes its toll. And think of your mother. If anything should happen to me, your husband must be able to manage Chiaramonte and take care of you both. We are not immortal, *cara*. I want to know that you have a husband and protector while I am alive to bless you."

Stefania was dismayed. "But, Papa, I hardly know either of them well enough to say anything in their favor . . ."

"Pah! A girl only truly knows her husband after she's married. Time enough for your husband to court you then. Just tell me which you like best and I'll . . ."

This was hopeless. Stefania expostulated, "Oh, Papa!" and left, nearly colliding with Linney in the doorway. Linney looked startled, and angry, as if she'd been listening.

Oh why, thought Stefania, *if Papa is so eager to have people do his bidding, couldn't he contrive to marry Gustine to Linney?*

Within a week, an exasperated Stefania was recounting all this to Peach and Little Molly at the trading post. "Now it's clear why Mother wanted me to put my hair up, and the purpose of the new dresses. It's as if I were a horse being trotted past by Henry so someone will buy me!" she spluttered crossly.

Peach sympathized, and Little Molly hooted with laughter. Then they commiserated over having a father with old-fashioned ideas about choosing a girl's husband until Stefania finally stopped feeling cross and agreed with them that it was too ridiculous to take seriously. Of course she wasn't going to marry either one of them. Papa was determined, but she'd enlist her mother's help and he'd change his mind. Her mother was the only one who could deal with Stefano.

"Is your mother's cough better?" Peach asked.

"No." Stefania stopped laughing. "She isn't looking as well as usual."

"Annie's baby Gareth isn't well either, poor little thing. Annie is up all night with him trying to get him to feed, hoping he'll get some strength. She looks awful."

CHAPTER 10

ROSALIA

January 1792

The year began badly with the baby Gareth's death. On a raw day under leaden skies, Stefania, Little Molly, Peach, and Magdalena supported Annie, who sobbed helplessly while George laid his son's small coffin in a grave marked with stones. Snow began to fall, thick heavy flakes that soon coated the mourners' heads and shoulders and dusted the new grave until only the wooden cross carved with Gareth's name and the dates of his birth and death marked where the baby lay. Caitlin sang "Guide Me, O Thou Great Jehovah" in a trembling voice heavy with sadness both for her grandson and her husband who'd never returned home. Rosalia contracted a heavy cold afterward and her cough grew worse. A fortnight later, Stefano's shout brought Stefania running to her parents' room, to find a nightmare scene: Rosalia gasping for breath, holding a handkerchief to her mouth. When Stefano lit the candle,

Stefania saw the handkerchief in her mother's fingers was no longer white, but dark with blood.

"Papa! What's happened?"

"Send someone across to fetch Robert! Your mother has consumption," Stefano cried, holding a fresh handkerchief to his wife's lips. "I know the signs, that cough, many suffered from it in the prison. But not all died. She hoped, I hoped . . . Oh, Rosalia!"

Consumption! Was her mother under sentence of death? Stefania threw a cloak over her nightdress and ran to wake the Pines and send one of the boys for Robert.

Robert came before daybreak but could do little. "The course of the disease can be unpredictable," he said, shaking his head. "But I fear this case is too advanced for any cure."

"Advanced?" whispered Stefania.

The disease followed a cruel course. Some days Rosalia would seem better, and her husband and daughter would think Robert had been wrong, that Rosalia had been reprieved. Then suddenly, she would be worse. The house revolved around the invalid's health, and Stefania found herself resenting Jane Pine's attempts to take over in the sickroom. Spring and then summer came, and Rosalia seemed improved by the change of weather and by being outside in the fresh air. Stefano had sent for a bath chair, and Rosalia reclined on it in a protected spot from which she could watch the horses and Henry and Stefano's visitors. Stefania was her constant companion and nurse, arranging pillows and cushions, coaxing her mother to eat a little soup, reading to her or covering her when she fell asleep.

Stefano aged suddenly. He confessed sadly to Stefania that he feared he had brought the illness with him from the prison. They took turns watching by Rosalia's bedside at night. Or sometimes he lay by Rosalia's side as she slept, whispering a wish they might die together.

Stefano urged Stefania to choose between the colonel and Gustine.

Stefania didn't have the heart to defy him outright. "Papa, I can think of nothing but Mother now. Neither can you."

She couldn't bring herself to say, *Wait until Mother dies.*

But in September both Stefano and Stefania were heartened when Rosalia insisted she wanted to attend the Blackberry Picnic. Stefania helped her dress and Rosalia chose her prettiest bonnet. Stefania piled pillows and quilts into a wagon to make her ride up as comfortable as possible. Rosalia lay still, her cheeks flushed in her white face from the effort of dressing, but she enjoyed the outing, exerting herself to talk brightly with the neighbors who made their way to the wagon to ask how she did, and eating more than usual. "It's done me good," she told Stefania as they prepared to return home.

But the excursion took its toll. A night of violent coughing and bloodstained handkerchiefs followed. By morning Rosalia was flushed and feverish again.

One golden September day that felt out of joint with the pall of sadness and approaching death that enveloped the Albanisi household, Stefania had left Stefano talking softly to Rosalia in Italian, and ridden out for a breath of air. She felt weary to her soul and desperately wanted a short respite from the sickroom, to compose herself for the increasingly painful nightly vigil by Rosalia's side, for her mother's inevitable end. She wanted nothing so much as to hold sturdy little Rembrandt for comfort and drink tea with Anna. She saddled her horse herself, quickly, looking over her shoulder for Gustine. But thankfully he was busy elsewhere.

Anna's small cabin was shabby but peaceful and tidy, full of autumn sunshine and a crock holding a bunch of witch hazel and Queen Anne's lace. Anna welcomed her kindly, made sumac tea, and said Secondus had taken a fancy to sketch his son. Stefania spent a pleasant hour with Rembrandt on her knee, telling him stories in an attempt to keep him still enough for his father to take a likeness.

She left reluctantly, refusing Anna's offers to come and help nurse Rosalia. Anna said she didn't trust Jane Pine to look after Rosalia properly, and Stefania assured Anna she never left her mother to anyone but Stefano. Approaching her home, sadness enveloped her again. She pulled up outside the barn, feeling the weight of her nursing duties descend again onto her shoulders and for a moment was almost too weary to dismount. Then Gustine suddenly appeared and was pulling her down from the saddle. She felt a flash of anger—how dare he try such a thing, again! But the sensation of being held up by a man was comforting, and this time she let herself fall into his arms. Then he bent his head and kissed her hard in a manner that left her dizzy and breathless, sending a shiver all down her spine. For a moment despair and sadness were banished. She put her arms round his neck and kissed him back, fervently.

"See, you're mine," he said, drawing back, half smiling. "You want to be mine." His breath was hot on her neck, and his arms were like steel. "Tell your father you'll marry me, Stefania!" he ordered. He kissed her again.

She almost murmured, *Yes, I will.* She wanted the moment to go on and on—anything to stay in his arms. He dragged her into the barn and pushed her back against a bale of hay. Stefania had no energy, no will, no desire to resist . . . until a scream brought her to her senses. Linney Pine stood at the door, her face a twisted mask of fury. "You call *me* a harlot, Gustine? You'll have her quick enough and then . . ."

Gustine let go of Stefania and went to Linney, who screamed again and tried to claw his face like an angry cat. He grabbed her arm, then slapped her hard. Linney's head snapped back as she shrieked and sobbed and spat jealous curses, kicking out at Gustine.

On the back steps of the house, Jane was calling Linney's name. Cheeks aflame with shame and anger, Stefania stalked out of the barn toward Jane with as much dignity as she could muster in the circumstances and pointed backward. Then she ran toward the house, shaken by the sordid scene, wishing never to see Gustine or Linney again.

But she couldn't avoid Gustine. He waited for her everywhere. The air around him felt the way it did before a violent summer thunderstorm. And nearby Linney was always hovering. Watching her. Watching Gustine. Hissing "Whore" as Stefania passed.

In this febrile atmosphere, the colonel and his formal manners were a relief. She felt nothing whatsoever in his presence, and Gustine and Linney kept their distance when the colonel was there.

Robert Walker visited Rosalia regularly. She was suffering now, and he'd produced a tiny bottle of laudanum to ease the pain of her last days. He explained to Stefania how to measure the correct dose, enough to bring ease, not enough to induce visions. He'd told her that it comforted the dying to speak, to recall old memories, to voice their dying wishes and farewells. If her mother chose to talk, Stefania shouldn't try to stop her.

A few nights later Rosalia was so poorly, Stefania saw it was time to give her the laudanum. She persuaded her father to snatch a little sleep, saying she'd keep watch by the bedside.

Stefania was certain she'd been careful with the laudanum, but she'd been so tired, after nights spent lying sleepless next to her mother's bed, listening for the next deadly crescendo of coughing, the bloody choking. The fire burned brightly through the night in the sickroom, and there'd been light enough to see the dose . . . five drops. It had looked like such a little bit in the spoon, but she'd resisted the urge to add more. Hadn't she?

After taking it Rosalia grew tranquil. She ate a little milk toast Stefania fed her, then lay quietly, propped up on pillows, her hair braided to one side, eyes bright and cheeks flushed deep red. Stefania held her hand, and they shared a peaceful moment, staring into the fire.

Rosalia said, "*Cara,* I want to tell you a Sicilian story and ask you to carry out my last wishes."

"Mother, don't . . ."

"Hush. I will go soon and I must tell you . . . When I was a child in Sicily, I found an old Greek shrine deep in an olive grove . . . Inside was a broken statue of a goddess with waving hair and a crown. The peasants were superstitious, there were rumors some still paid tribute to the Goddess of Many Crowns who protected women, who'd come to Sicily with the Greeks, long before the Virgin. I saw dishes of oil, flowers, olive branches. Four little figures on a kind of altar. You know what your father suffered at the hands of the church . . . I thought how powerful she must be, if women defied the Inquisition to bring her offerings." Laudanum made Rosalia's voice dreamy and slow . . .

"My father was an evil man. The Chiaramontes had been rich, but by the time I was born, their palaces were crumbling and estates were being sold to pay his gambling debts. The Albanisis were wealthy, so wealthy Stefano wanted to marry me even without a dowry. We were awaiting your birth, joining my family at their summer palace in the mountains, when my father sent Stefano to Palermo on the pretext of business. Stefano's servant returned alone. Stefano had been arrested by the Inquisition. Sicily was Spanish then, and intensely Catholic. Their Inquisition tortured those arrested until they confessed. To heresy, to being a secret Jew or Muslim, anything. There were many executions. And Stefano sent me warning that my father intended him to die, but I was in danger too. If Stefano died, I would inherit Stefano's fortune until our child came of age. But if I perished, my father would become legal guardian of the child and the fortune, and the child would be at his mercy. At best, the child would be locked away in a monastery or convent, parted from its inheritance. At worst, its death would be blamed on the fever or the smallpox. So many young children died, no one would question it. Stefano wished me to flee to his cousin in New Orleans."

"Mother, sleep now. Have you forgotten? I know the rest."

"No, not all. I was terrified to go, terrified to stay. There was no one in the house I could trust. So I went to the shrine and, like the peasant women, begged the Goddess of Many Crowns for help. And she answered me."

"What?" Stefania felt the first stirring of alarm. Had she misjudged the laudanum?

"Yes, I heard her say I must trust the servant Stefano had sent to warn me and to go. She would protect me. I promised that if I survived I would make her another shrine, and I took the votive figures with me."

"You should rest now, Mother."

"I left them in the old bear cave on Frog Mountain, on a rock like an altar. I went back from time to time, leaving you with Caitlin, to pray to the goddess to keep your father alive and send him here. And he came."

"Hush, Mother, you've tired yourself with talking." *The laudanum!* Stefania was racked with guilt as she wiped her mother's burning face. How sunken and hollow Rosalia's dark eyes were! "You're so hot. Sleep now."

"Promise, *cara!*" Rosalia's voice was faint. "Make an offering, pork . . . fruit . . . a flower . . . These please the goddess. And promise, obey if she speaks to you." Rosalia's eyes closed. "Promise," she whispered, struggling for breath.

Stefania sighed. "I promise."

Rosalia seemed to sleep at last. But Stefania saw a change come over her face and realized it was the end. She cried out, "Papa, come at once!"

CHAPTER 11

GIDEON

1792

Ten days ago I watched as a coffin was rowed across the river to the cemetery. It was followed by the girl Stefania, her father, and the men who work there, so I know it was Caitlin's friend Rosalia. It is another sorrow for Caitlin, who will believe I did not return home because I am dead as well. But Death will wait longer for me, my work is not finished.

Nearly two winters ago, I left my daughter Rhiannon after the Great New Moon Festival. She was very heavy with another child and is of an age when birth can be hard. It is a time that a woman should be with her mother. But Caitlin and Rhiannon are enemies. Sophia was a sister to Caitlin, and Caitlin cannot forgive Sophia's death at the hands of Rhiannon's husband, Two Bears.

Caitlin would avenge Sophia if she could, just as our people avenge the death of a clan member, taking a life from the killer's clan. Since Rhiannon takes sides with her husband, Caitlin swore she will never see Rhiannon again. Yet Caitlin's longing for her grandchildren is as great as her hate for Two Bears, and since she is cut off from them, she can find no peace. I cannot return to her until I know how to end this war between my wife and daughter. If I do not, grief and anger will bind Caitlin's spirit, prevent it from joining mine in the Darkening Land when we are both dead.

Rhiannon—or Singing Wind, as she is known—had a fiery light in her eyes, and when I looked at her, I did not see Rhiannon, and for the first time in my life, I knew fear, not for myself or Caitlin but for something greater and vengeful that is waiting in her to bring our people death and lamentations for many years and generations. In my dreams I see riverboats filled with our people going west on the river, hear wailing and death songs.

I do not know what to do to avoid this curse.

But I know it will be connected to Singing Wind. She became a beloved woman, one possessed by a fierce spirit. She speaks of battles and courage to the young braves in words that set their blood on fire, makes them eager to attack the white settlers, take scalps and prisoners, lay waste to their homesteads even when the chiefs and elders of the tribes wish to negotiate treaties and avoid war. They know, as the young men do not wish to hear, that what Singing Wind urges will bring the wrath of soldiers, like leaves borne on a great wind.

In a dream I saw the tribes swept away by such a wind. The mountains will echo with grieving and death, not victory songs. I am still a beloved man, and know my duty. I must continue to try and waken the powers I once had and persuade the people not to heed Singing Wind.

I am an old man now and long for our cabin where the fire is warm and Caitlin's songs and quilts and bread make life sweet, where she speaks to me with the same voice as she did many years ago when I wooed her. But I have not forgotten how to endure cold and hunger like a brave. So I did not go home but came to Frog Mountain to seek guidance from the spirits, to ask what spell or magic would ward off the evil that holds her fast. I must endure the separation for her sake and the sake of my people, for our children and their children.

I spent the winters alone in the mountains. Unless I am cut off from the white world, the guidance I seek will not come. I have hunted for my food and sacrificed in the fire. I have sought the counsel of my mother and grandmother and uncles in the wind carrying spirits that blows around the great rock, where I came as a young man and saw the spirits of white strangers hovering too. They come back to revisit the place of their deaths. Little by little the spirits I call approach to speak.

The answer does not come clearly, not yet. The whites are always impatient, but I know the spirits cannot be forced; they will answer when it is time.

I watch the valley change below me, the new buildings at the far end by Slipping Creek where the rocks are covered with moss, land that Seth Hanover bought from Rufus. There's a school now, a large, low cabin with smaller cabins around it where some of our people take their children and leave them between harvests so they join the white children and learn their ways. Already some of our people wish to live among their white neighbors as if they were white too.

The Drumheller girl was the teacher until so many children came that more teachers were needed. Young men and women arrived on riverboats, bringing many boxes and trunks with them. Brother Merriman goes there on horseback in the morning and leaves as Iddo Fox comes in the afternoon on foot. A bell above the largest building rings and can be heard along the valley, even up here. I cannot decide if it is a good sound or another way the whites signal possession of yet more land and the souls of the tribes' children.

I remember my father the long hunter, who kept a Bible with him and taught me to read from it. My mother said it would benefit me to know by what magic paper could speak. The children of the tribes will learn that magic, as I did, and they will walk between the white and

Indian worlds as I have, unsure of whether to cross to one side or the other. I want to tell them, *Be careful.*

From the rock I can look down and see the trading post and the valley where our people once hunted and planted crops, built towns, went to war. But the valley has changed since I was a young man, no longer a place with trees and buffalo and deer and our people. It is almost bare of trees, marked by divisions—fences separating it into fields and homesteads. It is not the same. I know the land has changed as the people on it have changed.

I think the spirits do not recognize it either. Sometimes I long for the time of my death, to lie down on the earth and let my spirit rise free.

Again last night I sacrificed tobacco in the fire, and a lock of my hair, called again the spirit of my mother and my grandmother. I have done this many times, but this time, they answered. In the smoke I saw that Singing Wind gave birth to twins and, since then, that she is bewitched by an evil spirit that will not allow her to move. The children are well and in the care of a wet nurse. All this I saw because the children are old enough now to come back with me. My waiting has not been in vain.

I must go back and say to the council, *Give the twins to me—the children belong to the mother's clan.* In return I will do what I can to release Singing Wind from the spell. My mother had a ceremony she performed for women who were possessed after childbirth. She will tell me what I must do.

My mother's spirit reminds me the children are still young enough to need their wet nurse, who is a woman of our clan, Fawn in the Water. Her own baby died, and she had milk. I will ask if she will come too.

Caitlin will cry when I return with the children and Fawn. She will cry to welcome them and from sorrow she cannot voice for the loss of Rhiannon, but these tears and the children will heal her heart. And my purpose will be accomplished.

After that, my death will come for me, and I will go to the Darkening Land. I am ready. Later Caitlin will come to me there. We have one heart, one spirit. Always.

CHAPTER 12

STEFANIA

December 1792

On Frog Mountain, above Wildwood, the path leading up to the big clearing with the rock like a man's profile was well trodden, wide enough for a pony trap. The lone woman stopped from time to time to look up toward the ridge, shading her eyes with her hand, racking her memory for the location of the cave she knew was somewhere above the clearing. From there the path up to the ridge was narrower, steeper, and overgrown.

Stefania remembered she'd been there before, as a child, once, with her mother and Magdalena and Sophia. They'd had a picnic—there had been wild strawberries, she recalled—and after the steep climb to the ridge, the little girls had fallen asleep on a quilt. Later the two children had shouted their names into the cave, to hear the echoes. *"Magdalena, Magdalena, Magdalena . . . Stefania, Stefania, Stefania,"* the cave cried back at them.

Stefania and Magdalena had gone a little way into the cave but decided it was too spooky to go farther and begged to leave.

Years later Magdalena confided that Kitty and Cully used to court in the cave before they were married—she'd followed and spied on them once.

Under normal circumstances the old bear cave was the last place in Grafton Stefania would have chosen to visit alone. The Cherokees called it Breathing Rock because it was like the mouth of the mountain. In summer a breeze blew out of the cave, and in winter air was sucked in. It conjured up some living thing that crouched, inhaling and exhaling, in the dark. She tried to banish that thought, told herself firmly that there was a reasonable explanation, that probably another opening farther back in the cave drew air in and out.

And bears had hibernated in the cave once, but they hadn't been seen on Frog Mountain for many years. Hunters had trapped and shot so many at the cave that it was said the animals had been scared off, had gone deeper into the mountains. She hoped that was true and no bear had changed its mind.

Stefania heartily wished she hadn't promised her mother to go there. She hadn't told anyone of her last conversation with Rosalia. It made Rosalia sound deranged and Stefania feel guilty for giving her mother too much laudanum.

She'd set off on impulse today, anxious to get this excursion over with. But the closer she got, the more she wished she'd asked Little Molly.

She had the comforting weight of a rifle on a strap across her back in case of an unexpected bear, a hungry mountain lion, or a wolf. She knew enough to be alert for wild animals and was a good shot.

She muttered crossly that this was nonsense, it was cold. She looked up again. How much farther? White pine and chestnut oaks up near the ridge had grown taller in the years since she'd been there, and it was going to be the devil to find the entrance.

She paused for breath at the clearing halfway up. It was windier up here. She leaned her gun against the rock and loosened and retied her new shawl tighter with cold fingers, thinking how beautiful it was—a warm, thick, soft India shawl of blue-and-green wool that had come in the last order placed with her father's agent in New Orleans.

She refastened the shawl with a brooch. It was an emerald-and-ruby scorpion with diamond eyes that flashed as if it were alive, part of her Sicilian grandmother's wedding jewelry. Her father had brought it to America for the child he'd never seen, if she was a girl. Had the child been a son, the brooch would have been given to the son's wife.

Thirsty from her climb, she stopped at the spring at the clearing's edge and filled the battered pewter mug chained to an iron ring set in the rock. The cold water tasted of iron. She straightened up and looked round the clearing. Children came up here to pick persimmons and beechnuts and fox grapes that grew on the mountainside, and in September it was the site of Grafton's annual holiday, the Blackberry Picnic. People said the blackberries grew bigger and sweeter on Frog Mountain than anywhere else, and the clearing was a pleasant spot for a picnic, the air fresh and cooler after the sticky heat and mosquitoes in the valley.

Now, in December, it was just bleak and empty. Years of picnic bonfires had left blackened patches in circles of stones, and the trees were bare of leaves and stripped of fruit and nuts, save for a few orange persimmon globes still hanging too high to reach. There was a smell of rotting fruit from overripe persimmons that had fallen with the swollen weight of their own flesh, lying squashed among the dead leaves.

From the clearing, the path up to the bear cave narrowed and grew steeper, almost invisible as it wound between laurels and leafless chestnut trees.

She sighed and reluctantly started up, negotiating blackberry brambles that reached out to snag her skirts.

Then her foot slipped on a loose rock, and she slid noisily off the narrow path, nearly dropping her basket. By clutching a mountain laurel, she stopped her slide down the incline, and beyond the branch she'd pulled aside she saw a flat ledge and the cave mouth just ahead. Hauling herself up onto the ledge, with the cave mouth gaping behind her, emitting a whiff of damp air, she caught her breath, looking down at the settlement on the river's bend, and across the river, where Chiaramonte looked neat and small from this distance. The cave mouth was dark and uninviting. She tried not to think of some breathing thing lurking inside and fought the urge to run away down the path now.

"You can't turn back! Just go and look," she told herself firmly.

She struck her flint and set a pine knot alight. She lifted it and peered cautiously in. She shouted, in case there was a bear to wake after all. She lit another pine knot and another, tossing them in to follow her echoing shouts, but no disturbed animal growled a warning from the cave's depths.

Very well, she thought. She stepped in cautiously, pine knot aloft, and felt her way along the cave wall. Deeper and deeper, into the silence, her flickering pine knot making shadows jump like living things between pillars of rock, catching sudden unexpected gleams and sparkles of quartz. The cave was dank and quiet and smelled of something rank. From farther ahead in the dark came a faint sound of dripping water.

Were there bats? She imagined bats being roused by the torch, flitting past her head . . . getting tangled in her hair with their little claws . . . ugh! She waved the pine knot above her head, ready to hide under her shawl if there was a sudden swoosh of wings and darting figures. Nothing flew at her. Cautiously she raised her pine knot higher and looked up, to be sure about the bats. Above her head the cave rose into a kind of vault, covered with a tracery of black and red lines.

As she gazed, the lines came to life. She clapped her hand over her mouth, turned and looked and turned and looked, craning her neck.

"Oh!" she gasped. In the flickering, snapping light, the lines became winged hunters chasing birds, running animals that resembled deer and bison across the cave walls and over her head.

But she dared not linger over the strange spectacle. She went farther in, hand on the cave wall. Indentations. She held the pine knot close. There *were* steps, of a sort, quite narrow but regular—carved into the wall deliberately. As her mother had described. They led up to a ledge above her head.

She sighed, hoped nothing that needed shooting would be up there, and propped the gun against a rock. She hitched her skirts up and carefully set her foot on the lowest step. She had to press against the cave wall for balance, awkwardly holding the basket and pine knot as she carefully climbed sideways up the narrow stairway . . . She didn't want to fall when she was all alone in here.

She was relieved to reach the ledge. It was bigger than it looked from below. She could stand easily. She held up the pine knot and looked around. There didn't appear to be any bats here either. But there was something else . . . On the cave wall were imprints of hands, their five fingers pale and distinct against faint patches of red.

A single hand outline was low enough to touch, as if reaching down to her from somewhere she could not see. It was oddly friendly and reassuring. She caught her breath, marveling again, rewarded for her decision to come. She was thinking she'd bring Magdalena and Peach up to show them this curious place, when her light fell on a flat rock. And four small objects in a line.

She bent to look, then picked them up, one by one. She hadn't believed Rosalia's story, but just as her mother had described them, here they were, four terracotta female figures, their only features a pointed nose below dark holes for eyes. Each held something. Stefania could make out a flower, a kind of jug, something that might have been a flaming branch, and half a pig with its back legs broken off. Could her mother really have brought them from Sicily and put them here? Had Rosalia *really* believed in the goddess?

The unseen water dripped.

She replaced the figures carefully, knelt, uncovered her basket, and took out the things she'd promised her mother to leave there. She'd taken them from the kitchen when Jane and watchful Linney weren't looking. She laid down a small piece of salt pork, apples, an ear of corn, a small dried nosegay.

Impulsively she said, "Goddess, my father wishes me to choose one of two men as my husband. I don't want to marry either. But my mother, whom he loved dearly, is recently dead, and I cannot refuse to do as he wishes without causing him further pain. My mother believed you helped her and will help me. She made me promise to make these offerings, and to obey your advice."

Silence, only the water dripping deep in the cave.

"The younger suitor has become like a son, my father finds him diligent and clever and certain to succeed in life. He is compelling, as if he would bend me to his will just as he bends the will of animals. When he is near, I can sense him, he casts a spell that's agreeable but dangerous because I want him near. He knows this, says that I am his, and I am drawn to him without loving him, this power he has makes me fearful of what would happen if I married him. I am myself and mine now. I would not be if I married him, he would . . . devour me in some way," she said. "And yet, I think of him constantly." She sighed. "I would rather I did not, because I can think of nothing else.

"The other is almost my father's age. With most people, he is somber and reserved. My friends find him stern, and even Peach is quiet in his company. He's been unhappy or, perhaps, rather lonely in his life. But with me he talks in a lively fashion and unbends, even laughs. I surprise him, I think, and that makes him animated. I am at ease with him. But should I become his wife? He regards me with affection, and hopes that I will be his wife. But he casts no spell, and I do not love him. I do not . . . think of him constantly. Or at all."

Silence.

Her knees hurt. She was too reasonable not to feel the absurdity of what she was doing. "Very well," she muttered; she'd promised; she'd kept the promise. What had she expected? She stood, brushed off her skirts, picked up her basket, and lit another pine knot. She took a last look round. To her surprise she felt faintly exasperated at the lack of an answer.

"I think Papa would be best pleased if I married both!" she said to the emptiness.

She started and spun around as a voice and yet not a voice broke the silence.

"*What?*"

But it was only a puff of air—like a breath, wafting through the cave from an opening somewhere farther along, carrying an echo between the rock formations.

"*Married both . . . married both . . . both,*" sighed the cave.

CHAPTER 13

TWELFTH NIGHT

January 1793

The English custom of celebrating the twelfth day after Christmas had always been kept by Sophia de Marechal and the Drumhellers, and tonight there was to be a party at the Vanns' big cabin at the trading post.

In preparation Peach and her children had decorated it with ivy, pine branches, and mistletoe. Caitlin had no need to consult the recipe written in her mother's hand on the flyleaf of her Bible, but felt her way through the making of a large raised game pie. Malinda Drumheller had made a boiled suet pudding with dried fruit soaked in her father-in-law's powerful liquor. Later more liquor would be poured over the pudding and set alight. It was always an exciting moment—the flaming liquor sometimes caused the pudding to explode.

As the night drew in, Bryn was tuning his fiddle, and his two boys tuned the dulcimers their Welsh grandfather had made them. Henry de Marechal held an instrument Meshack had made him, called a ban-jar, that Bryn had taught him to play. They began to play softly to welcome the arriving guests. Gradually the de Marechals, the Vanns, the Drumhellers, the Albanisis, the Stuarts, Venus accompanied by Iddo Fox, the Hanover women and their families, the Conways with Rembrandt, and even the Pines crowded into the Vann cabin and store-room. Old Meshack Tudor was already dozing in a rocking chair he'd once made for Caitlin.

On the wooden mantelpiece lay two mistletoe crowns fashioned by Annie, one to be given to the man chosen as the Lord of Misrule and the smaller crown with a ribbon for the girl who was his lady.

Mattie and Brother Merriman made a point of staying away with Mortify and Endurance. Brother Merriman disapproved of Twelfth Night as a godless pagan festival celebrating the Prince of Darkness. He would preach a vehement sermon about it in the coming weeks.

Each arrival brought a gust of cold air, a flurry of snowflakes from shoulders and hats, greetings between neighbors separated for much of the winter by bad weather, a sense of anticipation. The cabin smelled sharp with pine boughs and sweet with baking. A fire blazed, a haunch of venison roasted, turned by one of Meshack's ingenious weighted spits, and the guests set down pies and cakes, even a trifle made by Kitty to her mother's recipe, on every available surface. Furniture had been pushed back to make room for the dancing.

The children grew wilder by the minute. Annie tried to shush hers into better behavior. Magdalena held her new baby, Lorenzo, and tried to keep up with her daughter, Fanny, toddling rapidly after Rembrandt into any openings between the adults.

Jack and Toby and George had mixed a cauldron of hot punch, strong enough to make the women gasp and cough, but warming after the cold outdoors. Little Molly saw Zebulon edging away from his mother toward Mariah, so she asked the girl to help get the children upstairs to practice a carol they were to sing in rounds as a surprise for Rufus.

Caitlin sat by the fire, on either side a small, black-haired, black-eyed child. The twins had Indian names, but she'd called the girl Rachel and the boy Caradoc.

At the hearth their wet nurse, Fawn in the Water, did up the buttons on her bodice after feeding them. When Fawn's last baby had died, a shaman told her the baby's spirit would be comforted if another child thrived on her milk. When Gideon came home at last, followed by Fawn on a horse leading another horse with two cradles slung across the back, Caitlin had forgiven Gideon at once for his long absence and welcomed all three with delight and open arms, acknowledging Gideon had brought her another daughter as well as the twins.

Fawn's husband, White Owl, had come afterward, bringing their son so he could attend the new mission school. Tonight White Owl was dressed as usual in deerskin, but Fawn wore a new calico dress Caitlin had given her, and instead of a long braid down her back, her dark hair was tucked up under a cap like Caitlin's, while her fourteen-year-old son they called Joseph, because it sounded like his Cherokee name, wore homespun breeches and boots. He'd outgrown the deerskin garments he'd arrived in, and at the school, children were required to dress alike—high-buttoned frocks and aprons for the girls; loose shirts, breeches, and boots for the boys.

Colonel Charbonneau and then Gustine St. Pierre arrived. Both looked around at once for Stefania, who was by the fireplace, talking intently to Caitlin about the twins, as if there were no one else in the room. Stefania looked very pretty in a dress of dark-green wool and her salamander brooch. Her cheeks were flushed from the fire and agitation. Her father had made it clear he expected an answer tonight or he'd make the choice for her. Stefania wished time would stand still to prevent her from giving him one. If only she dared refuse to marry either. But he'd aged so since Rosalia's death, and his face was deeply lined with years of suffering. She couldn't bring herself to cause him more distress.

Tonight in the crowded room, she was determined to avoid Gustine, who she could sense in the crowd. When she sat down, putting Caitlin between her and the rest of the room, he finally turned away as if to ignore her, drinking heavily from the punch as he talked to Henry.

Finally Bryn began to play a carol in earnest, and the crowd stopped talking and, led by Caitlin, began to sing "Shepherds Arise."

Thierry pushed past Caitlin and leaned down, holding out his hand to Stefania. "Come," he said. "Some air." She went reluctantly.

He led her away from everyone, just outside the storeroom, where they could hear the children practicing through the wall. "Marry me," he said abruptly. "Your father forbade me to ask you directly, but tonight I am out of patience with waiting. It's been impossible to find you alone, to say that my every hope of happiness rests with you, and if you accept me as your husband, I will do everything in my power to make you as happy as I will be." He lifted her hand to his lips, then held it. "I must know, Stefania. Will you marry me?"

"I will," she heard herself say. She was tired of resisting her father. "I will."

And it was as easy as that. Stefania felt a burden drop from her shoulders. It was decided. It didn't matter that she wasn't in love with the colonel. She'd accepted him now, and that put her beyond the strange power Gustine exerted. She needn't worry about him any longer, or Linney.

Thierry kissed her cheek and said, "My darling, I am so happy."

Stefania looked up at him and smiled, mostly with relief at having done with Gustine. "Come. We'll tell Papa."

They returned to the crowded kitchen just as Little Molly had managed to hush everyone, announcing her pupils would sing now. The children fidgeted themselves into three groups. Bryn played a chord on the fiddle, and the children sang.

Angels holy, bending lowly
Bright star leading
Wise men slowly
Infant in a manger lowly
Gloria!

Gold and myrrh and frankincense
At the Virgin's feet they lay
Mary smiles
The infant blesses
Gloria!

Around the room firelight flickered on faces of the listeners as the children's voices rose. They sang the simple old country carol in rounds, ten times, and Jack then Toby and even Rufus joined in. Rufus, who everyone thought was much too hard for tears, was crying openly, thinking of the small church with stone walls thick enough to keep out the sea winds, where he'd last sung the carol with his first wife, Molly.

Stefania whispered to Thierry, "It's an old carol from Suffolk, where Rufus came from and Toby and Jack were born. Rufus said it was his favorite but couldn't remember all the words. Little Molly found it in an old singing book donated to the mission school and had the children learn it to surprise Rufus."

Bryn put the bow to his fiddle and began to accompany the singers, the boys picked up the tune on their dulcimers, and Henry strummed the banjar. When the last round ended, Rufus wiped his eyes, hugged Little Molly, and said over and over she was his good girl and a credit to her grandmother.

After that, Bryn, Henry, and the boys played more carols, and people sang, joining in ever more lustily on the choruses as more punch was drunk. The playing and singing grew livelier, until the guests were clapping and calling for a dancing tune. The young people looked around, the boys to choose a partner, the girls to be chosen, all suddenly self-conscious.

Gustine pushed his way toward Stefania, half smiling and intent. Stefania suddenly thought, *He's like a wolf stalking its prey.* His eyes held hers, and he was reaching out his hand to take hers for the dance. She lifted her own without thinking, against all reason suddenly wanting him to seize her again as he had before, to feel his heat . . . Too dangerous! And too late.

She drew back and turned her face resolutely away from Gustine. "Congratulate me, Papa, I've just told Thierry I'd marry him," she said to Stefano, who smiled and put an arm round her shoulders. From the corner of her eye, she saw Gustine halt. He wouldn't dare pull her from her father's side.

Stefano said, "At last! Your future and that of the business are assured."

"As if marriage were a business agreement, Papa!" she sighed.

Stefano laughed. "In France, my dear, the colonel's homeland, that is precisely what marriage is. But I believe he will make you a satisfactory husband. He is a good and sensible man, Stefania."

"Of course, Papa."

He beckoned Thierry to his side, and the two men exchanged a few words, smiled broadly, and shook hands across Stefania.

She didn't want to look up, but she couldn't help it. Gustine was watching. And his eyes narrowed and grew cold as he grasped what had happened.

Stefania glanced up at her fiancé. Thierry looked happy, and he looked solid and, suddenly, much younger. *Yes,* she thought, taking his arm, *yes, a satisfactory husband. Married to him, I will still be myself. And Papa is happy. Mother would be pleased.*

She silently vowed never to think of Gustine's kisses again. In fact, she would never think of Gustine again at all.

There was a pause in the music while Bryn put down his fiddle for a drink of punch, and Stefano shouted to be heard above the chatter. Forgetting his customary dignity, he climbed onto Caitlin's table, to cries of "The pies! Mind the pies!"

"*Silenzio!*" he cried. "Silence, please, my friends! I wish to say my dear Stefania is to marry my partner, Colonel Charbonneau!" He held a mug of punch aloft, and though the alcohol made his tongue burn, he raised it in a toast: "To Stefania and Thierry."

The company cheered and raised their pewter or wooden tumblers. "Stefania and Thierry!"

"Then they shall be the Lord of Misrule and his lady," roared Toby, stumping forward on his crutch with the two crowns. They were settled on the heads of Stefania and Thierry, and Stefania shrieked as she and Thierry were lifted onto the shoulders of the strongest men and borne around the room as the guests cheered. Stefania flashed an apprehensive glance in Gustine's direction, but he was gone.

"Now the lord and lady must begin the dancing," someone cried. Bryn picked up his fiddle again, and people crowded past to congratulate Stefano and wish the couple joy. Led by Bryn, there was a surge into the storeroom, where there was more room for dancing. Lines of dancers, merry with punch, formed as Bryn began playing "Soldiers' Joy." Henry and Bryn's boys abandoned their instruments to dance with the girls.

The elder Pine boy pulled Mariah Stuart away from under Zebulon's nose, and Mariah flashed him a grateful smile. The dancing began, and everyone joined in, with or without partners, even Stefano, even White Owl and Fawn and Joseph, even the children.

Despite the music and noise, Rachel and Caradoc nodded off against Caitlin, and she and Fawn each carried a sleeping child to Caitlin's bed and covered them with a quilt.

In the general merriment, no one except Gideon noticed when the cabin door pushed open a crack, and a breath of cold air was let into the room. For a moment a pair of eyes glittered in the firelight, held Gideon's, then disappeared. Gideon slipped outside, unnoticed by the throng. He walked away from the cabin; the sounds of music and the noise of the revelry was muffled by the falling snow. He sensed the presence of a warrior, then saw the shapes of men. One came to meet him.

The two men stared at each other. The eyes in the firelight had been blue.

"Father," said the blue-eyed brave. "Do you remember your son?"

Gideon reached out and held the brave by his shoulders, staring into his face. "Cadfael?" he said wonderingly. "Cadfael, Son, are you come back? Are you a spirit?" How tall he was, taller than Gideon.

"Your winter feast. I remember it."

"My son. My son . . . you are alive . . . alive . . . You and your companions are welcome here. Come, your mother—"

"No, I will not see her. I cannot."

Gideon was silent.

"I cannot, Father."

"Cadfael. I am an old man and never thought to see you again. Your mother has suffered. My son, we must speak."

"I know. But I cannot wait. I have come to fetch you with a purpose, Father. My wife is very ill, and I would keep her from the Darkening Land as long as is possible. I have come to ask your help. Our shamans have tried, but she gets worse, and is in great pain. They say your mother knew spells and cures for women. I have a blanket and a horse, if you will come."

Gideon didn't hesitate. "I will come, Cadfael."

The next morning at the trading post, the world was white and silent after the heavy snowfall. People woke groaning on pallets or quilts, on chairs or stretched under the table, covered by their coats and shawls. Caitlin had managed to tumble many of the children onto her bed beside Caradoc and Rachel and Fawn's son, Joseph. She rose from among them to build up the fire for breakfast before sending everyone on their way. Snow or not, cows had to be milked, livestock fed.

Gideon was nowhere to be found. "Why in all the world would he go off *now*?" an exasperated Caitlin asked Peach.

Gustine had disappeared too. When Stefano reached Chiaramonte, he went at once to Gustine's cabin behind the kennels. The dogs were howling for food, but there was no sign of Gustine, and his few belongings were gone.

Days later Peach told Stefania she'd seen Gustine on the river trail with a bundle on his back. She hoped he'd be safe from Indians. A half-frozen long hunter who'd found his way to Susan's tavern just after Twelfth Night reported he'd seen a small group of Indians, possibly scouts from a war party, in the valley. Linney Pine was red-eyed and so sulky Stefania wished Gustine had taken the girl with him.

Stefania very much wanted to be married to the colonel and done with everything connected to Gustine. She hoped he'd find another girl to marry, as Stefano assured her he would.

Thierry told Stefania they ought to have a priest to perform the marriage, but he didn't want to delay the wedding to find one. "Neither do I," said Stefania. She was beginning to think she might be happy after all.

CHAPTER 14

February 1793

Brother Merriman refused to join a papist in matrimony, so Iddo Fox led Stefania and Thierry through a Quaker-style ceremony at Chiaramonte in February. At twilight, an extravagant number of candles were lit throughout the house, and it was the turn of Peach, Magdalena, Annie, and Little Molly to stand up with their friend. Stefano had generously insisted Stefania make each of them a gift of a new silk gown when ordering her wedding clothes. Their measurements were sent to the New Orleans dressmaker with a request to complete everything as quickly as possible.

The door between the sitting room and the kitchen was kept open because so many guests had to squeeze in, and they all agreed that the four young women flanking Stefania before the sitting room fireplace looked elegant and very pretty in fashionable narrow-skirted gowns with high sashed waists: Peach in royal blue, Little Molly in cherry red, Magdalena in pale green. Even worn Annie looked younger and softer in a pearly pink.

Everyone agreed the bride and groom made a handsome couple. Stefania wore a new gown in the same high-waisted style of pale shot silk that glimmered in the candlelight, and Thierry was upright and distinguished in a brocade coat. They stood together before everyone while Iddo explained to the guests that among the Quakers, a couple married each other and didn't require the services of a third party. But as the couple were not Quakers, he would lead them through what should be said, the vows that should be given and received.

Stefania said her vows, but the thought of Gustine came unbidden, accompanied by a flutter of guilt in her heart. She was relieved he was gone—seeing him now would have been terrible—but she hoped he hadn't met the war party.

Jane and a scowling Linney laid out the food they'd prepared in the dining parlor, and the champagne Stefano had sent for to toast the couple was poured. As the guests drank to their health, Stefania smiled nervously and blushed, remembering Peach's advice about her wedding night. Would she please him? She had a new nightdress. Perhaps it would be all right.

She decided to begin her marriage by acceding to her husband's preference about where they should live. Stefano had assumed the couple would live with him at Chiaramonte, and Thierry also thought this best, but both men had been surprised when Stefania had been adamant she wanted to live at Thierry's cabin. At the time she'd thought Gustine would still be at Chiaramonte, and it was a way to get away from Linney. But after Gustine left, and seeing Stefano's disappointment, she had a change of heart. She mustn't give in to fancy. Gustine was gone, and however disagreeable, Linney was a servant. She wouldn't begin her married life intimidated by a servant.

Thierry was raising his glass of wine to his lips, toasting her, when Stefania said, "I've been thinking, you and Papa are right. We should live at Chiaramonte, as you and Papa wished."

Thierry was surprised. "But I thought you were determined we should have a place of our own! But of course, my dear, if you've changed your mind, it accords perfectly with my wishes. We can let the cabin or even sell it." Warmed by the ease of Stefania's capitulation, he drew her hand through his arm and kissed her forehead. "Thank you for letting me have my way so easily." He smiled at her fondly.

It will be all right, Stefania decided.

Months passed. Stefania was finding life easy. She seemed suddenly to have little to do. During Rosalia's illness, when she'd been occupied with nursing her mother, Jane had taken over the running of the house. Jane was efficient and had sensed that Linney irritated Stefania. She kept the girl working hard and mostly out of Stefania's way.

Thierry said it was no wonder Jane and Linney were so industrious; they were anxious the family not be turned out of the cabin Will had built. Will had ordered his family to give the Albanisis no cause for dissatisfaction.

"Ah," said Stefania, who hadn't thought of that. She was glad she'd never complained about Linney.

"And, *chère* Madame Charbonneau, for now you may be at your leisure and devote yourself to me. When the children come, you'll be busy enough."

The early weeks and months of her marriage passed pleasantly. Stefania sewed and worked in her herb garden and visited Peach, though both Thierry and Stefano insisted that now she was married she mustn't row herself about in a canoe like an Indian but have one of the Pine boys pole her across on the small ferry. Stefania sighed and gave in, though it meant she couldn't see Peach as often as she wished. She didn't like to take the Pine boys away from their work. Gideon didn't return. Thierry sold his homestead for a low price to White Owl, saying he didn't need the money now. Though Fawn weaned the twins, she and

White Owl wanted to stay in Grafton because of the mission school, where their boy was known as Joseph White.

White Owl made a living hunting and fishing and salting the meat and fish to sell at the trading post. Fawn was expecting another baby. She asked for the loan of a mule and a plow from Peach and Bryn and planted corn and beans and pumpkins in a field of rich bottom land near their cabin.

Without Gustine, Thierry and Stefano were very busy. News of the hunting dogs had spread. The sheriff Jonas Tyree purchased two of them, to Peach's alarm.

That summer turned furnace hot across the valley, as if the air were being sucked up. The river level sank, exposing muddy flats. Despite being pregnant, Fawn carried bucket after bucket of water to her field. In August, Caitlin and Venus helped when Fawn gave birth to another boy during the harvest. Days later she was back in her field, with the baby, named Thomas, on her back.

Stefania fanned herself. She told Thierry the heat was making her feel sick. Especially in the mornings. And why did everything smell so? Everything suddenly seemed to smell very strongly, especially the river. That made her feel sick too.

Jane smirked and said nothing when she took away the breakfast Stefania couldn't eat.

Stefano felt the heat as well. He said it reminded him of Palermo in summer. He looked very pale, thought Stefania, but when she urged him to rest, he brushed her concern aside, saying he had too much to do. She noticed he often needed to catch his breath.

Unusually she felt melancholy. She tried to reason it away, thinking it was the heat. She told herself she was happy, her husband was kind and attentive, her father was pleased to grant any wish she might have.

September came. While the laborers her father had hired were so busy with the harvesting, Stefania hadn't liked to ask any of the men to stop work and take her across, but she hadn't visited Grafton for weeks.

She was surrounded by men, and she wanted to see Peach very badly. "Once I would have rowed myself over, whatever you and Papa said," she grumbled to Thierry.

Thierry laughed. "I remember. But the younger Pine boy can ferry Madame across tomorrow if that's her pleasure."

"At such a time? Can you spare him?"

"For you, my dear, I can." He kissed her hand.

The next day at the trading post, Stefania and Peach sat on the jetty in the twilight. In the distance Fawn's baby, Thomas, wailed. "Peach, it's either the heat or I'm expecting too."

"You married, that's what happens." Peach grinned. "Aren't Thierry and your father pleased?"

Stefania sighed. "I haven't told Thierry or Papa. They're men, they don't understand how it feels to know you're having a baby. I'm frightened, Peach. I keep thinking about Anna and Rembrandt. It was terrible! I miss Mother." Stefania's lip trembled. "Jane suspects, I think, but . . . she's not Mother." A tear rolled down her cheek. "I want Mother," she whispered.

Peach took her hand. "It be fine. Mama knows what to do, she'll take good care of you. She said Fawn had an easy time. I'll come over and help too, if you want."

"Would you? I don't want Jane or . . . or Linney! Especially not Linney! And . . . if . . . if, if I die, don't let Jane care for the baby!"

Peach hugged her. "Don't be afeard. Babies come fine."

"They don't always. I'm sorry, Peach. I feel so . . ."

"It's the way it takes some women. Now go home, that Pine boy be up before dawn, needs to get his rest."

Stefania dried her eyes. She needed Rosalia to put her arms around her, call her *cara*, and tell her everything would be all right.

The next day, Stefania was in the garden when Thierry shouted her name. The urgency in his voice made Stefania drop the herbs she was cutting and run toward the house, where the Pines were carrying someone inside. Stefano had clutched his chest and collapsed in the paddock. Now he lay gasping for breath, his face twisted with pain. Thierry muttered that they'd sent to fetch Robert. Frantic, Stefania knelt by her father's side and chafed his hand. "Papa!"

"Too late for the doctor," Stefano gasped.

"Papa, I'm expecting a baby, you'll have a grandchild, as you wanted! Oh, Papa, don't leave us now!"

Stefano nodded. "Stefania . . . I fear . . . I must." He tried to pat her hand, groaned, and died.

CHAPTER 15

November 1793

If Stefania had felt anxious before, her spirits had been even more depressed by the death of her father. She was gloomy and tearful. Annie told her briskly it was common to feel this way when expecting a child; it was just a woman's lot.

Moody and whimsical, disliking Annie, irritated with Jane as well as Linney, she'd been short with Thierry, displeased with him, with everything. The noise of the chiming French clock kept her awake at night, listening for the next hour to chime. The dogs' howling set her teeth on edge.

Irritable and restless, she decided to climb up to the bear cave again. She was less nimble than previously, but the suffocating heat spell had ended, and cold weather had set in. She felt less lethargic. Indeed she had reserves of nervous energy. And she was in no mood to be ferried by anyone. She wanted to get away from all the men, from home, from everything.

The row across the river and the walk up Frog Mountain were tiring enough to dispel some of her ill humor. The lack of male company was a relief. She impulsively picked a small branch of persimmons, stopped for water at the spring in the picnic ground, walked resolutely up to the cave, and made her way in, teetering recklessly up the narrow steps to lay the persimmons on the altar in front of the votive figures.

"Mother. I wish you were here," she said. She sat on the rock altar, thinking of Rosalia, turning the votive figures over and over in her hands and listening to the silence that she fancied was listening to her, until she'd used up most of her pine knots. Before she climbed down from the ledge, she laid her hand against the lowest handprint for a long moment.

Afterward, instead of turning at once to go home, on impulse she climbed up to the narrow ridge above the cave, to look east, toward the distant place her parents had fled. A cold wind belled her skirts as she held her hand to her brow, elbow raised, shading her eyes, her imagination reaching beyond the mountains that rolled and folded into each other until they disappeared into the farthest horizon. She felt small and insubstantial, as if the wind might pick her and her child up and carry them away like dried leaves into the hugeness of the world.

"Mother, how far Sicily is, like the stars," she murmured. Her mother had pointed, beyond the mountains, across valleys, land, and seas, describing a world her daughter had never seen—vast, harsh mountains with jagged cliffs and ravines, unlike the rolling Appalachians, summer heat like the furnace of hell, churches with golden walls. A place of ancient things.

She was guardian of her mother's story now. She'd tell it to her child one day, pointing east, from this same spot, to Sicily. She'd show her the cave, tell Rosalia's story about the goddess. Not because Stefania believed in the goddess but because her mother had.

Her musing was interrupted. Far below in the valley, something was moving through the trees. She swung the rifle to her shoulder and stepped back to the shelter of a rock, then saw it wasn't Indians or a wild animal, but a caravan of long hunters with loaded wagons coming from the east valley.

She knew the type—hardened bearded men in filthy deer-hide leggings and garments and hats stitched together from raccoon and possum and fox skins. From her vantage point men were almost indistinguishable from their mules and their cargo of pelts—bear, deer, beaver, wolf—piled high on the wagons, spattered with dried blood and stiff in the cold. The caravan would be headed across the mountain and down to Vann Station at the Grafton river landing to meet the fur traders that came periodically, mostly from New Orleans.

Like timber and iron, the fur trade had brought prosperity to the Grafton settlement. Susan Hanover and Isaac Ozment thrived on it too, doing a brisk business in the tavern they'd built behind the trading post. Behind the bar were cubicles, separated by homespun curtains, where men could sleep two or three to a bed and eat dinner on credit until the pelts were sold or business done. At the side, behind a locked door was a room Susan and Isaac reserved for the traders and merchants to do business.

A group at the end of the procession caught her eye. She watched them start up the east slope of Frog Mountain toward the ridge. A skirt fluttered. Women? She counted. Four, close together and stumbling. Now she could make out they were Negro women, roped in a line.

From the base of the mountain, Stefania heard a long hunter shout to his companions that he itched so bad he'd a good mind to have a bath when they got to the tavern. This provoked derisive laughter. "A bath!" they shouted back. "Haw-haw-haw!" The sound rose in the cold air.

"Only a fool'd take a bath in winter, Zekiel, haw-haw!"

One of the men on a mule circled back to the slaves. "Step along there. Ain't reached the stopping place yet," he cried and swung a whip over their heads, making the women cringe and duck.

Poor souls. Stefania grimaced and turned to set off for home, stepping carefully down the west side of the mountain until she reached the path below the cave. It led down the slope past Wildwood. She could smell wood smoke from its chimney. She'd stop there, see Magdalena and little Fanny and Annie. She'd let them know there were long hunters traveling up the other side who'd probably head for Wildwood if the fog lifted. Annie would be glad of the advance warning so she could be ready with enough stew or soup and cornmeal and lard at hand to make johnnycake for the extra mouths. She'd have tea, warm herself at the hearth; they'd talk about Stefania's baby.

Then she'd hurry down to Grafton and row herself back across the river. Thierry would be anxious until she returned. Her free, frontier ways still startled him, as when she had picked up her gun and set off alone today. But he hadn't protested, afraid she'd make some angry retort. Now she was sorry for her bad temper earlier. Her call at Wildwood would be short. For the first time in months, she wanted her home and her husband.

It had been the longest trip the long hunters climbing up the east slope could remember. Animals were scarcer now than when long hunters first came to the valleys, before the war with England.

The tribes who depended on the game for food and oil and hides attacked hunters, tracking them for hours or even days until a good spot for an ambush meant scalps or prisoners to torture and kill or turn into slaves. Once, the river trail, or old buffalo road, as it was also known, had been a trading route between the coastal settlements and ports and the wilderness in the western part of the colony. Lately few hunters' or traders' caravans braved it, unless they paid for an armed escort.

They were relieved to make it to Frog Mountain without an escort. Indians didn't like it, thought it was haunted. They were halfway up the mountain when the scout shouted, "Fog's a-comin'," as a thin mist began to drift down. The whips cracked harder, and the wagon drivers jumped down and tried to pull the mules on faster to beat it, everyone hoping to make it over the top and onto the path down to Wildwood before the fog blinded them.

But the ridge above them was swallowed up before they could reach it. The fog settled wet and cold, trapping them in a dense white embrace. They were isolated until it lifted. It might drift and thin a little, here and there, enough to see a landmark a short distance away—a tree, a rock—but just as suddenly it would close around them again, confusing all sense of direction.

Cut off from the world, they would halt, stay where they were. Splintered boards of smashed wagons, human skulls, and mule skeletons on rocky outcrops below the trees bore witness to the risks of a loaded wagon driving blindly off a cliff edge.

It felt unnaturally quiet.

The uneasy long hunters quickly tethered mules to trees that seemed to disappear, taking the mules with them into the whiteness. "Tie the women up to a tree too," said the leader.

"Don't think you can go escapin' in the fog," he said. "You do, you likely to fall off a cliff."

"Please, don't leave us 'lone," begged one.

"I'se scared," said another. "Let us sit with you, Massa!" But the long hunter had a longer chain he put round a tree; then he locked their wrists to that. "Please!" the woman pleaded, almost invisible in the creeping mist. "Please!"

"Hush," said the man, walking back to his companions. They could no longer see the slaves, but they could hear the women's anxious voices.

The men knew there was nothing to do but hunker down to wait. There was a Cherokee word for the mountain fog. *U'nika.* It meant fog draped, but like so many Cherokee words, it was layered with meanings and even warnings.

"How much farther we got?"

"Lifts 'fore dark, we kin make it down to the de Marechal place," said the oldest long hunter. "Ef you ain't been this way a'fore, they's good people, lets hunters sleep in the barn there. Robert'll even doctor you, ef you need it, doctored Zekiel once when he got snake bit by a copperhead, leg swelled up bigger'n his belly. Women always got stew and corn bread. Got to remember to spit in the fire, though. Spit on her floor, Annie de Marechal'll tear a strip off your hide."

"That she will," said another man from the whiteness.

"Was George de Marechal's mother the woman owned the whole valley? And give land to some free niggers? English woman?"

"Thass so. Rumored they was Tories. So Injins who had a pact with the Americans attacked the place, kilt the woman and one of her boys. Remember that half-blood Gideon Vann and the trading post in Grafton, married the Welsh girl? Gideon was Annie de Marechal's pa. He 'us s'posed to be a medicine man, claimed he could talk to animals and spirits an' such. Some folks thought he's crazy, some folks said he really had powers. Anyhow, after the de Marechal woman and the boy was kilt, Gideon's wife took on so bad they say he kilt some braves or stole the bodies of some been kilt, buried 'em deep round the place. Put a curse on any Injins crossed them graves, curse said they can't go to no Dark'nin' Land. Injins musta believed it, 'cause they's stayed away, never attacked Wildwood again even when they's attacking up an' down the valley."

"Injins is superstitious."

"Ain't they! I've heard that Injins b'lieved the white settlers brought Death with 'em to live on the mountain, you know, when them de Marechals first come here."

The man named Ezekiel spoke up. "Old Gideon said when this *u'nika* come, only the higher bein's can see through it. Maybe them bein's is watchin' us now."

"I hopes not. I can't tell up from down, so I hopes they can't," said one long hunter, hunkering down with his rifle. "The mules is disappeared."

"Slaves too."

"Can't see as far as I kin spit," said another, and hawked a tobacco gob into the whiteness to prove it.

"Can't hardly see you," said a third, himself a suddenly indistinct shape in the whiteness.

From somewhere in the fog, mules snorted and stamped their feet. One brayed restlessly. There was a wailing from the women.

"Darkies is superstitious, like Injins," a man said.

"I been up Frog Mountain in the fog a'fore an' never seen it this bad. Sounds like somethin' disturbin' the mules, don't it? You feelin' it, Zekiel?"

Years in the wilderness had honed a sense for danger that didn't depend on sight. A twig snapped.

Instinctively the men groped to make contact with each other and huddle facing outward. Rifles primed and ready, braced to fire in case an animal prowled out of the whiteness.

The invisible mule brayed louder, spooked.

"Mountain lion?"

"Could be, or a pack o' wolves got our scent. They get close, we kin get us more pelts, boys."

"If we see 'em in time. 'Fore they sees us. Wolves can see good. Better'n folks. And them mules carryin' wolf hides."

"You reckon they after the slaves? Be terrible, 'cause we paid the slave trader good money for 'em, made the trip a lot better, eh, boys?"

"Hope whatever it is don't like dark meat," said Ezekiel, and snickered at his own witticism.

The men shifted closer. "Could be Injins."

"Injins couldn't see any better'n we can."

"If it's Injins followed us up here, we in trouble, 'cause they'll be bent on revenge after that militia from Fort Constant kilt all them squaws and children gettin' firewood, militia thought they was braves.

All they got to do is kill someone from the killer's people, so same number of people's dead. Not too particular about who."

"Can't say the militia was wrong, considerin' what them Cherokees done upriver at Caradoc Station last year. The other two old Caradoc brothers kilt, an' the grandson Bryn Vann went and sold the place to an Irishman. Militia found the bodies. Was settler fam'lies musta put in there, jumped off their narrow boats when Injins attacked, and tried to get to the trading post, but weren't no use. Tradin' post, barn, narrow boats all burned, and Irishman's fam'ly, all them settlers, children, women, two of 'em with babies, tomahawked. Varmints scalped everybody, even the babies."

"Wished the militia killed more Injins. Militia's lazy. I say good growin' land belongs to those that takes it, militia ought to protect them as takes it. I say good thing the militia shot them squaws, kids too, boys'd only grow up to be braves killin' white folks in their beds, girls just breed more damn Injin babies. Hell, shoot 'em all."

"Hush, fool! Higher bein's is Injin. They hear you, no tellin' what they kin do."

"Ain't no higher bein's, Injin or other kinds. That's just foolishness."

"Injins b'lieve all kinds a things is up here. Gideon Vann said an old witch woman lives in the mountains, creeps up behind folks, stabs out their livers with her fingernail. Eats 'em. Couldn't nobody kill her 'cause she had a stony hide. Could be her, a-sneakin' up with her long, sharp finger pointin'.'"

There was a wail from the tree where the slaves were attached.

Another twig cracked.

"Hear that? Might be her . . ."

"Zekiel! Stop blabbin'! Gideon was a crazy half-blood. Never know why old Caradoc didn't run him off 'stead o' lettin' him marry the girl. Gideon claimed he talked to the dead, talked to animals. Injins all b'lieved he got powers."

"White folks did too. He'd us'ta guide long hunters to Kentuckee. They say he knew a spell kept the Creeks from attackin'. They say he kep' ever'body went with him alive."

"Gideon'd be real old by now. He dead?"

"Folks say he brought home some twin babies his crazy daughter had, so his wife could look after 'em. Then he left again. Maybe he was drunk—you know how Injins get—an' walked off that jetty of his and drowned in the river. Maybe the Creeks got him, who knows? They's been fighting all summer, was a big battle farther south, lot of white folks got killed.

"His boy Bryn runs the trading post now, rebuilt it some, made the landin' bigger, 'cause they's more riverboats puttin' in. Married a free nigger girl."

"Shh . . . Fog's movin' back and forth . . . What's that dark thing?"

"I kin see somethin'."

"Don't shoot till you can see it good . . . Ain't no wolf, it's too tall. Wolf'd be slinkin' along down low . . . Hell, don't shoot, it's a mule's got loose, can't see good enough to go after it."

"Or that Uktena Gideon said lives on the mountain, drinks blood."

"Zekiel, you's my brother, but I kin see good enough to shoot you, and I will if you don't shut . . ."

Ezekiel's laugh was loud in the stillness. There was no sound from the women now.

The dark shape seemed closer. "Got to be a mule, grab him."

"Come thisaway, mule, lookie here, got some corn . . ."

"Whoa! Don't that look bigger'n any mule? 'Less it standin' on its hind legs . . ."

"The hell's that?"

Looming out of the fog, a head appeared on a feathered neck, the dark shape of its body still concealed by shifting mist. The head had a human face, an eagle's beak, and dark hollows where a man's mouth

153

and eyes belonged. Taller than a man, half walking, half hopping, the creature came toward the men, wings extended, beating the air to drive needles of icy fog into the men's eyes. It opened its hooked beak and slit the air with its scream.

"Hell's arse!"

"Ain't no eagle."

"Ain't human!"

"A shape-shifter!"

"Gideon said they's up here . . ."

"Shoot it!"

"Sleet's a-blindin' me."

"Shoot, fool!"

The long hunters fired, blindly, and the creature screamed. It lifted off the ground, hovering, wings beating at the crouching men.

Then it gave another cry and seized Ezekiel, sinking its talons into Ezekiel's head, and rose, dragging him off the ground.

"Aaaaiee . . . it's got my head, help me, boys, oh, oh, oh, help. Grab me! Bein' scalped!"

Two of the long hunters dropped their guns and grabbed Ezekiel, but the creature held on as Ezekiel screamed and struggled in the air, and hot blood splattered his rescuers. Then there was a long cry of agony and a heavy thud as the creature flew away into the murky whiteness, dropping Ezekiel. They could see a hat and a long bloody flag of hair and skin swinging from its claws before it disappeared from view.

The hunters fired again, their shots drowning Ezekiel's screams. "I'm scalped! Head's tore off!" The hunters made their way to Ezekiel, jerking and twitching violently, blood gushing over his face and into his eyes, a dark patch under his head. His head looked smaller than it should be, an odd shape.

"Can't kill no shape-shifter," one of the long hunters whispered. "It kin kill you, but you cain't kill it."

"Help me, boys! I'm bad! Can't see nothin'." Through the searing pain, the top of Ezekiel's head felt cold, despite the hot wetness on his face and neck. "Help me!"

"Is them his brains?" he heard someone mutter.

"Never seen anything like that."

"Dear God in heaven! Top of his head's gone. Worse'n scalped."

"Robert Walker's a doctor, git him to the de Marechal place."

"Tie him on his mule to get him down there and the insides of his head'll fall out! Lookit that, oh God!"

"Help me!" Ezekiel gabbled, his voice high and shrill now. In the fog the dark patch spread under his head.

"What kin we do?"

"H . . . he . . . help meee . . . he . . . hel . . ." Ezekiel's voice was high-pitched, no longer human.

"What kin we do?"

The awful screams increased.

"Only one thing kin help you, sorry, Zekiel." A shot rang out, and the screams stopped. The men stood in silence.

"Fog's liftin'."

"Snow's all red around Zekiel."

"The slaves . . . slaves is gone!"

When the long hunters reached Grafton the next day, they unloaded Ezekiel's body, and Ezekiel's brother paid the preacher a wolf pelt to bury him in the graveyard there. They weren't praying men, on the whole, but they stood with their hats off, shifting from foot to foot, while Brother Merriman read a psalm and said the Lord's Prayer over the grave.

Afterward they told the tale at the Ozments' tavern, calming their nerves with liquor and bemoaning the lost slaves. "We paid good money to have women," they kept saying.

"I'll never understand how they got away," said the man who'd chained them. He shook his head.

They relived how they'd felt something lurking in the fog, then how the apparition had struck so fast they half thought they'd dreamed it, except that Ezekiel was dead and the slaves were gone. "Terrible," said one over and over. "Wished I ain't seen it, thing comin' out the fog like it did, all of a sudden. Screamin'."

"Wished we had the women back. Could use a woman right now to forget what I seen. You reckon it got them too? Didn't find no blood."

"Wasn't no trace of them slaves. Maybe it carried them away, chains and all."

"Somethin' evil livin' up there on the mountain."

"I reckon it's from the Devil."

"Considerin' it's scalpin', likely from Injins."

"Maybe Gideon Vann come back. Injins always take revenge."

CHAPTER 16

PEACH

August 1797

Grafton had a jail. Peach averted her eyes from it every time she went onto the porch. The sheriff and a justice had ridden through not long after the attack by the eagle man or the shape-shifter or whatever it was and said it was the law every town had a jail, for lawbreakers and murderers and runaways, so Bryn and George and Jack had built one of logs. The sheriff was fairly certain Indians had stolen the slaves of the long hunters who'd been attacked, but in case the four women had somehow managed to slip their bonds and run away, between wild animals and Indians, he doubted they'd get far. He and his men had searched the lower slopes of Frog Mountain and found no trace. The de Marechals hadn't seen anybody.

At his forge Toby had fashioned bars and a huge bolt for the dark room that was the cell. There were leg irons as well. So far the cell had held two drunken long hunters and a man accused of murdering a homesteader family. The former had been released when they sobered up, and the sheriff had taken the accused man away to stand trial. Peach hadn't had runaways under her porch—that she knew of—in some time. She hoped they'd stay away.

But one hot August afternoon, through the slapping paddle of the mill wheel and the hot hum of cicadas came a faint, low, steady sound . . . Puzzled, she went to the door of the trading post. "What's that noise, Mother Vann? Sounds like they singing at church but nobody in church now. Coming from the river trail like a swarm of hornets, singing hornets . . . Oh, sweet Lord in heaven!"

A low chanting noise grew louder, interrupted by another sound at intervals. Armed men on horseback appeared first; then behind them came a shuffling coffle of barefoot slaves, young men and women, marching chained together at the ankle. Men in three abreast, women in four. The chains made a rhythmic rattling noise because the slaves were marching. One of the male slaves at the front was keeping up a singsong cadence to keep them in step.

A young white man on a horse, accompanied by armed and mounted overseers with whips, seemed to be in charge. He rode back and forth, keeping an eye on the slaves. The overseers cracked their whips over the slaves' heads and occasionally across a back, shouting to move along. The sounds punctuated the singing without interrupting it.

"Peach? What is it? Tell me."

"It's slaves, Mother Vann. A slave trader and guards and a line of slaves, walkin', all shackled together, comin' along the river trail," gasped Peach. "Like the sheriff said we could expect comin' through. They're takin' 'em south to sell." Peach's mouth was dry.

"Listen—you can hear the chains. Can you make out how many?" asked Caitlin, clutching the porch rail.

Peach counted in a whisper. "Must be thirty or more. Comin' this way. They stoppin'. Oh Lord!" Peach shrank back in the shadows of the trading-post porch. She wished she were invisible.

One of the overseers shouted a question to the young white man, who gave an order, and the slaves shuffled onto the jetty to rest. He dismounted and started walking toward the store. "One comin' this way," muttered Peach.

Caitlin reached for Peach's arm. "Peach, you go in the storeroom. Don't come out till he's gone, not for all the world!"

"Mother Vann. I can't leave you alone, you can't see enough to serve him."

"I'll manage." Caitlin gave her a push, then groped her way to stand at the door. "Go on! Before they see you! Go, I say!"

Peach turned and hurried to the storeroom. She was shaking. She put her head in her hands. She'd left Caitlin all alone with these men. Peach opened the storeroom door a crack. Somebody had to watch these men, see they didn't hurt Caitlin, see they didn't take advantage of her blindness and steal.

She saw the trader remove his hat when he entered, heard him say, "Good afternoon, mistress," and heard him give Caitlin a big order for cornmeal and salt pork cut into portions. While Caitlin felt her way to the supplies and then a knife, he stepped outside and called to the overseers. The guard replied, "Yessir," turned to the slaves, and gave an order. Line by line, those chained together shuffled forward and dropped their shackled feet over the jetty into the water.

"Might's well let the niggers cool their feet in the river. I find it's best to treat them kind, when you can," he remarked pleasantly. "Then they're less likely to cause trouble."

"Is that so?" said Caitlin, slicing through salt pork and stacking the pieces into a small mountain. "Is that enough for you?" she asked.

"A little more—I make it a rule not to skimp on their rations, like some would. Slaves in good condition, not too thin and worn out from the journey, fetch a better price."

The knife cutting more salt pork hit the counter hard.

Peach watched Caitlin cut and cut till she had a big pile of salt meat. Then she felt her way to the barrel of meal, picked up her wooden measure, and began filling a sack.

"Remarkable how you cut that meat, so exact, how you manage not to spill meal, being blind, ma'am, if you don't mind my saying," said the trader.

"Not quite as blind as all that!" snapped Caitlin.

"I mean it politely, ma'am."

"And so I understood you, sir," said Caitlin, filling and refilling her measure and emptying it neatly into the sack.

Peach thought her mother-in-law sounded different; her warm Welsh lilt had been replaced by an icily polite tone that said the trader was rude and coarse and unfit for polite company. The trader, who held himself a cut above the guards and was anxious to prove he was as good as any gentleman planter, tried to ingratiate himself in conversation. "A Virginia planter near Winchester's obliged to dispose of some of his people. Gambling debts, they say. We're bound for Louisiana, hands fit to work in the cane fields fetch the best price, but good breeding women do too."

Caitlin's intake of breath was sharp. "I beg you will not speak coarsely, sir!"

"They're just livestock!" he protested. Then, trying to regain ground as a gentleman, "If that was indelicate, I apologize, ma'am. Perhaps you can help me. I have a couple of slaves who're weaker than I thought, might not last in the cane fields, where the work's hot and hard. If I could find a buyer, I'd sell 'em now. They're good enough for field work here, in your trading post or that mill you got. If I get shut of them now, could get the rest to Louisiana faster. You'd get a bargain," he wheedled.

"I don't believe so," said Caitlin with frigid politeness.

"Your neighbors, then, ma'am? I could set up an auction block on the jetty."

"I think not," Caitlin said dismissively.

Peach suddenly realized Caitlin sounded exactly like Sophia de Marechal when someone provoked Sophia's English pride. Caitlin said it was because Sophia's people in England had been very grand that Sophia could make the tone of her voice sting like a slap. "With an expression on her face to match. Haughty. As if she were queen of all the world," Caitlin said. Now Caitlin looked and sounded like Sophia. It would have been funny. In other circumstances.

Caitlin told the trader how much he owed her, and there was a jingle of coins and a crackle of a bill as he paid. "It's the right money, ma'am, on my word as a gentleman. I didn't cheat you, being blind." Then footsteps in the silence as he walked out.

Peach crossed the storeroom to the window and watched as he carried the food to the jetty and portioned out meal and salt pork to each one. The slaves each took the ration and stored it in the sacking pocket tied to his or her waist to keep until they could cook it later.

She opened the door to rejoin Caitlin when she heard the trader again on the trading-post steps. "I almost forgot, ma'am. I have a letter to send to the planter's wife and children. Back home we hear so much about the Indian attacks on the road to Louisiana that they're anxious about the welfare of two of their favorite house slaves who had to be sold. I want to let them know Nancy and Jenny are well, not grieving for their children."

"Their children?" Caitlin gasped.

"The youngest were weaned," he explained patiently. "It's of little consequence, ma'am. Tenderhearted people don't realize, slaves don't feel things as we do. Mothers might shed a few tears at first—but they forget soon, don't feel it more than a cow misses her calf the day after it's taken away. They'll likely be singing tonight."

Peach closed her eyes and imagined standing over the trader with Caitlin's knife in her hand, the trader gasping his last breath in a pool of blood gushing from his throat like when they butchered the pigs in December. Only not quick like the pigs, but dying surprised and slow enough to understand what was happening to him . . . Peach imagined herself telling him not to worry, whites didn't feel things like Negroes did.

The trader asked Caitlin to send the letter north by any boat going upriver. "Here's a shilling to pay for its carriage. We'll spend tonight by the river, and maybe by morning people will have thought more about buying a slave cheap. If anyone wants to inspect the slaves first, they should come to me."

"Certainly," Caitlin replied in a voice that said, *Never.*

Next the trader recollected he needed a little whiskey, because moving slaves was thirsty work. Caitlin replied they had no whiskey, her husband refused to keep it. Finally the trader asked if there was a blacksmith, because his horse had thrown a shoe. Peach heard Caitlin hesitate. Then she told him the way to the Drumhellers' smithy at Rattlesnake Springs. Peach hoped he'd disturb a rattler. Then as an after-thought Caitlin said primly that Rufus Drumheller had liquor for sale. Peach thought Drumheller liquor was what he deserved.

Later she saw the trader return to the jetty with a jug, leading his newly shoed horse. He gave an order, and one group of male slaves went shuffling off under guard to collect firewood, until each line of slaves had a fire going and busied themselves cooking the food the trader had distributed.

After they'd eaten, she watched the trader pass the jug around to the guards. Then he called they'd take turns resting at the boardinghouse, and some could go now; then they'd change places.

The first group of guards went among the slaves, who'd suddenly fallen silent. Each guard chose a woman, unshackled her, and took her away with him. Most of the chosen women kept their heads bowed as the other slaves silently watched them go. One young girl resisted and cried out, trying to pull away as she was dragged off, but the guard slapped her so loudly Peach put her hand to her own cheek. The blow caused the girl to stumble and fall, but she was dragged roughly upright.

All night campfires flickered in the field by the river where the slaves were camped. Peach made supper and kept her children and the twins by her side until bedtime, threatening to whip any child who set foot outside her kitchen. They were not to go to the storeroom or the porch. Bryn would do everyone's chores tonight.

The children were all accustomed to Peach's vigorous mothering, but when Caitlin and Fawn, usually so indulgent, sternly repeated the threat, the children were sufficiently cowed to obey. Fawn and Peach put the children to bed, and Peach went restlessly back and forth to the storeroom with its view of the field, where the campfires flickered here and there. She saw the first set of guards change places with the trader and the second set of guards. A sound came from the field where the slaves were camped. Like singing, or a sorrowful wind.

Peach lay awake while Bryn snored, listening until the sound ceased. She prayed for the slave women dragged away, wondered if they were listening too, if the singing was meant to comfort them, the sound to make them feel less alone. She thought about Iddo, who'd preached abolition and been scorned for it. Iddo was dead now. She wished she hadn't made a fuss about him.

Next morning Bryn insisted on piling the children in a wagon and taking them up to Little Molly's school by a route that avoided the field. Peach continued to watch the guards as they reshackled the women from the night before. Then they cracked their whips, and the slaves groaned and pulled each other to their feet from their sleeping places on the ground. Peach watched them hurriedly devour corn pones saved from their supper, and a guard passed between the manacled groups with a bucket of water and a dipper.

Then the trader gave an order for them to line up. The slave at the head of the procession stepped in place to set the rhythm and called out his cadence until the chains were rattling and all the feet stepped in time. They moved off.

Peach came out onto the porch as the procession disappeared on the trail. She fell to her knees beside Caitlin's chair and prayed as hard as she could, "Please, Jesus, let Indians get the white men and do terrible things to them. Their worst things. And let the slaves loose to help. Amen."

There was a long sigh from Caitlin. Then she laid her hand on Peach's shoulder. "Amen, Peach. In all the world, amen," she said.

The slave trader's letter lay on the counter, like a dead poison toad. Peach wanted to burn it. Caitlin said, "No. We'll put it in the pie safe for now. We may see him again. If he gets back and hears they didn't get his letter, we'll give it back and say there was no one to send it by."

"I wish we could do worse," said Peach.

"I know."

Days later when Rufus came to the trading post, Peach and Caitlin heard him tell Bryn he'd sold the trader whiskey all right. Had pissed in the jug before filling it and plugging the neck with a corncob. He slapped Bryn on the shoulder, and both men guffawed.

"What use was that? Didn't help anybody," Peach told Caitlin.

"I know. But men think it does," said Caitlin.

The passing slaves made it blindingly clear to Peach how narrowly the people she loved escaped the same fate—her sons could have been shackled, the women the men took could have been her sisters, her daughter, herself, all bound for sale if they hadn't been lucky enough to be free. Her spirit began to rise up. If, being free, the best she could do was just be afraid, it wasn't any more help than pissing in the whiskey jug. If she was free, if her mother had run away, if people had helped Venus—and Sophia and Henri had helped—she had to do more than that. Even if she didn't want to, she had to help folks too. She muttered, "I swear before God to *do* somethin'. Don't know what yet, but I swear to do *somethin'*."

And as she thought about it, she realized how dangerous it would be, not just for herself but for her whole family, maybe for all the Negroes, for Cully, for Kitty, for everybody. White people were terrified of a slave uprising, and helping runaways could get the helper hung. Everything would depend on keeping it a secret. From Bryn, from Caitlin, from her friends. She mustn't let on to anyone.

CHAPTER 17

MESHACK

March 1807

Meshack Tudor was prepared for death. He'd been poorly for much of the winter, and his bones ached all the time. He was failing, he knew that. Fortunately he'd got his coffin ready in time. He couldn't trust anyone else to make coffins like he could—he'd made many coffins in his day. He'd seasoned and polished the oak so it would be watertight, to keep him safe and dry until he rose on Judgment Day, like Brother Merriman said was God's covenant with the elect. And he counted on rising; it was the only way he'd see his children again.

Meshack had found religion, thanks to an unlikely bond that had somehow strengthened over the years, composed of something approaching friendship on Brother Merriman's part and something approaching pity on Meshack's.

It had begun when Meshack had been obliged to consult a much younger, unmarried Brother Merriman over the funeral of Saskia Stuart.

Saskia had died in her chair, her arms full of laundry she'd been folding. Her husband, Nott, who'd taken the laundry off the line to save her the trouble, had gone to feed the livestock and come back to find her body before it had grown cold. Nott was too undone to do anything but sob helplessly in the corner as the women came to prepare Saskia's body and dress her for the funeral. Meshack had delivered the news to Brother Merriman. Saskia had felt sorry for Brother Merriman, an uncomfortably sanctimonious young man with a gift for irritating his neighbors. She'd given him some good advice about how not to do that if he wanted to show people the way to the Lord. Brother Merriman had managed to bury Saskia with dignity.

Afterward Meshack had been quietly receptive to Brother Merriman's evangelizing, especially the part about Judgment Day and the Rapture and the souls rising from the grave. There were many people Meshack wanted to see again, and he believed Brother Merriman's message because he had to if that was going to happen.

Nott, who'd come to live with Meshack after Saskia died, could never concentrate for long on what Brother Merriman was talking about. His eyes were permanently red rimmed from missing Saskia, and he mostly passed the time in Meshack's rocking chair, chewing on his pipe and thinking quietly to himself. If asked if he wanted something—food or even a little whiskey—Nott would shake his head and say, "No. Just waitin' till it be time to join her. Just sittin' here ready, so the Lord know where I am. He ready to call me, don't want to be elsewhere and keep him waitin'."

Sometimes Nott asked Brother Merriman for his opinion of whether it would be long before God called him. At the time it got on Meshack's nerves. "You mighty impatient! We just two old fools—why you think God in any hurry to have us for company?" he'd snap. But when Nott died, Meshack missed him. It was a comfort to think Nott was with Saskia again, though. He'd doted on her.

Meshack had company almost every day. Malinda Drumheller and Little Molly came and brought him food and saw he had a good supply of firewood and a bucket of water and a dipper handy. Malinda sometimes boiled a load of laundry and hung it up for Little Molly to get in and fold when it was dry. Malinda had never been able to talk, but he was used to her silent presence. Little Molly talked to him, but he was getting deaf, so her voice now sounded like birds chirping far away. He smiled and nodded as if she were making sense and was grateful for what they did for him.

Gradually, though, when Malinda and Little Molly had been and gone, he became aware of more visitors. Sometimes these appeared so briefly he wasn't sure they'd been there at all. Once he thought Nott was back. Another time he saw Sophia out of the corner of his eye, looking at the shelf of plates she'd given him, the ones with the roses painted on, as real as life, and gold trim. He loved those plates and told her again how beautiful he thought they were, and she smiled and nodded and disappeared.

Malinda brought sweet fritters. He roused himself to eat a few bites, could taste nothing.

Saskia came and sat for a while. Seth too, who'd been killed by the rattlesnakes.

He was cold. Little Molly swept the fireplace, laid kindling, and lit the fire. She left him watching the flames dance.

Malinda was sitting by his side with a bowl and a spoon, and fairly certain she was real, he opened his mouth obediently.

Then Malinda was gone and his wives came, the women who'd been sold away from him, or he sold away from them. The last with the rope still around her neck. She'd hung herself when the slave trader came and took the children. They came and sat with him, along with others he didn't recognize but that his wives made him understand were his children. The slave catcher he'd trapped and burned to death, along with the slave catcher's companions, was there. They stared at him balefully. Meshack chuckled. *Can't do nothin' now, can't catch nobody now.*

Malinda and Little Molly were back, and some others he thought were Sophia's daughters, but he wasn't sure. They bustled around his cabin doing whatever it was women do around a tired old man. Someone pulled a quilt up to his chin. The fire held his eyes, his field of vision had narrowed until that was all he could see, but he sensed those waiting, still and patient, for him in the shadows beyond.

Finally his last wife stepped forward and held out her hand. "I'm coming." With a sigh of relief, Meshack reached out and grasped it.

CHAPTER 18

BROTHER MERRIMAN

They carried Meshack's coffin from his cabin to the cemetery. There had been a week of warm days, a green haze of new leaves had appeared on the trees, and the orchard and dogwood buds were opening.

Eyes closed against the sun, Brother Merriman leaned on his cane, supported by his sons, Endurance and Mortify, waiting by the open grave as the procession made its slow way toward the cemetery below the orchard. He suffered badly from rheumatism and no longer had the stamina for one of his funeral sermons. After several years of being obliged to help their father at the mission school, both Endurance and Mortify felt a call to circuit preaching and were often gone from home to preach and baptize in distant settlements.

Today his sons were taking it in turn to read psalms, and each had prepared a homily. As funerals went, Brother Merriman thought it lacking.

Brother Merriman was lonely. Mattie was dead, as was his archenemy, Iddo Fox. Now Meshack, the closest thing he'd had to a friend, was gone too. Brother Merriman wondered how he would weigh up in the heavenly balance when he was called to give an account of his earthly ministry. Had Meshack been his only success? Sometimes it seemed so.

As a young man he had set out to spread Christian light through all of Kentuckee, and possibly beyond, bringing thousands to Jesus. Looking back on his life's work, it seemed to him that the only real successes he could claim were his small wooden church and the mission school. Iddo Fox's Quakers in Pennsylvania and his own Congregationalists had both sent teachers to bring Cherokee children into the light of the Gospel, and there'd been many baptisms, whole families sometimes.

It had surprised Brother Merriman and Iddo Fox to observe the teachers and see how Quakers and Puritans had mellowed toward each other in the next generation. They'd discussed this, in their usual combative way, whether it was a good thing. But then Iddo had died.

Sometimes, on days when he could get about, he'd go to the cemetery and stand by Iddo's grave and carry on a one-sided argument, as if Iddo could still hear him. He always did it with the intention of having the last word with Iddo. He talked and talked at the bare earth that covered Iddo's grave, as if the force of truth would penetrate down to where Iddo lay in his coffin. But it was never a satisfying experience.

He'd done everything he could to bring the settlers and heathens to repentance in this wild place. In church on Sunday and at midweek prayer meetings, he still delivered sermons, shorter than before, denouncing sacrilegious superstition and Cherokee beliefs, threatening hellfire for the nonelect. When he caught the Indian boys talking of Gideon and his powers to speak with the animals, or telling the shape-shifter story at school, he gave them a whipping. Joseph and Jesse White, sons of Fawn in the Water and White Owl, renamed the White family in the census, had been the boys most frequently beaten for this.

None of the Cherokee boys whimpered or cried, no matter how hard he tried to whip the Devil out of them. Afterward Brother Merriman made them recite the formula: There was only the word of God. The stories were nonsense, and Gideon had been a heathen medicine man with a wild imagination. There was no Uktena, no Darkening Land, and no such thing as a shape-shifter on Frog Mountain or anywhere.

If he could have whipped the scorn out of their eyes, he would have.

He felt his sons nudge him out of his reverie. He blinked. Where was he? Oh yes, Meshack's funeral.

Brother Merriman had realized that his days in charge of the mission school were numbered. He was tired. He'd written several times to the church in Massachusetts where he'd been ordained, requesting an assistant to train to replace him. Little Molly should have succeeded him, but he was fairly sure she was not among the elect, and in any case, she was female, with all the weaknesses attendant upon that sex. Not to mention lacking what he regarded as the feminine virtues, especially modesty and the habit of silence. She was inclined to express her opinion too freely and too forcefully until opposition gave way. No, a weaker vessel, as he thought of women, should never have a position of authority in the school. It set a bad example for the Cherokee girls.

Mattie had been a much better model of a Christian wife. Mattie had admired him.

Mortify and Endurance nudged him. "We're going to sing now, Pa. 'Rise, My Soul' . . ."

From years of habit, Brother Merriman sang as the first line was played.

"Rise, My Soul, and Stretch Thy Wings." It had been Mattie's favorite hymn. Brother Merriman led the call-and-response singing from memory and by long habit, though after so many years, everyone knew the words. He continued leading the mourners through hymn after hymn until his voice gave out.

Earth was being shoveled over Meshack's coffin. He hoped Meshack had been saved. He was hungry now. His thoughts turned to the funeral meal. The mourners were drifting away, and he and his sons turned toward the trading post, where it was to be held. If Mattie had been alive, she'd have baked a scripture cake for the funeral meal. He bent his head and swiped his eyes with his handkerchief. If only Mattie had been spared a little longer.

CHAPTER 19

MESHACK'S FUNERAL

Gathered at the trading post, everyone was hoarse from singing. Meshack was one of the last original settlers, and they'd sung hard. Only Venus and Caitlin were left now.

Malinda and Little Molly and Caitlin were busy setting out food. Malinda had prepared a mountain of the fritters Meshack had loved, and Annie, who was talking to Little Molly and Peach, had been holding one for the last ten minutes like she'd forgotten it was there. Annie was too thin.

"Eat it, Annie!" urged Little Molly. Poor Annie, she thought; at thirty-eight she looked twice the age of her friends and sister-in-law. Beneath her cap, gray hair was straggling from its bun, and teeth lost with each of her eleven pregnancies had left her cheeks hollow and sunken. Little Molly only needed to look at Annie to be satisfied with her lot as a spinster teacher.

Nor did she envy Stefania. Marriage had mellowed her friend, who had been such an independent spirit, always ready for an adventure as a girl. Now Stefania led a sedate, well-ordered life as mistress of Chiaramonte, with two children; an aging husband who doted on her; a capable housekeeper; and time and money to be a generous patroness of the mission school.

Today Stefania was in a high-waisted gown with a short velvet jacket, a funeral bonnet with feathers, and jet earbobs. She always had very pretty clothes. Thierry was a Frenchman and believed his wife should dress becomingly. Stefania always acceded to her husband's wishes, just as Rosalia had indulged Stefano.

Little Molly reflected that she need please no one but herself. As always, she dressed in black. She claimed it was because black made her more of a figure of authority at school, helped her stand up to Brother Merriman and his lecherous son Mortify. It was also suitable for funerals when the occasion arose.

But Little Molly had her private vanities, and she looked wonderful in black. It set off her slender waist, fine complexion, and blue eyes, and with her grandfather's legacy to draw on, she could afford new gowns in the high-waisted style featured in Stefania's fashion books. From these she also learned to gather her abundant brown hair into a sort of loose bun, held in place with some pretty tortoiseshell combs Stefania had given her. Rufus had made her a present of some gold earbobs, and Peach had pierced her ears so she could wear them.

"Lo, how our days are numbered," Annie murmured, before finally biting into the fritter.

"Yes," said Stefania. She looked down at her children—a solemn, dark-eyed girl named Rosa on one side, a small boy named Lafayette clinging to her skirt on the other—and put a protective arm round their shoulders. Her youngest child, a daughter of two, had died the previous year of fever. People spoke of coming out of mourning, but Stefania knew it wasn't possible to do that, and she was beginning to live in dread of Thierry's death. He'd aged and was too poorly to attend today's funeral. Stefania feared what was coming.

Magdalena brought over her children, Fanny and Lorenzo, and suggested the four children get something to eat and take it outside to the jetty. Happy to be released from the solemn adults, the children walked off, agreeing, "Let's just have cake!"

Little Molly sat down beside Venus and handed her a plate. Brunswick stew. "Squirrel stew. I made it," Little Molly said diffidently, "because Mother was too tired." Venus frowned at the stew. Little Molly hated domestic tasks, including cooking, and at an early age she'd gleaned that if she cooked badly enough, someone else would take over. It was another reason she liked teaching—at school, meals were prepared by helpers who were often orphan girls who felt a missionary calling and were sent by the northern congregations. They were sort of servants but not exactly.

But sometimes cooking had to be done, and it was an unwritten law that women, married, single, or widowed, never attended a funeral empty-handed.

Venus took a bite, made a face, and put the plate down. "Toby have to make you iron teeth 'fore you could chew that squirrel! Tough like it still alive! You so smart with that school of yours, got everybody doing what you say the way you say do it, an' still cain't cook stew? Fetch me some of Susan's corn bread, dish me some o' those crab apple preserves," she snapped.

Little Molly flushed, and tears rose in her eyes.

Venus put a hand on her arm. "I spoke too hard. Stew don't matter, child. I know you and your mama was with Meshack when he died, nursed him good. Your mama loved Meshack like he was her daddy. She was his child."

"It was hard. Meshack wasn't himself anymore, was wandering in his mind, Aunt Venus. He didn't know Mama. He kept talking over and over about something he buried where his old cabin used to stand. One minute it was money, next it was bones. And he laughed like someone just told him something funny, but like the funny thing was also bad."

Venus looked sharply at Little Molly. "Buried? Don't you go repeatin' what Meshack said," Venus ordered. "You hear me, girl? Don't say nothin' about Meshack buryin' nothin'!" Peach was crossing the room with a slice of pie. "Not even to Peach. 'Specially not to Peach." Venus hissed. "Never know who hear what's said at the trading post. Sheriff always stop, pass the time of day. If she mention somethin' Meshack buried, he go lookin' for it, and we have trouble. No, we don't want the sheriff sniffin' round."

Peach came up in time to hear her mother mention the sheriff. "No indeed! Mama's right about that man. Sheriff got a way of askin' questions about this and that, like he tryin' to find something, only he don't know exactly what yet. An' you talkin' 'bout one thing, he change the subject next minute, wait to see what you say, like he hope you confuse'. Las' time he here he talkin' about the church, next breaf askin' me about some slave tracker, s'posed to've disappeared somewhere in the mountains when the sheriff was a boy. Famous slave tracker, a half-blood got rich, had a plantation in the sheriff's neighborhood. Went off after some slaves, never came back. Wife never knew whether she was a widow or not, the sheriff had said. And he askin' me if I know anything 'bout *that*? How would I? You know anything about it, Mama?"

"Hunh-un," said Venus, eating pie. "Might of heard of that slave tracker, but never seen him. Slave trackers be gone south now."

Newspapers came through the trading post, usually left behind by riverboat travelers. There'd been a slave rebellion in Haiti. Slaves there had revolted and succeeded in killing their owners or driving them to flee the country. The slaves were in charge now, and there were lurid accounts of their revenge. Coffee and sugar planters had fled for their lives to New Orleans.

"Sheriff say they busy catching folks tryin' to get to Haiti, don't know they got to cross the water," Peach reported. "I don't think he likely to bother us for a while."

She had perfected a facial expression of dumb innocence when she saw the sheriff coming, and she'd learned to hold it even when the sheriff put runaway slaves he'd intercepted into the jail overnight. Peach had that same expression now. Venus stared at her daughter. "Why you lookin' like that?"

Peach shrugged and turned away. Mama was too sharp. Runaway slaves had been sleeping under the trading-post porch more and more lately. They'd be there, just breathing, not saying a word. After the first few times, Peach didn't say anything either, just fetched some food when she could slip out and leave a plate. If it was cold, she tried to leave a blanket if she could spare one from the stock. She hadn't told anyone.

But soon she was forced to tell Little Molly.

CHAPTER 20

LITTLE MOLLY

November 1807

Little Molly liked living at the mission school. Women teachers occupied a large dormitory cabin off to one side of the school yard, close to the woods so their privy could be decently hidden. Male teachers had another as far away from the females as possible. The female teachers shared domestic chores in their building, went to meals together, and at night sat at their long wooden table with benches and corrected students' work or did their mending or wrote letters home as the fire crackled. Female teachers tended to be young, usually earnest, fresh-faced girls from up north who'd felt the call to devote themselves to spreading God's word among the heathens for a year or two until they married.

Thanks to her grandfather's insistence, as the senior female teacher, Little Molly had the privilege of a room of her own. The dormitory cabin extended into an L shape, and the short leg of the L was hers. It had its own entrance, a stone fireplace, a pleasant outlook down the valley through a glass window her grandfather Rufus had installed, curtains and a feather mattress her mother had made, a cheerful quilt, a rocker Jack had made for her, a worktable, and shelves for her cherished books.

She never entered it without a rush of satisfaction at its harmony and neatness and delight in having a place of her very own after growing up in a cabin bursting with children. It was Little Molly's private territory, and no one else was to enter it, but even so, Rufus had insisted Toby make a lock for the door. He didn't trust Indians not to steal, not even children. Molly protested this wasn't really necessary, but when some of the young teachers took to sitting there during their free hours, the invasion on her privacy grated on her nerves so much that Little Molly took to keeping her door locked. The other teachers were offended at first, but as the years passed and a succession of young women took their place, it was accepted that Little Molly was a spinster set in her ways and she had an eccentric liking for privacy.

But Rufus had recently died, and Little Molly suddenly wanted the comfort of her family. She'd often saddle up her mare, a last gift from Rufus, and ride back to her father's house on Little Frog Mountain to eat supper and spend a night with her parents, even though this meant getting up in the dark to ride back to Slipping Creek in time for prayers and breakfast.

This time Jack had gathered the family, including Toby, Patience, Zebulon, and Zebulon's wife, Linney, for a reading of Rufus's will. Jack and Toby were astonished at the assets in money and property their father had amassed. Jack whistled in surprise. Rufus had divided his estate between his three sons and Little Molly. Her share was in money while his sons' was mostly in land and animals. *Why . . . I'm rich!* Little Molly thought, astonished. But she'd kept her countenance, not giving away her surprise or looking pleased.

Zebulon was furious because he'd always been encouraged by his mother to believe he was his father's main heir. Patience had wailed it wasn't right and accused Little Molly of being a sly baggage, cozying up to her grandfather to deprive Zebulon of what was rightfully his. He should have inherited her share. He needed it to keep his wife, Patience spluttered, while Little Molly was unmarried, had her board at the school and no need of money. As for Toby, he had his still where he made his whiskey and the smithy—very well, Zebulon didn't want those—but Toby wasn't married either, so didn't need his share of Rufus's money any more than Little Molly did. And Jack, she protested, had all the land he needed, didn't need money either! His family were nearly grown. It wasn't fair, Patience whined.

Linney Pine Drumheller sat silently during her mother-in-law's diatribe. Little Molly thought she saw her smirk, but Linney ducked her head, and when she lifted it again, her lips were set in a line like her mother-in-law's. Everyone knew Patience had been furious when Zebulon insisted on marrying her to spite Mariah Stuart.

Little Molly knew Stefania had overheard Linney boasting to her mother, Jane, still the Chiaramonte housekeeper, that when Zebulon came into his inheritance, she and Zebulon would have a better house than Chiaramonte, better than Wildwood. She'd have house servants. Maybe she'd persuade Zebulon to buy slaves, she'd gloated.

Little Molly had wondered aloud to Stefania what Gustine could ever have seen in Linney.

When it was time to go home, Linney gave Little Molly a false smile and followed an indignant Patience and a surly Zebulon out of Jack's cabin.

Malinda slammed the door behind them, and Jack laughed.

"Pa wanted you to have this as well," Jack had said after Zebulon and his wife and mother were gone. He pressed a bulky stocking into Little Molly's hand.

"A stocking?"

"Look inside. Patience made Pa write a will so she and Zebulon would be provided for—Toby and I agreed it was only right—but after the will was drawn up, Pa got it into his head to keep the money he made after that out of Patience's hands. When he was dying, he told me about hiding a sock of money in the barn for you. It's in addition to what he left in the will. He said you'd probably spend your inheritance on books, and this was for dresses and hair ribbons like Stefania has. He liked to think of you looking pretty, not just serious and thinking all the time. Said you'd never get a husband otherwise."

Little Molly put a hand in the stocking and withdrew a handful of dollars. "Papa, there's loads of money," she exclaimed, astonished. "With all this I could buy a husband. Several husbands."

As she saddled her horse in the early dark hours the next morning, it began to rain, and there were distant claps of thunder, but she had an oilskin cloak and didn't mind a little rain. And even if she had minded, she had to get back. The stocking of money lay heavy in the deep pocket of her cloak. Ten minutes down the road and it was pouring down so hard she could scarcely see. She pulled the hood low to keep rain out of her eyes. The mare knew the way and plodded along. The weather and the muddy ground muffled her horse's hoofbeats as she passed the trading post, envying Peach, probably still warm and dry in bed.

Blinded by the driving rain, she didn't see the figures emerge from the space under the porch, but suddenly someone was practically under the mare's hooves with a lit lantern, and she tried to pull up abruptly. "Bryn?" she exclaimed as her startled horse whinnied and shied, slipping in the mud, and she lost her seat. "Oof!" she cried as she landed in the muck.

The lantern was quickly covered, and she heard voices muttering, "Who that? Somebody here!"

"Go before they sees us!"

"There's a horse, must be patrollers!"

"Oh Gawd, if they is! Let's go!"

"How? We s'posed to follow the stars south but can't see no stars, can't see nothin' . . . Which way you spect we go?"

The wet mud was slippery, her skirt was sodden and heavy, and her oilskin cloak was twisted round her legs. Little Molly couldn't get a purchase to stand up. It wasn't Bryn or his boys or long hunters out on the road before daylight in this weather. "I'm not patrollers. Help me up," she said.

A black hand held the lantern up close to her face.

"You must be runaways. Where do you want to go? I'll help you if I can."

A muttered voice said, "Haiti. It far?"

"Yes. Help me up out of this mud. I'll explain."

The people in the dark hesitated.

A hand reached down. "Please, missus . . ."

Little Molly took it and was pulled upright to find herself surrounded by three Negro men, a boy, and a woman with a small boy tied to her back and holding a baby wrapped in a shawl, all soaked. The little boy's teeth were chattering.

"Haiti's in that direction." Little Molly pointed south. "But I wouldn't advise going that way. It's a long trip south to get to the coast, then there's a sea to cross before you reach Haiti. Slave owners know that's where runaways want to go, and they have militia patrolling everywhere. And they've caught many. You have a better chance if you head north."

"North! But Haiti ain't north!"

"If you can get north to Pennsylvania or Vermont, the law there says you're free."

"Where's that?"

"The shortest and best way is over Frog Mountain there, down the other side to the river. Don't go now, wait till there's a clear night and you can see the stars. After you cross the mountain, you follow the big north star. The river goes north for a while too. Then it goes east through a pass in the mountains, and you stop following it and just go by the star."

"How you know that the way? You been there?"

"No, I haven't, but I'm a teacher and we have a map at school. I know where the mountains and rivers are. I've showed the children the route the first settlers took to get here. But if you wait another day here, I'll get you some food. I'll come back tomorrow night and guide you over the mountain myself. I promise. There's a trail the sheriff doesn't know, the patrollers won't either . . ."

The Negroes talked among themselves. "We got to cross the mountain? Don't sound right to me, Haiti be better."

"No, maybe she right. Folks talk about Haiti but Moses talk about norf, sent us this way. He say a woman at the trading post would feed us, let us hide for a night. He right about that."

"Moses ain't here to show us, I say she wrong and we go to Haiti."

"Got to go, missus."

The boy was shivering, and the woman's shawl round the baby was soaking. The mother looked from man to man, fear and despair in her eyes.

One of the slaves had caught Little Molly's horse. For a moment she debated whether to give the runaways the horse and think of some story to tell when she eventually got back to school about it being spooked by thunder and running off. Instead she reached into her pocket and held out the stocking full of money. "Take this. There's money inside."

"Why you want to give us money?" asked one man suspiciously. "We ain't thievin' you!"

"I know. Take it! It was part of my inheritance and I have more. Please listen to me. Go north. Whoever Moses is, he's right," she said to the man who'd returned her horse. "You can buy food, maybe even a horse, but if you're caught, throw the money away. It'll go worse for you if the patrollers catch you with money and think you're thieves."

The man took the stocking. "Thank you, missus. But got to go, can't stay."

"Here." Impulsively she unfastened the oilskin and wrapped it round the soaked woman with the child on her back and the baby. She pulled the hood down across the woman's brow. She could buy another. It didn't matter if she was wet; she'd get dry when she reached school.

"Thank you, missus," the woman whispered.

"We go now, missus," said a man, offering his hand to help her mount.

The little group walked away, disappearing into the dark and the rain, probably doomed. Little Molly watched them go, feeling helpless and angry. She hoped they'd get north safely and could build new lives with her money. The futility of giving a wet woman her oilskin, though! In despair, shivering and soaked herself, and knowing she would return to her fire, dry clothes, and breakfast, she swore to think of something better to do.

She came back the next day and confronted Peach.

Peach denied she helped runaways. But Little Molly described the group she'd seen emerge from beneath the porch. "Those poor people. I can't get that baby in the wet shawl and the little boy out of my head, probably catching their deaths in the rain and no idea where to go. I'm going to help, Peach. Stefania will too."

The strain of keeping her secret, never knowing from one night to the next if anyone would be hiding on the premises, was wearing Peach down. She hadn't been responsible for them coming to the trading post in the first place, and she couldn't stop them now—word seemed to have spread. She was afraid to sleep in case some noise from below woke Bryn or the children, fearing the appearance of the sheriff and his men at any moment. She broke down and agreed Little Molly was right; she was helping runaways.

"Sits heavy on me! I can't tell anybody, can't tell Bryn, 'specially can't tell Mama or Mother Vann. Was Iddo who know about people helpin' runaways, he didn't say nothin' to Mama 'bout it, but one time he say to me, leave some food and a blanket under your cabin, act like you don't

185

know nothin'. Trading post is on the river, people hide on the riverboats if they can. So I do. Most nights I put it in a bucket under a plate, ram a piece of wood in over it tight so the raccoons don't get it. Sometimes it's gone. I leave a blanket if it's real cold but can't leave too many or Bryn will notice what's gone from the storeroom. On cold nights I hate thinkin' somebody under the porch, lyin' in the cold and we got a fire."

"Do you ever see who it is?"

"I talk but make sure I don't look, so if the sheriff asks have I seen any runaways, I can say no and my face won't tell no lie. That sheriff watches you real close. But there's a man, they call him Moses. Sounds like he goes back and forth, takes a few folks at a time, knows different ways, he uses one for a time and then changes when he thinks they may be watchin' it. He say better they go north, 'stead of Haiti, jus' like you told those poor folks you saw. Hard to go south without running into patrollers. That's why so many folks come past here lately. They come hidin' on the packet boats when they can. Moses supposed to know which folks along the way will help. If they catch Moses, won't just be a whippin', won't just hang him, they bury him alive."

"A man mentioned Moses, and how he'd told them to go north instead of to Haiti, but they couldn't wait long enough for me to show them which way to go to find the path."

"You smart, you could draw a map, show where the river go, trails over Frog Mountain, where the drinkin' gourd star is they say show the way north," said Peach. "So folks could see where they meant to go. You'd figure how to do it."

"Hmmm." Little Molly considered. "We've got a map at school I can copy."

Little Molly thanked heaven she had a room to herself and enough money to send for paper along with her last order of books. She spread out paper on her worktable and sketched, copying the school map in a reduced size, carefully drawing landmarks on it because she was sure most of the slaves couldn't read.

She rode up Frog Mountain and meandered up and across, noting the landscape to the north and east.

She talked to long hunters, said that it was part of her teaching to show the children how to draw a map. Could they help her by describing what was north of Grafton? How would she show a route to Philadelphia? She flirted. The long hunters, mostly illiterate, and all woman hungry, obligingly drew her simple maps to compare with her big one, described landmarks and trails, told her where the Indians were dangerous, tried to put an arm around her waist or pull her onto their knees. To their annoyance, Little Molly would slip away with a smile and profuse thanks.

She showed Peach and Stefania. "You workin' it out, how they goin' north over Frog Mountain. How long till the sheriff work it out too? He can see trails as good as you can," worried Peach.

"He doesn't know where they are yet."

"He get dogs, he find them quick enough. Dogs find everything."

Stefania said, "Why didn't I think of it before! The bear cave! The mouth is overgrown, but there may be a second entrance. I was there once . . . er . . . because of Mother. I felt a breeze. The Indians call it Breathing Rock. Come up with me, Molly, we can see."

"Stefania, no! You know how dangerous caves are! We tell the children if they set a foot in the bear cave, it means a whipping. They could fall in a hole or get lost and never find the way out."

"Molly, let's just *look*, for mercy's sake! We can tie a rope to the entrance and spin it out as we go, so we can find our way out again. If we come to one of those places where the cave floor turns into a hole, we'll come back. But we must *try*, Molly!"

Molly sighed. "Have you any rope, Peach?"

"Riverboats always needin' rope, we got plenty in the storeroom. Take that big length in there. You'll need the wagon to haul it 'cause it heavy. And get it back before Bryn lookin' for it."

Little Molly and Stefania agreed to go the following Sunday, when Little Molly was free from school duties. If they weren't back by night-fall, Peach was to raise the alarm.

By sundown Sunday an increasingly anxious Peach was preparing to do exactly that and wondering how to explain it to Bryn when Stefania and Little Molly appeared, filthy, stinking, and spent.

"Stefania was right, but it was horrible," said Little Molly. "If you go in at the mouth, the cave's not so bad and you can feel wind, though it was hard to find where it came from. But we finally found a narrow opening through the rock, and we crawled and squeezed along a passage that's just big enough for a person if you go in deep. The passage has a high ceiling, and there were bats roosting. All crowded together. Droppings everywhere. The smell burns your nose, like smelling salts, but the passage came out on the other side of Frog Mountain.

"The smell is so strong it hurts to breathe, but it might make it harder for dogs to track people through the cave if bat droppings were spread at the entrance. I'll put the cave on the maps I give the runaways."

"I got to clean this rope before I put it back," said Peach with disgust. "Ugh!"

Little Molly and Stefania both gave Peach money for supplies—jerky and strings of dried tomatoes, apples, and pumpkins—so that Peach could leave a parcel of food under the porch if runaways came. Stefania bought blankets. Thierry was the kind of Frenchman who would not inquire into housekeeping matters—that was his wife's province—it would never have occurred to him to question her expenditure. There was plenty of money, he liked his comforts, and Stefania could spend what she liked. He failed to notice that although Stefania bought a great many blankets from Peach, few reached Chiaramonte.

Meanwhile Peach did what she could to keep the topic of the fur trader and the shape-shifter going. Every time the sheriff came, she'd talk on and on about a shape-shifter that would come creeping down to Grafton in the night. She wrung her hands and said she was frightened to death of shape-shifters and haints. She protested she was too scared to set foot on Frog Mountain now, even to visit her friends at Wildwood.

The sheriff decided Peach was at a time of life when women were particularly irritating and irrational.

In part thanks to Peach, rumors of the shape-shifter wouldn't die. Occasionally a long hunter would even claim he'd seen it, coming over Frog Mountain. People agreed there'd always been something odd about Frog Mountain. An old Indian story said shamans would conjure up the dead there. And look at the way the fog closed in around the top. Peach was so vexing and querulous about the shape-shifter that the sheriff stopped at the trading post less and less often. He hadn't found any trace of runaways passing through Grafton, and the free blacks didn't want trouble. And the shape-shifter story would provide its own discouragement to runaways thinking to cross Frog Mountain.

"Niggers as gullible as Indians," Peach heard him say disgustedly to his men. It was music to her ears.

So the shape-shifter story persisted. Shape-shifters were part of the local lore, but people with any sense thought they were a product of long hunters' drunken imaginations.

"Up at the school any child caught mentioning shape-shifters or the bear song gets a thrashing," Little Molly reported to Peach when she went to pay Peach for a new supply of food to be left out for the runaways. The weather had been fine lately, clear and frosty at night. The north star could be seen clearly, and there had been two groups of runaways in the last fortnight.

"Brother Merriman says heathen nonsense will be beaten out of them if necessary. I see why Sophia de Marechal hated him. He's a mean old fellow. Besides, it does no good, thrashing the Cherokee children. Their parents don't hit children, they shame them when they do a bad thing. The children think the thrashing and whipping is some kind of white ritual to build endurance, so of course they never whimper or cry."

"Brother Merriman too old to run that school."

189

"We've had a letter from a mission board up north. They're sending some new teachers and a temporary replacement for Brother Merriman. Mortify and Endurance keep saying they're called to go out on circuit, preaching. That's good. I don't care for either of them. Mortify especially. I caught him praying with that pretty new Indian girl Amelia. With his arm around her waist, telling her to 'feel the power of the Spirit.'"

"I know what he got her feelin'! Some folks come through here sayin' how Mortify sowed his seed at a camp meeting upriver last summer. Four girls expectin' babies, each claimed the visitin' preacher got to prayin' with 'em, all alone, till they in such a state they were overcome. He denied it, of course."

"I keep a close watch on the older girls now. And even Brother Merriman is uneasy about him. I overheard him telling Endurance that when they go on circuit, to keep an eye on Mortify, guard his brother from temptation."

"Fornication!" exclaimed Peach, and laughed. Little Molly laughed too, just a beat behind Peach. She couldn't help wondering what fornication would be like.

"You think anybody come while this weather lasts? Stefania say she pay for everybody to have blankets, but I just don't dare, Bryn will notice."

Little Molly looked around to be sure no one else was in earshot. "I made some more maps." She handed Peach a sheaf of small folded papers. "We have a Fry-Jefferson map of Virginia now. The bookseller I send to in Kingsport sent it when I wrote to ask for his best map. I draw the way north from that. I wish we knew how many make it to Pennsylvania."

"We got no idea about anything, whether we do any good," agreed Peach. "But we can't stop."

CHAPTER 21

MOSES

March 1810

The sheriff hadn't been to Grafton over the winter, which had been unusually hard, with ice on the river. But the fact that there was a free black community in Grafton made people elsewhere uneasy, especially after the slave revolts in Haiti and Santo Domingo and the horrible stories of massacres and reprisals and arson that white refugee planters spread in New Orleans and Washington. Patrols to catch runaways had been increased, and the Pine boys said a number of sheriffs had been to Chiaramonte to buy tracking dogs.

There'd been a late snowfall, and Peach saw footprints that led to the space under the porch. She quickly scuffed them up and chose her moment when Bryn and their two sons were at the mill and stopped by the porch.

"Don't want to see you, just tell me, how many need to eat?" she'd murmured. She could hear breathing.

No answer.

"How many! I know you there! Speak up, nobody here but me and I ain't got all day!"

"Three."

"Man's sick. Has you any tea, missus?" There was a sound of muffled coughing. Followed by a murmured order to hush, then whispers: "Don't die on us, Moses, please don't go dyin', we got this far, our wives waitin' for you to go back and bring them."

Moses? "I fetch you some lard and turpentine on a rag, put that on his chest," said Peach. "And I got a little honey left. I boil up some hops and put the honey in, you give it to him, that good for the coughing."

Oh Lord! she thought. Usually runaways stayed no more than a night. Now here was Moses himself sick, maybe too sick to travel, and there was nobody the sheriff wanted to catch more than Moses. Moses was taking runaways north under the sheriff's nose, and the sheriff had sworn to see him hung.

Moses needed to leave. The sheriff had dogs now. They'd easily track Moses to the trading post if they came. Peach felt sick with fear. The sheriff would arrest her and Bryn, maybe the boys too, maybe her sisters and their husbands. Penalties were severe—prison and branding and fines. Hanging. She *had* to get rid of the people under the porch. She needed to see Little Molly or Stefania and work out what to do. But she daren't leave the trading post—if the sheriff came, she'd have to distract him somehow.

Peach caught and killed a chicken and set about making soup while she worried.

Little Molly had worked out that the river, the buffalo trail, and any number of lesser Indian and animal and trading trails in and around the mountains were possible escape routes north fanning out from Grafton. And if runaways made it to the cave, they could exit by the opening on the east side of Frog Mountain, and there were more trails from there. Which was the best way to send this group? How soon would they be able to go? But she had to wait, nerves stretched taut. Little Molly was out of reach at the school, and while Stefania still came to the trading post sometimes, it wasn't as often as before. She was recently widowed and in mourning. Thierry had taken ill with pleurisy and died in the cold spell—and Stefania was overwhelmed with the Chiaramonte business accounts and correspondence. She'd realized the children's education was suffering and had sent fifteen-year-old Rosa and fourteen-year-old Lafayette to school in Natchez. Will Pine transported them there and back.

Will and his sons still took her across the river when necessary. Stefania felt too matronly to leap into a canoe as she had when a girl, but she disliked interrupting their work too often.

Peach was nervous feeding three extra mouths and preparing her mother's cold remedies when none of her household were ill. She gathered Moses was in a bad way, and she desperately hoped he wouldn't die under the porch. A week passed. She took as many blankets as she dared, but it was no place for an invalid, and Moses grew worse. His companions whispered to Peach that Moses told them to go on and leave him, that he feared he was dying. They didn't want to leave, but Moses said he was giving the orders.

Would one dead slave be less incriminating than three live ones? "Do what he say," said Peach finally, "while you can see the sky good at night. I get him better if I can." *Unless I have to drag his body off and bury it,* she thought. She slipped the two men as much stew as she could from that day's cooking and parceled up jerky and dried apples and one of Little Molly's maps. Next morning they were gone.

Peach was overcome with relief to see the ferry coming across with Stefania's black-clad figure later that day. Peach hurried to the jetty and arranged her face in a smile for the Pine boy's benefit. "Been a while, been a while!" she greeted Stefania as the Pine boy handed her onto the jetty with a "Mind your step now, Miss Stefania. Shall I wait?"

Peach widened her eyes and shook her head ever so slightly.

"Thank you. I'll signal later."

"Yes, ma'am," the young man said, and started back.

"Thank the Lord you're here! I need to tell you something!" Peach hissed as soon as he was out of earshot.

"Shall I buy more blankets?"

"No, come inside!"

Peach told her about the three men hiding under the porch, that two were gone but the one still there was dangerously sick. And it was Moses. He'd die on the damp ground unless they could get him away somewhere warm.

"Just as bad if they find him dead as find him alive," hissed Peach. "Sheriff likely to ride past any day now. Other two said they's folks waiting for Moses to come back and take them north. Men went first, he get them to Pennsylvania and then he supposed to go back for their wives and chillum. He won't take many at a time 'cause it too dangerous, so he been going back and forth. What can we do?"

"Do you still have Gideon's old canoe in the barn?"

"But Moses too sick to paddle himself on the river. And where he can go till he's better?"

Stefania thought for a moment. "We can't leave Moses there."

"No indeed!" said Peach with feeling.

"And it would be hard to hide him at Chiaramonte . . . but . . . Peach, help me hitch up one of the mules to your smaller wagon. I'm going up to the school. I'll take a load of . . . of . . . What can I take a load of?"

"Got some new bolts of calico and homespun needin' to go up for the girls' sewin' class, but can't worry 'bout that now . . ."

"Material for the sewing class! That'll do. I'll take it up in the wagon, say I'm donating it. I often give the school things like books and blankets and food. Usually one of the Pines takes whatever it is up to the school, but no one will think it's odd if I take material. It's bulky enough that we can hide Moses underneath. And if he's in the wagon, dogs can't follow his trail."

"Take him up to the *school?* That's a terrible idea!"

"No, it isn't. Little Molly can hide him in her room, look after him there. She likes her privacy, won't let the other teachers in. She's even got a lock on her door—Rufus insisted. The other teachers think she's an old maid set in her ways. It'll be warm there. It's too cold and wet outdoors, he'll die."

"They'll see you."

"No, they won't. The whole school—the teachers, the cook, everyone—has to attend evening prayers. If I go now, I can be there before prayers are finished and slip him into Little Molly's room. I know where she hides her key."

Peach thought it sounded like the worst plan in the world but agreed reluctantly because she didn't have a better one.

An hour and a half later, as dusk was falling, Stefania drove the wagon past the school and stopped by the door of the women teachers' cabin. From the main building came the sound of a rousing hymn. Stefania climbed down and entered the women teachers' cabin. No one there. She slipped around the corner to Little Molly's locked door, pried the key from its hiding place in a crack between the boards in the floor, and opened the door.

She returned to the wagon and awkwardly lifted a bolt of cloth, letting it unravel slightly to make a screen.

"Now," she muttered, and a man groaned and rolled out from under a pile of homespun and crawled behind her and the cloth into the cabin. If anyone had spotted what looked like a man, Stefania would claim it was just the bolt of cloth.

"Around the corner," said Stefania. "The door's open. Hide under the bed for now, no one but the lady who lives there ever goes inside."

She was laying the last bolt of cloth on the wooden worktable in the main room and out of breath from carrying the heavy load when Little Molly and the other three teachers returned from the evening prayer meeting, surprised to find Mrs. Charbonneau calling at such a late hour.

"You must have thought I'd forgotten my promise to donate material for the girls' sewing class," said Stefania pointedly.

Little Molly gave her a surprised look. "When did you promise? I must have forgotten."

"*Peach* ordered it for me, and it just came in," said Stefania firmly, "and *Peach* said I should take it at once. So many people coming to the trading post asking for calico and muslin!" Stefania was babbling the first thing that came into her head. "She'd be tempted to cut into it. So I said, I'll take it up right away. I knew how it was needed. And . . . my evenings, you know, are a little lonely . . . we widows . . . the children away at school . . . I just thought it would be nice to . . . see you."

The lonely widow in search of a little companionship touched her handkerchief to her eyes.

Bewildered, Little Molly watched this performance and imperceptibly raised her eyebrows.

But the teachers were inspecting the cloth, delighted the girls could make themselves new frocks. The school depended on donations. Baskets of apples, salt pork, buckets, nails, tools, watermelons, feather comforters were all useful and welcome. As with every donation, the teachers effusively praised God and thanked the giver, exclaiming how good it was of Mrs. Charbonneau to come so late in the day with such a grand gift.

They weren't surprised when Little Molly invited her generous friend into her private sanctum for tea. The teachers were in awe of rich Mrs. Charbonneau, who had lovely clothes and sweet ways and quietly paid for some of the poorer pupils whose parents couldn't afford the tuition.

"Stefania dear, of *course* you'll stay the night," said Little Molly firmly. "You mustn't think of going back in the dark. I'll brew some tea, and we can have a nice visit. Poor dear, you must be *quite* lonely at Chiaramonte, to come all this *way* at this *hour*," she added.

"Yes, I confess I am," sighed Stefania. "Thank you, perhaps I should stay. But have you some sage to put in the tea? My throat's a little sore." She took out her handkerchief again and coughed. "I fear I'm taking one of my colds. The weather's so changeable in spring. Oh!" Stefania was suddenly fluttery with oncoming illness as she touched her handkerchief to her nose.

Why on earth are you behaving as if you'd taken leave of your senses? Little Molly's expression said.

The teachers were solicitous.

"You poor dear!"

"The night air is generally the cause of colds, you can depend on it."

"It is indeed, you must avoid the night air at all costs. I'll make up the fire in my room," Little Molly chimed in, taking her friend's arm and almost dragging her away before Stefania could indulge in any more theatrics.

As the door to Little Molly's room closed behind them, Stefania explained hastily. The two of them got a half-conscious Moses into bed with the sage tea, a poultice for his chest, and a hot brick for his feet. He was burning hot to the touch, and his breath rattled.

"Whatever were you thinking, bringing him here!" Little Molly hissed in a whisper as she tucked a quilt under his chin. "What will we do if he dies? And talk quietly."

"There was nothing else to do," Stefania whispered back, wiping Moses's brow with a damp cloth. "The sheriff's likely to come any day now, and we had to get him away from the trading post. No one dares to come in your room. No one will find him here. He'd die under the porch."

"What will we do if he dies here? How shall we explain that? You'll have to stay and help me."

"We'll say my cold got worse and I'm in bed here."

"Perhaps that will work. Help me make up pallets on the floor for us."

So Stefania stayed put for a fortnight while they did their best to nurse Moses back to health, one or the other sitting up with him nights. He coughed a lot at first. The other teachers knocked on Little Molly's door, bringing honey and apple vinegar and mallow water because widow Charbonneau's cough sounded very bad. They offered to take turns with Little Molly sitting up with her at night.

Little Molly thanked them and opened the door just wide enough to take their offerings. She agreed Mrs. Charbonneau's cold was very bad, but that was always the way with her friend—very ill for a time, then a quick recovery. The best thing was for her to rest quietly. At mealtime Little Molly was assiduous in carrying tea and soup and hominy mush to her patient. Locking her door as she came and went, in case her housemates were overwhelmed by their zeal to nurse their benefactress.

Bryn Vann came to fetch his mule and wagon, exasperated that his wife and Stefania had taken it into their heads to use them to deliver cloth to the school on the spur of the moment, and then he'd been put to the trouble of going all the way to the school to fetch it. "I'm so sorry, Bryn—er, Stefania felt poorly all of a sudden."

This sounded like a feeble explanation even to Little Molly, and she was relieved that all Bryn did was mutter, "Damn fool women!" crossly as he drove off.

Finally Moses's fever broke, and he opened his eyes and took in his surroundings. He was astonished to find himself in a bed with quilts and what looked like one white woman asleep wrapped in a quilt on a braided rug on the floor, and another one dozing in a chair by his side.

"Who are you? Where am I?" he muttered.

Little Molly woke and put a hand over his mouth to shush him. "Whisper!" she ordered in his ear. "You're at the mission school in my room. I'm in charge of the female teachers, so I have my own room. More teachers are asleep next door. Don't wake them! You've been very sick, and we couldn't leave you outside to die. This is the only place we could hide you until you're better."

Moses was incredulous and insisted he had to leave at once. Little Molly and Stefania protested he must stay, to get his strength back, and after trying to get out of bed, he felt so weak he agreed.

The next morning, a worried Rosa and Lafayette drove up in the chaise to fetch their mother home. Will Pine had brought them back from school at the start of their holidays, and Peach had sent word to Jane Pine that Stefania had been taken ill while visiting the mission school. Stefania had no choice except to leave with them. The other teachers gathered to wave goodbye. She held a handkerchief to her face and coughed piteously as she took her leave. "Thank you, Molly," said Stefania as her children helped her into the chaise. "I'm sorry to have burdened you."

"Not at all," insisted Little Molly. "I'm only sorry you're going before you've recovered." The two women exchanged an anxious look.

"Poor Mother!" cried Rosa, solicitously tucking a buffalo robe around Stefania. "Don't worry, Aunt Molly, we'll take good care of her," she called as Lafayette turned the chaise round.

Little Molly waved goodbye to her accomplice. Now she'd have to live alone in the room with Moses until he could leave. Her heart sank.

CHAPTER 22

LITTLE MOLLY

So Little Molly was left to nurse Moses, smuggling food from the school's kitchen, as she no longer had the excuse of her ill friend. She was terrified at the situation in which she found herself but had to admire Stefania's thinking—a spinster schoolteacher's bedroom was the last place on earth the sheriff would come looking for him. She was doubly careful about locking her door and keeping her homespun curtains drawn.

Moses was better, and awake, complaining that if he was found in a white woman's bedroom, he'd be hung on the spot. Little Molly retorted it hadn't been her idea and he was welcome to leave as soon as he liked. He was impatient, trying to walk around the room and regain some strength, but tired easily, not well enough to leave yet. Both were edgy and irritable. And being closeted in close quarters was awkward for both of them. They adopted a wary, strained politeness. He turned his back when she was dressing, just as she turned hers, or went outside when he was washing. In the evenings, she prepared lessons, and one night, to her surprise, he asked if he could read her books.

"Help yourself," she said, wondering how it was he could read.

But in their forced intimacy, they grew curious about each other. During the long nights, when neither could sleep because they were listening, alert for patrollers or slave catchers, they began to talk in whispers.

"Why you helpin' us?" Moses whispered in the dark one night.

Little Molly told him about the morning she'd seen the runaways from under Peach's porch and how they'd walked away in the rain, the woman holding a baby wrapped in a soaked shawl, how it wasn't much help giving away her oilskin cloak, though she'd meant well. How she'd given them money too but hoped they hadn't been caught with it and hung for thieves. How she wished the people had made it to Pennsylvania. How Peach had told her about the other runaways. How she and Stefania wanted to help then, though they weren't as brave as Peach.

She told him they'd figured out a route over the mountain through a cave and sent runaways that way. The sheriff didn't know about it yet.

"What? What route you talkin' about?"

She explained it had been Stefania's idea to look for a passage through the cave, how the two of them had gone up to the cave with a length of rope and a basket of pine knots, looking for a back entrance.

"Just you two women went in a *cave*?" He was incredulous. "Women in a cave, you got to be careful in caves. They're dangerous places."

Little Molly was irritated. *He* was telling *her* to be careful? "I know how dangerous! There are a lot of caves in these mountains, children are warned to stay out of them, get a whipping if they don't. It's easy to get lost," she hissed indignantly. "But Stefania was right. The second entrance comes out on the east side of Frog Mountain. It's almost impossible to see it from the outside because it's low down behind some bushes. It looks like an animal hole. But there's just enough room for a person to wriggle through. Stefania and I both managed. Though we had to . . . um . . . remove our dresses and do it in our shifts. Our skirts were too full. Anyone who's not fat or wearing a big skirt could do it."

In the firelight she could make out Moses's skeptical expression.

"I made a map. I'll show you. I give them to runaways."

She lit a candle, sat beside him on the bed, and showed him her map, with pictures of the mountain and the cave because few of the runaways could read.

Moses asked, "What give Miss Stefania the idea in the first place?"

"I think she went up to the cave with her mother one time. Her mother liked caves."

"Why she like caves?"

"I don't know. Her mother was from Sicily. She wasn't like most people. She wouldn't kill snakes, said they belonged to the goddess."

"Never knew anybody liked snakes. She a witch?"

"Well, Rosalia was beautiful, and she had a way of making people like her, so no, I never heard anyone say she was a witch."

"Who else know the cave's got a back door?"

"If anyone does, it'll be Indians, but they keep away from Frog Mountain. Spirits live there, they say."

"Hmm." Moses calculated. He had to keep changing the way he took people. Any route the runaways used was figured out before long, especially when the patrollers had dogs. Or when runaways were caught, they were forced to reveal them. Any new route was worth looking at. "Show me again, on the map."

Together they bent over Little Molly's drawing, while she traced it for him again with her finger and told him about the bat droppings being a protection if dogs were used to chase runaways.

"Never knew anybody make a map like that before."

"Do you want one?"

"You and Miss Stefania done good, figurin' it out," he said grudgingly. "No, won't take no map, I'll try it for myself, memorize it."

The next night as they lay in the dark, he asked if her family owned any slaves.

"No." She told him about her grandfather who'd committed a crime in England and been transported with his wife and boys to be indentured servants, how her grandmother she was named after had died on the voyage over. How Rufus and his boys had suffered at the hands of their masters and had run away, which made them criminals in Virginia.

"Like slaves," remarked Moses. "But only for a while. If you white you get free eventually. Most places niggers never free. Even up north in Philadelphia and places, lookin' over their shoulders. Is still slave catchers don't care what the law say about bein' free there. They catch you and take you away to where niggers ain't free, say you a slave. Nobody stop 'em. And that makes you a slave again. Best protection is have some white blood, pass for white. But no easy way to get that white blood . . . Mos' times somebody's mama pay a high price for that white blood in her chile."

"Why ain't you married?" Moses asked the next night. "Looks to me like somebody ought to of married you. You ain't ugly."

Little Molly sighed and said she'd never wanted to keep house and raise children, she hated household chores, her cooking was terrible, that it suited her living here with her own room with her fireplace and books, and she liked teaching. She supposed she was meant to be an old maid. Some people felt sorry for her, but she didn't feel sorry for herself. Then, because it was comfortable talking to him in the firelight, she said she'd never met a man she liked enough to hope he liked her.

"You not too old. Might meet a husband yet 'fore you too far gone."

"Perhaps. But the thing I mind is not knowing what it's like to . . . to lie with a man. I was always curious about that. And Brother Merriman used to go on so about fornication, sometimes I thought of nothing else . . ."

Little Molly immediately regretted her candor. In the dark her face burned with embarrassment. How could she have said anything so awkward! Moses was quiet for a minute, then said that was something to miss all right.

She heard muffled laughter.

To change the subject, she asked him about himself. Men always liked talking about themselves.

Moses told her he'd been a house slave. "My mother was . . . a fine-looking woman. Master was my father, she the one persuaded him to give me work in the house, not send me to the fields. But Master give my mother another baby, so the master's wife had her sold when he gone away one time." He was quiet a moment. "Master was angry she'd done it, wouldn't sell me and my brother too, like she wanted. He kept us workin' in the house, right in front of her. My master's wife love her flowers in the garden, my little brother helped the gardener. I was a body servant to the master's sons."

There'd been a tutor who lived in the house. Moses played at being stupid, got his half brothers to show him how to read and write and figure, over and over and every time by claiming lessons went in one side of his head and out the other and he couldn't remember what they'd just told him. Trying to teach their stupid body servant became an amusing game for the white children. Moses let himself be a figure of fun. He made stupid faces, until the children were howling with laughter.

He studied their primers in secret when he could, and if they found him, he'd hold the primer upside down and declare, "See, Marse Billy, I'm readin' just like you is!"

Their mother had laughed at him too and told her children the Negro mind was very small and couldn't, unfortunately, be made as big as a white mind, even with instruction. She said she really didn't understand the necessity for a law prohibiting the education of Negroes. Educating them was an impossibility.

So by this ruse, he'd learned to read and write and figure as well as the master's other sons and, an equally useful lesson, how to dissemble.

He told her about running away after forging free papers. He was wearing some cast-off clothing of his master's and had saved a little money because from time to time, his father would give him a few coins. He'd cut a respectable enough figure, and the ruse succeeded long enough for him to hide away on a boat bound for Philadelphia. He'd heard of Philadelphia, that it was a place where slaves could be free.

He hadn't believed it, but when he reached the city, he learned that there was a gradual abolition law, and under it a Negro man his age was free. It had seemed that the air of Philadelphia was the sweetest he ever breathed.

He'd used the skills he'd learned as a house slave and hired himself out as a butler, saving his wages and meeting other free blacks who'd run away who told him about their experiences, what routes they'd taken, landmarks, people along the way willing to offer food or a hiding place in their barn, and where the patrollers were most likely to be along the way.

He bought a map and worked out what they told him on it. He attended a Negro church and read his Bible. Then one day he heard the voice of God telling him it was time to leave Philadelphia, to go back and help others to freedom. He'd taken the map, bought a pistol, and gone.

Moses wasn't his real name. He took the name Moses because slaves often knew the Bible stories. Their owners thought teaching the Bible to slaves taught them it was God's will for Negroes to serve white masters and mistresses, to serve their owners. He'd first thought of calling himself Daniel, who God saved from the lions' den. Daniel was a powerful name, and he liked the association with lions, but Moses gave him authority to lead people. And he'd learned from the community of runaways in Philadelphia that leading slaves north required authority. One of the most dangerous things that could happen was for an escapee to refuse to obey the leader's orders, to say he or she was too tired to go on, to say they'd make their own way. Runaways like that were sure to be caught, and when they were, it was a certain thing they were beaten and tortured until they gave away who'd helped them escape, where they'd come from, who the leader was, what route they'd taken. He took along only a few at a time, showed his pistol, would threaten to shoot anyone who couldn't keep up or didn't obey his orders.

"Did you ever shoot anyone?" asked Little Molly.

Moses frowned into the firelight. "One man." He was quiet for a minute, then said softly, "My little brother, not one of my white half brothers. My mother's other son."

Little Molly was horrified. On her pallet she rose up on one elbow. "Why?"

"When I left, he was ten years old. I hated leaving him behind, but I didn't know what would happen to me. I'd promised myself if I made it to freedom, I'd come back for him one day. Time I did, he was near grown. I was taking him and three other men—I always take men and women separate, can manage it better that way. Time I went to take my brother and three other men, he insist a yellow girl he half-crazy about had to go too. Didn't want to take her, not yet anyway, because we had a hard way ahead of us, too hard for a woman. And she a house slave too, not strong from workin' in the fields, she sew for her mistress.

"But I agree, and before long my brother was dissatisfied with everything I say. I got a rule: those I take do what I say, no arguing. But my brother want to impress his gal, want to look like he in charge and he the one gon' save her. He challenge me every minute. I try not to show he make me angry, and I tell him to be quiet but don't do nothin' else. Usually, anybody else talk against me, I send 'em back or leave 'em behind to find their own way.

"But he my brother. He a good talker, other slaves start wonder if maybe he right. Girl lookin' at him like he the angel Gabriel. She can't go fast as the rest and he carry her sometimes. Slows us down.

"One day he say we got to go a different way than the way I'm sayin' go. Where I want to go is swampy and got snakes. His gal afraid of snakes. I don't know everything, he say. I tell him what I know is they's patrollers everywhere it easy to go, and they worse than snakes. Runaways get caught in the easy places. Don't want to be caught if you're a runaway, Miss Molly. They don't hang you, rather punish you so bad make an example to the other slaves, you wish they had hung you. My fool brother won't listen to reasoning.

"Or maybe . . . I start to think he settin' a trap. A bad thing to believe about your own brother, and I wanted to get him free, but that happen too sometimes, one of the runaways get everybody to go a certain way, where he know patrollers or militia waitin' and ready."

"But why?"

"They scared slaves get guns and revolt, kill the owners, like in Haiti. So they set a trap, confuse people. Get a slave pretend he a runaway too, then help the others get caught, he get a reward. Maybe get to have a wife, they promise him they won't sell her away, maybe they even tell him his chillun be free. So I get to thinking, what if my brother gon' lead us into a ambush, 'cause they promise him if he do, he and his gal get to be married.

"My brother arguin' with me, talkin' 'bout snakes, the girl standing behind him sayin', 'That's right,' like she know anything about it, until others want to go with him too. I say no.

"He say I actin' like I'm his master 'cause I'm older. Say he ain't goin' with me, 'cause I ain't Master. He goin' the way he think is right. Ask do the slaves want to go with him or me. I warned him, but he just laugh, say, 'Come on,' to the others.

"I couldn't let him go. Even if he wasn't leading us into a trap, he was bound to be caught, and I knew he'd tell the patrollers what way we'd taken, who'd helped us along the way. He don't tell them, they torment it out of him. I give him one more chance, and he just walk away, pullin' his gal by the hand. Others say, 'Sorry, Moses,' and start up to go with him.

"Next minute he dead. I shot him, killed him with one shot. Can't take no wounded with us. He lie there, girl screamin', 'No! No!' and not wantin' to move until I hold up my pistol and say I shoot her too. And I say I'll shoot anybody else think they ain't comin' my way. So they turn around and say they come with me. We bury him as best we could, scrapin' at the ground 'cause we got no shovel.

"I get everybody safe to Pennsylvania. Yellow gal she cryin' all the way and half dead by the time I leave her, but she free. I do what I have to do, Miss Molly. I warn folks 'fore I'll take 'em. I want folks scared of me, enough so they do exactly what I say."

"Should I be scared of you?"

"You? We been livin' in the same room for weeks. From what I can tell, you ain't scared of nothin', be wasting my time. An' why I want to shoot you? All I want to do is get well enough to go, 'fore we both caught."

A few days later when the morning bell rang to wake the school, she woke to find him pacing the room. "I'll leave tonight when it get dark. I'll go up and through the cave so I know that way."

"Oh. Of course." Little Molly's heart sank unaccountably.

That evening, as night fell and they waited for the other teachers to blow out their candles and go to sleep, she silently packed a quilt and some corn pone and apple pie taken from her dinner. The waiting stretched her nerves tight.

Finally Moses whispered, "Be time to go soon."

"Yes."

"Have a care, you and Peach and Miss Stefania. Thank you for all you've done."

They looked at each other, and Little Molly wondered if she'd ever see him again. Impulsively she held out her hands to him. "Moses, I'm sorry you're going."

Moses took them and raised each one to his lips and didn't let go. In the firelight she could see a question in his eyes. She allowed herself to be pulled closer.

"I remember what you told me," he said. "About lying with a man. I got nothing else to give you. If you willing, that is."

Little Molly said nothing for a long moment. Then she nodded.

"Moses," she said as he kissed her.

And then it was just she and Moses.

Later, when he was about to leave, she whispered, "Go safely, Moses." And stopped before she said, *Come back if you can. Please. Oh, how I want you to come back.*

In the months that followed, three more groups of runaways took refuge at the trading post. Two got away safely up the mountain, headed toward the cave, but Sheriff Tyree and his men were in pursuit of the last ones, this time with their two *tricolore* hounds. The huge dogs bayed and sniffed and pawed under the porch, while the sheriff and his men talked loudly about how many other runaways the dogs had caught. Then the dogs bounded toward the orchard at the foot of Frog Mountain.

Sheriff Tyree shouted he'd been right and, as soon as they caught the runaways, they'd be back to arrest Bryn and Peach and their two sons. The sheriff and deputies rode after the dogs, ropes swinging on their saddles.

That the dogs had been chasing something was plain. At the trading post, they could hear them baying above the orchard, then above Wildwood heading toward the Old Man of the Mountain, and up higher. Then there was silence.

Peach was dizzy with fear. Two hours later, the sheriff and his men were back, on lathered horses and swearing, the bloody bodies of two of the hounds slung behind the sheriff's saddle. No slaves.

"What . . . what did you find?" asked Peach, emboldened by the fact the men hadn't captured anyone. The sheriff removed his hat, wiped the sweat from his face, too angry to speak.

One of the deputies answered for him. High up on the mountain, the dogs had disappeared into a thick patch of mountain laurel. There'd been an almighty commotion, barking and growling and a terrible scream, and then they couldn't hear the dogs any longer. By the time the sheriff and his men reached the patch of mountain, expecting to find cornered slaves hiding, they found the dogs lying with their bellies ripped open and eyes gouged out.

"Don't know what got 'em, most times these dogs ain't afraid of nothin'," said one of the deputies. "Thought it must have been a wild pig at first, but I seen 'em kill a wild pig with a litter to protect, and ain't nothin' more dangerous than old mother pig. Whatever it was got away before we saw it good. Big and dark, heard wings flapping. Must have been an eagle, to kill a dog that big."

"The shape-shifter!" Peach shrieked hysterically, and burst into tears, knowing it was a good idea to look as scared as she felt, pleading and swearing she'd never seen any runaways, all the slaves they saw were the ones getting driven to Mississippi and Louisiana, and they just camped next to the river overnight and went on. Why, that was good business for her and Bryn, the slave traders always stocked up with provisions. A bewildered Bryn protested they'd never seen any other slaves come past. With genuine puzzlement in his voice, he asked what made the sheriff think they helped runaways?

The sheriff paused. He'd been chasing runaway slaves for much of his life, and he was good at catching them. It was profitable collecting the rewards. He could think like a runaway now and what direction they'd take, had developed a good sense of where they went, when they traveled, and who helped them. And what he couldn't track the dogs could. His instincts told him runaways came through Grafton and someone was being helpful, but maybe the Vanns weren't the ones. Even runaways would be too canny to trust a silly woman like Peach Vann who was carrying on about an eagle man.

"You tell everybody, we find runaways hidin' here, we'll hang you all," threatened the sheriff for good measure. He was under pressure. "South of here a cotton planter named Gustine St. Pierre's lost over a dozen field hands from his cotton plantation. Big place, married a woman with five thousand acres and over two hundred niggers. He's lost a dozen or more, and that's with some of the hardest overseers alive in charge. Other plantations near his have lost slaves too. They say some-body's comin' and goin' tellin' people to go, guiding runaways north. St. Pierre's a powerful man, offered a big reward to get his slaves back. You tell everybody, make sure word gets passed in Grafton. A big reward."

Word spread about how Peach and Bryn had nearly been arrested and what the sheriff had said about Gustine St. Pierre. A few people remembered he'd once worked for Stefano Albanisi, looked after the dogs. There'd been some gossip about him and Linney Pine, but most people expected he'd marry Stefania. He'd been a handsome young man, and her father had liked him, treated him like a son. That Stefania chose to marry an old Frenchman instead surprised everyone.

"Moses freeing Gustine's slaves!" marveled Stefania to Peach. "Isn't it wonderful!" She and Little Molly had been worried and gone to the trading post when they heard about the sheriff's dogs.

"I can't stop nobody comin' if Moses send folks this way," said Peach. "And I sure hope he don't come back."

"Moses," murmured Little Molly, and squared her shoulders. She couldn't keep it to herself much longer.

"I have to tell you both something," she said in a low voice. "I'm going to have a baby."

Stefania and Peach stared at her, shocked.

"You keepin' company with somebody?" asked Peach.

"Who? Did he say he'd marry you?" asked Stefania.

"Not a teacher, and there'll be no marriage. It was Moses," said Little Molly.

"Moses!"

The other two stared at her as if she'd grown a second head from her shoulders. She stared back defiantly. "It's Moses's baby."

"How dare he take advantage when you were hiding him!" Stefania was outraged.

"No," Little Molly protested. "It wasn't like that. Not at all. I . . . we . . ." There was no explaining it to the others; she could barely explain it to herself except to acknowledge she didn't regret it. "But he mustn't know. Not ever."

Peach's mouth was open, but for once Peach was speechless.

"What am I going to do?" Molly asked them.

"Well," said Stefania faintly after a minute, "we'll think of something."

CHAPTER 23

STEFANIA

June 1810

After considering Little Molly's dilemma for the next week, Stefania had a plan by the time the Saturday riverboat pulled away. It would mean leaving Rosa and Lafayette for a long time, but that couldn't be helped. Jane Pine would look after the house. Jane was proprietorial about the house, Stefania thought, half-amused and half-irritated by her housekeeper.

The children would be boarding at school most of the time. Rosa was a sensible and steady girl, but Lafayette got up to mischief when he could, slipping off to the horse races Zebulon Drumheller organized. Jack Drumheller, whose wife, Malinda, had died the previous year, was bereft and restless, anxious to fill his time with anything. He agreed to look after Chiaramonte in her absence and keep an eye on Lafayette as well as the horses.

She waited until Saturday afternoon when Little Molly was free from her school duties and, as she usually did, came to the trading post to do errands for the school and eat supper with the Vanns.

As the Saturday riverboat pulled away from the jetty, Stefania put on her bonnet and asked one of the Pine boys to row her across, saying she wanted to go quickly and they needn't wait for Rosa and Lafayette. The afternoon sun reflected on the water, half blinding her. As they pulled in next to the jetty, a man in a hat just off the riverboat was standing with his back to them, smoking and staring at the river.

The Pine lad said, "I'll just tie up and help you out, Mrs. Charbonneau."

"Don't bother tying up," said Stefania. "Your father needs you. I can manage. I'll signal later." The glare from the water left black spots in her vision, and she blinked to clear them. The boat wobbled as she reached blindly for the jetty post and the step, and she almost lost her balance.

"I really ought to help you," the Pine boy was saying, when the gentleman, who'd been within earshot, turned.

"Allow me," he said, and offered his hand.

"Thank you, sir," said Stefania. She looked down to gather her skirts and clasped the outstretched hand. The stranger pulled her onto the jetty next to him and steadied her as the Pine boy swung his boat around and started back. She was surprised he kept a grasp on her hand, too long for courtesy. She struggled to withdraw it, but she was held fast. "Sir, I have my footing now," she remonstrated.

The man held her fast and with his free hand doffed his hat. "My compliments, madam."

Stefania raised her head and gasped in astonishment. "Gustine!" His hand was cool and dry as snakeskin as he bowed and lifted her hand to his lips, not brushing the back of the hand with his moustache but turning her hand over, kissing her palm, flicking the sensitive skin inside her wrist lightly with his tongue. Stefania shivered and tried to pull her hand away.

216

For a moment, he looked as if he'd pull her into his embrace as he'd done so long ago. For a moment, she wanted him to.

"I trust I find the widow Charbonneau well," he said, half closing his eyes in the way she remembered, smiling with the mouth that had kissed her so passionately.

His grip on her hand was like iron. "If you'd only married me, Stefania, you'd be fifty times richer than you are now. Slaves and jewels and carriages instead of paddling across the river with a hired man. You should know, Stefania, your father's confidence in my abilities was justified. Cotton is king, and I, madam, am king of cotton. I am very rich."

"Let go of my hand!"

"Don't you remember the last time I saw you? I wanted you, and you were nearly mine. Yet you married the poor old colonel. I married too, a widow, rich and charming, also old, with a very large property. Barren, alas, despite my best efforts to make her otherwise. But the fruit out of our reach is always the sweetest. I have thought of you all these years. Have you no words of welcome?"

"Sir, you are as welcome in Grafton as any man of business," said Stefania with a show of bravado, though she was flustered. "You can have no reason to think of me. I trust your wife is well. Now you must excuse me."

"My wife is dead. A terrible fever, which afflicted many on our plantation and left me short of hands for the cotton, took her away from me. She was buried a fortnight ago. Alas."

"I am sorry to hear it. You are in mourning, then. Why do you go abroad so soon?"

"I'm here for the slaves, of course. Did you think I came only for you?" he asked. Stefania flushed, and he laughed. "How convenient that they drive slaves through Grafton now. Between the fever and runaways and new cotton fields ready for picking, I'm in need of slaves. I received news a consignment will pass through Grafton this week. If I can buy before they reach the slave market, I shall have first pick of the strongest at the best price. The traders like to shed some as they go. I'll take the best and one or two of the weakest. That always drives the price down.

"While I wait for them to come, I'll do myself the honor of calling on you. I will make the boardinghouse my home for the time being. And who knows, perhaps I will return to my plantation with a new wife as well as slaves. If I want a new wife, I shall have her, Stefania. I am experienced in having my way now."

"Impudence! Let me go!" Stefania hissed again. Still smiling, Gustine released her hand, and Stefania turned on her heel and strode purposefully to the trading post. She'd glanced back at the door to make sure he wasn't following her, but Gustine was nowhere in sight.

She and Little Molly and Peach had gone to sit on the bench on the jetty, out of earshot of anyone at the trading post. Stefania was flushed and agitated and for the moment couldn't remember why she'd come. She fanned her hot face.

Little Molly was looking pale, nibbling a biscuit Peach had given her. "Made it two days ago, so it good and dry. Sometimes that helps," said Peach.

"One minute I want to vomit, the next I want to eat a ham dinner," murmured Little Molly, gnawing on the biscuit. "My ankles swell when I stand up to teach the children. It's so hot! Oh God, what am I going to do!"

"Er . . . I have a plan," said Stefania, struggling to concentrate on Little Molly's predicament and not Gustine St. Pierre. Then she realized her plan would put a distance between her and Gustine while helping Little Molly.

"We'll go traveling, Molly."

"Traveling? Where?"

"Yes. After Thierry died, I felt very low, and I thought of going away for a time, perhaps to Saratoga Springs for a change of air. But Thierry had so many business matters that needed attending to, plans had to be made to send the children off to school, and the business of finding someone to manage Chiaramonte while I was gone—I felt overwhelmed and didn't go then. But what would you think of our making a northern tour together now?"

"But I can't just leave the school!"

"You could if the purpose was to gain support and funds for the school's work. It's grown so much that it's short on everything, and most of the teachers are young people. Most of them only stay for a year or two before they go home to get married or help their parents on the farm. I propose we give public talks about the work of the mission school, try to attract donations from the mission boards and appeal for more young people to come and teach.

"We'll go by boat from New Orleans or Natchez to Washington and call on as many churches there as we can, to arrange public gatherings to speak about missionary work among the Indians. After Washington, you and I will go by stage to visit Iddo's Quaker meeting in Philadelphia. We can see the city and speak about the good work with the Indian girls."

Little Molly no longer looked incredulous. "They did support it. But they stopped after Iddo died. And it's true the school needs money. Most of the buildings need repairs and we have to pay the teachers a stipend, though it's very small. And then so many pupils board and there's the cost of their keep. Few of the parents have money, so they pay in kind, but it's never enough. And we need books and slates, and the stove in the big classroom is broken."

"We'll do our best to raise the money. We'll stop in Baltimore too, there are big churches with mission boards there. We'll do as much as we can, Molly, before you start to show so much you can't hide it with a shawl or your cloak, and eventually you'll have to become 'unwell'—a woman can always rely on being believed if she claims to be in delicate health. We'll end our lecture tour then, and I'll take you to Saratoga for a change of air. No one will know us in Saratoga. I'll lend you some of my widow's clothes and a mourning veil—they're conveniently long in front. In Saratoga we'll no longer be speaking about the school. We'll say you're recently a widow and in your condition you require quiet and privacy. There are comfortable hotels there, I hear, and you can have your lying-in."

"But then what once the baby's born? I refuse to abandon the baby to an orphanage."

"You needn't. We'll bring the baby back with us and say . . . its mother was a poor woman we found dying and we brought it back to Grafton in an act of Christian charity. And if it's obviously a mulatto baby, it's less likely anyone will suspect it's yours."

"Stefania, I can't return to school with a baby! Teachers can't stay after they're married, let alone bring orphaned babies to raise . . ."

"No," Stefania said. She took a deep breath. "I've thought of that. I can raise the baby with me at Chiaramonte. I'll adopt it. It would seem natural, I think, if I've rescued an orphan. Everyone knows I'm lonely while the children are at school, and people are used to my doing things like paying for Rembrandt's schooling. That way you won't have abandoned it, you can see the baby anytime you wish."

"But how can you bear the responsibility for my child?"

"I can, Molly. I have a large house, my children are nearly grown, and Jane Pine manages the house as she pleases. I often feel I'm in her way. I have little to do and should love to have the baby. You know I lost my youngest to the fever." Stefania could never mention her dead little girl calmly, and tears rose in her eyes now as she said, "Please. It's a good plan, Molly."

Little Molly sighed. "Yes. It is. When . . . when will we go?"

"There's no time to lose." Stefania didn't mention that the sooner she left Grafton while Gustine was there, the better. "So, we'll go at once."

"Riverboat to Natchez due on Thursday," said Peach. "You be ready to go in two days?"

"Well, I don't know . . . ," said Little Molly, trying to think through a sudden wave of nausea.

"Yes!" said Stefania firmly. "The answer is yes."

CHAPTER 24

DANIEL

January 1811

"It's still snowing," said Stefania, looking out the window and trying to hide the anxiety in her voice. The hotel gardens were buried under a blanket of white beyond the swirling snowflakes melting on the windowpanes. Saratoga was in the grips of a blizzard, and there was no sign of the midwife who should have come two days ago. Other than Stefania and Little Molly, the hotel was empty of all but a few elderly guests and the skeleton staff of chambermaids, cook, porters, and errand boys who'd been kept on to look after them when the season ended.

Little Molly and Stefania had been marooned in their quarters since Christmas. The chambermaid had lit huge fires in their bedroom and adjacent sitting room, where they took their meals. The grand dining room was too large to heat comfortably in this storm, she'd said, the hotel was mainly a summer destination, and the ladies would be cozier here.

"And the poor widowed lady needn't exert herself," the chambermaid had whispered solicitously to Stefania. "She'll be wanting to keep to herself until her time comes."

"You'd think any midwife who lived in Saratoga would know how to get about in such weather," said Little Molly irritably. "You'd think she would use a sleigh." Reclining on a chaise, she massaged her mountain of a stomach, which was definitely tightening and relaxing, tightening and relaxing.

"Will it be all right, Stefania?"

"Of course, Molly, don't worry."

"What if the midwife doesn't come?"

"We . . . we'll manage."

"How?" There was a note of panic in her voice.

"The midwife is sure to arrive any minute," said Stefania as calmly as she could.

Little Molly tensed with the next sensation, then let out her breath.

"Stefania? I'm glad you'll raise the baby. I've never said how grateful I am."

"It's all right, Molly. We'll raise it together as much as we can." She put another log on the fire as a gust of wind rattled the windows. She looked outside again, hoping to see the midwife at last, but even the garden was no longer visible. There was nothing to be seen outside but a cloud of swirling white. *Oh God,* thought Stefania, *the midwife really isn't coming!* She racked her brain to remember Rembrandt Conway's birth, what Caitlin's instructions had been.

Little Molly cried out, "Stefania? Ring for the chambermaid! Something is happening!"

Three months later the blizzard and Little Molly's surprisingly quick delivery were a distant memory. The last of the snow was melting in April sunshine, and light streamed through the chapel window onto the small group at the baptismal font. The baby in the christening gown was sleeping soundly when he was rudely woken by a cup of lukewarm water poured over his head of soft dark hair, and someone said, "I baptize thee Daniel." He howled lustily in protest for a moment but was soon lulled back to sleep in familiar arms.

Afterward Stefania and Little Molly took turns to push the baby carriage back to the hotel through the street running with rivulets of melted snow. They walked slowly and both gazed fondly at the baby.

"I see nothing of Moses in him yet," said Stefania, stopping to tuck a blanket under the baby's chin and considering as she stroked his cheek. "Perhaps Daniel will pass, Molly. Moses's father was white, and you're white. His life will be easier if he can."

Little Molly sighed. "I know. But I hope he has Moses's courage."

"I hope he has his mother's. Are you really determined to go tomorrow?"

"Yes, I must. The weather's changed, and I've no excuse to stay longer from the school. We've spread the word about the mission, we've raised money, and any number of young women have expressed their willingness to travel south to do the Lord's work when the weather turns warm enough. I ought to be there when they come, or it will be chaotic."

"You're right, I suppose. I know you don't want to be parted from Daniel, but we agreed it would attract the least suspicion if I bring him back later. Very few people exist who could give us away, only the chambermaid and the colonel's widow at the hotel who helped with the birth. We hired the wet nurse."

"I know," said Little Molly, who'd been forced to bind up her leaking breasts in preparation for leaving Daniel.

"You'll be so busy the time will pass quickly. I'll follow you when the baby's weaned. I'll send you a letter when to expect us."

"Oh, Stefania. Send me more letters than that, tell me everything he does. Yesterday he smiled at me . . ." Her voice broke.

"I know, dear. But what else can we do?"

CHAPTER 25

REMBRANDT

August 1815

The Grafton settlers had begun to hold town meetings at the end of every summer. Mostly it was the men who attended, but a few prominent ladies were admitted on sufferance. The first of these was Stefania, in recognition of her generosity to the mission school. Little Molly, as the head female teacher, always accompanied Stefania, though no one could remember how she'd been formally asked. In her capacity as the consort of George de Marechal, Annie de Marechal had attended until her death during the fever epidemic three years earlier. Magdalena Walker had taken her place.

Thus privileged, the ladies, in bonnets and shawls, sat quietly at the back of the meeting room that had been built on the back of the late Brother Merriman's church. Stefania always brought her adopted child, Daniel, with her—she took him everywhere, reluctant to leave him with Jane Pine. Daniel sat between Stefania and Little Molly, who was fond of the child, and he'd sit quietly on her lap as often as he sat on Stefania's.

The assemblage heard a report from the mission school on its finances, now in a healthy state thanks to the efforts of Stefania and Little Molly. This was followed by a discussion about who was responsible for ensuring the network of dirt roads that linked the homesteads remained passable, the reports on hostile Indian activity, and finally the vote on whether to hold the Blackberry Picnic that year. On this matter, the ladies were requested to cast their votes along with the men.

The preachers were in favor. It was important to demonstrate to the Indians—especially the Cherokee children at the school—that tales of shape-shifters didn't have the power to deter Christians, and it was important to bear witness that they looked only to the Lord for protection. Jack Drumheller, Bryn Vann, and Cully Stuart snorted that when the Lord wanted the settlers to be protected against Indians, he generally sent the army to do the job. Some said Gideon Vann had used his powers to become a shape-shifter and God had punished him by turning him to stone, though the last explanation made little sense, considering the boulder had been in the same place since the de Marechals came and didn't look any different. Everyone laughed and voted to hold the picnic.

At the end of this meeting, Stefania stood and suggested they take up a collection to pay young Rembrandt Conway to make a pictorial record of the gathering this year. Stefania had seen his drawings and thought Secondus had taught him well. Rembrandt was struggling to support his mother, Anna. A commission would help them, and everyone who attended would have his or her likeness made. The sketches Rembrandt made at the picnic would later be turned into a grand panoramic painting to hang in the courthouse. Stefania would not only contribute money, but undertake to provide whatever artist materials Rembrandt needed.

There was a murmur of excitement as people agreed. The Blackberry Picnic was a civic occasion, carried out in style. It would be fitting to have a painting to mark the event and show the world Grafton at its best. The motion was passed.

These picnics had become more elaborate occasions with each passing year. They now required carts drawn by mules or horses to carry the picnic baskets and buckets the children would fill with blackberries. There was a prize, a storybook, given each year by Little Molly Drumheller to the child who picked the most. Women wore their best bonnets and shawls and insisted their men wear fresh cravats. Earlier in the day, the older boys had gone up to string lanterns in the trees to be lit at dusk and laid a fire, ready to light for the ladies' tea and coffee. The men laid makeshift tables of planks end to end in a long line.

Jugs of lemonade and raspberry shrub for the children and whiskey and brandy for the men were unloaded. The older children brought water from the spring to boil for their mothers' tea.

There was a ritual that had grown up over the years. Before any tea was drunk, whiskey taken, or children lined up to begin their picking race, singly or in groups, the picnickers all walked up to the Old Man of the Mountain and stood for a minute contemplating Grafton, agreeing with each other that the first settlers would be astonished if they could see it now, the patchwork of farms and fenced, tended fields of corn and wheat and sorghum and livestock stretching down the valley. If people still lived in cabins—and most did—those of all but the latest incomers had been extended, with porches and shutters and shade trees, tidy barns and neat vegetable gardens behind them. Privies were set well back behind bushes. The women shared cuttings from their herb gardens, and some even managed to acquire roses and lilacs to plant.

Grafton had its mill, blacksmith, boardinghouse, tailor, and livery stable. Thanks to the river landing and trading post, it was prosperous and growing.

The fine sight swelled the viewers' hearts with civic pride they could hardly express in words.

Then the women drifted back to the tables to lay out the food they'd prepared: fried chickens and salads, light breads, hams, pickles, preserves, apple stack cakes, syllabubs, and fruit pies. Fawn White and other Cherokee homesteader wives added bean bread, venison stew, and grape dumplings. The women complimented each other on the work of their hands, spread out so invitingly. Stefania and Magdalena were each assisted by a hired girl. Linney Pine's shrill voice let it be known that her new brick house was so large she required *three* hired girls. "Zebulon's very particular, and of course, I have to have things nice for him. But he doesn't like to see me fatiguing myself."

People didn't like Linney any better than they'd liked her late mother-in-law, Patience. Now that she was married and rich, Linney mostly ignored her parents. Will and Jane Pine and her younger brothers still worked at Chiaramonte, and Linney cherished an old resentment against Stefania, either because Gustine St. Pierre had wanted Stefania more than he'd wanted Linney or because Stefania had sent him away when she chose to marry the colonel. Linney wasn't sure which was worse, but she'd hated Stefania and all her family ever since the day she'd seen her kissing Gustine.

Rembrandt arrived early and settled on a fallen log on the sidelines. It was his first actual commission, and Secondus had warned him an artist lived and died by the opinion of the people he painted. Rembrandt was shy and self-effacing, and now he was nervous about pleasing everyone. He set out his new sketching materials with trembling hands. He wanted more than anything to paint for a living, and today was the great test that would determine more commissions, and he'd better do a good job.

He began sketching his parents from memory, something he often did to loosen his hands. He drew Anna, who was too frail now to attend the picnic, her face etched with lines and hollows, but her eyes lit with adoration for her son, who'd inherited his father's gift. She'd always been in awe of Secondus, the *Meisterkünstler*. Sketching Secondus from memory, recalling how his father's eyes narrowed in concentration, Rembrandt heard him saying, "Hold the pencil just so, a line here, just so, you're setting down a soul on paper, boy, look with your eyes and your heart." His strokes grew firmer.

He finished Anna and Secondus and turned his attention to the active scene he was commissioned to draw. As often happened to him, as he stared, everything and everyone came slowly together, a swirling mass of baskets and people and trees and rocks and carts, colors and movement all linked together with the long white line of the tablecloths in the center, weighted with food, until they were not single things but shapes and colors, each part of something whole that he saw and felt and wanted to replicate on the paper, but hesitated to try. He feared the people for whom he was recording the picnic would not understand or see it through his eyes.

He felt a moment of despair that he'd fail before he'd begun. It was like trying to draw bees in motion, swarming on the hive. He blinked hard.

After a moment the scene before him began to resolve itself into manageable images, and he could draw the individual objects and people, not the bustling whole. He felt the familiar, reassuring twitching in his fingers, and before he knew it, he was sketching the line of a bonnet, the drape of a shawl, a child's excited face.

There was a quilt spread on the ground, a baby laid on it next to a pie and a basket with the legs of a cooked chicken showing. He'd start with the baby. Its parents were Captain Henry Stuart and his cousin and pretty wife, Fanny. Fanny and her mother, Magdalena Walker, were both bending over the baby. The composition was pleasing, the baby reaching up to catch her young mother's bonnet strings, the smiling grandmother reaching her finger into the baby's other hand.

He forgot time and the fact he was hungry and that the log wasn't very comfortable and just drew. If one of the men drinking whiskey happened to catch Rembrandt's eye, the man would self-consciously strike a pose to look grave and important, sometimes raising an arm in an awkward gesture pointing to the valley as if to say, *I did this.*

Sometimes Rembrandt would cry mischievously, "Sir, please don't move before I catch you, so dignified, such authority! Hold still for a moment," and the man would freeze with his arm awkwardly upright in midgesture, deprived of his drink for an uncomfortable length of time but willing nevertheless to hold the pose for a week. Despite the discomfort, it was gratifying to be preserved in a noble moment. Rembrandt grinned down at his sketch taking shape very slowly.

The ladies were less vain, easier subjects. The fluid lines and colors of their skirts and shawls and bonnets were pleasing, and they were too busy making tea, talking among themselves, hurrying after crawling babies, or quieting hungry children with apple slices, cookies, and cold biscuits to preen because he was drawing them.

He drew Stefania Charbonneau's adopted son, Daniel, a sturdy, cheerful child self-confidently making the rounds of the ladies setting out food, who laughed and gave him hugs and cookies. Rembrandt smiled as he sketched Daniel with crumbs around his mouth. Observing Daniel's features, Rembrandt wondered if Stefania's foundling had Negro blood.

The impatient children were dispatched to their blackberry picking. When they returned with their wooden buckets filled to overflowing and purple hands and mouths, he drew that too.

Then it was time for a lengthy patriotic address extolling the virtues of Grafton and America. It was the custom for the more prominent older men from the Vann, Stuart, de Marechal, or Drumheller families to draw straws for the honor of delivering it, but this year, for the first time, Lafayette Charbonneau had been allowed to join the draw, and he had won. Young as he was, he was successfully managing and expanding the Chiaramonte enterprises and was now breeding racehorses. When he stepped up to deliver his address, Lafayette cut a dashing figure in a handsome frock coat and launched into a lengthy—some murmured too lengthy—speech. The theme of his address was the singular opportunities for wealth in America, where any man of an industrious turn of mind could prosper. Thriving towns like Grafton were leading the way, with its enlightened businessmen who, in increasing their own fortunes, conferred a public benefit and were the very pillars of their community. Its bold entrepreneurs had made American commerce the envy of the world, he concluded. "America leads the way now. And Grafton leads the Commonwealth of Virginia!" He was roundly applauded.

Rembrandt caught him in the pompous oratorical pose he'd struck, clutching his lapels. Rembrandt's fingers itched to draw the weakness around Lafayette's mouth, but he refrained. After Lafayette, the ministers from Grafton's two churches prayed at great, competitive length, thanking God for the harvest, for the food they were about to eat, for business, and to lay before the Almighty the achievements of the mission school. Rembrandt drew them with their mouth open, arm raised to point at heaven, and resisted the urge to draw God looking bored.

"Amen," said people at various points in the prayers, hoping they would end. He drew in a crowd of heads and shoulders of listeners, attentive faces except for two in the back of the crowd, rolling their eyes with impatience.

Little Molly was reading a book hidden under her shawl.

"When can we eat?" groaned the children, hungry after their berry picking.

Finally, the last amen was said.

Stefania and Rosa called to Rembrandt to rest from his sketching awhile and eat his dinner. Rembrandt looked up and blinked, owl-like and abstracted. Rosa patted the seat beside her. Rembrandt blushed. Rosa was very pretty, and he hardly dared speak to her.

After supper there was call-and-response hymn singing, and Rembrandt went back to work. The men detached themselves from wives and children and gathered on top of the Old Man of the Mountain to pass their jugs of whiskey and apple brandy. The smaller children fell asleep on their mothers' laps. Older boys and girls gravitated away from their families to a spot overlooking the valley to watch the sun go down. The lanterns in the trees were lit. Rembrandt drew all this too, his supply of sketching paper nearly exhausted by the time the light faded. He felt suddenly drained, as if the pencil had drawn his soul from his body onto the paper.

Or perhaps he was merely hungry again, he thought, and went to see which ladies had food left and to listen to the different conversations taking place, to rest his mind and his satiated eyes.

Mothers were warning their daughters not on any account to let a boy persuade them away from the group of young people clustered by the edge of the clearing and into the woods for a spot of courting. Alone, Rembrandt moved among the families, eating the chicken and ham biscuits he was offered, wishing he was the sort of young man mothers warned their daughters about, but he knew he wasn't.

The stars came out, and a full moon shone over the valley. Crickets sang. Campfires were replenished, more tea and whiskey were drunk, and conversation hummed across the clearing.

The men who were gathered at the Old Man of the Mountain spat tobacco and repeated approvingly what had been said in the patriotic address, agreeing over their whiskey that America was the finest place in the world. The more prominent citizens, the Drumhellers and de Marechals and Vanns and Stuarts and Walkers, talked the loudest, while the Pines and some hired hands and a group of Irish laborers who came up from New Orleans every year, traveling to work between harvests, were less vocal and were content to be quiet and drink steadily.

"This country's all about progress!" the men kept exclaiming. "Can't say the same about England and Europe, had their day. They're worn out, I guess. Little England wouldn't fit into a corner of America."

"Commerce, that's the thing!"

"If we could just get rid of the Injins once and for all. I hear there's gold been found down in Georgia. Land don't belong to Injins. Government should move 'em."

Commerce and land were their favorite topics. They talked about the opportunities now that territory west of the Mississippi had been acquired from the French by President Jefferson and how it drew more land-hungry settlers through Grafton. The news that gold had been discovered on tribal hunting grounds farther south attracted more settlers and speculators of settlers who said the Indians should go or be driven out and who sent delegations to Washington to make their views known.

Snatches of conversation about progress and commerce reached the ladies, who saw progress less in terms of commerce and more in its manifestations such as Sunday school, midweek prayer meetings, hymn singings, committees, a Bible society, and quilting parties. It meant tablecloths and hired girls. Prosperity had given rise to not one but two wooden churches that vaguely preserved the old doctrinal disagreements between the first preachers, Calvinist Brother Merriman and the Quaker Iddo Fox. Though the particulars of these theological disputes were forgotten by most people of Grafton, Brother Merriman's church was now designated Primitive Baptist, and Friend Fox's one-room meetinghouse became officially Methodist.

The tension between Brother Merriman and Friend Fox lingered on, in a manner of speaking, in the particular and distinct way the congregations sang hymns or the preachers vied to deliver the longest, most terrifying Sunday sermons and attract the largest congregation. The quiet of a traditional Quaker meeting had been forgotten. The congregations of both churches were composed mainly of women and children, none of whom were interested in the finer distinctions of theology. Men stayed outside, passing the churchgoing hours discussing horses and business.

Enjoying the blackberry wine her sister Patsy had brought to the picnic, Peach told her Hanover sisters the latest gossip from the trading post about Mortify Merriman. He'd been caught seducing young girls at camp meetings again. His impressionable young listeners were aroused to a fever pitch by fiery sermons heavy with innuendo such as calling on sinners to lay themselves bare before God and experience spiritual ecstasy. When he offered to pray with them afterward, the girls were in no state to resist him and always claimed the power of the Spirit had overcome their inhibitions.

The churchgoing Hanover women shook their heads and wondered if Brother Merriman had addled Mortify's head, going on about fornication the way he'd done.

"He just talk about it, though. Mortify do it," said Peach. "But I heard Mortify had his comeuppance. They say the family of one girl he got in a family way turned up at his last revival and kidnapped him. Just climbed up to the platform where he preachin' and hauled him away, threatened to shoot him if he didn't marry her. Had the girl with 'em. They found another parson waitin' his turn to preach, and they pointed their guns at him, so he married her and Mortify. Then they took Mortify back, make him work on their homestead. Won't let him leave to do no more preachin' now. He stuck like a fly in molasses," said Peach.

Her sisters approved.

They had more sympathy for Endurance, who'd continued circuit preaching on his own. No breath of scandal had ever touched Endurance, a lonely figure in his dusty black suit, with his Bible in his saddlebag. He was still waiting to be called to head the Slipping Creek Mission School when the current principal, Brother Merriman's temporary replacement, went back north. It was taking a long time, and occasionally Endurance reappeared in Grafton to preach a guest sermon to the Primitive Baptists and see if the temporary principal was gone yet. The congregation took turns putting him up, but he was a dour, oppressive soul to have around, and they were usually glad to see him go.

Still, Endurance had his defenders among the women who said Endurance wasn't to blame for his brother's sins. He lived a decent life, had even tried to rein in Mortify, and he deserved to get the job as principal before it was too late. They agreed it would help his case if he were married, but none of the girls liked him at all.

People commented on Zebulon and Linney Drumheller's new house. Rufus's old cabin had been torn down, much to Little Molly's disgust. In its place stood a brick house, painted white like the one Stefano Albanisi had built at Chiaramonte, only much larger. Linney talked constantly about the difficulty of finding furniture good enough for it. There was a new courthouse, where Annie Vann de Marechal's widower, George Marshall, had been appointed a justice of the peace. George was regarded as Grafton's most prominent citizen by everyone, except Zebulon Drumheller, who resented not being chosen instead. Linney Drumheller agreed and complained shrilly about George and his self-important family, who claimed to be descended from counts and princes and had changed their name trying to sound American but still pretended to be better than other people.

It was true the Marshalls had changed their name. The last gravestones carved with the name de Marechal were Kitty de Marechal Stuart and her sister-in-law Annie Vann de Marechal, who died within days of each other in the fever epidemic of 1812. But out-of-date newspapers that occasionally reached Grafton had carried accounts of the Napoleonic wars in Europe and inflamed reports of diplomatic tensions between America and France because American ships and sailors had been seized in those wars. The de Marechals' name was deliberately Americanized to Marshall by a census taker because he thought it more patriotic to note it as Marshall. George de Marechal complained, but the authorities claimed once it was written down in the census book, there was nothing anyone could do about it.

Conversation turned to the Frog Mountain shape-shifter. People said it caused the Marshalls' hunting dogs up at Wildwood to howl on nights when the fog settled in and there was no moon to set them baying, and dogs in general, even the big hunting dogs Lafayette Charbonneau bred at Chiaramonte, could only be driven up Frog Mountain with whips. Look what happened to the sheriff's dogs that time. Something big got them.

Rembrandt Conway tried a few sketches of what the eagle man might look like. At the end of the picnic, one or another of the old men—Toby or Jack Drumheller or Cully Stuart—would gather the children somewhere out of earshot of their parents and the preachers and tell them stories of Indian spells and lost travelers who'd seen ghosts and finish with the one about the long hunters and the eagle man. The story always ended with a warning not to get left behind on Frog Mountain tonight and to look over their shoulders as they went down the path home, lest the shape-shifter creep up and snatch them. The older children went home in a pleasurable state of dread and the younger ones in terrified silence, both disinclined to stray from the path and get lost in the dark. "It's just a story from the Indians," said their parents. "Just a Cherokee story." But at night, going down the Frog Mountain path in the dark, more than one person was sure they felt a presence.

CHAPTER 26

1815–1834

The Cherokee stories woven into the fabric of Grafton reflected the way Cherokee families had mixed in with the settlers. Fawn and White Owl had been baptized, along with their son Joe and their second boy, Thomas. Joe had married pretty Mariah Stuart within two years of his return from the academy in Tennessee, and George Marshall gave his niece and her husband a fine piece of land down the valley as a wedding present. It was a valuable gift. The Marshalls had made a great deal of money selling similar parcels of land to incoming settlers.

Sweet Rachel Vann, educated and baptized and a Sunday school teacher, had married at seventeen in a high-necked calico frock to the boy of her choice, a fellow Cherokee pupil. Though the school discouraged any adherence to clan ways, Rachel remembered what Fawn had taught her about Cherokee customs. She thanked God in her nightly prayers that the young man was not of her mother's clan and forbidden to her as a husband. Caitlin insisted Rachel be given money as a wedding present, and the couple bought a piece of land from the Marshalls, next to Joe and Mariah's homestead, but not so big.

The two couples helped each other raise their log cabins and a barn, and a year later Rachel's daughter, Nancy, and Mariah's son, Lucas, were born within weeks of each other.

Mariah's older brother, Henry, had joined the cavalry, been made a captain, and cut a dashing figure in his uniform. He'd worn it at the Blackberry Picnic in 1812 when he'd stood on top of the Old Man and called for congratulations; his cousin Magdalena's daughter, Fanny Walker, had agreed to marry him. Fanny, blushing and smiling, had been pushed forward by the other girls to stand by his side while everyone clapped and cheered. Fanny resembled her pretty grandmother Sophia, and the ladies declared it would be hard to find a handsomer pair.

Bryn and Peach weren't ready to relinquish their successful trading post to the next generation, so their two sons packed up their families and went off to set up a bigger trading post at Cincinnati on the Ohio River. This left Bryn Vann's nephew Caradoc to inherit the trading post eventually. In the meantime, Caradoc followed Henry's lead and joined the army.

With no husband or children of her own, it was perfectly natural that Little Molly took a special interest in her friend Stefania's adopted son. When Daniel was old enough for the mission school, he boarded in the boys' dormitory during term time and won prize after prize for memorizing and reading and spelling correctly. He called Little Molly Aunt.

In 1818 Gustine St. Pierre paid another visit to Grafton, and this time made an extended stay. He took up residence in Susan Hanover and Isaac Ozment's boardinghouse, commandeering the parlor there for his exclusive use. He bought Chiaramonte horses and hunting dogs and timber, which he sent on to his plantation, and called on Stefania so frequently that people speculated how soon the widow and widower would marry.

Stefania surprised everyone by quietly remarrying Jack Drumheller at Chiaramonte, with only her children and Little Molly present. Jack was a quarter of a century older than Stefania, and everyone agreed it was unexpected, but her first husband had been much older too. Gustine St. Pierre took the news of the marriage badly. According to Isaac Ozment, he called for a bottle of brandy, drank it, and smashed up the boardinghouse parlor before departing, looking murderous, on the next riverboat.

Linney Drumheller left no one in doubt that her brother-in-law Jack had no business remarrying again at his age, and as for Stefania—she rolled her eyes scornfully—hadn't her mother been some sort of dancing girl? And hadn't Gustine, Stefano Albanisi's former hired hand, been sniffing round her like a male dog around a bitch?

Though later when she learned how very rich Gustine had become, Linney contradicted herself and said Stefania was a fool to let him get away.

Toby Drumheller was found dead in his lean-to beside his smithy in the fall of 1820. He left a crude will, bequeathing his savings, a considerable sum of money buried in a box under his bed, to his "god-daughter Magdalena de Marechal Walker." Magdalena wept when she heard the news, saying she wished Toby had got over his anger with her for championing poor Anna Conway.

Magdalena spent some of this inheritance commissioning Rembrandt to paint a portrait of her daughter, Fanny Stuart, holding Magdalena's granddaughter, the same child Rembrandt had painted years earlier at the Blackberry Picnic. The double portrait was much admired, and Jack asked Rembrandt to make a marriage portrait of him and Stefania, to hang at Chiaramonte. Linney demanded to have a portrait too, only bigger, of her and Zebulon. She forced a grumbling

Zebulon to sit still through long posing sessions in a cravat and stiff collar.

After his mother's death, Rembrandt made his way to New Orleans and within a few years wrote to Stefania that he was making a living from portraits. Later he returned to Grafton much richer than he'd left it. He repaired and expanded his parents' dilapidated cabin and turned the rickety shelter Secondus had once built for his donkeys into a studio, where he continued to paint. He brought with him an exotic wife, Ella, whose parents had been sugar planters in Haiti. Stefania paid a formal call on the new Mrs. Conway. Ella said her family had barely escaped the slave revolt with their lives, managing only to salvage a few of the family's collection of paintings, purchased on a tour of Europe by the planter's grandfather in the previous century. She had met Rembrandt when he was employed to restore those damaged in the family's flight.

Ella missed having slaves and was shocked there were none in Grafton. She avoided Peach and the Hanovers and was scandalized to learn dashing Captain Henry Stuart was the son of a Marshall daughter and her mulatto husband. She snubbed Henry and his wife, Fanny.

Then Ella gave birth to a son they named Angelo Conway. To her chagrin, Angelo was darker than his mother, and his features plainly testified to Negro blood. Stefania knew it hadn't been inherited from Rembrandt and surmised that one of Ella's ancestors must have had a Creole mistress.

Little Molly's hair turned completely gray by the time she turned forty-five, though she was still a slim, handsome woman, elegant in her black clothes and gold earbobs. Years of teaching had given her an air of authority, and she continued living alone at the school despite being urged by her brothers and their wives to return to the Drumheller enclave. Little Molly knew an unmarried woman living with her family would be expected to shoulder many domestic and child-rearing chores, and declined.

People found her intimidating and a little odd, as a spinster fond of teaching and the solitude of her book-filled room. There was a general sense that Little Molly was too smart and independent, had put men off, and had missed her chance.

Rachel's only child, Nancy, was married at sixteen to Jesse Bonney, a full-blood Cherokee and distant cousin. Rachel had an uncomfortable sense that the clan relationship customs might have prevented their marriage, but she could no longer remember the rules, and the cousin was her daughter's choice.

Rachel's husband had died of the fever when Nancy was a child. Rachel gave the couple a fine parcel of land from her own homestead, and Jesse built a good four-room cabin with a porch, within sight of Rachel. The couple plowed and planted their fields, and Rachel brought spare quilts and cooking pots and a cradle for the child Nancy was expecting. She congratulated herself that her daughter was happily settled.

Peach Vann had grown stout and was a grandmother several times over. Her mother-in-law, Caitlin, was a little dried-up cricket of a woman who, unless Peach deemed it too cold or wet, spent her days on the trading-post porch under a buffalo rug. She could identify passersby by their voices, and people made a point of stepping over to wish her good morning, ask how she was today, and tell her the news, if they had any, of their children and grandchildren. Caitlin would smile and nod and wonder where she'd put her mending basket. It had never been her habit to sit in idleness, and she automatically still groped for her sewing, her mending and quilts, to make torn garments whole or fashion an intricately pieced coverlet out of scraps, forgetting her hands had been too stiff to hold a needle for years. She liked to feel the sun and asked to have her chair turned to face the mountains she could no longer see. She'd never given up hope Gideon was still up there, somewhere.

One day an old, old woman dressed in deerskin came hobbling along the river path. She passed slowly by the trading post, where

Caitlin dozed on the porch. Peach came out to check Caitlin's buffalo robe hadn't slipped to the floor when she looked up and saw the newcomer.

The old woman turned and stared at her for a moment. Peach gasped. "Rhiannon?"

"My name is Singing Wind."

Peach hurried down the steps and dragged the woman out of Caitlin's earshot. "Rhiannon, have you come back to see your mother at last? She's old now, your father has gone. She sits waiting for him. Let me tell her you're here—I spect it be a shock, but I'll tell her gentle."

"No," said the woman with an impassive expression. "I will not set foot in the trading post. I am looking for my daughter. Rachel, they say you call her. Gideon took her and my son away." The old woman's eyes narrowed.

Peach protested and begged her to come inside, but the woman was adamant.

"Rachel lives that way; her daughter, Nancy, and her husband do too. You can see their cabin."

"Do Nancy and her husband not live with Rachel? A Cherokee husband goes to his wife's house."

"Rhiannon, please."

The woman pulled away from Peach's grasp. "Rachel and Nancy need me. I will tell them the old ways," she said. "My mother, who raised them, will have filled their heads with nonsense, taught them nothing, wishing them to be white." She hobbled away toward Rachel's homestead.

On the porch, Caitlin's dream was interrupted by a familiar voice, she was unsure whose. She murmured, "Gideon?"

CHAPTER 27

CAITLIN

1834

Caitlin's hearing was still keen. She was woken by Peach whispering to someone that Mother Vann hadn't been well but she'd never liked to make a fuss. They hadn't realized . . .

"Hadn't realized what?" asked Caitlin.

"Mother Vann," said Peach. "Are you awake?"

Caitlin was momentarily surprised to find herself in bed. She tried to get up, but Peach was settling her back against the pillow. She tried to protest that she mustn't stay in bed in daytime. She only did that when she was giving birth.

A moment ago in her dreams, she'd been young, hurrying up the orchard path to Wildwood with a baby on her back, Indian-style, to see Sophia. Sophia?

Why, I'm an old lady! Caitlin thought with dismay, surprised anew by that discovery each morning.

Slowly she gathered her thoughts. She remembered Sophia was dead, that Rhiannon had married and gone, that Gideon had left for a long spell but returned with Rhiannon's children Rachel and Caradoc, that Rachel was married and a mother of a grown daughter and . . . Gideon . . . She couldn't remember where Gideon was.

Caitlin strained to hear for Rachel's voice in the hum of voices around her. Rachel had been her comfort and joy from the day she arrived. She'd clung to Caitlin's skirts as a small child. By the age of five, she was leading Caitlin everywhere, watchful for anything that might trip her grandmother and keeping up a constant stream of chatter describing everything Caitlin couldn't see.

She told her grandmother who was passing on the river, who'd come to the trading post, what the weather was like. She read Caitlin's Bible aloud to her, made her tea, and fetched the sewing basket.

When Rachel and Caradoc were eight and old enough to make the trip to the mission school on horseback, Rachel was sent off riding behind Caradoc every day. She'd cried bitterly at the time, and Caitlin whispered in her ear that she wanted Rachel to bring home one new interesting thing to tell her from school every day, like a present.

Rachel was soon brimming over with news about her lessons; the other children and the teachers; how Miss Drumheller was very strict; what she and Caradoc were learning; which of them was better at their sums; that the Charbonneaus were paying for Rembrandt Conway to attend the school because everybody knew the Conways were poorer than the Pines; that Fawn's son Joseph White, who'd once won the prize of a Bible for memorizing the most Bible verses, had returned to the mission after three years at the South West Point Academy in Tennessee as a teacher.

"And there's a secret, Grandma," Rachel had told her earnestly. "Joe's sweet on my teacher, Mariah Stuart! He always sits by her in morning and evening prayers. He says, 'I want your opinion, Miss Stuart,' like she's special and knows everything, even though she hasn't been to any academy. Miss Stuart gets so red in the face when he talks to her that the girls get the giggles. And once"—Rachel's voice dropped to a conspiratorial whisper—"we saw them kissing!"

"Kissing!" Caitlin had acted suitably shocked.

"And, Grandma, what do you think! Zebulon Drumheller has married Linney Pine! I heard the teachers say he did it to serve Mariah right, but Mariah just laughed, so I can't see how it serves her right, can you, Grandma?"

Her memory of Rachel's voice, like an excited baby bird, was drowned out by Peach saying that Mother Vann had taken a bad cold last winter and hadn't been herself since. Was that true? Caitlin wondered. She couldn't remember.

"Wouldn't eat," Peach continued to whoever it was she was talking to.

Who wouldn't eat? Caitlin tried to think. Susan had come with custard and broth, Caitlin remembered that. "Sophia's recipe," a shadowy presence would say in Susan's bossy voice. She would feel a spoon on her lips. "Mama used to say it's good enough to raise the dead, ought to mend what ails you, Aunt Caitlin."

Sophia had made soup and custard too, sometimes out of nothing, for Caitlin after the birth of all Caitlin's babies, to keep Death from the door and give her strength and, after Caitlin's three stillbirths, to help her body and spirit to mend from the grief of the dead babies.

Childbirth had been terrible, each time. She'd been so afraid she'd die. She'd made Sophia promise to raise her children and look after Gideon. She had always tried to make her peace with heaven and prepare her soul before she was brought to bed, but the prospect of leaving her children motherless meant she had struggled and struggled to live.

"I won't let you die, Caitlin, I won't!" Sophia would encourage her, gripping her hands during the terrible labor, wiping her brow, bracing Caitlin's back when the baby came out, insisting she eat afterward.

She would lie bleeding and sore and spent afterward, astonished to find she was still alive, with Sophia by her side, praising whichever baby had just been born, if alive, or holding her hand and reading a psalm from her godmother's prayer book after the stillbirth, and making sure Caitlin ate.

"Eat this! You *will* get your strength back," Sophia would order, holding spoon after spoon to her lips. "For the baby. For the children. One for Gideon, that's right, no, you're not finished yet, one for me." Sophia had imperious ways, and Caitlin had always obediently opened her mouth, even though she never felt like eating when she was so sore and bleeding and exhausted. She smiled faintly. Sophy had been so good at making people do things. The fragrant steam of soup, the silky custard on her tongue had been the taste of life.

But now Caitlin couldn't swallow. "Perhaps a little tea," whispered Caitlin, turning her head from the spoon and falling asleep.

When Caitlin opened her eyes again, she sensed the presence of many women around her. Magdalena and Peach were smoothing the covers. Someone laid a cool cloth on her brow.

Was she giving birth again? Caitlin waited for the pain to take her in its grip; there would be pain, and she would struggle and scream, then push when they ordered her to do that. But there was no pain today . . . How sad everyone sounded . . . Was it over? Had this baby died? Please, God, no! She loved her babies so much!

A man's voice somewhere in the background.

She strained to identify the figure leaning over her. Someone said, "Robert."

Robert had married one of the girls, she couldn't remember who.

She wanted to ask someone, where was the baby? Shouldn't there be the sound of it crying? It was bad if the baby didn't cry at once.

She fell asleep.

She woke again, and they were asking if Rachel and Caradoc had come yet. Then there was a quick step. "Grandma," said Rachel. "I'm here." Rachel's hand closed over Caitlin's.

Rachel and Caradoc. Venus and Susan. Kitty. Magdalena. Cully. So many children. Robert Walker's voice, a spoon of something to her lips, saying it can't be long now. She tried to swallow, but her throat wouldn't obey her.

It's not a baby, Caitlin realized. She must make herself understood. It was important.

She made a mighty effort, like she had when pushing the babies out. "What did you say, Mother Vann?" Peach bent close.

Caitlin patted her hand. "My good girl . . . will . . . ," Caitlin whispered. "In the Bible." Peach opened the Bible and found a folded paper. "Front page. Names."

Peach opened the Bible to the frontispiece where Caitlin had recorded the dates of birth and death of her mother, father, aunts, and uncles together with those of Rhiannon and the three stillborn babies who followed her. She'd stopped after the stillbirths.

"Bryn and you. Cadfael."

"Oh, Mother Vann!" There was a sob in Peach's voice. Caitlin had rarely spoken of Cadfael.

"Cadfael." The image of her sweet, sturdy little boy passed through Caitlin's mind. It was an image she'd clung to for many years, fiercely and painfully, determined to keep him with her. Now she said his name, it would be written, and she could let Cadfael go. Just as she'd let Rhiannon go when the twins came.

She asked Bryn to read her will out loud.

"To Bryn and Peach, half the Vann cows, the trading post, the landing, the gristmill, the cooking pots, and the churn, and to Bryn and then his eldest son, Tad's fiddle. To my grandson Jericho Marshall and his wife, Rosa, my two best feather mattresses, my pie safe, and the remaining cows. Fawn to have my best blue-and-white quilt. To be divided among the grandchildren, including Rachel and Caradoc, the rest of the quilts I made. To Rachel, my Bible. And I wish Bryn to allow Caradoc an equal share of the trading post with Bryn's sons."

Caitlin knew her affairs were in order. She had believed in order and tidiness, her weapons against the anarchy of the wilderness.

She summoned the strength to say, "Bryn, I want . . ."

"Yes, Mother."

"Sing 'Guide Me, O Thou Great Jehovah' when they bury me."

Bryn's voice said, "Of course, Mother."

She struggled for breath to say, "Loud . . . so Gideon will hear." Gideon possessed an ability to slip between worlds, the human and animal worlds, the worlds of reality and the spirit. It was why for so many years she'd cherished the hope he was still alive in the mountains, in some form, waiting for her. It was the only way she knew to send him a final message, to let him know that she understood, that her spirit would find his.

From far away, Bryn was saying, "We will, Mother."

Her work was done. "Gideon, in all the world . . . one heart," Caitlin murmured, and closed her eyes for the last time.

CHAPTER 28
THE REMOVALS

They had been given an opportunity to go voluntarily. Few went. In 1837 the army came and built a stockade, then rounded up the Cherokees in the valley and corralled them inside the stockade until enough flatboats came to take them away to the west, where they'd been promised new land. Zebulon Drumheller had personally chased down those trying to evade deportation. The Cherokees hadn't come quietly—a pregnant woman had died, and her small daughter had disappeared in the melee. Afterward Zebulon bought up many of the vacant Cherokee homesteads for a good price from the government. For a time the valley felt strangely unpeopled, and there were sightings of Indian ghosts who refused to leave their homesteads and farms and hunting grounds.

Bryn Vann, being only a quarter Cherokee, was allowed to stay. He decided it was time to give effect to Caitlin's wish for Major Caradoc Vann to take over the trading post. Bryn bought Fawn and White Owl's old cabin, empty since the removal. Caradoc had married a young teacher from up north, a pretty redheaded girl named Adelina. The little Cherokee girl who'd disappeared had been one of her favorite pupils, and they said the child had drowned. The Removals were soon after the wedding, and Caradoc had taken Adelina away to the hot springs. He called it a wedding trip, but grief and shock had overwhelmed his bride with melancholy. Bryn Vann and Jack Drumheller took ill and died of quinsy within days of each other in January 1839. Little Molly's hair turned from gray to white, as did Stefania's. Little Molly had to send away for spectacles. People said she'd put her eyes out from too much reading.

Stefania's daughter, Rosa, and Rosa's husband, Jericho, had gone to live at Wildwood. Lafayette was still unmarried, and Stefania almost despaired of him settling down and raising a family at Chiaramonte. Lafayette seemed to live for enjoyment—horse racing, cards, and, she suspected, women. He would disappear for weeks at a time to Kingsport or New Orleans. He was wealthy enough, thanks to his father and grandfather, to do as he pleased and seemed happy to leave management of Chiaramonte to Will Pine. Stefania tried not to think what would become of the place when Will died.

Stefania's only companion at Chiaramonte was taciturn Jane Pine. She often had one of the Pines row her across to the trading post to see her friends and keep loneliness at bay.

When they met from time to time, the old ladies concurred that Grafton was passing into a new era. That they must leave it to the next generations now.

CHAPTER 29

MOSES

July 1839

Early that summer, Rembrandt Conway made a sketch of the four old ladies, writing, "Miss Little Molly, Miss Magdalena, and Miss Stefania with Miss Peach on the Porch," underneath. He signed it and presented it to Stefania on her birthday.

With Caradoc and Adelina still away, the three women kept Peach company most evenings, when the weather was fine, gathering as Rembrandt had sketched them. They sat on the porch to catch the river breeze, drank tea, exchanged news, sewed, and watched the light fade on the river until Stefania hung an old white sheet from the porch railing as a signal to the Pines that one of the men should come and row her home. Until then they watched children skipping stones on the river, playing hide-and-seek in the orchard, chasing lightning bugs.

All but Little Molly were widows, but their tangled network of family ties among their Stuart, Drumheller, Vann, Marshall, and Charbonneau offspring gave them plenty to talk about.

Magdalena usually had the most news. She often had letters from Fanny, who led a transient life after marrying her cousin Henry Stuart, now a colonel, moving around the country as he went from one posting to the next. Henry and Fanny were now settled in his latest posting to New York, and their children were grown and married.

But Fanny had surprising news—she was expecting again in the new year. Magdalena fretted, concerned about this development at Fanny's age. Nevertheless, Magdalena was at work stitching a rather lopsided dress for the new baby. Her sewing hadn't improved with time.

Peach asked when they'd see Fanny's brother, Lorenzo, again. Who was *surely* on his way home by now, the ladies exclaimed each time his name was mentioned. He'd been sent to South West Point Academy in Tennessee, thanks to Magdalena's inheritance from Toby Drumheller. After the academy, the family of a rich Kingsport classmate had employed Lorenzo as a tutor to their younger son and subsequently decamped to Europe to spend a few years broadening their son's education. Lorenzo had gone too. He sent interesting letters home describing places they'd been, what they'd seen and done and eaten. Magdalena read these out to the others and sighed. It was good he was enjoying himself.

At least, Stefania reminded her enviously, Magdalena didn't lack for company at Wildwood. Rosa and Jericho lived there and were expecting a baby, which would make the house livelier. Annie's unmarried daughter, Martha Washington Marshall, lived there too. She suffered from rheumatism, but when she felt able, Martha sometimes came down to the jetty with Magdalena in the evening. Years ago Martha's possible marriage prospects had been a constant topic of conversation—unless she was present—but these had come to nothing.

They discussed poor Adelina Vann. Peach reported Caradoc had written that the hot springs seemed to be having a good effect, and he hoped to bring Adelina home soon, to be among her friends in case she discovered there was to be a certain event.

"That would be the best thing for dear Adelina, I'm sure," said Magdalena, hopelessly snarling her thread and giving up on the baby dress for the night. "A baby is the best cure for sorrow."

"You seem happy about something, Stefania," said Little Molly. "You keep smiling to yourself."

"I am. You must congratulate me—Lafayette and his wife are expecting too." There was a murmur of "So many babies coming! How wonderful . . . So pleased . . ." In the course of a trip to New Orleans after Christmas, Lafayette had married. He'd astonished his mother by returning with a bride, a beauty named Aimée.

With her dark hair and eyes, graceful ways, and olive complexion, the girl could have been Spanish, and Stefania was curious about her, but Lafayette was vague about her people. All Stefania could learn was that the girl had been provided with a substantial dowry. Stefania had raised her eyebrows at this news, but Lafayette had always been too fond of money and too self-important to think beyond his own immediate concerns of pleasure or business. What of his wife?

Aimée was soft-spoken and beautifully mannered, obviously well brought up. Care and money had been lavished on her convent education, and she'd brought with her a large trousseau of stylish clothes, in which she looked very pretty.

Stefania suspected her son's account of the matter—that she'd lately left school and had been living with her guardian when Lafayette was introduced to her—wasn't the whole truth.

Stefania surmised she was the love child of a wealthy white man and his quadroon mistress, and her father was paying to secure her respectability away from New Orleans. A quadroon's daughter, no matter how beautiful, was unlikely to find a white husband there, but Lafayette seemed to be enchanted by his bride, and if the girl was "passing," he was oblivious. For all this Stefania was reconciled to the match. She'd despaired of her son ever settling down and was relieved Lafayette was married to anyone. She discerned that for all she was twenty years younger than Lafayette, Aimée was adept at pleasing him, always quick to anticipate his wishes, to say the right thing to him, to be always fresh and elegant in her person. Amused as she was by this management of Lafayette, Stefania wondered what Aimée's prospects were for happiness with a man as monumentally self-absorbed as Lafayette. She hoped motherhood would be Aimée's consolation.

But Stefania said nothing of her doubts to her friends. "Aimée will be an excellent mother, I am sure. It's wonderful to see how . . . how marriage has settled Lafayette. He's now as fully engaged managing Chiaramonte as I have ever wished, instead of leaving everything to the Pines. It will be good to have a family in the house. Children will steady Lafayette still more."

There was a murmur of agreement that it was bound to.

Little Molly, as always, asked if Stefania had had a letter from Daniel. Peach, Little Molly, and Stefania had kept the secret of Daniel's parents, but Daniel, who was three-quarters white, resembled Little Molly in his complexion and coloring, which the women had felt made everyone's life easier. And Lafayette had accepted his adopted brother and had actually grown fond of him in a patronizing way, as Daniel didn't stand to inherit any of the Charbonneau fortune and was often useful to Lafayette.

To prepare Daniel to make his way in the world, he'd been sent to South West Point Academy, like Lorenzo, and Little Molly cherished a hope he'd return to teach at the mission school.

But when Stefania read out Daniel's latest letter, it announced he had arranged to read law with a judge in Kingsport.

All the friends had something to say about it. Peach had sniffed, said he'd do better to come home and help Lafayette. Magdalena said you could never tell with children. She'd hoped Lorenzo would follow his father's example and become a doctor. Grafton felt the want of a doctor since Robert died. "But it's hard to know what Lorenzo proposes, since he's not here to tell us," she murmured. *Would he ever be?*

Stefania defended Daniel. Grafton had a jail and a small courthouse where Jericho Marshall, like his father, had been appointed the magistrate. The court sessions had become more and more frequent, and they needed a lawyer. "He's got a sharp mind. Perhaps he'll be a judge one day," said Little Molly, stifling her disappointment.

The friends made a plan to piece a quilt for Aimée's baby, discussing whether she'd like a star of Babylon or a shell pattern best. They wondered if Daniel would end up marrying a Kingsport girl, and shared their opinions of what he and the rest of the younger generation ought to do. They sewed and listened to the millrace in the distance. In mid-July there was a smell of hay in the air, and the corn would be ready to harvest soon. Occasionally cattle lowed. The river ran with its deceptive serenity, and some of the older boys were fishing.

First Peach, who had the best hearing, then Stefania, then Magdalena sat up and grimaced. Little Molly, who was a bit deaf, looked up over her spectacles, saw the others stirring, and said, "What is it?"

It grew louder, and they all stiffened. They'd heard it too many times. Singing, deep and low and sad in the twilight, traveling ahead of many shackled feet.

The coffles were a too-familiar sight. Over the years, Peach and her friends had come to recognize some of the guards and slave traders. The women made it a point to be polite to the men. Dignified and ladylike but never cordial. And praying no runaways would arrive at the same time.

Resignedly, Peach rose from her seat as the procession emerged from behind the trees. If the guards and traders weren't familiar, she'd direct them to the stopping place in the field next to the trading post, where there was a spring and circles of stones where captives had built campfires over the years. She reminded herself that showing deference, calmly selling the slave traders and guards what they needed, was the only thing she could do in the circumstances. The procession passed close enough to see the dark, drooping, tired figures, close enough to see the dust that they tried to swipe from their faces. The slaves averted their eyes. The women on the porch wondered if any among them had heard this was a place that offered shelter and sustenance and maps to runaways, and they continued their sewing with fixed expressions. *Remember us, remember how to find us, when you go on tomorrow,* they said in their hearts. *Perhaps you will find us again.*

The guards on horseback circled back and forth to herd them past the porch, toward the field. One of the guards dismounted and headed into the trading post, and Peach got up to serve him. She wanted to cry to the slaves, *Forgive us. Forgive us for letting the guards take you past us into the field to make your fires, forgive us for selling the food you'll eat. Forgive us our courtesy to those who drive you.*

At the back of the coffle came two slaves chained at the ankle, half carrying a third.

"Good evening to you, ladies," said the leading guard, riding toward the porch. He took off his hat. "Miss Magdalena, Miss Stefania, Miss Molly. I apologize for disturbing you after supper like this." The three women acknowledged the apology with a slight inclination of the head and a forced smile.

"They say there's a doctor in Grafton. Where would I find him?"

"I fear there's no doctor here now, sir. My husband died three years ago," said Magdalena.

"Pray tell us the nature of the emergency," said Stefania graciously, putting down her sewing, "and perhaps we can help."

"One of the slaves can hardly walk. He ran away from his master over twenty years ago. Fool that he is, he came back last month, trying to entice other slaves away, promising he'd lead them north to Philadelphia. The owner was obliged to administer punishment, to discourage the other slaves from such a course of action. The slave should have been hung, but his owner was content with merely cutting the man's tendon. The owner felt especially provoked, both by his going and then by his return to compound the offense and lead others away. It was unsurprising he was overzealous in his chastisement.

"Niggers are fond of inventing excuses, you know how lazy they can be, but his leg's swole up and it's slowing us down. He can't walk no matter how I help him along with the whip. I've even had to loosen the leg iron, which I dislike doing."

"How trying for you, sir, to have a fellow ill and inconveniencing you with the consequences of his own misdeeds," said Stefania evenly. "Peach Hanover"—Stefania knew better than to call Peach "Mrs." to the man—"has bandages and some excellent salve," she said, rising. Like Peach, she had to be civil. "Molly, Peach is busy, do you remember where she keeps . . ."

But Little Molly was looking toward the field, her mouth open, her eyes wide, her face a mask of horror. "Come, dear, help me find it," said Stefania briskly, moving to block the guard's view of her friend, pulling her out of her chair and propelling her into the trading-post storeroom, out of earshot of the guard buying salt pork from Peach.

"What's the matter?" Stefania hissed. "Your expression's going to give us away! You mustn't look at them like that! They mustn't suspect we sympathize with the slaves or feel sorry for a lame slave, or they'll think we're abolitionists. It won't help anyone if you let your feelings show!"

"The . . . the injured man . . ." Little Molly was shaking. She took off her spectacles to wipe away her tears. "I saw his face. Oh, Stefania! It's Moses! He looks older, his hair's white, but it's him. They caught him! What can we do? Can't we offer to buy him, relieve them of the trouble?"

Moses! Stefania thought, then shook her head. "No, I don't think we should."

"Stefania! How cruel! Surely we could do it as an act of Christian charity, one of us could say we need a gardener."

Stefania shook her head. "Molly, just think! There'd be something suspicious about old ladies buying a troublesome runaway slave, even charitable old ladies. And you know Moses wouldn't be here long, crippled or not. And since we've seen these same guards many times, next time they'd be bound to check that Moses was still here and not causing us trouble. And they'd find out he was gone. Sheriff Tyree could never prove we've helped runaways, but according to Jericho, the authorities still suspect runaways pass through Grafton. Now help me find the salve and bandages. And dry your eyes, Molly!" she added fiercely. "We mustn't appear to know him."

"I'm going to the cabin," said Little Molly abruptly. "Tell Peach to stay here tonight."

Lying in bed in her old room at the trading post, kept awake by the mournful singing from the field, Peach heard a splash by the jetty toward morning. *A bullfrog*, she thought.

The next morning the guards were angry, shouting and cursing, cracking whips as the slaves began to stir. One guard stormed into the trading post demanding to know if Peach had heard anything in the night or seen who helped the injured slave escape. He'd somehow slipped his leg from the manacles loosened to accommodate the swelling. The manacles were greasy with salve.

And Moses was gone.

At the Whites' old cabin, Little Molly rinsed Moses's teacup as day broke. She'd lit the candle she'd taken from Peach and sat by the window with her book. The wooden shutter was pulled up on its rope, and she'd been visible in the candlelight to anyone in the field. She'd sat, listening to the cicadas and the singing until the candle burned down and the room went dark. She'd continued to sit until there was a faint scratch at the door.

When she opened it, Moses was there. He limped in quickly, favoring his good leg, and they'd embraced and held each other tight. She whispered urgently he had to go. He shook his head.

"Please! Go!"

"No. I spent years talking to you in my mind, like we used to lie and talk in your room that time you hid me," he said. "Wishing we were there again. Wishing I'd appreciated it. I need to hear your voice again, before I go. You married now?"

"No, I'm not married! Peach lives here alone. And I told her to stay away tonight." Little Molly sat him down and cut ham and bread and butter. "How did you get loose?" She put a full plate in front of him.

"That good salve," he said, grinning. "Got bear grease in it. Slick up anything."

He fell on the food. Little Molly made him as comfortable as she could. She stood behind him as he ate and massaged his shoulders. "I must tell you something. We have a son."

"*What?*" He turned to stare at her in disbelief.

"A fine young man. Stefania helped me—we went north, and he was born in New York. Saratoga Springs. Stefania brought him back and explained he was an orphan baby she'd adopted."

"How did she manage that? Didn't folks ask questions?"

"He can pass," said Little Molly, kneading his neck. "He passes so well that he's fixed it to read law with a judge in Kingsport."

"We got a boy! A lawyer," said Moses, shaking his head. "Our son." His hand swiped across his eyes, and he was quiet. "An' he passes."

"I know," she replied. "But he's like you, Moses, in his sharp mind, in his good heart. That's what matters."

"You gon' tell him?"

"I . . . I don't know yet."

"Be light soon. I have to go," he said. "While I can." She threw her arms around his neck from behind and laid her head against his. He put his hand over hers. "I have to go," he said, as if he was telling himself. They were silent for a moment.

"I know. Be careful, Moses."

He turned and stroked her face. "A boy! Thank you," he said, and was gone.

The next morning the guards raged, and a party set out to hunt for the fugitive. Little Molly hitched up her horse and refused to stay for breakfast. "New teachers are coming," she told Peach. "One is the younger sister of poor Adelina Vann, and I want to be there to welcome her. I think her name is Hezziah."

She drove away and didn't allow herself to cry until she was well down in the valley. If they caught Moses, she couldn't bear to be there to see what they'd do to him.

CHAPTER 30

SLIPPING CREEK MISSION SCHOOL

GRAFTON

Hezziah Maury to her parents, June 1840

Dearest Ma, Pa, and Sisters,

I am pleased my first letter contains the news you are anxious for, of the improvement in Sister Adelina's condition after her first happy expectation of a certain event was so cruelly dashed soon after Major Caradoc brought her home. Thankfully, I can report she is expecting again. Our journey south was uneventful— we were not the least savaged by beasts or Indians, as our neighbors assured us was often the case. With the help of Miss Molly Drumheller, who is in charge of the female teachers at the mission school, I'm finally beginning to take the measure of this place and its inhabitants, to know who the principal families are who have supported the mission and the great work the mission did in civilizing the Indians and turning them to Jesus. This has helped me understand how the events surrounding the removal of so many of her Indian pupils and their parents by the army three years ago were such a shock and the destruction of Adelina's health and comfort for a time. As you know, she was devoted to the Cherokee children, who were the focus of the mission, and she labored tirelessly to bring them to the light of Jesus.

She struggled to reconcile herself, but it was, by her account, a terrible thing when the army came and built a stockade and forced our Cherokee and mixed-blood pupils and their families onto boats that bore them away to be resettled in the west. The shock, as you know, precipitated the great crisis, both of body and of her faith. She was unable to grasp how a just God could have permitted it to happen when the good work of the mission was proving successful.

For a long time afterward, she suffered from low spirits, and though her husband, Major Caradoc Vann, is an estimable man and devoted to her, the early days of their marriage were overshadowed by a dark cloud in her mind.

Major Vann has also been deeply affected by the removal of the Indians, though as a man he shows emotion less. But he is part Cherokee himself, so it is natural for him to regret the forced departure of so many of his connections, especially his own sister, Rachel, and his niece, Rachel's daughter, Nancy, married to another Cherokee, Jesse Bonney. Nancy Bonney was expecting a baby and died, they say, from the rough treatment by the soldier. Some even say it was at the hands of Zebulon Drumheller, who led them to the Bonneys' hiding place. That loathsome man (forgive me, but he is loathsome) has now acquired from the government a title to a great part of the land owned here by the Bonneys and other Cherokee families. And at a very favorable price, they say.

Miss Drumheller told me Adelina was particularly affected by the fate of her favorite pupil, little Dora Bonney, the major's relation, possibly a great-niece, although it is hard to tell the relationships between Cherokee families, and thus Adelina's relation by marriage. The child had a fanciful Indian name, Dancing Rabbit. She was lost in the melee that ensued when her family, the last of those doomed to transportation, were dragged on board the departing boat. They said the child must have fallen or been knocked into the river and drowned. The river here appears calm, but there are undercurrents that they say are strong enough to sweep a man away. The thought of the child drowning was horrible to Miss Drumheller, who is nothing like her uncle Zebulon, but it preyed on Adelina's mind.

Only a few mixed bloods—that is, those with both Cherokee and white and even Negro blood—were suffered to remain on their homesteads. It is thought that this was due to their very long connection with Grafton. Others say it was because money changed hands and bought a reprieve, and indeed, if you knew Zebulon Drumheller, you would find this credible. It was he and a band of newer settlers who are convinced they'll find gold here as settlers discovered gold on Indian lands in Georgia. They say Zebulon had used the money that bought the reprieves to buy up the Indians' abandoned homesteads. This injustice too has troubled Adelina profoundly, and it does seem very wicked. So much evil we are powerless to prevent!

One of these suffered to remain for what I daresay was the former reason was Mariah Stuart White, along with her Cherokee husband, Joseph. Joseph White was one of the earliest pupils at the mission school, along with Major Vann. The two have been friends from boyhood.

Though most of the White family were obliged to go, including the aged grandparents Fawn and White Owl at the last moment, there was a concession from the government in the case of Mariah and Joseph only. Mrs. White is a granddaughter of the Marshalls, one of the old leading families of Grafton. The Marshall family seat at Wildwood is a large and very handsome log cabin of white oak, set on an eminence halfway up Frog Mountain, with a fine porch and smaller out-buildings dotted neatly around the property, all in the same style.

They say at the school that the Marshalls were connected to an English lord on one side, French aris-tocracy on the other. Though I have often heard men boast that one person is as good as another in *this* country, I cannot help observing that the Marshalls and all connected with them are spoken of with what *sounds* very much like deference.

The Wildwood ladies have been most kind to Adelina in her illness. Miss Magdalena Marshall

Walker is a widow, who presides over the household. Her niece Miss Martha Washington Marshall is a spinster lady in her forties, and Rosa Marshall is married to Miss Martha's brother Jericho. They sent broth and arrowroot jelly when Adelina felt too low to eat.

Jericho Marshall manages the estate when not occupied by his magistrate's duties. Rosa and Jericho's older boys are married and living in Richmond, but their youngest boy, Charles, is still at home. He attended the mission school only briefly, as the Marshalls hired a tutor to live with them and prepare Charles to enter the College of New Jersey at Princeton.

Miss Magdalena is very sweet and a little melancholy, I fancy. Miss Martha is rather terrifying and stern, and her manners are imposing. Miss Rosa has a softer way about her. Her mother, Mrs. Charbonneau Drumheller, who has been widowed twice, poor lady, is wealthy and a generous benefactor of the mission school. Over the years she has paid for many poor children to attend. People say Miss Rosa is as handsome as her mother was, and if you met her, you would think Miss Rosa is a young matron. I was surprised to learn that she expects to be a grandmother soon. It seems the custom for girls to marry quite young in this region.

I trust that in time Adelina will present a similar countenance. Her nervous debilitation is improving, she is now strong enough to sit by the window and sew for the baby—I encourage this as much as I can, as much because the infant needs to be dressed when it comes as for the soothing effect preparing for this second baby seems to have on her mind. We pray together every evening now.

Her home, like most of the homes here, is a large cabin near the trading post. It began its existence as a very small cabin—it is still possible to mark the original outline—but has been expanded over the years, with rooms laid out round a large and very convenient kitchen with a great stone fireplace, and a bread oven built into the side. Surrounding it is a pretty and well-laid-out garden of flowers and herbs all growing together, the work of another of the first settlers, Caitlin Vann, who was the major's grandmother. This residence was obligingly yielded to Adelina and Caradoc by Miss Peach Vann and her late husband, who moved to a smaller cabin nearby. But Miss Peach remains the mainstay of the trading post and prefers to spend her days there, where she gets news and visits and insists on keeping stock according to her particular system.

On fine days Adelina takes her sewing to sit on the porch. You will wonder, dearest Ma, how a daughter of yours can "sit" when she should be about her housekeeping, but in her present condition of both mind and body, the major will not allow her to stir more than absolutely necessary, to prevent a second misfortune. He has insisted on hiring one of the young settler girls to keep house.

I am of less assistance to Adelina at home than I intended to be when I left you. On my arrival I discovered that instead of being a sort of helper and willing pair of hands at the school, Miss Drumheller believed I had come to take Adelina's place as a teacher for the youngest class. Miss Drumheller has quite an air of authority and is not to be refused, but my heart misgave me at the time.

How well-founded my apprehension was. I have not Adelina's gift. At nineteen, I lay no claim to experience with large numbers of children, and I confess I am less fit than I thought to be a teacher! Dear Mother, you were right. It is wearying. I never imagined a class of the youngest children would be such a difficult thing to manage, but they bob up and down and chatter and fight when it is necessary for me to attend to hear one's reading or to correct another's slate of sums.

A particularly naughty boy, five-year-old Tom Stuart, brought a field mouse into the class today—it was let loose and it scampered round and round the classroom to smothered laughter until it scuttled across my boots. I detest mice, and I screamed. The children shrieked with glee, and before I knew it, the entire class was out of their seats, scampering after the mouse. Tom is a little imp, always bouncing up from his bench, but he is also very sweet when not up to mischief, and he is, I think, the cleverest child in the class, already able to read and figure. So disagreeable as the experience was, I was loath to name the culprit to the principal, Endurance Merriman.

Endurance is the son of the original principal, and while his father was alive, he was a circuit preacher traveling far and wide in these mountains to spread the Gospel. That fact ought to inspire respect and esteem, but he is a dour individual and too inclined to thrash the children when they misbehave. He is unmarried too, a fact which would not surprise you in the slightest if you were to meet him.

I finally thought to open the classroom door and allow the mouse to escape to its fate, which is doubtless to be eaten by the school cat, and continued with the lesson.

Such accounts of what happens at school make dear Adelina laugh now, though rather wistfully, I think. She loved teaching.

For the time being, I am keeping order in the class with the promise of a holiday outing when the school year ends, provided they are very good and quiet, make some progress with their lessons, and there are no repeats of today's incident. I can only take the younger children in my class. Their older brothers are needed to help get in the harvest, and the older sisters assist their mothers and aunts with the endless cooking and baking for the harvesters, as well as the preserving and drying of peaches and wild plums and cherries that all come ripe at the same time and must not be wasted. But the smaller ones are in the way this time of year, and the mothers are grateful to see them occupied elsewhere.

I am striving to appear strict and stern now that the treat will seem less certain, and the combination of an outing to be earned by good behavior and a stern face has had a beneficial effect. I do not know how long it will last.

There. I must pause now. I will continue my account until there is happy news of the baby. But as that will not be for some months yet, you may expect a good thick letter packet when it is finally possible to send this north by a trusty messenger.

 Your loving daughter,
 Hezziah Maury

July 1840

Dearest Ma, Pa, and Sisters,
As the school year has ended, I must describe to you the two engagements that closed it very pleasantly.

 The first was the school's graduation ceremony. This year we had ten girls and eleven boys, who stood up at the front of the school, the numbers being less than in previous years, as the Cherokee families have mostly been driven away. But it was as fine a ceremony as can be contrived here.

 The building where we take our meals had been filled with fragrant wintergreen branches and the oddly named rattlesnake orchids, which are beautiful little white flowers on a plant the Indians used to treat snakebite, and the last of the mountain laurel, which is just coming to the end of its blooming season.

 The teachers did up each other's hair, and in honor of the occasion, I wore my flowered muslin gown, matching hair ribbons, and my locket from Grandma. Miss Drumheller looked very well in a black silk gown with her white hair piled high. Reverend Merriman, to my surprise, had gone to the trouble of writing out a certificate for each of the graduates, testifying to their completion of the course of study, and a Bible verse chosen for each student. These verses were all of a kind to admonish the students against sin, as if he expects they will do nothing else when he can no longer watch them. His penmanship is very well done, and this is a much nicer act on his part than I would have thought him capable of. I must strive to feel more charitable toward him.

There were prayers and singing. My class had practiced an old song from England to be sung in rounds. They were divided into three groups, and at first there'd been great difficulty in persuading the little ones to sing only when their group's turn came, and not all together. But on the evening, they performed it commendably. And wonder of wonders, Reverend Merriman smiled!

The singing was followed by addresses from the two ministers and then an even longer one from our reverend principal, together with much exhorting and congratulating of the young people. Finally, almost fainting with hunger, we were allowed to sit down to a dinner to which all the graduates' families had contributed. The most delicious part of it was a whole wild pig slowly roasted over a bed of coals for nearly two days, attended to by the male teachers, who doused it throughout with apple cider.

But there was a great quantity of other things—great dishes of vegetables, berry puddings, sweet potato puddings, Indian puddings, and pies. We finished the evening with a little concert, though you would have judged it very rustic. There were three fiddles, a banjar, and another stringed instrument called a dulcimer, played by some of the younger men. The musicians played in an increasingly lively way, and the young people were hoping for a dance—their toes were tapping—but Reverend Merriman ended proceedings before that could happen.

Rustic or not, music lightens the heart and provided a most satisfactory end to the day. Because it was dark, Reverend Merriman insisted on saddling his horse and seeing me home to Adelina's when all was finished.

Unnecessary, as there is not the least danger. I have a very pleasant ride every day from the trading post to Slipping Creek, as Major Vann is able to spare me a horse for this purpose. I even wondered about the propriety of riding home in the company of a man with no chaperone, but I have observed propriety takes second place to necessity and convenience here, so I hope you will not say I was wrong to accept his offer. Adelina was asleep when I returned.

Now for the second thing. The other female teachers and I were invited to drink tea at Wildwood last Saturday evening! Adelina was included in the invitation but, alas, felt her condition made it impossible to accept.

We understood such a thing had never happened before, and the other teachers came early to the trading post so we could dress together. First we bathed in a secluded spot in the river—in our petticoats, of course—then put up each other's hair, sharing hair ribbons, polished our boots, and freshened our collars and cuffs.

We walked up to Wildwood through the orchard, arriving at the appointed hour of five o'clock. Down by the river on summer days, the air is very heavy and muggy, but up at Wildwood the air feels much fresher and there is a breeze.

It was delightful. Miss Martha and Miss Rosa seemed very pleased to see us and had prepared a grand feast—cold chicken, beaten biscuits with ham, which are a great favorite and appear at every gathering, a very delicious salt-rising bread, cherry tarts, a great variety of cider cakes, almond sweethearts, together with a delicious sassafras cream. Finally after we were finished eating, Miss Martha pressed us to try her special blackberry cordial she puts up every summer. Her rheumatism troubles her considerably at times, and she swears her blackberry wine relieves it.

I praised it and regretted there had been no leisure to do any blackberry picking or wine making last year, when Adelina was so indisposed and needed my constant attention, but I was planning a day's holiday with a berry-picking expedition for my class of little ones, and if Miss Martha would kindly give me her cordial recipe, I could put up some for Adelina and Major Vann.

Miss Rosa asked where we were going and how we intended to pass the day. I told her we would go up to the interesting rock they call the Old Man of the Mountain, which I have not yet visited. They say the view of the mountains is delightful from that spot. We are to have a fine holiday from lessons and chores, with lunch and singing and games and prizes for the best students.

Miss Martha exclaimed that I'd never manage so many children, a picnic, and many buckets of berries unless there was some means of transporting the food and the baskets and probably some of the children. She offered the use of their pony trap for the day, and I accepted gratefully, on the condition that we bring them several buckets of berries.

Berries grow thick on the mountains, but they ripened inconveniently early this year, when most people in Grafton are too engaged with the harvest to have an afternoon's leisure for going up Frog Mountain or Little Frog Mountain on picking parties. There is even a sort of festival they call the Blackberry Picnic, a custom similar to our Harvest Home, which was begun by the original settlers. Now it has become an important occasion, a very grand and festive picnic supper, which by tradition takes place in September, at the selfsame rock where I proposed to take the children.

As you know, berrying was always a favorite task when Adelina and I lived at home, and it would be a real trial to see an abundance of berries and be denied the satisfaction of filling my bucket. I am looking forward to the excursion with as much pleasure as any of the children.

There will be twenty in our party. How I wish Adelina were well enough to go too, but she prefers to keep to her cabin at the trading post. When she feels well enough, she helps Miss Peach there.

The trading post has expanded since the major took over from Bryn and Peach Vann, whose sons set up another post a hundred miles west on the river, and it is very busy with a constant flow of river traffic. The major has hired several women and boys from the settler families to help Miss Peach. The major has much other business to compel his attention, in respect of the land he owns, the mill, and his connections in Washington who are trying to influence Congress on the matter of compensation for the Indian lands seized.

I must close, dearest Ma and Pa and Sisters. Tomorrow is the day of the great picnic. All is prepared—a plentiful lunch contributed by the mothers and grandmothers is waiting in baskets, quilts to sit on, and buckets galore—and the Marshalls' hired man is to drive the pony trap down early in the morning.

How I miss you all! But a sense of being called here to labor for the Lord is growing in me. Adelina and I pray together about it often. There is talk of a Sunday school for the children at the Methodist church when a new wing is added, and Reverend Merriman has asked if we would be willing to teach in it. Of course we agreed. So as you see, I am busy and content. If only I could be sure no more mice were to be set loose in my classroom.

In the next installment of this missive, I shall give you a full account of our happy day.

Your loving and dutiful daughter,

Hezziah Maury

CHAPTER 31

THE RICHMOND DAILY INTELLIGENCER

December 1841

CHOICE READING

We hasten to lay before our readers the facts of a curious and tragic event of which we have been recently apprised. It occurred two summers ago in the former Cherokee territory in the Bowjay Valley from which the Indians were removed four years ago at the instigation of the government after the Treaty of New Echota was signed by the Cherokee delegate, agreeing to relinquish their tribal territory for a fine and vast grant of land in the west, a treaty generally acknowledged to be much to the advantage of the Indians.

It is accepted that the policy of removing the Cherokee from contact with whites of the states in which they resided was a wise expedient. The Treaty of New Echota, under which the Cherokee accepted removal in exchange for resettlement on new lands in the west, was agreed between Congress and Cherokee representatives. It must be admitted that many of the Cherokee Nation regard the aforesaid treaty as fraudulently signed by a few interested parties who did not represent the views of their people in accordance with custom and tribal law. They claimed the lack of process rendered the treaty invalid.

This claim was adjudged meritless, and the necessary removals according to law took place, with those unwilling to go being obliged to do so with the assistance of the army. Yet those in military authority used their best endeavors to carry out their duties to enforce the removal with justice and humanity. Nowhere was this truer than in the town of Grafton on the Bowjay River, where boats were provided for the convenience and comfort of the Cherokee, to carry them part of the way on their journey to new lands provided for them in the west.

Nevertheless, there were distressing and affecting scenes, inevitable at all times of parting, as Cherokee were taken away from fields they were in the act of planting or mothers in the midst of performing their daily household chores. Many were the hearth fires extinguished, many the loaf of bread left to burn in the bread oven, while the milk was left to sour in the churn.

Whites, who numbered Cherokee among their friends, exchanged sorrowful farewells. And our informant has not sought to conceal that there were three sad occurrences on that day, which nevertheless cannot be laid at the door of the army or the men of Grafton, who performed no more than their civic duty in assisting the military in seeing that all were on board.

Despite the care that was exercised, a young Cherokee girl, Dora by her baptized Christian name, a pupil of great promise at the Slipping Creek Mission School, was lost and believed drowned. Her mother was in such a condition herself as to be unable to sustain the shock and tragically succumbed to death from grief at the loss of her daughter. The poor Indian family suffered a further affliction when the aged grandmother yielded also to death, as much from shock as from her greatly advanced years, which render death mournful though not unexpected.

Every assistance that could be given was rendered to the family by those in authority, but they could not prevail. Distress was the inevitable result.

And among those affected by the tragedy—or tragedies, we should say—was Dora's young teacher at the mission school, Miss Adelina Maury, daughter of worthy and devout parents, who had resigned the comforts of her father's home in Maryland in obedience to the precepts of our Savior to "go ye therefore and teach all nations" in a spirit of true Christian servitude. She, in her anxious care for the spiritual well-being of her little Cherokee charges, was so distressed by their leaving that she, calling and calling their names in despairing and weeping tones, especially that of little Dora, was finally rendered temporarily insensible and fell prostrate upon the jetty even as she waved her goodbyes to the departing riverboat.

That the emotions of the day were felt keenly cannot be denied. But though the Cherokee were successfully removed, they left behind many of their beliefs and superstitions, which, *notwithstanding the strength of Christian belief among the inhabitants of Grafton, have persisted.*

Nowhere is this superstitious legacy stronger than on Frog Mountain, where there are intimidating stories of a mythical creature the Cherokee called a "shape-shifter," part eagle and part human, which long hunters claim to have seen or felt over the years. This mythical apparition may be a useful story to frighten the children of the town into good behavior, but the more rational of the inhabitants ascribe sightings of it to the strong drink produced locally in the form of whiskey and hard cider, to which the rough long hunters are inclined.

There arose a story, born of forlorn hope, that little Dora had not drowned, as her corporal body was never recovered for a Christian burial. Since the Cherokee departures, there are those who claim to have seen a little Indian girl on Frog Mountain. One of these was Dora's former white schoolmate, one of the Marshall children, who claims to have seen her little friend running on the mountain slope, wearing Indian doeskin clothing instead of her school dress. She ran after her friend, calling out, "Dora, Dora, wait for me!" Her cry brought no answer. Then recalling Dora's Cherokee name, she called out, "Dancing Rabbit! Dancing Rabbit!" And Dora/Dancing Rabbit stopped, turned her gaze on her former friend, held out her hand, and called in coaxing tones, "Come with me to the Old Man of the Mountain, and we will fly away together."

The child halted in her tracks, suddenly alarmed. There was something strange in her friend's visage. "I don't want to fly," she cried. "Dora, come back!" Dora looked over her shoulder, gave a most awful laugh, and disappeared.

The Marshall child cannot of course be accused of a liking for strong drink, so her account cannot be ascribed to that cause, but children have lively imaginations and often conjure up fantastical stories for their own amusement. The Marshall child was roundly scolded.

Yet last summer, something startling occurred that may incline readers to view these stories in a more sinister and as yet unexplained light.

An entire class of young children from the mission school, in the care of their teacher, who had planned a day's outing with a picnic and berry picking as a treat, disappeared entirely while her back was turned, and no trace of them has yet been found.

The teacher, Miss Hezziah Maury, followed her elder sister to the mission school after the removal. By then Miss Adelina had become the wife of Major Caradoc Vann. Since married women are disqualified from teaching, Miss Hezziah, with the blessing of her parents, traveled south to take Miss Adelina's place at the mission school. Dedicating herself to the promulgation of the Lord's word in the wilderness, she did all in her power to supply the little ones in her care with assiduous instruction that had been given by the capable elder sister in the past.

It was with the kind intention of giving her young charges a treat, and their busy parents a respite during the labor of the harvest, that the younger Miss Maury conceived of her outing, with a picnic and games and prizes.

The day of the excursion dawned fair and fine, the children duly gathered at the trading post at the early appointed hour, and amid the happy chatter, mothers bade their small ones to be good, enjoy themselves, and bring home an abundance of berries so their mothers might put up their jams and cordials.

They were then relinquished to the care of Miss Maury, and a pony trap was loaded with baskets of comestibles, berry buckets, and the smaller children. Miss Maury led the pony, the children dancing round her, as the gay party set off on the path up Frog Mountain, where the little merrymakers and their teacher were bound for a picturesque rock known as the Old Man of the Mountain.

Alas, what a difference a few hours were to make.

The children were the youngest in the school, all between the ages of four and eight, from most of the families in the valley.

Our informant had the next part of the story as it was told by Miss Maury to the sheriff. However, the reader will readily surmise that Miss Maury's account of what happened will have been rendered almost incomprehensible by her distress at being obliged to give it.

When they reached the broad and sloping clearing around the Old Man, where the bursting ripeness and particular sweetness of the berries that grow there have made it a favorite location for similar berry picnics for many years, the teacher distributed pails and baskets. Although the children were familiar with the spot, and where the blackberry bushes grew thickest around it, Miss Maury sternly admonished them not to wander off too far, to stay within hailing distance, and to keep her in sight at all times. Lest the children forget, she impressed upon them that any who failed to obey her would have the dreadful prospect of no lunch.

She then released them to their picking while she got busy unharnessing the pony, building a small fire, filling her teakettle from the spring and a pail with a dipper ready for the children. Then she set about unpacking the baskets of lunch.

When all was ready and the picnic spread out on a quilt brought for the purpose, Miss Maury looked up and to her amazement couldn't see a single child. She couldn't hear them either, though twenty children make a lot of noise, and some of these children, like the young scholar Tom Stuart, rarely ceased their noise. And she was certain the children had been making a great deal of noise when they set about their picking. But it was strangely quiet, and afterward she was unable to recall when she had ceased to hear the children.

With a feeling of exasperation at being disobeyed at first uppermost, Miss Maury called and called their names, but the only thing she heard was cicadas singing in the trees. In the expectation it was a prank, Miss Maury searched the bushes where she'd seen them picking, but they weren't there. She went deep into the bushes around the clearing, walking in until she could scarcely see it, then returning to search another section, but there was no sign of the children, no answering call, no sign of the berry buckets.

She looked at the slope under the Old Man to see if any had fallen off. Indeed, it was her hope that this was the explanation, because directly under the rock a thick stand of pine trees spread their boughs, and any child who tumbled off the Old Man would be caught safely. Indeed, jumping off the Old Man into the trees, though strictly forbidden by parents, was nevertheless frequently indulged in by the older boys, who would dare each other to jump when their parents weren't looking. None of the jumpers had ever come to harm save for scratches from the branches or a thrashing from their parents.

But there were no children in the branches or beneath the trees.

The poor teacher called and called until she was hoarse, but not a single young voice did she hear in reply. Exasperation was replaced by fear and a conviction some accident had befallen them, though she was at a loss to imagine what sort of accident could account for the disappearance of all. If one had fallen or been bitten by a snake, the others would have rushed to her immediately. There had been no cries for help.

It was with a growing sense of dread she harnessed up the trap and whipped the pony all the way down the trail, hastening back to Grafton to see if the children had gone back down the trail and home, though she could not conceive of a reason they should do so, especially as they were all looking forward to their lunch and games. Why they would do such a thing was beyond her.

But they hadn't gone home. The alarm was sounded by ringing a bell that hangs on the trading-post porch, a summons in times of emergency such as when the river floods or, formerly, to warn of an Indian attack. As word of the children's disappearance spread, families abandoned the harvest and set out to search the woods around the Old Man. The men armed themselves, and Jericho Marshall fetched his hunting dogs from their kennel at Wildwood. The mountain rang with mothers' pitiful cries of "Tom, Ella, Lizzie, Hetty" and fathers' threats of a whipping if the children didn't step forth at once.

But there were no answering shouts of "Here, Mother!"

They searched and called until sunset, and continued into the night with lanterns and pine torches. A number of the men camped that night by the Old Man, lighting a bonfire that could be seen from a distance, and calling and calling the children's names into the forest through the night until they were hoarse.

The dogs could pick up no scent to follow, just whined and chased each other.

The search continued for days, but never was any trace of the children found. No bodies, not so much as a hair ribbon or a shoe button or even a berry basket. Twenty children vanished, gone without a trace.

Out of desperation some parents pointed the finger of blame at Miss Maury, but the principal of the school, Reverend Endurance Merriman, hastened to her defense. He vouched for Miss Maury being an exemplary and responsible young female who had come south in the service of the Lord, and he was insistent that she had been devoted to the children in her care and had asked his permission and that of the parents to give the children their treat.

Despite the minister's warm commendation of her excellent character, Miss Maury was herself so much affected by the terrible, tragic, and inexplicable loss of the children that for a time it was feared her reason would give way entirely under an overwhelming sense of sorrow and guilt.

Our informant has lately added a curious twist to this tragic account.

It must be remembered that the Bowjay Valley was formerly Cherokee land; Cherokee beliefs and superstitions still cling like mist to the mountains. A theory had been advanced, though your correspondent cannot accurately pinpoint the source, that eagles, a sacred bird of the Indians, took the children, and this explains why no trace of them was ever found.

Application of common sense disproves this at once. Of course an eagle couldn't fly away with a child, let alone twenty of them. One possible explanation that presented itself was that the children found a cave, were unable to resist exploration, and went in too far to find their way out or met with some accident deep inside.

The people of Grafton, however, have been quick to dismiss this possibility, saying there weren't any caves near the Old Man of the Mountain, except an old bear cave high on the slope above the clearing. The children wouldn't have been likely to abandon their berry picking or venture so far up a steep slope, especially as from an early age they've been sternly warned against exploring caves if they found any, because of the dangers of getting lost, deep holes, and underground pools. But even if one or two naughty ones had done it anyway, what about all the others?

Men roped themselves together and looked in the bear cave, but found no trace of the children.

In the following months as it grew cold, mothers mournfully ascended the mountain to spend lonely hours in the last place their children had been. Some claimed to have heard a child's voice up there, and some claimed laughter, though all, when questioned, said they could not tell from where the sound came—they hastened to look behind bushes or trees or rocks, only to hear it coming from elsewhere.

While these mysterious accounts have been attributed to the mothers' inconsolable grief, they have fanned the superstitions about Frog Mountain. It's said the clearing around the Old Man of the Mountain is haunted. And others claim to have caught fleeting glimpses of a small Indian girl running.

The mission school where the lost children were the youngest pupils never reopened after the tragedy. Since then the two ministers of Grafton and Reverend Merriman, the former principal, have struggled to reassert the triumph of Christian faith over Indian superstition, such as the older legend of the eagle-man shape-shifter and now the ghost of the Indian child.

The three clergymen decided on holding funerals for the children in the hopes it would put an end to speculation about haunts and apparitions. Funerals were held, but they had nothing to bury, and the little graves in the cemetery lie empty as the broken hearts of the mothers.

The young teacher, we understand, has led a quiet life of retirement at the home of her elder sister since the distressing event.

CHAPTER 32

HEZZIAH

April 1842

Adelina shifted the fretting baby on her hip and said, "Reverend Merriman's here again, Hezzie. You must come and speak to him a little while I feed the baby. I felt I must ask if he'd stay to supper, poor man. He has no one to do for him in his father's old cabin. You can start the supper while you talk."

"Adelina, I wish he'd stop coming. He reminds me of a black crow. A very persistent black crow." By the window, Hezziah stitched away resolutely on some mending. On the window ledge lay a creased newspaper.

"He means well, Hezzie, he means to be kind. He says the newspapers are dreadful and we mustn't mind. That you mustn't mind."

"But I do mind, Adelina. How can I not? The poor children! Their families! The horror of it never goes away. And now to think the story we've just seen has been circulating for months, read by many, before we even knew it had been written. I can think of nothing else! And to think our parents will see it! I haven't dared write to Ma and Pa since . . . since . . . I wish I'd disappeared with the children, Addy! At least then I'd know what happened."

"But since you didn't, God must have another purpose for you. Accept his will and carry on. I did!" Adelina had a note of exasperation in her voice. "Hezzie, you came to help me in my hour of need and were my rock when I felt very low. Now I have Joshua and Caradoc, and looking after them has fortified my heart and my spirit—prepared again to do the Lord's work however he intends me to do it. Reverend Merriman means to support you under this trial in the same way, if only you could see it, to encourage fortitude on your part. He understands you were not to be blamed for the tragedy and has defended you unfailingly."

"But who else is to blame, Adelina? I'm not going to help him restart the school, and that's final," she said, deliberately misunderstanding her sister.

"I think, Hezzie, he has a different purpose today."

"What purpose? The mission school was his purpose, his life work. I'm to blame for that loss as well. No parent in the valley would leave a child in my care for a moment. People look at me as if I were a murderess. So I do not see there is anything to discuss. Leave me to the mending, Adelina, I cannot do any harm while occupied with that, sitting here alone."

"According to Caradoc, Zebulon Drumheller and Lafayette Charbonneau propose a new enterprise on Little Frog Mountain that requires building a turnpike, and Will Pine's sons have been engaged to get it built. That's put Reverend Merriman in mind of a scheme of his own now the school is no longer in use. Whatever he wants to do also requires a turnpike. And that's his purpose in calling today. He believes you can help."

"Help? Turnpikes! What have I to do with *turnpikes?*" Still it was a relief to hear that turnpikes were the subject of his visit. Lately she had begun to suspect that Reverend Merriman's frequent calling meant she was the object of . . . of something she'd prefer not to think of but that Adelina seemed to be urging upon her without actually saying so.

"For goodness' sake, ask him, Hezzie!"

The baby began to howl. "Hush, Joshua, Mama's going to feed you." Adelina jiggled the baby. "Go on!" she urged. "He's waiting in the kitchen. I told him you'd come. And there's a basket of ramps that need trimming," she said over her shoulder before disappearing upstairs with the baby.

There was a small looking glass in the room Hezziah occupied. She observed her reflection for a minute. She looked gaunt. She frowned. The four redheaded, blue-eyed Maury girls had always been thought pretty. Then she sighed and repinned her hair because her wayward curls always escaped the bun at her neck, like Adelina's.

Reverend Merriman's visits were another trial to be borne meekly, she thought. She was trying to bear everything, in the hopes of finding forgiveness one day. She disliked seeing people; it was painful the way they looked at her, as if she were a murderess . . . but if she suffered, she must bear it and not complain at God's chastisement. She smoothed her collar and cuffs and settled her skirts, noticing how her bodice and the waist of her dress were too big for her now. She'd have to take them in.

At least Adelina was pregnant again. That was fortunate, she thought, because that gave her the opportunity to be of use to her sister and brother-in-law, so she had a reason to stay. So she needn't go home. She dreaded going home to her parents and sisters above everything. So Adelina, needing her help, would stop hinting that if Hezziah would get married, everything would be better when she had children and a husband of her own.

She resisted the thought that Adelina had grown unfeeling. This was followed by a thought that marriage and motherhood had made Adelina bossy.

These uncharitable reflections were another thing God would need to forgive her for. Adelina was happy. It was only natural that she wanted Hezziah to be happy too.

She tried to submit her will to God's and went to the kitchen, where Endurance Merriman was hunched by the fire, his hat on his knees.

"Good evening, Reverend," she said briskly, taking the chair on the other side of the fire, setting to work on a basket of ramps.

"Miss Maury. A chilly evening for April. I hope I find you well?" Endurance sat up straight and pushed his spectacles up his nose.

"Well enough, I thank you. Adelina says you've brought us interesting news of enterprises and turnpikes."

Turnpikes! she thought. *Could there be anything more tedious?*

"Indeed!"

"Do tell me," said Hezziah, feigning interest, resigning to bear his discourse.

"Ah yes, the Lord works in mysterious ways. A scheme conceived by Zebulon Drumheller and the Pine boys gave me an idea for a scheme of my own. Perhaps *our* own."

She looked up, taken aback by the *our* and startled by the unlikely convergence of any scheme involving Reverend Merriman on one hand and grasping Zebulon Drumheller and the Pine brothers, equally quick to see their material advantage in anything, on the other.

"What?"

"I'll begin with Zebulon. I see from your expression you expect I'm part of his scheme, but that's not the case. Or not exactly. But many elements may come together in ways we do not anticipate for the glory of the Lord, and we—"

"For heaven's sake, just tell me!" Hezziah snapped, ripping outer leaves from a ramp.

"Zebulon has his furnaces on the lower part of Little Frog Mountain, but higher up near the top, out of sight of the furnaces, he's just discovered a hot mineral spring. He's heard there's a good business in hot mineral springs. Saratoga Springs in New York and Berkeley Springs in Virginia are just two places where invalids go to take the waters, and in the process have contributed greatly to the finances of the towns.

"He proposes turning his mineral spring into a similar enterprise."

Hezziah raised her eyebrows and murmured, "Does he, indeed."

"His ideas are very grand. He's studied how these things are done elsewhere. He proposes a building where people can take the cure, where the waters can be drunk, and perhaps bathing pools, separate, of course, for male and female invalids, sufferers from rheumatism, from dyspepsia, from all the illnesses and suffering that hot mineral waters can soothe and alleviate.

"Along with that he wishes to build a boardinghouse—no, something grander, a sort of hotel, with verandas. The fresh mountain air he believes will be restoring and add to the beneficial effects of the water cure, particularly in the hot months, which are almost unendurable at the lower elevations, such as New Orleans or indeed anywhere along the river."

"But how would visitors ascend to this hotel unless they fly?"

Endurance smiled. "As you know, Zebulon's wife was Linney Pine before her marriage. And no sooner had she mentioned Zebulon's idea than they began to see a way to lay a road up the mountain, to be paid for by toll."

"I imagine she did. No one is more forward than Linney Drumheller to boast of her husband's business sense and how much richer it makes them," Hezziah said tartly.

The reverend tried to look disapproving. "Don't be uncharitable," he said without conviction. Hezziah looked up and thought being uncharitable felt satisfying.

"The Pine brothers heard what he was proposing and approached Zebulon to go into partnership in the scheme, to the extent that in return for investing in the building of the turnpike to the top of Little Frog, they will oversee the work, maintain it, and then levy and collect the tolls on it once it is in use. After some haggling, Zebulon and the brothers agreed upon it."

"But, Reverend Merriman, why are you taking an interest in a mineral spring and a hotel for invalids?"

"Because their scheme set me thinking. There's a good deal of land around the school that is part of the gift Venus Hanover made, and of course the school itself is no longer in use."

Hezziah flinched.

"And there's a sloping stretch of land behind the school, near the top, on the southern end of Frog Mountain between Slipping Creek and the Old Man of the Mountain that would be suitable for camp meetings. I looked at the deed from Venus Hanover, and the large parcel of land she donated includes it."

He removed his spectacles and gazed earnestly at Hezziah. "Since the closure of the school, I have striven not to be idle, I have prayed for guidance, how best to serve the Lord in a new way, to be a faithful servant. And God has answered me. In the past months I've corresponded with several ministers in the burned-over district of New York, a place that's seen a great burst, an intensification of Christian endeavor in the expectation the Rapture will come soon. There they are striving to lead the way, to purify mankind for what is to come, with revivals and prayer meetings, awakening sinners to the peril they're in, unless they repent! Spreading the great news!"

Hezziah couldn't resist and said sarcastically, "Great news of their peril, do you mean?"

His eyes were glowing with fervor. "No. I mean a message of hope, Miss Maury! In short, the millennium is coming, Miss Maury, and after that Christ will return to earth to usher in the time of peace and harmony and brotherhood. We don't know precisely when, but the call has gone out, we must awake from our slumber, awake the nations from theirs, and prepare. Revivals, Miss Maury, camp meetings, to make ready! A great awakening! 'Prepare ye the way of the Lord!' as the Bible bids us. And I came to see that was God's purpose for the school land."

"Reverend, of course I've read of the Christian awakening in that part of New York, but—"

"It gathers force, Miss Maury! It will spread! It is right that it should, and it is right that we play our part. I will dedicate the school land for the use of revivalists in the service of that great awakening. And I have spoken to the Pine brothers about building a turnpike to the top of Frog Mountain, on the same terms as they agreed with Zebulon, that they may take and keep the tolls when the revivals and camp meetings take hold there. They have agreed! Even Zebulon approves of my plan, because he thinks it will bring business to his hot spring when the revivals are done. I am not deceived as to his true self-interested motives, Miss Maury, but no matter. Among those who come to take the waters, we may gain souls for the Lord!"

His words rang with such passion that Hezziah was startled, even impressed. She'd never seen him like this.

"God on one mountain, mammon on the other," she ventured. But when she considered it, the plan made sense. It would certainly be advantageous for Adelina and Caradoc too—the trading post was doing very well and had expanded, but more business would be welcome, and she calculated, there was the mill, more flour to sell . . . salt . . . some of the homesteads would sell milk and eggs to the campground visitors, supply the hotel.

It was almost refreshing to contemplate the business aspects after months of grieving over the lost children.

She didn't draw back when the reverend leaned closer and took her hand. "Dear Miss Maury, I've felt unable to speak before. With no prospects to offer you, I felt unworthy. And I am more than twice your age, and I cannot expect you will love me. But if you will agree to be my wife, I'll do everything in my power to make you happy while we embark on this great work together. Universal peace and happiness! The ascendency of Christ! Say you will, Miss Maury, say you will!"

"I . . . I suppose . . ."

The next hour passed in a daze.

Reverend Merriman had shaken hands with Caradoc and asked his permission to marry his sister-in-law. Adelina was surprised but delighted and hugged her. Later that night in her room, wavering, Hezziah wondered why she'd whispered yes so quickly. It was as if someone else had spoken through her lips. Someone who, unlike Hezziah, wanted to marry Reverend Merriman. Adelina brushed her regrets aside and told Hezziah she must like the reverend better than she'd thought. During a sleepless night, Hezziah tried to convince herself that was the case. "What have I done?" she asked herself over and over.

By the following day, she was striving to keep alive the memory of her fleeting feeling for Endurance Merriman. She agreed to a wedding as soon as possible. Two weeks was settled upon. Adelina said she would write to their parents and sisters to give them the news. They would be delighted, she assured Hezziah.

To be able to face her parents again as a respectable minister's wife was more in favor of the marriage than anything, Hezziah thought when she wavered, which was constantly. She prayed for her wedding day to come soon. Then everything would be decided and secure and out of her hands.

As Endurance's wife, she would once again be on the path of righteousness. That ought to be enough.

CHAPTER 33

HEZZIAH AND ADELINA

September 1844

On a golden autumn afternoon, with the cicadas singing loud in the heat, Hezziah Merriman, with her baby daughter on her hip, and Adelina Vann, holding the hand of her elder son, Joshua, and her baby, Jonathan, Indian-style on her back, reached the foot of the newly completed turnpike. They waved to the Pine brother hoeing his vegetable patch by the toll cabin as they started up.

"No charge for human feet—just horses and mules and oxen," the Pine brother called gallantly.

"We're not going far, just up to the mission school," Adelina called back.

"Yes, ma'am. Pretty overgrown up there. Watch out for snakes." He touched the brim of his hat.

The turnpike was a steep switchback, and though the school hadn't been very high up the slope, by the time they reached the overgrown path leading to the classroom building, both women were out of breath.

"Well!" said Adelina, surveying the remains of the mission school. The log buildings—the dormitories for boys and male teachers at one end, the dormitories for the girls and female teachers at the opposite end, the dinner hall, and the classroom cabins—all were in various stages of dilapidation. Chinking crumbled from gaps between the logs, hand-hewn shingles were missing from the roofs, and out from between the logs, creeper vine and honeysuckle and wax myrtle grew thick everywhere.

"I thirsty!" said Joshua.

"There's the springhouse and pump. Let's see if the old tin bucket and dipper are still there." Grasshoppers jumped out of the long grass as they walked toward it.

Hezziah pushed the pump handle. It groaned several times before a trickle of water finally came out, looking rusty. She worked the handle till it gushed clear. The dipper was still attached by its chain, rusty now. "Here you go, Joshua, Mama used to drink from this dipper too."

Hezziah's baby began to cry, and they found the bench made from half a log where teachers had sat to supervise the morning and afternoon playtime. She sat and unbuttoned her bodice and fed the baby while Adelina sliced an apple for Joshua with her pocketknife, pointing out to him what all the buildings had been used for.

Hezziah hadn't wanted to come up here, but Adelina said they both needed to make peace with the past. The camp meetings would start soon.

Joshua put his head in his mother's lap and dozed off. The baby fell asleep on Hezziah's shoulder.

The sisters listened to the hot, dry hum the cicadas made. "It used to be the scene of such bustle and activity—the children and the school bell and the noise from the kitchen, mules bringing food, braying, the school chickens," said Adelina.

"Singing, reciting you could hear through the windows," said Hezziah. "Quiet as . . . as the graveyard now. We meant to serve the Lord, Addy. I wonder if we did. Seeing what's happened here."

"My purpose was also to get away from William Henderson when he chose Cousin Mary over me," said Adelina, smiling. "My heart felt broken at the time. I found a better husband, I think, in Caradoc. He's very good to me, though he appears grave to others, I know. I have no regrets. But do you, Hezzie? I sometimes sense you do."

"If I do, they never last long," answered Hezziah lightly. "And if the autumn camp meeting is a success, we expect to have our first great revival in the spring after the planting's done, so there is much to do. Letters to be written, notices to be sent, announcements in the papers. To determine how people and wagons can fit conveniently into the campground. We expect to be very busy. My regrets are of no importance when God's given me another chance." Hezziah kissed the sleeping baby's head. "I named her Mercy, lest I forget."

"Reverend Merriman's undertaking will surely be a great success," said Adelina. "Already I see the Lord's hand in it, in the way you've truly become your husband's helpmeet. Praise the Lord for his goodness, Sister, in raising you up from despair."

"Praise the Lord," responded Hezziah. "Praise the Lord."

CHAPTER 34

AIMÉE

June 1851

His chest has swelled with such gratified pride at his own importance that I half expect my husband to topple over. All Grafton is here, turned out in its best clothes at too early an hour on a hot morning to welcome Grafton's first train, and it is Lafayette's doing. I try to brim with dignified wifely composure as I look around me. In the first line to officially receive the dignitaries and distinguished visitors arriving by rail: Zebulon Drumheller is leaning on his cane beside Lafayette. Zebulon's son, Preston, with his heavy gold watch chain draped across his chest and his plain wife from Kingsport, wearing far too much jewelry, beside him. Then Jericho Marshall and his wife, Rosa.

But Lafayette is first.

Daniel and I stand slightly behind him. Because he is a lawyer and accustomed to speaking publicly in court, Daniel will give the speech of welcome. Preston and his father believe Preston should do it. Preston is put out and is looking angrily at Daniel. Lafayette doesn't care about the speech. Daniel, I know, is amused.

Daniel looks very distinguished in his high collar, wide cravat, and frock coat. He is clean shaven, so that while his eyes and heavy brows would give him a stern countenance, there is always a smile lurking on his lips, ready to appear.

All the men, even Daniel, look hot and perspiring. It can only be a matter of time before one of them keels over.

Rembrandt Conway should draw them quickly while their cravats are still in place and before their collars wilt. He is sitting on a stool in the shade with his son, Angelo, standing by to hand him materials as he requires them. Rembrandt must work quickly to get everyone in—everyone will want to see themselves represented at this occasion. His wife, Ella, is pointing out my gown admiringly, and Rembrandt has turned and is, I believe, sketching me. I hold my parasol in such a way that my face is framed for his convenience. My parasol will give the effect of a large halo.

Then I look around to see everything is as it should be. That is my task in life, to ensure that Lafayette's home, my toilette, his daughter, Malvina, his dinner, and this occasion that is so important to him are all as they should be. So that he will appear to advantage.

It is a perishingly hot day. The pansies the Ladies Committee had chosen to be planted in containers and baskets have been well watered and tumble prettily over the sides, with tendrils of ivy. Very tasteful and refined and fresh. For the moment. Unless they give up and wilt in this heat. You can only water so much before there's a puddle on the floor.

The committee has made sure the waiting room for ladies on one side of the ticket office and the one for men on the other had been swept, and the floors are temporarily clean, free of brown patches. There are spittoons discreetly placed, but men are blind to spittoons.

The black ironwork was painted white at my request. To offset the flowers, I told Lafayette. It amuses him to grant such small, pointless requests, so I make them occasionally. Nothing that will cause him inconvenience. It allows him to feel magnanimous to indulge my whims. As he would a child.

He was equally amused, and even gratified, by the attention I gave to my appearance on the occasion. I talked of flounces and veils and bonnets to echo the colors of the flowers we ladies had planted, and he laughed, saying how charming it was that, when an event of such economic significance was about to take place, the female mind was fixated on clothing.

"Ah, but the wife of the leading figure of the occasion must do her husband credit," I simpered prettily, and he thought for a moment and conceded I was right to consider how it reflected on him.

So I have a lovely gown of light silk with tiers of ruffles. Yellow and blue, like the pansies, with the faintest edging of green to echo leaves and ivy. A sample came from New Orleans along with the latest fashion papers from France to show how it should be made up. Fabric with printed borders *au choix* is the latest thing, and each ruffle of the skirt displays the printed border. I sent an order at once to the dressmaker along with a picture of the dress I wanted. It proved to be no end of trouble to make. I have a worked-lace chemisette and a repeat of the printed border on my collar and cuffs. A light straw bonnet with ribbon flowers to match the border, lace gloves, and some pretty green silk slippers complete my ensemble. It was all, of course, immensely expensive.

That is what my husband wants, so that I outshine Linney Drumheller, who is solid as a cow, and Preston's overjeweled wife, who mistakenly trusts what passes for style in her hometown of Kingsport and looks gaudy. Lafayette was satisfied with me. This morning when I was dressed, he turned me this way and that and said I'd done him proud. He gave me a pearl brooch set with a lock of his hair to mark today's occasion, which he believes confirms his position as the leading citizen of Grafton, ahead of Zebulon and Preston Drumheller and Jericho Marshall. He is happy.

I thanked him sweetly, gave him a kiss, and pinned the brooch on my bosom. Approaching the new station, Lafayette stopped the buggy, and we descended. He wished to go the rest of the way on foot. I picked up my parasol. He gave me his arm. He likes having me on his arm, like a butterfly, he says.

I make it a point never to cling.

Then Lafayette stopped and offered Malvina his other arm, as if she were grown. Delighted, she stopped skipping and took it, gazing at Lafayette with adoration, trying to match her steps to mine. I can't deny that sometimes Lafayette surprises me. He set a slow and digni-fied pace, walking majestically toward the new station, as became the investor of importance.

Daniel had dressed and gone ahead earlier. He dresses swiftly.

Malvina was quivering with excitement. She had a dress similar to mine, made up to be suitable for a ten-year-old girl. Also very expensive. She is to present a posy to Charles Marshall's new wife, whose name is Comfort. A name that reeks of Quakerishness. I crane my neck to make sure Ella Conway has the posy with her in the shade. Ella nods to me. I nod back. We each recognize the other and of course never mention it. We must all live.

Because the Marshalls are regarded as the founding family of Grafton, Charles and Comfort Marshall will be the first of the dis-tinguished passengers to alight, followed by a general, two senators and their ladies, and reporters from Richmond and as far away as Philadelphia. Comfort arouses the most interest, and as a bride she can expect to be deferred to.

Charles Marshall is very handsome and rather dashing. They say he resembles his great-grandfather, who was a Frenchman and a favorite with the ladies. Also a spy, they say, before the War of Independence. The couple were recently married quietly at the bride's home in Richmond and cut short their wedding trip to Niagara to grace the inaugural train.

The wedding was rather quick—Jericho and Rosa weren't informed of it until too late to make the journey in time for the wedding.

When it became clear that the railway would come through Grafton, there was a great rush of activity. It seemed the town expanded overnight; there were suddenly great numbers of workmen and their families. Riverfront land was purchased from the Vanns and the Marshalls, and buildings to house workmen were thrown up with such haste that no thought was given to the way that part of Grafton floods if the river runs high, and it is very marshy and plagued by mosquitoes in summer. The riverfront echoed with hammering, and timber planks were stacked everywhere. The livery stable was extended, and the Ozment boardinghouse added a new story. A courthouse was built next to the jail. Of brick. That is where Daniel practices, in an office on the side.

The quarter called Darkie Town is farther down the river. The Hanover family sold parcels of land in town next to their own homesteads so the free Negroes who came here could build cabins. There are many new cabins in the shadow of the large one they say belonged to the matriarch Venus Hanover. Two of her granddaughters live there now and keep a boardinghouse. Darkie Town is all free blacks. They stick together. As well they might.

Across from it are some houses for Irish workmen, who keep themselves separate.

Comfort Marshall will be the first Quaker I have met. Quakers do not own slaves and favor abolition.

The train is late! Oh, the heat! I neglected to bring my fan.

I wonder how Comfort will like Grafton.

There will be a collation at Ozment Hotel afterward. The Drumhellers bought the Ozment boardinghouse after Susan Hanover and Isaac Ozment died and changed it into a genteel hotel. There is a parlor with velvet drapes and carpets—though the last are somewhat stained from tobacco despite the brass spittoons. And potted plants. White cloths are spread on the long dining table in the saloon at mealtimes, but when a dinner bell is rung, guests crowd in to find a seat as best they may. Men think nothing of elbowing ladies and children out of the way in the rush to fork up their chops or beef. Hardly genteel—more like a herd of buffalo stampeding to the feeding trough.

Still, people feel a hotel confers distinction on the town. Daniel takes his midday dinners there because it is easy to eat quickly and he has a great deal of work.

The hotel hires cooks and waiters and porters from Darkie Town, many of them the wives and children of the free black railway workmen, in preference to the Irish. They cannot hire both, because the Irish look down on the Negroes and the Negroes look down even more on them, and the antagonism prevents any work being done at all.

The hotel guests are business travelers or those bound for the mineral springs. The Drumhellers and Marshalls get richer and richer.

So do the Charbonneaus. That is why Lafayette could invest so heavily in bringing the railroad here. There was a sudden accession of money—more money!—a few years ago that came in such a peculiar manner from such an unexpected source that it has convinced me, as no amount of convent education and priests could do, that God is all-seeing and sometimes deigns to arrange human affairs.

It was indirectly the doing of my mother-in-law, Stefania. I was fond of her. She was very kind to me from the first, withdrawing little by little as head of the household after I came, saying that as Lafayette's wife, I should preside at Chiaramonte. She intended only to give me time to see how the house runs. Or more exactly how Jane Pine, her housekeeper of many years, ran it.

But Jane fell ill a week after I, the mistress in waiting, arrived. I could feel the anger at my being Lafayette's wife building in her until she collapsed, paralyzed on one side, her mouth twisted.

When I took a glass of cool strawberry shrub to her bed, saying it would be refreshing, she glared at me and said thickly out of the good side of her mouth, "I told Will, if they take the cabin back, they take it back. Won't take no orders from a nigger slut ought to be living in the quarters, not upstairs in the master's bedroom. I won't work for a nigger or a slut."

"I doubt you'll have to," I replied coolly, and left the shrub on her bedside table. I was trembling. If this was my reception from a servant, what could I expect from the rest of the ladies? When she died the next day, she hadn't touched it. Lafayette hired two girls from Darkie Town. They like me only a little better than Jane did, but they need their wages and do as I say with only a little show of insolence. I am patient. We must all live, however we can manage it.

At first I feared I would occupy a sort of desert between Darkie Town and being mistress of Chiaramonte, belonging in neither. But Stefania did not allow that to happen. Her friends Peach Vann and Magdalena Walker and the Drumheller schoolmistress, who frightens me a little because she is so clever and is impossible to fool, all pieced a quilt for the baby before Malvina was born. Miss Martha Washington Marshall visited me, which means I have been recognized to an extent I doubted was possible, and I returned the visit after three days, just as I was taught. Miss Martha is quite formal. Just like the head nun at convent school.

Rosa is reserved, but we may be friends one day. She has lost four of her children at young ages to fevers and various illnesses, and after having Malvina, I pity her.

Malvina means everything to me.

Daniel and I each recognized what the other was at once, having both passed through a gate so constricted and narrow that most are left on the other side. He called Stefania Mamma. He was an orphan, from the streets in Philadelphia, and has never known who his parents were.

He shares the Charbonneau name. Lafayette is genuinely fond of him. It is one of the few things I like about Lafayette. That and the fact he gave his arm to Malvina.

Stefania only cared that Lafayette was happy. Lafayette is happy enough, I see to it. She can rest in peace on that score.

I am in charge at Chiaramonte now, as Lafayette's wife accepted by the Wildwood ladies. For that I would put up with anything Lafayette did. Otherwise, without Lafayette I would be kept by a man in New Orleans, perhaps one of my father's wealthy friends, if I was lucky, or if unlucky, in a place like the Darkie Town brothel in Grafton that everyone pretends does not exist, and that I know Lafayette visits.

My father advised me always to think of Lafayette with gratitude if I could not think of him with love. I think the arrangement my father made, that meant Lafayette married me and brought me here in exchange for my dowry, is no different from his arrangement with my mother, whom he did not and could not marry. We were both bought, or rather exchanged, for reasons of convenience and lust. My mother for money, I for a chance to marry and pass into white respectability.

I remind myself, we must all live.

I think, I think . . . It has never occurred to Lafayette to consider me as thinking at all.

But Stefania I loved. When she fell ill, I nursed her, sitting up with her at night while she told me stories of her parents and Sicily. Then one day she received a letter that made her stare at the envelope as if it contained snake venom. She opened it with a trembling hand and cried, "No!"

When I asked what was wrong, she said that when she was young she'd had a suitor she'd been very drawn to, but who at the same time frightened her. She had rejected him in favor of the colonel, who was her first husband, and for a long time wondered if she had betrayed her heart. The answer, she always concluded, was that she had not, that she had done well not to bind her fate to a man who roused fear as much as he roused longing. The suitor went away but returned to Grafton and pursued her again after her first husband died, again with a degree of intensity that seemed unlike love. She'd gone traveling with the Drumheller woman to escape him. When she returned, he tried again, came back to Grafton, declaring she'd always had a hold on his heart, and he would not let her get away this time. He said she was the one thing he wanted in life that had eluded him, and this time he would have her.

She thought he sounded obsessed. Dangerous. It became clearer to her why she'd refused him. She said her guardian angel had prompted her to accept the colonel when she was young. To escape the unwelcome attention, she'd married for the second time, to the widowed father of her Drumheller friend.

Then she confessed to me that despite twice refusing him, there was something about her old suitor that stirred her blood; *demonic* was the word she used. "Old as I am, I wonder that the Devil can be so compelling."

I asked the suitor's name.

I concealed my surprise when she said Augustine St. Pierre. I asked if it was the hugely rich cotton planter by that name, who also owns property in New Orleans, and she said he was. According to my mother, who was raised in the orphanage run by the nuns who also ran my school, the nuns told her Augustine St. Pierre had singled her out for his "protection." He had a habit of observing the orphaned girls through a louvered window as they walked to Mass and then made what the nuns believed was a charitable offer of guardianship when they left the orphanage. My father rescued my mother from him just in time, and she taught me always to be grateful. It was rumored that he kept the girls he chose prisoners on his plantation. An older girl at the orphanage who had been my mother's closest friend had the misfortune to be very beautiful. After six months on the plantation, she hanged herself.

I kept my knowledge of Augustine St. Pierre's predatory ways to myself. I spent what time I could spare from Stefania with Malvina. Each day I checked that she had learned the lessons I set for her. A girl must be educated. I encourage her to learn but not in such a way that she complains to Lafayette that Mama is too hard upon her over her lessons. We make it a game. Lafayette does not want his daughter to become a bluestocking.

Mr. St. Pierre wrote to say he'd learned Stefania was again a widow and he was coming to visit her. I saw the phrase "will not be cheated of you a third time."

"But I am nearly dead!" muttered Stefania. "What can he be thinking!"

"Revenge," I said. "Augustine St. Pierre does not like to be thwarted." I told her about my mother. He went to great pains to ensure that he had his pick of the girls at my convent, just as he had at the orphanage. He was a patron of my school, the guest of honor on feast days. We were obliged to sing for him. He made a large gift to the school and the orphanage every year. The Irish nuns were a poor order. I don't know if they suspected what was meant by his offer of guardianship and, if they had, what they would have done. There were few schools for girls like us, and he is a very rich and powerful man.

Stefania looked at me sharply then. "I know what you are, my dear," she said.

"Yes," I said. "You've always known. And Augustine St. Pierre preys on girls like me. There is no justice for us. There was no justice for my mother's friend." But there was no time to write and forbid him to come. The day he was expected, she was quiet and thoughtful. I helped her put on her best nightdress and her prettiest dressing gown. I plumped her pillows and aired the room, placed a chair at the bedside.

"Will you require a chaperone?" I asked, hoping she would ask me to stay, and she shook her head.

"You'd best leave it to me," she said. "Alone."

When he arrived at the house, fortunately he did not recognize me. I led him up to Stefania's room. He bowed and kissed her hand. I left them alone, but with the door open. I was consumed with curiosity.

Later I heard Stefania calling me, and when I came in, she said, "I have agreed to marry Mr. St. Pierre."

I couldn't believe my ears or contain my astonishment. "But you are too ill to manage the stairs, how will you get married!" *And you have rightly feared this man,* I wanted to protest. *What are you thinking? Whatever power he has over you, do not trust it.*

"I know there are no priests here. Send for the minister. I will get a priest to come on the next riverboat, but I don't wish to wait," he ordered. He was holding Stefania's hand. "We'll marry right here. Now." As if he would settle an old score by demanding a husband's rights immediately. I shuddered.

Stefania nodded. "I yield at last," she said. "But send for Daniel as well. We need a lawyer present."

I sent one of the maids for Reverend Merriman and another for Daniel. The two men arrived within the hour, with the reverend expecting to officiate at Stefania's deathbed and Daniel astonished by the news Stefania was bent on marrying. Stefania insisted she and Augustine speak to him privately before the marriage could take place. Daniel closed the bedroom door, leaving Endurance and me in the corridor. Waiting outside in the corridor, Endurance was as shocked as I had been by the request he marry them, was on the point of refusing, and talked of the banns that must be announced. That takes weeks.

I said that there may have been something very improper between them once, that Stefania was dying and Mr. St. Pierre was very old, and it would be wrong to deny them this chance to make amends. Uniting them in marriage would expunge the sin, if there had been one.

"But . . . but . . . this is hardly the purpose for which marriage was ordained," spluttered the reverend. "Irregular! A bedside wedding . . . I cannot . . ."

"Shall I send for your wife? Perhaps she can persuade you," I muttered.

The reverend sighed. Hezziah Merriman has a sharp tongue when she is not speaking of her own holiness. "Oh, very well."

After a while Daniel emerged and beckoned us in. "My sister-in-law and I will serve as witnesses."

Words were said, the vows exchanged, and Reverend Merriman admonished the new couple to live in godly love and made his escape. Daniel and I went downstairs. "You'd better fetch Lafayette," I said.

When Daniel returned with my husband, I asked the men to sit down and sent the maid for whiskey. I began to explain as best I could a marriage that was inexplicable, the details of which were unclear but were bound to make Lafayette furious.

Lafayette's bluster that his mother had gone mad was interrupted by a cry from upstairs. We all ran to Stefania's bedroom to find Mr. St. Pierre collapsed across her bed. When the men tried to move him, they discovered he was dead.

A very trying half hour followed the removal of the body. Stefania explained, Lafayette raged and swore, and Daniel expressed the opinion the marriage was legal, and finally both men shouted until they were out of breath.

When they fell silent, I widened my eyes in my stupid expression and asked if Stefania still inherited her new husband's estate, despite the brevity of the marriage. Lafayette looked at Daniel. Daniel tried not to smile at me. He sometimes says I should have been a lawyer, only that would have required me to be a man and he prefers me as a woman. He arched his back and patted his stomach, rolled his eyes to the ceiling, and thought.

"It might indeed. It depends on the terms of his will. And, Lafe, your mother called me in, saying she and St. Pierre wished to marry and she would only agree if their wills were in order and would I write out a new joint will and testament. St. Pierre has no children, no legitimate ones, and he was impatient and agreed that if he predeceased your mother, she would inherit his fortune in its entirety for the rest of her lifetime, and after that, half of St. Pierre's estate would go to you, half to me."

Lafayette had opened his mouth for another tirade.

"Lafe, St. Pierre's fortune is considerable," said Daniel, looking at the ceiling in a calm and thoughtful way. "Your mother's heirs would probably benefit beyond their wildest dreams."

Lafayette shut his mouth abruptly.

"I was only doing as your mother asked at the time—I have no idea whether the will I drew up before the wedding will stand up legally. There was no time to investigate. The circumstances in which St. Pierre died are . . . unusual. I'll examine the legal position more minutely at once. But keep the possibility in mind, Lafe. In the meantime, my felicitations on your recent nuptials, dear Mamma," Daniel said mischievously.

"Mother Drumheller, or perhaps I must now say Mother St. Pierre, is fatigued," I interrupted. "It would be wise to let her rest after such an afternoon. Go along, let me settle her."

The two men left. As he went past me, Daniel couldn't suppress a chuckle.

The excitement and uproar had left Stefania looking pale and tired and, suddenly, diminished and frail. Understandably. I sat on the bed and began to brush her hair that was still thick, though white.

"What has happened today?" I asked.

"We came to an understanding, my dear. A late understanding. Too late perhaps for some things. A bargain, if you like. He has brooded for years, beyond reason, over the one thing . . . the one person he could not have. Such intensity! Such . . . a will to have me in his power. He wants all women in his power, I think. Perhaps that's what I saw all those years ago, when I was almost intoxicated by his presence, yet knew it was dangerous. He was dangerous. Especially to girls like you."

"Yes."

"And now . . . when Lafe inherits half his fortune, be sure you out-live him. Justice, I think, that it will be yours in the end. And justice that the other half will be Daniel's. Daniel is like you," she said sleepily. "Like you. He passed."

"I know," I said. I blew out the candle and pulled the coverlet to her chin. She feels the cold.

"But as I have arranged things, you will have the benefit of Augustine's will through both Lafayette and Daniel . . . With either of them, you will have your carriage, your pretty gowns."

I started back.

"Marry both. Marry both," she was muttering as I left the room.

I went to see Malvina in the nursery.

"Is Grandmother better?"

"No, darling. I fear not."

The next day Stefania was poorly. She asked about the funeral, and we told her Augustine had been buried in the cemetery.

"If a Catholic priest comes through Grafton, please see he blesses the grave," said Stefania. Then she added, "I shall soon follow him."

The day after that she seemed to lose interest in everything, barely able to smile at Malvina when the child came to offer to read to her. And when she read, Stefania didn't praise her, as usual, for being the cleverest six-year-old in America. As the week passed, Stefania couldn't be troubled to eat. She seemed detached from those of us around her, sleeping and waking at intervals to mutter things that made no sense. She talked of a goddess and crowns, someone holding a torch and a pig. That she should have told Rosa about them.

Once or twice she stroked my cheek, thinking I was Rosa. "The shrine," she said. I have no idea what she meant, but it was obvious she was entering the realm between this world and the next. The family gathered to wait. Lafayette and Daniel, Rosa and Jericho Marshall and their boys. The youngest Marshall child, Catherine, is Malvina's friend. She crept to Malvina's side and sat holding her hand until we sent the children to sleep for a few hours. We passed the next day and most of the night watching.

Molly Drumheller, Peach Vann, and Magdalena Walker arrived together. In tears the old ladies each held Stefania's hand for a moment and murmured farewells. Molly was the last. She bent over, kissed her friend, and murmured, "Thank you, dear, dear Stefania. He's a credit to you, to his father."

Stefania opened her eyes. "To you as well," I heard her whisper hoarsely. Her eyes closed again.

Who was? I wondered.

And then I knew, looking at Molly's face. The features so like Daniel's. Daniel . . . And that meant Molly . . . Daniel's father was a Negro! Not his mother. And Stefania had raised him.

A great secret had come to my keeping.

Stefania's breathing grew labored, a horrible sound, yet she struggled to speak again. We crowded round the bed for her last words.

"Both . . . both . . . both . . ."

After the funeral Daniel found there was nothing to prevent Augustine St. Pierre's widow from inheriting his estate. There were no other heirs, as he'd never had children, and an old will he'd made when married to his first wife left everything to his spouse without naming her. "Cunning devil" was Daniel's assessment.

I assumed he meant Stefania.

Stefania left most of her own Charbonneau and Drumheller fortune to Rosa and Lafayette, but with the prewedding will valid, the St. Pierre estate went in halves to Lafayette and Daniel. Lafayette sold the St. Pierre cotton plantation—with all the slaves—and invested his share of the money in the railway. I imagine for a moment that the train is approaching, not on tracks but on the backs of slaves chained to the ground.

This is what I am thinking of as Malvina and Lafayette and I stand in the hot sun, waiting for the train we now hear whistling in the distance. I wonder who Daniel's father was, why Stefania raised Molly's child as her own son. I thought about the forms and twists and turns love and passion take. How people must live as best they can.

I can see smoke in the distance. There's a murmur of excitement. Everyone is waving. Malvina is practicing her curtsey. Her friend Catherine is watching her with an expression of envy, wishing she'd been chosen for the honor of presenting flowers to her new sister-in-law. Ella Conway hands Malvina the posy. Mercy Merriman, who shares lessons with Malvina and Catherine, and her cousins Joshua and Jonathan Vann are jumping up and down with excitement. Their two redheaded mothers, who sing together as a feature at their camp meetings, are craning their necks for a sight of the iron horse that can carry them on a visit home to Maryland at last.

Reverend Merriman and the other two preachers are clearing their throats and will all pray at great length. Each of the three wants to step forward first, but will politely gesture that one of the others should precede him.

Miss Martha Washington Marshall, leaning on her cane but very upright despite looking frail, and her cousin Lorenzo Walker, back from his long European travels and wearing a rather exotic long embroidered waistcoat, are crowding in to welcome Charley's bride. Miss Martha is wearing a fine dickey of white lace like a spiderweb, probably Belgian—a present from Lorenzo?—that I can tell cost a fortune.

Colonel Henry Stuart, in uniform, and his wife, Miss Fanny, are beside them with their grown sons and their last boy, Lawrence, only eleven, a late surprise for his parents.

The train has slowed for the final approach. Hopefully it will arrive before we all die in the heat.

There is already cheering. The conductor waves. Charles will get down first, then reach his hand up to assist Comfort onto the platform.

He will smile proudly. She will blush and look shy. Malvina will step forward, curtsey, and present her posy. Daniel will make his speech. I will cut a ribbon.

Finally Lafayette will step forward to applause and cheers, tip his hat, bow, strut like a turkey cock, and say a few words of approbation for this great work of progress.

I will give a dazzling smile to all and, for a moment, allow myself to lock eyes with Daniel. To send him a message.

I am pregnant. The baby is yours. I love you.

CHAPTER 35

December 1860

In later years, those who had been young on the Christmas of 1860 would recall it wistfully.

That year it snowed heavily in mid-December, turning the valley and mountains white. Every approaching train's whistle announced it was bringing holiday letters, parcels, one or two more young men home from college for the holidays. There was a general air of expectation and excitement. The engine steamed importantly into the little station, which the Ladies Committee had decked with pine boughs and holly, and the train disgorged boys into the joyful arms of their mothers, who exclaimed how their sons had grown taller since they'd left.

Among them were Joshua Vann and his brother, Jonathan, returning from Washington College in Lexington, along with twenty-year-old Lawrence Stuart, who attended the Virginia Military Institute in the same town. On the way they speculated whether their friend Jacky Drumheller was home yet from the university at Charlottesville. Jacky had a reputation as a great attender of horse races and an avid player of cards, rather than a regular attender of classes or studier of his books, and there was even a rumor he and his university friends kept company with actresses in Washington.

His three friends speculated whether it was true what they'd heard, that Jacky had been expelled. If so, his mother would be furious. She was a difficult woman who regretted exchanging the elegance of Kingsport for Preston Drumheller's river valley, whose name she subsequently discovered, translated from the French, meant "wild pig mud wallow." She was determined Jacky not appear a wilderness bumpkin among her former, refined circle. She intended for him to marry a girl from among the nice families of Kingsport, and meanwhile, the university at Charlottesville was a gentleman's seat of learning.

If they anticipated any fly in the ointment of their pleasures this Christmas, that fly resembled Mrs. Drumheller.

The girls didn't have so far to travel, as better-off girls in Grafton between the ages of ten and eighteen attended the Female Academy, which now occupied the site of the old Slipping Creek Mission School, since the revivalist grounds Reverend Merriman had tried to establish there had come to nothing. But in token of his former efforts, Reverend Merriman was engaged to teach Scripture there once a week, and his daughter, Mercy Merriman, attended for free. The academy taught English and mathematics and religion, and the older students had lessons in Latin, music, needlework, and deportment. They read suitable works of literature, and Rembrandt Conway came once a week to teach them flower painting. The girls groaned ritually that all this was far too much for their poor little minds.

Now classes were suspended until mid-January, and the girls all agreed it was heaven not having to decline Latin verbs, read Shakespeare, commit endless poems to memory, or practice the piano two hours daily during the holidays. They could concentrate on parties and carol singing and the Twelfth Night Ball that always ended the holiday festivities.

In their bedrooms, so warm and comfortable after the dreary cubicles at the school, the girls had time to experiment on each other's hair with hairpins and curling irons and combs, compare their dresses for the ball, and deny any intention of sending secret Valentine verses to any boy in the world when February came. All insisted, laughing, they weren't acquainted with a single young man worthy of their notice.

The enjoyment and anticipation of more enjoyment was contagious. Parents and older people smiled on their offspring, who seemed to be constantly on the move. Charley Marshall; his wife, Comfort; and his sister Catherine had driven his trap to collect a large, mysterious box marked "Fragile" he'd ordered from Philadelphia. The stationmaster reported that Catherine was pestering her brother to tell her what was in it, but he'd just laughed and said they wouldn't know until Comfort opened it.

Comfort and Catherine gasped with delight when they finally saw what was inside. From a bed of sawdust, he unpacked an assortment of thin glass balls with ribbon ties, small gilded candleholders with clips on the bottom to fasten on branches, and angels with tinsel haloes.

Having spread out these treasures on the dining table, Charley said a decorated tree in the house was essential now. It was a custom fashionable in England and had been taken up in many households up north. He'd seen them when he was at Princeton, and this year there would be a tree at Wildwood.

The three of them trooped off to hunt for the perfect tree after lunch—a matter of some deliberation that took most of an afternoon. By suppertime a fine pine tree stood in a bucket of damp earth, little candleholders attached to the branches, glass balls spinning on their ribbons with every footfall, and flights of angels sparkling through the branches.

A general invitation, spread by word of mouth, was promptly issued by Comfort, Charley, and Catherine to an evening party to see their creation and drink eggnog.

The following days saw a pine tree erected in many Grafton households at the instigation of their younger members, gamely decorated with berries and candle ends and ribbons and any pretty scraps young people could lay their hands on.

Much visiting was necessary to admire the trees and have a glass of shrub and a slice of Christmas cake. Despite the cold, an excursion was organized to climb up to the Old Man of the Mountain to hold a séance at sunset to see if the shape-shifter or the little Indian girl, Dancing Rabbit, would make themselves known. There were tea drinking and suppers, dances and taffy pulls, carol-singing parties and bonfires. Jacky Drumheller proposed getting up an amateur theatrical performance with costumes, but it came to nothing as everyone was too busy.

And there was the usual ball to look forward to on Twelfth Night at the hotel, before they dispersed again. If a couple had become engaged over Christmas, they usually saved the announcement until then, which added to the anticipation.

Two nights before the ball, there had been a great snowfall, followed by a freeze. The following day a bright sun in a cold blue sky shone on branches encased in ice and made every blade of grass sparkle. A group set off at midday for a sleigh ride, bundled in rugs and packed into Preston Drumheller's sleigh. Jacky claimed the honor of driving, as was his right. Every so often he would whip the horse to go faster so the girls would scream.

Mercy Merriman, Malvina Charbonneau, and Catherine Marshall cried that if he did that just *once* more, he shouldn't have a bite of the picnic they'd brought.

"Then you'll be sorry because I won't dance with any of you tomorrow night at the ball!" shouted Jacky gleefully, and whipped the horse to go even faster.

There were louder squeals from the back.

"Never mind, I'll dance with each of you three or four times to make up for Jacky," cried Lawrence. "Can't have you sitting with the chaperones until you're old and ugly."

"Girls, I'll do better than that, I'll dance with all three of you all at once," said Joshua Vann, poking his nose from under the blanket keeping his face warm. "I'm a better dancer than Jacky or Lawrence. Lawrence dances like a military man, as if he's on the parade ground, and Jacky jigs about."

"I do not jig about," yelled Jacky over his shoulder.

"You jig a little," the girls chorused.

"Dance with me, girls, one at a time. I've my dance card with me, who's first?" said Joshua's younger brother, Jonathan.

"Let's stop and have our picnic before the horse is tired out. I'm starving," said Lawrence.

Jacky and Joshua and Jonathan agreed they were starving too.

They pulled to a halt beside the river that was frozen along the bank. Jacky unhitched the horse and walked it up and down before giving it some feed and then broke the ice to draw it some water. The girls unpacked their basket and handed round ham biscuits and jumbles and slices of dark fruitcake heavy with spices. Everyone's face was glowing and rosy, and for a moment they fell silent as they ate, appetites sharpened by the fresh air.

"I say we should stretch our legs," said Lawrence, who was the tallest.

"Let's," agreed the others.

The boys helped the girls out. Their hooped skirts were awkward to manage. The girls drew their pelisses tighter across their shoulders and stuck their hands in their muffs, as if to keep them safe from being held.

Gradually they paired off across the riverbank to observe the ice. The boys tested it with their boots, and the girls cried, "Careful!"

Jacky and the Vann brothers competed to see who could throw a snowball the farthest across the river. Lawrence and Catherine somehow walked off to the side, away from the others. They moved closer and closer together with every step until Lawrence put an arm around Catherine's shoulders and took the glove from his other hand, slipped into Catherine's muff to clasp hers.

"Catherine, have you missed me?"

"Lawrence, I . . . perhaps. A little. Sometimes."

He stopped. "Have you? Only a little? Is that all? Because I've missed you, every day, every hour."

"What would the institute say to that? You're meant to spend every hour of every day learning to be an engineer. Not missing girls." She laughed nervously.

"Not girls. You. And you wouldn't let me write."

"You have important work ahead of you, you shouldn't be distracted."

"What's distracting is thinking of you here with other men! I'll finish soon. As you know, regulars like me have to teach for two years in Virginia after graduating, and I've arranged to stay at the institute to teach. I don't mind staying in Lexington, it's an agreeable town. You'd find it congenial."

"Would I?"

"Then afterward, I shall build bridges and roads and military things, and the institute's very sound in training one to do that, so I shouldn't lack for work or an appointment."

"Lawrence, still there two years after . . ."

"Catherine, I'll be in a position to marry! At last. You always say it's imprudent to talk of engagements before there's a possibility of marrying, but everything changes when I graduate then. I'll have a stipend from teaching, and Father says that as I'll be of age I shall have an allowance. Say you'll marry me then! Say you'll marry me and live with me in Lexington until I finish my teaching there, and after that we'll make an adventure of it and go wherever my work takes me. I ask you every Christmas and you put me off . . . but I think, I hope, you love me. Just a little? Eh?"

He put a finger under her chin and tipped it up. "I'm so tired of waiting. Aren't you?"

"Lawrence. You're . . . precipitate." She blushed and dropped her eyes, uncertain how to proceed in an encouraging but not excessively encouraging way. A girl mustn't on any account appear forward—it put men off. Her mother had drilled that into her. She certainly didn't want to put Lawrence off, especially since he had prospects that made her heart leap.

"Precipitate! What a thing to call your lover! I've been in love with you since we were children!" He swept her up in a bear hug and swung her around; then he held her with her feet off the ground as she laughed and struggled. "And you've been in love with me, though I understand girls aren't meant to admit it. But admit now, Miss Marshall. Don't be heartless! You can't get down until you kiss me. If you're going to be my wife, you should try kissing me to be sure you like it."

"Lawrence! The others will see and suspect . . ."

"All the more reason you should kiss me."

"Lawrence, the others!"

He swung around so his body shielded her from view, put her down, and bent his head. "Kiss me," he murmured. She wavered, then decided it wasn't being forward if a girl was going to accept a proposal. She lifted hers, and they kissed. Softly at first, and then they kissed as if there were nothing else in the world but the two of them, lips joined together, the vapor of their breath mingling warm together in the cold air.

Breathless, Catherine pulled back a little to look at him. "Come back," he murmured, putting his mouth on hers again.

"Marry me, say you'll marry me," he said into her cheek. "I shan't let you go until you promise. If I had my way, we'd marry tomorrow."

323

Catherine was shaking. If only his kiss could go on and on, no ball tomorrow, no going back to the institute, just Lawrence and nothing else.

"Have you spoken to Papa? Do you have his permission?" she asked at last.

"I understand that to mean yes. My darling, you haven't given me enough encouragement to speak to him before. But I will at once, tonight, before you change your mind. I'll call after supper." He wrapped her in his arms. "We'll announce it at the ball. Then you can't back out, it will be official. Oh, my dear Catherine! We'll have such a life together!"

"We will."

"Only six months, that's not long really."

"No."

"It is," he said, grabbing her by the shoulders. "It is, but we'll bear it. I'll study and study."

"Mama and I'll have to plan the wedding," she said, suddenly shaky with the happiness that seized her as she thought, *I'm going to marry Lawrence!* Was it really decided then, just like that? Her life decided, her happiness sealed in an instant.

"We'll write every day," he said.

"And every day will be one less to wait. We can't tell the others yet, though."

He tucked her hand in his elbow and laughed. "They'll guess, I expect. Come on. They're back in the sleigh, and Jacky's waving his whip and dancing about." He smiled down at her. "My own Catherine. Dearest."

"Dearest Lawrence," she replied, thinking *dearest* wasn't a big enough word for Lawrence.

"Tallyho," cried Jacky from the sleigh. "I thought you two were never coming!"

"You look . . . different," said Mercy with a significant look as they snuggled down under the blankets and Lawrence's hand found Catherine's. They headed back to Grafton at a brisk pace as the moon was rising, and it was shining through the bare branches of the orchard as they climbed to leave Catherine at Wildwood.

"Tonight," he murmured as he helped her down. From the expression on his face, she knew he was resisting with all his might the urge to kiss her again.

She looked at him with eyes full of happiness that said she was resisting too. She whispered, "Just remember, Papa's a Unionist. I know the institute are mostly secessionists, even if you aren't. But please, don't start talking politics and forget to ask about marrying me!"

Lawrence threw back his head and laughed. "Never fear! And I suppose I must provide you with an engagement ring at once, mustn't I?"

"Bother the ring," Catherine whispered and hurried inside.

"I expect you've claimed every one of Catherine's dances at the ball," said Mercy with a sly smile as Lawrence leaped back onto the sleigh.

"Yes, as a matter of fact, I have," Lawrence replied.

"What! Are we not to have a dance with Catherine just because you two are . . . ouch!" Mercy had kicked Joshua hard under the blanket.

Malvina giggled. "We saw you! We know your secret."

"For goodness' sake keep it to yourselves!" said Lawrence. "I still have to ask Jericho's permission."

CHAPTER 36

LEXINGTON

August 15, 1861

Dear Mama, Papa, Comfort, and Charley,
I left you as a bride of a few weeks, but now, I write
with all the dignity of a matron finally settled in her
new home.

By now you will have heard of the great Battle of
Bull Run. They say local people in Manassas turned out
to watch the fighting as if it were a theatrical arranged
for their benefit. When you consider the dead and
wounded and the misery of their families, this seems
not just heartless but utterly wicked. Here everyone
in Lexington is rejoicing at General Beauregard's victory. Many people think it means the war will be over
soon, though Lawrence is doubtful. He said the Union
soldiers there were young and untrained—poor lads,

it's said they died like flies—but the Yankees will be better trained for the next engagement.

There is a great deal of drilling and marching in Lexington, and some of the cadets have absconded to join General Jackson in Winchester. His wife remains at home in Lexington. I have not called on her on purpose, as I do not wish to, but I understand the other ladies attribute my reluctance to shyness! I can hear Charley whooping with laughter at the idea! Lawrence deplores the departure of the cadets, many of whom he teaches. Some are as young as sixteen.

I am very careful here to keep my counsel and not to say anything—Unionist people are passionate about Virginia's secession.

You will wish to hear of our new quarters. We have a sweet little brick house with black shutters at the end of a row of trees near the institute. It is surrounded by a garden that has been somewhat neglected. I am attempting to set that right, weeding and digging in new plants myself. This has shocked the Lexington ladies, as being beneath the dignity of the wife of a teacher at the institute, and one went so far as to insist on sending me Uncle Eli, her own slave gardener, to do this work.

I do not like this arrangement, but felt the reproof. Mrs. Dupree is very formidable and will not be denied. I give Eli a little money and a hearty lunch to salve my conscience.

Inside the house there are fireplaces in every room, each with a pretty plaster surround and mantelpiece. Lawrence has made the parlor his study, as it is the most pleasant room. His desk is by the window, and his books, as you can imagine, are piled everywhere. I have a sofa for my own use with a worktable, and we are very comfortable there in the evening, Lawrence working and me with my sewing.

There is a purpose in my industry, as we expect a sweet stranger to bless our little family early next year. Mother, you must make your plans to travel to Lexington after Christmas, as I am counting on you to be with me when the baby comes.

Please tell Malvina we are delighted by the news she and Jacky are married. We had half suspected their attachment before we left Grafton, but Jacky is so lively and full of nonsense, he can be quite distracting, and Lawrence says it is hard to tell what Jacky is really thinking. Malvina on the other hand is more thoughtful and serious. Lawrence says Jacky needs the ballast that Malvina will give him. But truly, we think it a happy match. Many wartime weddings are taking place in great haste just now, but despite that I'm sure Malvina made a beautiful bride—her mother will have seen to that. You must remember to describe her wedding clothes to me in detail when you come, Mother. And Jacky in uniform? It is most unfortunate that Jacky's mother obtained a commission for him in the Confederate army through her father's influence in Kingsport. I know Malvina must wish it were otherwise. Perhaps she will be able to visit me when Jacky is in camp.

Tell Mercy I hold her to her promise to come to Lexington. She and her mother would be welcome visitors any time it is convenient, though I know the summer months are a busy time for them, as they're traveling to camp meetings. She has hinted a fall visit to Lexington would be possible if she and her mother happen to be traveling to see Mrs. Merriman's people in Maryland then.

I have my suspicions that Mercy's willingness to visit is not entirely to do with me and Lawrence. I believe she has become attached to a certain young man who attended Washington College with her cousin Joshua Vann and paid the Vanns a visit last spring during the holidays. We shall see.

Lawrence had news Joshua himself has gone to Baltimore, where he is studying to become a physician! How wonderful to think the mischievous boy who chased Mercy and me with live frogs will emerge a sober, bearded, bespectacled, and solemn doctor in a few years' time. Jonathan Vann, I suppose, will manage the trading post since the major's sad demise.

It is nearly time for my daily walk. In the afternoons, without any formal arrangement, there appears to be a custom of ladies donning their hats and going out to walk near the green, watching the cadets drilling and meeting their acquaintances to exchange a few words. There is little standing on ceremony. I can scarcely take a step outdoors before being accosted by a lady or two exclaiming how delightful it is to see Lawrence Stuart married at last—he seems to be a great favorite with others as well as with me! Ladies are solicitous, asking if we have everything we need and urging me to call upon them if any assistance is needed. I must enjoy these while I can, as it will soon be impossible to appear in public in my interesting condition. I would think nothing of it at home, but in Lexington I tremble at the thought of what Mrs. Dupree would say.

Lawrence and I have made a delightful excursion to see the Natural Bridge and have a picnic. It is quite marvelous to think that the river that cut the great arch from the rocks so high above our head now runs below our feet.

The market in Lexington is well supplied, with vegetables and poultry of every kind, and good butter, so there is no lack of anything. Lawrence says to tell you I have become an admirable housewife.

In short, we are very happy—despite Mrs. Dupree—and would be happier still if this war ends soon, which most people here expect.

Give my best love to Comfort, who will have her own sweet stranger soon. I have embroidered a cap for her baby and will send it next time someone is traveling to Grafton. I trust Charley has said no more about going off to join the army—I should scold him severely for even thinking of it, especially as Papa has been so ill. I hope Papa's chest has ceased to trouble him after the bad cold you wrote of.

Please give my love to all inquiring friends and tell them to write me all their news.

Your loving daughter and sister,
Catherine Marshall Stuart

CHAPTER 37

SAMPIE

July 1864

The hounds at Wildwood were barking, straining against the ropes that tethered them to the porch. "Quiet down," said Jericho Marshall, waving a thin old hand from the quilt he was wrapped in, even though it was a warm day. He felt the cold no matter what the heat. At the far end of the clearing, two women in faded sunbonnets, Rosa and her daughter-in-law Comfort, stopped hoeing potatoes at the sound, looking toward the path that came out of the orchard.

They were expecting Aunt Polly Stuart, who lived just off to the side of the orchard with her two middle-aged daughters, whose husbands were off God knew where with General Forrest. Aunt Polly was the widow of a man who'd had a small homestead far down the valley.

She'd appeared at Wildwood a year after the war started. "Heard you folks own most of the land up here on Frog Mountain, so I guess I'm askin' the right person," she'd said to Rosa. Aunt Polly wanted permission to build a cabin on a flat spot next to the orchard, overlooking the cemetery. Her cabin in the valley had burned down, and anyway, their homestead had been so isolated she wanted a bit of company now, within earshot. Aunt Polly's chickens had been taken by some men she suspected were deserters, but they were so dirty she couldn't tell which army they were deserting from. "I'll shoot the next rascals who try and steal from me," she swore. "You hear a gunshot, you come help me clear up the mess and bury whoever I shot."

Rosa protested that the new cabin would be close to the cemetery, but Aunt Polly said she and the girls weren't squeamish about being close to the dead. She reckoned there were going to be more folks dead than alive before the damn fool war was finished.

"But who'll build a cabin if your menfolk are gone?"

"Why, me and the girls will!" Aunt Polly was a large woman who laughed heartily at the suggestion she couldn't build her own cabin. "Won't be where you can see it," she assured them. "Just you can maybe see the smoke from the chimney. That's a friendly sight." Rosa told her to go right ahead, they needed company too now that so many men were away. She insisted Aunt Polly and her strapping daughters sleep at Wildwood until their house was ready.

So they'd come with a wagon full of half-burned beds and charred pots, some chairs, a table, and a mule.

To the surprise of Rosa and Comfort, Aunt Polly and her daughters actually did all the work, felling trees and notching them, before their mule dragged the logs into place. The two daughters hauled stones and built a fireplace and chimney. They mixed the chinking and packed it into the gaps. "Way they did it in the old days, still a good way," Aunt Polly asserted when Rosa and Comfort walked down to view their progress.

Aunt Polly was a good forager. She'd found a hive of bees in an old hollow tree in the orchard and promised to bring them some honey when she got around to getting it away from the bees.

Rosa and Comfort agreed they'd give her one of their layers in exchange. They found it comfortable having a near neighbor. And that was who they'd been expecting when the dogs barked.

But it wasn't Aunt Polly that set the dogs off. Comfort and Rosa tightened their grip on their hoes and watched a man in ragged pants and a scrap of shirt made from coarse cloth walk slowly out of the orchard. Comfort swiped the sweat from her upper lip while they waited for him to get within earshot. There was something wrong with one of his legs, and he rolled when he walked toward them. Stopping before he got too close, the stranger took off a battered hat, revealing a head of wiry copper hair set off by his pale-coffee-colored skin. The dogs barked and snarled, and she shouted at them to hush. He was barefoot and looked old.

"Mornin', ladies," the old man said in a soft voice, casting a wary look at the man on the porch. "Wonder if'n I might have a drink of water?" He gestured toward the well. "Maybe something to eat if you've got to spare—ain't et nothin' for a spell." He sat down suddenly, and they saw the wide scar on his ankle. Rosa and Comfort looked at each other. A slave who'd escaped once and been caught. His Achilles tendon had been cut.

He was free now. But they'd heard freed slaves were roaming the country, no longer able to count on their masters for food and housing and clothes, and with few means to obtain the necessities of life.

Like their Grafton neighbors, the Marshalls didn't own any slaves. Comfort's family hadn't either. Her father, though born and bred in Richmond, was a Quaker and an abolitionist who'd made himself unpopular airing his opinion that Christians should shrink from owning another human being. Her mother, from a wealthy Philadelphia Quaker family, was quieter about it but just as firm in her views. She'd been snubbed by the ladies of Richmond until the day she died.

When he was courting her, Charley had promised she'd be happy in Grafton. The only sign she'd seen of slaves was an old cabin at Wildwood with a collapsing stone chimney built for a slave who'd been left behind by her owner many years ago. And he said he suspected Grafton had been a route for slaves escaping north. His Vann cousins thought Peach had helped them evade the sheriff and patrollers.

When the war came, they'd had a fierce disagreement over Charley going. He was a Unionist, he said. It was worth fighting for. Comfort didn't hold with war. But he went.

Well, at least the slaves were emancipated now, though she had heard most were left high and dry in their freedom, not knowing where to turn for work or food or a place to live. So she wondered how much use Unionism or even emancipation was if you were starving. The stranger saw their eyes on his ankle and knew they knew. "I'll work for some food. I'se a good worker," he said in a hopeless voice. He struggled back to his feet. "Maybe you ladies and the gentleman"—he nodded respectfully in Jericho's direction—"have need of a good worker? I can hoe and plant and cut logs, plow, shoe a horse even, just once I get a little strength back."

Comfort remembered her father telling her about criminals in olden times who, if they could reach the altar of a church, could place their hands there and cry, "Sanctuary," to claim protection against those pursuing them. She thought about that, looking at the man. Though he didn't need sanctuary as a runaway now, just a means of keeping life together.

"No horses left to shoe, but thee'll find plenty of other work here," said Comfort finally, gesturing at the garden and the field of corn and the big cabin whose porch was sagging.

She shifted her weight, trying to stand in a way that eased the ache in her back. Neither she nor Rosa had been brought up to do hard physical labor, and it had been almost four years of an ever harder struggle to keep up with what needed to be done, let alone feed themselves, especially since Jericho could no longer help and the children were too young. All the hired hands were off fighting.

Every day she and Rosa set to work before the sun rose, trying to win the struggle for survival. There were the chickens and cows to see to; the milking; the kitchen garden to weed; and the vegetables all coming ready at once the way they did, needing to be dried and put up for winter; wood chopped and water drawn; a little soap made with ashes and grease, and grease was in short supply; a few candles made with beeswax that burned fast and were in such a meager supply they hardly dared use one; patching and mending their clothes with any pieces of material strong enough to hold together; washing their dwindling stock of clothes; foraging for mushrooms, for anything edible, before the light failed in the evening. Passing soldiers had killed the pigs and taken them when they stripped the orchard of apples and peaches.

Comfort tended the children, the baby Priscilla, whom they called Teeny and who was born in the last year, after Charley came home on a brief furlough, and Ben, who was nine and ought to be in school, but there was no school. She taught him to read Bible verses and songs and told him stories. It was the best she could do. Ben helped with Jericho and minded Teeny.

The collapsing pasture fence needed mending before the cow wandered off and broke her leg. There seemed to be more and more to do before they could finally feed the little ones and collapse into bed themselves for a few hours' sleep.

At least exhaustion kept sorrow at arm's length. After the defeat at Chickamauga, from the Union army camp across the river from the Confederate lines, Charley had watched helplessly as two of General Forrest's men executed some black Union soldiers they'd taken prisoner. Some of his fellow Union soldiers took revenge on a young Confederate bugle boy. Charley hated it all.

Charley was ill when he came home, coughing blood and burning up with what he said was camp fever. "I'll go back soon as I'm over it," he said between nightmares.

Aunt Polly came to help nurse him through the long winter nights. "Don't matter him and the girls' husbands on different sides," she'd said.

"Man with a gun is pretty much all the same when you get down to it, honey. They all crazy."

Still, she'd got pregnant. Aunt Polly and her girls helped when Comfort gave birth sooner than she should have done. She'd heard them saying the baby was small, a tiny little thing. A girl. They hoped it wouldn't die. Comfort felt despair at everything gaining a hold on her heart. Other than nursing the baby when it was handed to her, she couldn't remember much about right afterward—just that the spring buds had frozen on the branches in a late cold spell. When she next took notice, the wild plums were shedding their blossoms. And the baby lay beside her, breathing gently.

While Comfort lay inert and sad, Rosa had grown fearful and sharp under her burden of work and her own failing strength. "Comfort, those children going to starve unless you get out of that bed this morning and we get the garden planted. The chickens have taken to laying their eggs in the woods. The cow's gone off again. If she hasn't been stolen, someone has to go after her. Jericho keeps calling someone to help him to the privy, and the children need looking after. Trust the Lord to look after Charley, but it's your Christian duty to get up and stop moping."

Comfort had stared blankly up at her mother-in-law and noticed the new lines crisscrossing the older woman's face, the pinched look pain gave you when it lingered too long. Feeling stiff and empty, and wanting to turn on her side and sleep, she got up. Comfort still felt like ice inside, no matter how hot it got in the middle of the summer, working in the sun and all. She tried to reach for the light, to feel the Lord had given her strength enough to carry on.

"First, name the baby," said Rosa. "You couldn't do that before. Name her and you'll feel better."

"Priscilla. My mother's name," said Comfort.

But from the start they all called her Teeny because she'd been so small. But she'd lived.

Now Comfort looked over at her children. Ben sat with Teeny on a quilt in the shade under a tree. He stared solemnly at the stranger. "Teeny's fixin' to cry," said Ben, and there was a wail from a woven basket.

"I'll get him some water first, then see to her," said Comfort, putting down her hoe and tucking her straggling braid back under the bonnet. "Sit awhile with Ben, Mother Marshall." Rosa seized the chance. She sat down and picked up the baby.

Comfort went to the well and cranked up the bucket. "Help thyself," she called to him. "Dipper's right here."

The man stared desperately at the gourd dipper. "Ma'am, you got another dipper, 'cause I cain't go usin' same one as white folks."

"No one here cares what thee uses," Comfort said tartly. She took Teeny from Rosa. "I can't think where I could find another gourd at the moment," she muttered. "And if we had one, it would have a hole in it, like everything else. I'm going in the house to feed the baby," she said. "I'll bring thee a corn pone and buttermilk, maybe a spoon of beans if any's left, when I come back. Thee can have thy dinner and then help us with the corn. If thee can do that, neither of us cares what thee drink from." She disappeared up the steps.

"Yes'm."

His name, they learned, was Sampie. Short for Sampson?

He had yellow eyes.

He didn't know how old he was, but he called himself Old Sampie. They gave him a quilt and a pile of clean straw and pushed open the door of the old slave cabin that was on the property from long ago. Comfort swiped the cobwebs away with a broom, and they warned him not to sleep under the place where the roof leaked. On impulse Comfort snatched up Charley's patchwork breeches and boots and left them at the cabin door, trying not to think about Charley wearing them.

Sampie was stronger than he looked, a good worker like he said, and when he put his hand to something, it got done almost before Comfort and Rosa realized it needed doing. In a few days he had mended the fence, picked all the ripe beans and tomatoes and squash so more would grow, weeded the vegetables, hoed corn before sunup, fed and milked the cow, chopped wood, built a lean-to for the chickens from some old boards, and put straw inside so they would nest there and lay their eggs. He picked and found some windfall apples from the overgrown orchard.

Comfort and Rosa and Ben spread corn and beans and tomatoes and slices of windfalls, worms and all, to dry in the sunshine. One of the Drumhellers had driven her pigs into the forest on Little Frog Mountain when the soldiers came, so there was a litter, and she was willing to trade the runty shoat for eggs, dried apples, and some of Aunt Polly's honey.

Ben gathered acorns and corn husks and bean pods to fatten it. The women made blackberry cobblers with a thin cornmeal-and-water topping for supper every night, and in the evening, Comfort and Rosa sat on the porch of the now-tidy cabin with the neglected mending basket and wondered how they'd managed before Sampie came.

Sampie even helped tend Jericho, who could do less for himself with every passing week. He helped Jericho wash and to the privy and walked him between his chair on the porch and the bed. He was gentle with the old man. In the evening he'd play with the children catching lightning bugs or carve little toys out of wood until the light faded and Comfort called the children to come on to say their prayers.

Aunt Polly came to call one afternoon. She brought them a small basket of wild pears and a hickory-nut cake. She asked if Jericho was feeling better. He was looking better than the last time she'd seen him.

"No," said Rosa, "it's Sampie who looks after him. Don't know what we'd have done without him." She reeled off a list of tasks Sampie had done just that day.

"Humph!" said Aunt Polly, at where Sampie was smoking his pipe at the end of the porch and mending a hoe. Sampie looked up at her, and the last rays of the sun glinted off his strange eyes.

When Rosa went inside with the children, Aunt Polly took Comfort off to the other side of the porch. "Girl, get rid of that high yellow. He's trouble, I can tell. Maybe helping you, but don't trust him. He's got evil in him."

Comfort felt a flash of irritation. Aunt Polly was a dear, but she was always meddling in other people's business, whether that of her own daughters or anyone else. And such a way of talking about a Negro made her think Charley had done the right thing to fight on against slavery. "He's found refuge here, and he's more than repaid us," she said primly.

Aunt Polly shook her head. "You watch him, girl. And if you feel uncomfortable, you let me know at once. Fire that rifle you keep loaded above the fireplace. We hear a shot, we'll come. And keep an eye on Rosa. She trying to hide it from you, but she's poorly. Give her some catnip tea."

"I will," said Comfort.

In June they had seen newspaper reports that there'd been a terrible battle at Newmarket in May. A letter came to Rosa from Catherine in Lexington. Rosa began reading it to Comfort and then reached for Comfort's hand.

Catherine wrote that Lawrence had disappeared. Cadets from the institute weren't conscripted, but they'd been sent to the Shenandoah to act as drillmasters for the Confederates. Lawrence believed they were exempt from any actual fighting, but the boys were young, and he had gone with them to prevent hotheads from getting carried away and enlisting.

Lawrence had been at Newmarket with a group of young cadets who were meant to observe only. Catherine was certain Lawrence would have done anything in his power to prevent what happened next. General Breckinridge was so desperate for troops he reneged on his undertaking to keep the young cadets out of the fighting. He was supposed to have said, "They're children, may God forgive me," as he sent the young cadets into the line. A shell had exploded, killing many of the boys. No one knew what had happened to Lawrence. Catherine was praying he was in a field hospital or even had been taken prisoner.

The last thing Catherine wrote was "I know what Lawrence's feeling must have been as he watched his boys die, dear Mother. His pain is mine. I cannot rest until I know what's happened to him. I am setting off to Newmarket to find him. I will leave the baby with Mercy and her mother, Hezziah, who by the grace of God were visiting."

The weather turned cold in October, and Jericho died. They buried him, and Sampie carved a cross on which Rosa had written, "Jericho Marshall, beloved husband and father, born 1790, died October 21, 1864," for him to burn into the wood.

"'The Lord giveth and the Lord taketh away,'" said Rosa, bleakly. "We were married nearly fifty years."

As the winter drew in, Comfort watched with a heavy heart as Rosa struggled to get up in the morning and grew gaunt and bent over with the pain of whatever was gnawing at her.

It grew colder and colder. One morning they woke to find it had snowed hard, and ice crystals hung from the trees. Rosa's bed was in the parlor, where they had moved it when Jericho was sick, to be closer to the big fireplace. Comfort slept beside her at night because Rosa said she couldn't get used to sleeping alone in the featherbed she'd shared with Jericho. The children slept on a pallet in a little room at the back that had a fireplace. Nights were long, and Rosa was often in pain, waking Comfort by her tossing and turning to ease it. Comfort would poke up the fire and read the Bible aloud to soothe her back to sleep.

"Comfort, dear, I can feel my hour is coming," Rosa said one night. Her voice was weak.

"Mother Marshall, don't say that!"

"It's nigh." She gazed into Comfort's stricken face. "You're a good girl. You were good to Jericho and me, a good wife to Charley just as my Catherine is a devoted wife to Lawrence." Her voice faltered. No one knew what had happened to Lawrence or whether Catherine had found him and brought him home to Lexington. "Staying with us when you could have gone back to your family in Richmond."

"I couldn't leave thee, Mother Marshall."

"Read me a psalm, dear."

And before Comfort reached the end of the psalm, Rosa was dead.

Comfort closed the Bible and sat still. She tried to open her mind to the light. All she felt was despair.

She heard a noise and looked up to see Sampie had come in with a load of wood. He closed the door and walked over to the fireplace, threw it on the fire. He turned to her, and his yellow eyes were caught by the leaping flames. Then he came to where she was sitting.

"Miss Rosa dead?"

"Yes."

He was too close. She felt the first stirrings of fear. He put a hand on her neck, a strong hand, like iron. "Don't be afraid. Just Old Sampie, I won't hurt you none. Don't make a noise and wake the chillun."

"Get out," she hissed. "Have thee no respect for the dead!" Trying not to let her mounting fear show, trying to pull away, but they struggled and she realized how strong he was. He dragged her down onto the floor, and though she fought and bit with all her might, he was too strong for her. Through the long, terrible hours that followed, she prayed and thought of her children and managed not to scream, not once.

When dawn came and the window lightened with the new day, Sampie rose and arranged his clothes and closed the door behind him.

343

That instant Comfort rose too. Hardly knowing what she did, she went to the fireplace and snatched down the rifle Aunt Polly insisted she keep loaded there. She flung open the door and saw Sampie halfway to his cabin. She raised the rifle and fired, and Sampie fell forward into the snow. She saw him twitch and jerk, and a red stain spreading in the snow.

The children! She'd forgotten everything, even the children.

She put the gun down and hurried to the small bedroom. Teeny was grizzling, and Ben was sitting upright, his eyes wide. "Was that a soldier shooting? Are the soldiers coming?" He began to cry with fright.

The children mustn't see Sampie's dead body, she thought frantically. *If it is dead. Will I have to shoot him again to make sure? Yes, if I have to.* She'd have to drag it out of sight somehow.

She fought to keep her voice calm and steady. To smile, even. "No soldiers, darling, thee need not be afraid. It's cold, Ben. Let Mama build up the fire in the kitchen, the silly fire's gone out. Thee and Teeny stay here while it gets warm, and I'll get thee when breakfast is ready."

Ben nodded. Teeny wailed. "Here, let's put Teeny in thy bed, that way thee can each keep the other company." Ben moved to let Teeny snuggle next to him. She looked up at her brother and smiled.

"Now, thee must both stay until I come back." She'd explain their grandmother's death later. She swiftly pulled the quilt over Rosa's face.

She was putting on a pair of Charley's old boots, her hands almost numb with cold, when she saw two figures coming out of the orchard. Aunt Polly and her eldest daughter. Comfort rushed to meet them.

"What's wrong, child? We heard the gunshot and came as fast as we could. Good Lord, your face, what happened? Is it Rosa?"

"Take the children to thy cabin!" Comfort said through chattering teeth. "Please! At once. Please. Please! And don't let them look toward . . . toward S-Sampie's cabin!"

Comfort began to shake uncontrollably, and without another word Aunt Polly's daughter went to the back bedroom, dressed the children, scooped one up in each arm, and said they were going to her place to eat baked apples for breakfast and, if they looked way over in the distance, they'd see an eagle and could make a wish. What would they wish?

"For Papa to come home and be safe, like we pray every night," Comfort heard Ben say solemnly.

"For Papa," echoed Teeny.

"Keep looking," said the daughter as they crossed to the orchard with their heads turned away from the bloody mound in the snow. "Keep looking. Biggest old eagle in the mountains."

After she heard the story, Aunt Polly made Comfort drink some hot milk and eat a little, wrapped her in a quilt, and told her not to stir. Then the older woman went outside and stared at Sampie's corpse. She gave a low whistle. For a Quaker who'd never fired a gun before, Comfort had taken a good shot, hitting Sampie squarely in the back. Aunt Polly bent and grabbed Sampie's feet. She dragged him into the old slave cabin and over to the pile of straw where he slept. She went back to the kitchen, where Comfort was sobbing uncontrollably and rocking back and forth. *Let her have a good cry, best thing,* thought Aunt Polly as she lit a pine knot. She went back to the cabin and held the burning pine knot to the pile of straw. Soon flames were leaping, it was catching pretty good, she thought, and left to pour boiling water on the bloody snow. Black smoke rose in billows from the burning cabin. It was likely some other person in Grafton would see the smoke and come soon, thinking Wildwood was on fire.

She'd explain that the crazy old man Sampie had burned his cabin down, had probably got hold of some whiskey Jericho had.

She'd get whoever came by to help bury Rosa.

Three months later an ashen-faced Comfort whispered to Aunt Polly that she was suffering punishment for her act of murder. "God has truly deserted me," she cried. "I'm expecting a child!"

Aunt Polly's daughters took Ben and Teeny into their cabin for longer and longer visits as Comfort's stomach swelled noticeably. They cried for their mother, but the daughters said Ma needed to rest, the war had made her tired, and by the time Comfort gave birth with Aunt Polly's help, they were used to being there. The baby was a girl with a sallow complexion, curly brown hair the color of Comfort's, and yellow eyes.

Comfort turned her face away. "I will not feed it."

Aunt Polly was firm. "You have to. It's not the baby's fault," she insisted. "That's an innocent child. Innocent as you in all this."

"What will I do if anyone finds out, Aunt Polly? I won't look innocent, will I? And Charley . . . What will this do to Charley? If he comes home, if he isn't dead like I'm afraid he is. What will I do then? How would I explain without breaking his heart? Oh, it would have been better if I'd died!"

"That's a wicked thing to say!" Aunt Polly shook her finger. "You ain't dead, and while you're alive, you have to do right. Doing right brings right. If you want Charley home, you can't abandon this child. Now I have a plan. With the war over, there's plenty of people traveling, men going home, sometimes a woman with them. Lot of Irish enlisted, I hear, and now they're either going home or looking for land like all the other soldiers.

"We'll say an Irish couple asked to stay the night in the barn, and when they'd gone, you heard a baby crying and found this one. Christian charity to take her in, honey. Give her an Irish name, like Katie."

By the time Katie was two, Comfort had let go of hope of ever seeing her husband again. On a summer evening with the chores done and the supper cleared away, Comfort sat the children down to explain to Ben and Teeny that Papa was dead and couldn't come back to them, but they must keep him alive in their hearts instead. She had Katie on her knee and was trying unsuccessfully to keep from adding her own tears to the children's distress when Ben cried, "Somebody coming toward the house!"

Comfort looked up to see a gaunt man's figure and swiftly put Katie down to fetch the gun she still kept ready and loaded above the fireplace. Her inner light, she'd decided long ago, had been extinguished by the act of murder. She had ceased to live in grace, was no longer who she had been, who she ought to be.

Yet as she lifted the gun, there was something about the approaching stranger . . .

"No!" she choked. "It can't be . . ."

"Ma?" said Ben, alarmed at the change in his mother's face.

"Ma?" Teeny echoed, looking anxiously from Ben to her mother.

"I think . . . the man is . . . Papa . . . come home," Comfort struggled to say, lowering the gun and putting it back in its resting place with shaking hands. She could scarcely breathe for relief and terror. "Children, it's a miracle. Papa has come home!" She went down the porch steps, slowly at first with the shock, then began to run toward the approaching figure, crying Charley's name, making her decision, her bargain. If she was a good mother to Katie, she never had to tell Charley the truth. Only Aunt Polly and her girls would ever know that. She would have to shoulder a burden of deception and maintain it for the rest of their days together. And she'd do it. She'd do it a thousand times over.

That Charley was home was all that mattered. For that, and his peace of mind, she would pay any price.

CHAPTER 38

THE RICHMOND DAILY INTELLIGENCER

Summer 1880

Yellow Fever?

*July 14. The report that there may have been a case of yellow
fever in the town of Grafton will excite sympathy in our readers who remember the terrible epidemic of the dreaded disease
in Norfolk in '55 and the great loss of life there. However,
we understand from another source in Grafton that it would
be an exaggeration to cry the alarm. There have merely been
a few cases of indisposition, consistent with the discomfort
occasioned by an especially hot and sultry summer that has
turned our normally rushing rivers sluggish and brown and*

given rise to an unpleasant miasma arising therefrom with the dawn. At such times mosquitoes and flies thrive and are especially vexing. To the despair of the housewife or the cook, in such conditions the dinner spoils almost as soon as it is placed on the table, milk sours in the pail, and butter melts in the springhouse. These are uncomfortable trials to be borne, to be sure, yet it would be wrong to conflate these discomforts of summer with a more deadly scourge.

Such an ill-founded supposition would result in needless panic and a great disruption to the river trade.

Yellow Fever?

July 18: Yet another report of a possible case, perhaps two cases, of the yellow fever in Grafton has reached us, but the telegraph line to Grafton being down, it precludes our further investigation. Still, it is not judged an outbreak is at hand. We understand that the supposed incidences have been contained by quarantining the sufferers in their homes. We have no further particulars at this time, but there can be no cause for alarm among the wider public.

Yellow Fever?

July 23: We are now supplied with further information on this matter. A riverboat from New Orleans put in to Grafton on the thirteenth of this month, and was due to have repairs carried out before loading its cargo and passengers for the return trip. The captain, who was traveling with his son, thinking to give his boy a treat, put up at the Grafton Hotel for the night, where they dined. Many of the crew also availed themselves of permission to go ashore and lodge at a boardinghouse that welcomes sailors, though several crew members did not, either because they felt tired from the journey or because they had no wish to indulge in the sometimes reprehensible excesses to which sailors are regrettably prone.

In the early hours of July 14, the captain's son was taken ill. He woke his father to complain of a bad headache and pains in his knees. He was feverish, and when the worried father lit a candle to examine the boy, the light proved too excruciating for the boy to bear, and he begged his father to extinguish it.

The town physician, Dr. Joshua Vann, was sent for, who confirmed the boy was very ill, but he could not diagnose yellow fever as a certain thing and believed it would be better not to cause unnecessary alarm. The boy was returned to his bed, to be watched closely by his father, advised to partake of cooling drinks at regular intervals and a tonic the doctor left.

In that same night some of the sailors staying at the board- inghouse began to be unwell with the same symptoms. But as they had been carousing and drinking copiously earlier in the evening, not much was thought of their being indisposed, until morning when it was discovered they all ran a high fever, complained of aches everywhere, and began vomiting.

The woman who ran the boardinghouse sent for Dr. Vann, who advised keeping the sailors separate from the other guests as a precaution. The landlady and the hotel proprietress provided cooling drinks as instructed to their various patients, and it is reported today that all are in a state of recovery.

Yellow Fever?

July 25: The recovery that all appeared to enjoy proved an harbinger of mortality. Following the doctor's assurance to his patients that they were mending, the captain's son began bleeding from his nose and eyes and was soon racked with pains in his abdomen. A similar relapse was reported from the boardinghouse, where the sailors one by one had seizures and fell into a coma. Alas, sure signs that the dreaded malady concealed itself briefly, deceiving the sufferers all was well, then, cruelly, igniting again with great savagery. The next day the captain's son died, and after suffering similar horrible agonies, the crewmen died likewise. Nevertheless, our informant believes that this was a few cases only, half a dozen, and precautions have been taken sufficient to prevent the spread of the malady.

Yellow Fever?

July 29: Reports from Grafton of further instances of sickness grow daily more alarming. Since we first wrote of a suspected case, a fortnight since, the workingmen's quarters and an area of Grafton known as Darkie Town have seen a great increase in the number of sufferers and fatalities. People living in these parts of Grafton are many, and the fever spreads from one to another like wildfire. The first citizens of the town have retreated away to the higher elevations. A Female Academy at Slipping Creek is presently home to a number of mothers with young babies, and the hotel at Rehoboth Springs on Little Frog Mountain is occupied by a number of matrons and older children. Despite the exigency, the hotel owner, Mr. Preston

Drumheller, declined to abate his customary tariff for these refuges, and people must pay or go.

Yellow Fever

August 4: We cannot report the latest ravages of the fever in Grafton, as the telegraph line is again down, but we understand there have been many deaths. With the hot spell, the river level sank, and there are reports of a riverboat damaged by rocks that put in to the Grafton landing with a badly damaged keel that needed repairs. There was no one to carry out repairs due to the spread of the fever, and the riverboat and its crew were resigned to wait. Somehow the fever crept on board and left it a charnel house. It caught fire one night and burned where it lay aground. Arson may have been involved, but it is impossible to say so with any certainty.

Yellow Fever

August 16: The fever shows no sign of abating in Grafton, and the list of the dead grows daily. The "voice of Rachel weeping for her children" is everywhere heard, as little ones expire in their mothers' arms. The scourge is no respecter of wealth or position. Members of the Vann, Marshall, White, Stuart, and even Drumheller families die as surely as the poorest laborers. Death, when it comes, comes quickly to children and to the older people, a terrible mercy. There are reports of couples expiring side by side, of families with no one well enough to minister to their suffering members and forced to lie helpless, listening to the cries and supplications of their loved ones begging for a drop of water. An aged minister of the town, who had labored to bring relief to his suffering townspeople, and his wife, who went fearlessly nursing in the afflicted households, contracted the malady. Reverend Endurance Merriman and his wife, Hezziah, were found expired together, an open Bible beside them on the bed, by Hezziah's elder sister, Mrs. Adelina Vann. Mrs. Vann herself died soon after. There are too many dead to bury, and too few gravediggers. Much use is made of wagons to collect the dead and bury them in common graves.

Yellow Fever

September 4: Those who would flee Grafton and the pestilence find every door, every town closed to them lest they carry the plague with them. People who sought refuge elsewhere have been driven back by armed patrols who will accept no one from the Bowjay Valley. There the fever has spread beyond the confines of the town to the most distant homesteads. It is reported that a group of Quaker nurses and doctors volunteered to travel south to the beleaguered region and are expected any day.

Yellow Fever

October 10: We understand that the rate of infection in the Bowjay Valley is at last slowing with the cooler weather, and we note with sadness the deaths of some thirty of the Quaker Good Samaritans who themselves succumbed to the dreaded disease. A subscription is being got up in Boston and Philadelphia for their families.

Grafton can truly be termed the Valley of the Shadow.

CHAPTER 39

"VOICES FROM THE SPIRIT LAND"

July 1883

On the approach to the turnpike road leading up to the campground on the southern end of Frog Mountain, the procession of wagons bound for the campground had slowed to a crawl. It was hot, and the oxen and mules and horses stamped their feet, raising dust, shaking their heads up and down against the flies. Bella and Marietta Fairweather were glad the long trip up the valley from their homestead to Grafton was nearly over. It was the time of the annual camp meeting, and they'd been traveling since before dawn. The girls swung bare feet off the back of their parents' wagon and clung to the sides to keep from being bounced off as they stopped and started. "You smell 'em yet?" they kept asking each other. They sniffed the dusty air expectantly as the wagon lurched, stop-starting toward the tollgate, and finally were rewarded by a heady fragrance of hot butter, sugar, and cinnamon.

They turned around and craned their necks to see if the tollgate was in sight at the southern end of Frog Mountain. Up ahead, Burwell Pine, the toll keeper, grinned like a hound with a bowl of molasses, collecting tolls in an unhurried way. Nobody passed his tollgate without a "Good morning" or a "Y'all come far?" and a discussion of the weather they could expect for the next week. This tactic forced the travelers to linger long enough to decide the cookies smelled too good not to buy some.

Inside the house Burwell's wife had been baking as fast as she could get them in and out of her oven. The Pines' son, Jimmy, stood guard by the plank bench where the cookies cooled, a penny a dozen. Burwell fumbled with change and didn't hurry anybody, and people had to wait in line, tantalized by the aroma. Most bought some.

"Y'all too old to want cookies—big old girls now, fourteen and fifteen," said their father, looking back from the driver's seat as he took out his toll money. "Reckon we'll just drive on through."

"Paaaa! *Please!* We're half-starved! It's been practically a whole day since we et breakfast!"

"Bella Fairweather, hadn't been more'n two, three hours at most. I think you got worms again."

"She's got her a sweet tooth," said Bella's mother, "and she come by it honest, from her daddy." All four of the Fairweathers knew that when they reached the tollgate, Mr. Fairweather would gee up the horses as if to go straight on through as soon as he paid his quarter, then halfway through the gate would pull the team up, say he plumb forgot, and buy two dozen cookies. Bella imagined the first bite, always the best, when the cookie melted into a river of sweetness on your tongue . . .

"How y'all doin' today?" asked Burwell jovially, counting Mr. Fairweather's money for form's sake. "Yep, that's right, sure enough. Gonna be a hot day. Now lessee, you're the Fairweathers, from down the valley a way, almost didn't recognize you 'cause it's been a while since you come to the gatherin'. I remember them two girls in the back from when they weren't no bigger'n june bugs, and I almost didn't recognize them, darn if they are growed-up young ladies already, settin' there pretty as a picture! Be married before you know it." The girls blushed and giggled, and Burwell winked and tipped his hat.

The teams of oxen and horses strained on the turnpike's winding climb, and the Fairweathers called greetings to people they knew from previous summers. It was the eighth year the Spiritualists had held their annual camp meeting at the top of Frog Mountain, where Slipping Creek came tumbling below a broad, grassy place just level enough to camp on and mountain springs in the rocks provided two hundred people with fresh water.

At the first bend of the turnpike, Mr. Fairweather pointed out the first landmark, a cluster of overgrown buildings where there'd been a mission school in the old days, for the Cherokee, and then an academy for young ladies. That had caught fire and burned down just after the epidemic.

Above that the air grew fresher as they climbed. The spirits liked when everyone came to a high place; it was closer to where they dwelled.

The girls waved to their friends as the procession went slowly up the switchback. "There's the Marshalls," said Marietta, nudging Bella and pointing down below to Comfort Marshall and her son, Ben, coming up the turnpike behind them. Comfort was still a pretty woman, thought Marietta. She had all her teeth, and her white hair was so abundant that it was like a great cloud on her head. Her eyes were sad. Probably because she was a widow. They said her husband had been a handsome man, tall and lively, always laughing. Ben was handsome too, with a shock of hair that fell over his forehead. Behind Ben and Comfort sat Katie Marshall. From a distance Katie was pretty enough, with a lot of curly hair tied back with a ribbon and slim waisted. Only it was disconcerting when she looked at you.

Her eyes were strange. They reminded Marietta of a bobcat she had once surprised slinking under the chicken coop. The bobcat had turned and given her a malevolent yellow-eyed stare, and Marietta had screamed for her father to bring the rifle. There was some strange thing about Katie, something to do with where she had come from, Marietta knew. Aunt Polly Stuart, who'd been the Marshalls' nearest neighbor during the war, had told everyone Katie was a poor little war baby. They had found her wrapped in a blanket in the barn after some Irish people had passed by and spent the night there.

"In the straw, like baby Jesus in the manger!" was how Aunt Polly had put it in her booming voice. And since it had been left in Comfort's barn, Aunt Polly had told Comfort it was Comfort's Christian duty to raise it. When Aunt Polly had an opinion about something, it was better not to argue with her, so people could see why Comfort raised the child.

Except for her strange eyes, it was funny how much Katie resembled Comfort, Marietta thought, considering she wasn't blood kin.

At the overlook, Mr. Fairweather pulled off the road beside the Marshalls, lined up like many others, and let the horses drink after the climb where water trickled out of the mountain into a wooden trough. Everyone said, "How've you been?" and counted the family members with their eyes.

Marietta watched Ben Marshall from under her eyelashes, thinking how handsome and melancholy he looked, every inch the sorrowful lover. No wonder. He'd been engaged to Marietta and Bella's older sister, Bessie, and now, thought Marietta, like the old song about Lady Margaret and Sweet William, "his true, true love was lying in a cold, dark coffin, her face turned to the wall." Bessie's death had turned Ben quiet and made him look older. He didn't talk about it, though.

Ben stood with his back to everybody, not saying anything, as if absorbed in the view. She knew he'd come to the meeting in case Bessie's spirit would contact him, even though Marietta was sure he didn't believe in spiritualism; Ben was practical and reasonable and clever and funny, but not . . . sensitive to spirits. Suddenly Marietta understood how deep his grief went, that he was willing to try something he thought was nonsense, just in case.

She remembered the night Ben came riding down to their homestead three years ago. It was just before supper, and Bessie had been jumpy as a cat all day. She kept leaving her chores to look out the window.

The girls had watched through the window as he tied up his horse, raised his hat to slick his hair back, straightened his coat, and marched to the door to ask Mr. Fairweather if he could have his daughter's hand in marriage. He'd been too nervous to remember to say good evening, just blurted out the minute he stepped inside, "Sir, I've come to ask your permission to marry Bessie."

The girls had been hovering on the stairs in earshot. They all held their breath. Their father had a droll but unpredictable sense of humor. Mr. Fairweather had looked at him for a minute, then asked, "Why?" and Bessie had groaned, "Papa!" and put her head in her hands.

Ben's declaration of love had come pouring out, and he was just saying that the night they'd met at the Twelfth Night Ball when Bessie was staying with the Stuart girls had been the happiest chance of his life, when Bessie came running down the stairs, crying, "Papa, don't tease. Ask Ben to stay for supper. I told him that if the answer was yes, you'd invite him to supper."

Ben had nodded and put an arm around Bessie. "She did, sir. And I'm hungry."

"Well," Mr. Fairweather had said laconically, looking up at the ceiling like he wondered what it was doing there, "I was going to ask about his prospects, and how he's going to take care of you, but they say he's planning to start a newspaper. Is that right?"

Bessie and Ben nodded.

"A good idea. Newspapers are good business. So, Bessie, don't just stand there looking at me with such an expression, go tell your mother to set an extra place."

Now they were all thinking about Bessie. So the Fairweathers and Comfort and even Katie started talking louder and more enthusiastically than necessary about the view and how far you could see and the amazing fact you could look *down* on the birds flying over the valley. They agreed how much fresher and healthier it was away from the river, several times.

Mrs. Fairweather asked after Teeny Marshall. "In school in Philadelphia," said Comfort. "A Friends school for girls."

"This nice, clean air, I feel the souls lifted up and rejoicing, don't you?" asked Mrs. Fairweather, breathing deeply as the wind stirred the wisps of hair around her face.

"I do, Mommy," said Bella, retying her sunbonnet. "I feel them all around us, flying in glory and peace, praising the Lord they don't have to bump along in an earthly wagon. Just flying through this nice, fresh air." She tipped her head up and scanned the sky.

Bella looked pale and nervous, Marietta thought. Like she always did when she felt the spirits warning her to get ready.

Comfort nodded her white head. "May the Lord grant us grace to hear them," she said with a vacant look. Comfort had come from a Quaker family. Marietta was fairly sure Quakers were supposed to pray quietly and not go looking for spirits. They had learned about Quakers at school. They didn't go in for hymns and shouting, preferring to sit and think quietly about the Lord and what their inner light told them.

Well, the Lord must have approved of that way of worshipping, because no one could say he hadn't looked after Comfort Marshall. She had a new bonnet, plain gray silk, tied with large ribbons in a becoming bow under her chin. The buggy she was driving was sleek and black, and the pair of horses pulling it looked lively.

Comfort and her husband had sold some of the Marshall estate and managed to rebuild Wildwood after the war, get the fields and orchards producing again, pay their taxes, send Ben north to college in Boston, and then, when he came home, even buy a large lot in Grafton so Ben could start a newspaper.

The Marshalls had money because they'd inherited twice. They said Rosa Charbonneau Marshall had left her son Charley a small fortune of Charbonneau money and that Comfort's father, a Quaker from Richmond with Unionist sympathies, had invested heavily in railway stock before the war. Comfort had been adamant Ben attend Harvard College, where antislavery sentiment had been strong. Then she'd sent Teeny north too. Founding a newspaper was Ben's plan when he returned.

Comfort was only here for Ben's sake.

"There will be a great rejoicing, hallelujah! Come on now," said Mr. Fairweather, and clucked the team back into line. The girls clambered back on the wagon. Mrs. Fairweather sighed and retied her bonnet. "If only Bessie would send the boy a word or two!"

Marietta chewed her dusty bonnet strings resentfully and wondered why the spirits never spoke to her. She was the eldest now Bessie was gone. For some reason the spirits had never spoken to Bessie either, though Bessie had tried to attract their notice. She would go off by herself to the springhouse or hide in the barn and would shut her eyes and tell them in her mind where she was, in case they wanted her. But they never did, although they nearly always went for the oldest girl in the family. Of the three girls, they only spoke to Bella, who was the youngest.

Mrs. Fairweather told Marietta that with spirits it all depended, and anyway, now that Marietta had started having monthlies, the spirits were unlikely to speak to her any more than they spoke to Bessie. They liked young girls best.

Word had spread that Bella had the gift, and people came for miles around just to see and hear Bella get in touch with the beyond. They would bring her little presents—some honey in a comb or a fancy pincushion or a piece of muslin—and treat her like she was some kind of princess. They wanted to talk to their dead, were desperate to say what they hadn't said or thought of before Death parted them.

It had been the same with her mother when she was Bella's age, according to Mrs. Fairweather. Then she'd got married. Sometimes Marietta was jealous, wishing she had been the one to inherit her mother's gift and have folks come for miles, begging her to get in touch with their dear departed dead folks and making her feel important.

Other times she wished they could all just live in the normal world where you could see and touch and hear things for real, not trying to figure out what the spirits were doing every minute and whether they were present and watching you. You had to be thinking about them all the time, careful what you said in case they heard you. Careful what you *thought*! They could tell what you were thinking.

You couldn't get away from spirits. They were always hovering, wearing long white garments, never too busy to be watching and listening even if they weren't speaking to you at the moment. Even if they never spoke to you. Marietta knew her mother found this comforting, but she didn't much like to think of being watched all the time. Whole armies of spirits, she imagined, because so many people had died. Did they all watch while you were asleep? Did they wait politely outside the privy?

"Spirits can't eat cookies, though," Marietta muttered, biting greedily into her third cookie. *So there!* she thought, chewing, hoping the spirits were watching. Then, guiltily, she whispered, "Sorry, I didn't mean you," to her twin brothers and Bessie. The twins had only been three when they died. They'd been poorly the night before the three girls were due to take the train to visit their aunt in Danville.

Only two went. Bessie, who doted on the boys, had stayed to nurse them at the last moment. It was the yellow fever. Within a week the twins' tormented little bodies had been laid to rest, and Bessie was struck down too. She was stronger, had taken longer to die, gasped that they mustn't send word to Ben, because he'd come and he'd take sick too.

By late afternoon the campground was crowded with wagons. People unpacked blankets and coffeepots and skillets and sent the children to wash their dusty hands and faces in Slipping Creek. Campfires were lit, and suppers of bacon and skillet corn pone and coffee were prepared and eaten, followed by the bustle of women washing pans and cups at the creek's edge. Revived by supper, children splashed in the water and chased each other, shrieking, while the sun set. The men checked that the horses were firmly hobbled. Lightning bugs came out, and with families fed and chores done, women unrolled and fluffed the quilts they had brought. It would be cool in the early morning hours. Smaller children protesting they weren't the least bit tired were wrapped up and put to bed in the wagons.

Then one by one, or in family groups, people made their way toward the grassy area with a small platform the men erected every year in the middle. Mr. Fairweather carried a chair and a table and put them on the platform, and Reverend James set out a trumpet and a drum by a stack of *New Harp of Columbia* shape-note hymnals. A few people came forward to take one and began turning the pages, squinting in the dusk to look for this or that favorite. The air throbbed with anticipation and a low hum of conversation. Slowly everyone gathered round the platform in a semicircle. Dusk deepened into dark; conversation died away.

Resin torches had been lit by the platform, and there around the edge of the clearing they crackled in the silence, the light cast by the flames throwing faces in high relief against the night. They waited.

Then the hush was broken by a woman who began to hum a key. The sound was picked up here and there in the crowd; tentatively voices hummed to get the different notes right. Finally out of the crowd a soprano voice lifted tremulously:

> *In the silence of the midnight*
> *When the cares of day are over*
> *In my soul I hear the voices*
> *Of the loved ones gone before.*

The congregation joined in, swelling the hymn:

> *Hear them words of comfort whispering*
> *That they'll watch on every hand*
> *And I love, I love to list to*
> *Voices from the spirit land.*

Finding its voice, the congregation shifted into close harmonies and sang louder:

> *Loved ones that have gone before me*
> *Whisper words of peace and joy*
> *Those that long since have departed*
> *Tell me their divine employ*
> *Is to watch and guard my footsteps*
> *Oh it is an angel band*
> *And my soul is cheered in hearing*
> *Voices from the angel band.*
>
> *Voices . . . voices . . .*
> *Angel . . . angel*
> *Voices . . . voices . . .*
> *Voices from the angel band.*

The echo of the last harmonies drifted away into the mountain night, and there was silence again under the stars, this time tense with anticipation, broken only by the snap of the torches blazing in the darkness.

A night bird called, and Reverend James, who had been praying quietly, lifted his bowed head and bid the congregation welcome to their campground. He spoke for a long time about trials and afflictions, about the plagues of Egypt and about loved ones gone before. Reverend James had lost his wife of forty years to the fever, and this year, though his words were stirring as always, people shouted, "Amen!" just as often as they had in previous years. Marietta thought his voice was feeble, his words harder to hear. And she sensed the crowd growing . . . what? Restless? Impatient?

Finally Reverend James made way for a smiling woman in a white dress and a kind of veil on her head, who stepped briskly forward from the crowd onto the platform, and a sigh of expectancy and relief went up.

She threw her arms wide as if to embrace the whole crowd. Her voice rang out. "Oh, friends! Oh, brothers and sisters! Tonight the air is full of sounds, the sky is full of tokens! All speak to the intelligent. Open, oh open, your spiritual eyes, and see the shining ones that dwell in light who come among us now. Purify your souls, and you will hear, not the voices from the cold and lonely tomb, but the voices of those gone before who dwell in brightness and joy beyond the grave, beyond sorrow, cares, sickness, pain, and disappointment, and exalting in eternal love. Hear the angel band all around us."

People shifted and murmured, "Amen!"

"Amen, glory!" shouted Mrs. Fairweather in a firm voice. "Glory of the Lord be upon us!"

When word of the fever reached Danville, Marietta and Bella's aunt refused to let them return home until the leaves began to change and the first frost came. Mrs. Fairweather met Marietta and Bella at the gate, smiling too brightly. They found a house of mourning in a valley decimated by the fever.

Mrs. Fairweather's insistence that the three dead ones were still present, just invisible because they were on the other side, unsettled her two remaining daughters. She said they were right there in the house, just like always, dressed in radiant garments and content and smiling, sending spirit messages of love, if only the living would hear them.

Bella said at once she did hear something and called out, "Oh, Bessie! We miss you."

Marietta thought the house felt horrible, empty and silent with just the four of them. Though she tried hard to feel the spirit presence, she felt . . . nothing.

Tonight Mrs. Fairweather smiled bravely at Marietta, but as usual, when Marietta looked hopefully around her, she saw no light or radiance anywhere, and if Bessie and the boys were there, they weren't saying so. Instead she saw a tear trickle down her mother's cheek and slipped an arm round her protectively. "They woke to eternal life," Mrs. Fairweather whispered with a quaver, "from a world of sorrow and care. No hunger or thirst, no sickness, toil, or danger, never in sorrow to bring forth children."

"Now, Mama," said Marietta. Hugging her, Marietta could think of nothing but how Bessie had been looking forward to being married to Ben and didn't give a fig what sorrow and care lay in store, even the things to do with making and birthing babies that sometimes killed you. Bessie had made up her wedding dress, and Marietta wondered if she'd looked down from her heavenly bliss to take note of the fact they'd put the dress, finished except for the hem, in the clothes press with a branch of myrtle. As for the twins, how much sorrow and care could they have had to escape from in their small lives . . .

"Amen," whispered a similarly affected woman to Mrs. Fairweather. "As did my blessed angels. All five, took one after the other, they was. Same week. First little Susan, then little Joe, then Janey and Columbia and Minnow. Oh, I held on so hard to Minnow, he was my last, my baby, why could not one, just one, be spared?" The woman was thin, with eyes that looked too big for her face.

"The fever was God's handiwork for their good. Remember they dwell in bliss," said Mrs. Fairweather, patting her arm, "in a happier world."

"My husband wouldn't come this year," the woman whispered hoarsely. "I had to come by myself with my sister and her family. It's wrong, I know, but he says he just can't believe anymore, all five gone, but I had to come, in case . . . in case . . ."

"I know," whispered Mrs. Fairweather hoarsely, "of course you did. Remember, 'by the wife is the husband sanctified.'"

"There are pure and good spirits working among us tonight," intoned Reverend James loudly, lifting his right hand high. "Oh, I feel them around us, sweet human blossoms plucked to safety before they could shrivel and decay, moving among the crowd gathered to receive them, longing to communicate, to tell us to be of good comfort, they are near. Let us pray!"

The gathering sank to its knees. As they did so, there was a thud from the drum. It was shortly followed by a second thud, and there was a collective intake of breath. "Spirit music," people murmured excitedly. Everyone knew there had been many wonderful instances when the spirits had manifested themselves by playing instruments. Marietta repressed the thought the sounds might have been caused by pine cones falling from the tree overhead.

In the front row, Bella began swaying from side to side with her eyes shut.

Reverend James began a long prayer. Bella swayed harder.

Reverend James prayed good and loud this time, almost shouting, to the heavens, to let the spirits know where they were.

Bella began moaning, softy at first, as if she were just practicing, then louder until the people near them began to nudge each other hopefully. Finally Mrs. Fairweather said, "If they call you, Daughter, go and welcome them, don't keep them waiting!" She pulled Bella to her feet and gave her a push.

Other women whispered from behind, "Yes, go on if they're calling you!"

"Go!"

As if reluctant, Bella walked slowly forward out of the semicircle toward the platform, arms outstretched and staggering, as if her legs were heavy. "Hallelujah!" she whispered hoarsely.

"Hallelujah!" yelled Reverend James encouragingly, helping her to the chair.

"Hallelujah!" the cries rose hopefully. "Hallelujah! *Hallelujah!*"

When her mother began singing another hymn to encourage Bella, Marietta joined in.

> *In the words spoken I knew the sender*
> *Oh strange creation of times master*
> *We hear the message so much the plainer*
> *In the words spoken I knew the sender*

The harmonies rose triumphant with a livelier tempo than before, as Bella made her way with halting steps to the stone platform.

> *A vibration on the stillness of the night*
> *By the chemic masters of the spirit sphere*
> *Ignorance may seek to beat its sway in vain*
> *A condition it demands in nature's plan*
> *A vibration on the stillness of the night.*

Bella turned to the crowd, who fell silent almost at once, and sank slowly into the chair Reverend James placed for her. Her eyes were wide in her pale face, staring beyond everyone out to the dark starry sky. "Who is it that comes communicating with us tonight?" she intoned, looking up.

The sad-eyed woman next to Mrs. Fairweather strained forward and caught her breath.

There was silence, then Bella nodded. "I understand," she said in a strange, high voice. There was silence and the sound of five distinct rapping noises.

"I hear . . . I hear . . . Are you children?"

A single rap.

"How many of you, children?"

The five raps came again.

"And do you have a message for anyone here?"

Rap.

"Your mother? Is your mother with us?"

Rap.

There were eager, stifled cries among the congregation.

"Oh, spirits, what message do you bring?"

There was the sound of more rapping.

"You want your mother to know . . . all is well . . . on the other side?"

Rap.

"Your names, tell me your names so your mother will rejoice."

Rapping.

". . . Jenny . . . No, Janey . . . I'm sorry, *Janey*."

The woman by Mrs. Fairweather caught her breath sharply. "My middle girl was Jane, her daddy always called her Janey."

"Joe . . . ," repeated Bella slowly.

"Joe!" the woman cried out. "Mother's here!"

"Co . . . Co," said Bella hesitantly. "I can't understand you clearly . . . It sounds like a little girl."

"Columbia, are you indeed there? Oh, speak to me, darling! Speak to Mama one more time!" The voice rose shrilly.

"Columbia, yes," cried Bella.

"Min . . . Min."

"Oh, Minnow! Oh, my precious Minnow!"

Two raps.

"Su . . . Sukie . . . No, Susan?"

"Susan!"

"Janey," repeated Bella.

369

The woman by Mrs. Fairweather shrieked, hysterical now, "My baby! My Janey! All five! Together. A comfort! Shall I see you again in the hereafter, children? Speak to Mama!"

"Yes!" said Bella in a loud voice. "Yes! *Yes!*"

"Praise God Almighty," the woman screamed and collapsed, sobbing. Women nearby rushed to lift her up, saying, "Praise Jesus!"

"Thank the Lord, my dearie!"

"Your little ones have gone on before, showing you the way! Thank you, Jesus!" A woman looked up and shouted to the dark sky.

"They're waiting!"

"Rejoice, sister! They spoke! Oh, what joy you have tonight!"

"Joy," the woman sobbed. "Joy!"

On the ground she writhed and shrieked of joy and wept as others tried to support her. Marietta thought she didn't look comforted.

Bella sat still, staring into the darkness, looking dazed.

"Praise Jesus," said Mrs. Fairweather faintly. "A wonderful manifestation, we are blessed this night. But are there no more with you, Daughter?" she called wistfully to the front. Marietta knew her mother was waiting to hear about the twins and Bessie.

But Bella fainted.

Being guided by the spirits often had that effect. They wore her out. Mrs. Fairweather sighed and stood up and went toward her daughter, smelling salts already in her hand. She looked much older all of a sudden, and her step was slow. Marietta saw the glint of tears on her mother's cheeks and longed to shake Bella awake and scream at her.

Someone started singing "Amen, Amen, There's a Higher Power," and soon everyone was singing and clapping their hands and shouting, ecstatic, swaying in time, singing louder than ever.

Automatically mouthing the words "There's a higher power," Marietta stood too and slipped away from the circle, unnoticed in the commotion. It was always like this. These gatherings left Marietta feeling terrible; sadness engulfed her like the river. She was unable to rejoice or join the singing.

The torches flickered in the night breeze. She walked past the wagons with the sleeping children and then past where the horses and oxen were hobbled and then away from the camp. A rousing chorus of "Amen! Amen!" followed her, growing fainter as she saw the profile of the Old Man of the Mountain looming dark against the night sky. She kept walking, feeling angry and sad and doubting and helpless and wanting to put as much distance as she could between herself and the Spiritualists and her parents and the grieving mother of five dead children.

She heard an owl cry and an answering cry from another one.

Marietta looked up at the stars. She liked to hear owls calling to each other even if some people said that meant bad luck. She decided she was tired of struggling to believe what other people said about things you couldn't see.

She walked up and up toward the Old Man. On previous trips she'd climbed up here during the day but never in the night. She sat down on the top of the Old Man's head and looked out at the dark valley. The stone was still a little warm from the sun, and that felt friendly. Things rustled in the forest around her, but she didn't feel scared.

She jumped. The child sitting quietly at her elbow must have slipped away from one of the wagons where it should have been asleep and followed her from the campground. She had been very quiet, because Marietta hadn't heard steps behind her on the road. The child stared up at Marietta. She had dark eyes in a clever little face framed with long dark braids, wore a plain old-fashioned frock, and had beaded moccasins on her feet.

"I like looking at the stars," she said.

"Me too," Marietta said, looking up. "Seems like they go on forever." She was beginning to feel a little uplifted, even if she had company and she was now responsible for a child.

"Would you like to fly with me?" the little girl asked. "We can fly up to the stars if you want."

"That sounds like a nice game," said Marietta. The owls hooted again, and back at the campground they started another hymn.

"It's not a game, I can fly. I know a spell that will turn us both into eagles. We stand on the ledge up there, and I say the spell, and we fly off."

"What?" said Marietta.

"The eagles taught it to my uncle when he became their brother, and he taught it to me. The spell only works if there are two or more. I flew with him only once, from that cliff up there." The child pointed up. "He made the spell and told me to close my eyes, and we flew off the rock, and then he disappeared. I must go to the land where the darkness dwells and find my people who were taken away on a boat."

Marietta sucked in her breath as the truth dawned. The child was one of those "not right" in the head. She knew several families with a child like that. They often took fits as well.

Feeling suddenly out of her depth and wondering what her mother would do in these circumstances, Marietta asked warily, "How did your uncle get to be the eagles' brother?" She'd better take the child back to the campground before her family got worried.

The child sighed and swung her feet. "He was a beloved man of our tribe. He had powers. Then someone laid a curse on him, and evil followed him. The elders banished him to live on the mountaintop."

"And then he flew away and left you alone?"

The child shook her head. "No. My mother is here."

"That's good," said Marietta with relief. "Come on. It's late. Time for you to be asleep. Let's find her. She will be worried."

"She's over there," said the child, pointing into the woods. "But you won't be able to see her."

Marietta hoped the child with an eagle for an uncle was not going to say her mother was a bear or something. Anyway, what kind of mother would be sitting in the woods at this time of night? Maybe one that wasn't right in the head any more than her daughter.

"And sometimes I find people who want to fly, so I take them up to that cliff, and we fly off."

Marietta looked up again, then at the dark valley below. The shadows were suddenly ominously deep and black under the cliff.

"It doesn't hurt to fly," said the child scornfully.

"Have you changed many folks into eagles?" Marietta asked as conversationally as she could manage. She'd better take this odd child back before she upped and tried to fly off the Old Man and left Marietta to explain. Marietta didn't think she could stand any more dead children and grieving mothers just now.

The child nodded. "Children want to. I took a lot of children once, but none of them could fly for as long as I can. I have to find more soon."

"Er. Come on, we'll go back to camp now. What's your name?" asked Marietta, putting out her hand for the little girl's. Better hang on to her.

Instead of a child's hand, cold stung Marietta's fingers, as if they had touched ice.

The child grinned up at her, teeth gleaming white in the dark. "Dancing Rabbit," she cried, and then the rock beside Marietta was empty. "Dancing Rabbit," came the girl's voice from farther off. Marietta whirled round. Where was the child? *"Rabbit, Rabbit, Rabbit,"* echoed tauntingly. There was something that sounded like laughter and a rustling in the bushes. Then silence.

Marietta gaped at her empty hand. The hackles rose on the back of her neck.

A twig broke behind her, and Marietta nearly jumped out of her skin. She whirled round.

The dark form of a tall man walked toward her. "It's me, Marietta," said Ben. "I saw you leave the meeting. Don't blame you for going.

I'm fed up too. Came to see if you're all right, make sure you don't get lost. There's some strange old stories about a shape-shifter sits up here at night."

"Ben, you half scared me to death! Thought you'd be back at the meeting, carrying on with everybody else." Marietta was so relieved to see a real person she knew that she almost hugged him. "I don't believe in shape-shifters any more than I believe in . . . spirits."

He sighed. "Were you talking to someone? It sounded like you were."

"I thought so at first. Did you see a little girl . . ."

"'Cause there's another old story about a curse the Cherokees put on this spot when they were forced to leave. I heard talking, but I couldn't see anyone with you. I heard somebody laughing. You stood up and started looking around. They say a Cherokee girl got left behind when they carried the Cherokees west."

"Er . . . there was a child . . . but she's gone now."

"You got the sight, haven't you." It was a statement. "Bella doesn't, not really. I watched her."

"Well . . ." Marietta realized that if she did have the sight, she didn't particularly want it after all. "I never thought so before . . . ," she said cautiously.

He broke off. "We're leaving in the morning. Look, can you reach Bessie?" he asked bluntly. "I don't believe in it, but I've been waiting since the day we buried her to hear a message from the other side, in case I'm wrong. I want to believe she would send me some word, even if it's just goodbye, if she could. Can you try one last time? You're her sister, maybe she'll talk to you."

"Ben."

"Please! You don't know how hard it's been, knowing she's not here but people saying she is."

"Well, I'll try, but you've got to promise me you won't tell anyone if I get through."

"Cross my heart."

Marietta closed her eyes tight and tried to open her heart. She conjured up a picture of Bessie in her mind and concentrated hard. But nothing happened.

Come back, Bessie, just say something to him, Marietta begged silently, but nothing. *Please!* Silence.

"I'm sorry, Ben," she said finally. "Nothing."

"That's it! It's what I knew all along. This is all foolishness. Bessie's dead, and that's all there is to it. She's gone on. I loved her, but all the messages in the world don't mean I can still marry her. Man needs a real wife, not a spirit one. I hate this spirits thing! I hate that I try it when I don't even believe it."

Marietta sighed. "I know. I'm sick to death of spirits myself. It wears you out, always wondering what they're doing and whether they're near but you can't see them!" Marietta burst into tears. "We finished sewing her wedding dress, she fell sick before she could hem it." She sobbed, "It's all packed up in the cedar chest. It's so pretty . . . like Bessie was. When we closed the trunk on it, it felt like we were burying her again!" She buried her face in her hands.

Then close to her ear, there was a mournful whisper. "Don't cry. You'll get married. You can wear my dress to get married if you want . . . you hear? Live for me, Marietta. Take my place," said Bessie faintly. "It will be all right. You'll be happy. Goodbye, Marietta. Goodbye."

CHAPTER 40

LORENA

June 1885

I was almost late for the arrival. Misplaced my notebook. Again. Swore to clean up my desk sometime, or I'm liable to disappear someday underneath a pile of something, but it's a big desk, and it's astonishing how much mess two men and a newspaper can generate. A newspaper generates a lot of papers and mess. Finally found the notebook. Then my hat was missing. Late! Ran. By the time I got to the train station, there was a crowd. But thankfully no train yet.

I looked around me to make a note of the details. As a newspaperman, indeed, the only newspaperman and the proprietor of the *Grafton Messenger*, yours truly is obliged to record every detail of this interesting event for our readers.

A newspaperman must always observe the details. They are what make a story live or die. And stories are what make a newspaper live or die. Ladies, in particular, enjoy reading about the clothing worn to events, which forms the greater part of the newspaper's subject matter—school prize days, the Blackberry Picnic, weddings, and so on. This detail is regarded as somehow encapsulating the spirit of the occasion. Above all, our female readers are always gratified to see themselves mentioned and described in flattering, though respectful, terms.

It was a colorful scene, ladies in their Sunday finery, men in hats, children in their best clothes, and a line of grizzled Confederate veterans, some with a leg or an arm missing, most in their old uniforms, stood to attention. Those people who supported the Union—and there were many in Grafton, like my late father—are, unsurprisingly, not present. But since the war Grafton has seen an influx of former Confederates, and they are all here today to honor their hero, a man who led so many to death and defeat.

The band members were trying to line themselves up in some kind of formation on the platform under the Confederate bunting and a banner that said, "WELCOME to GRAFTON," but the Ladies Committee had organized stands with big arrangements of flowers everywhere. These took up so much room the band was squeezed into a corner, much to the disgust of the disgruntled musicians, who kept batting ferns out of their eyes.

The place of honor on the platform, a special enclosure festooned with ribbons, was occupied by the Charbonneaus. The late Lafayette Charbonneau was responsible for bringing the railway to Grafton—the *Messenger* did a long piece on the twenty-fifth anniversary celebrations in the first issue—and this family enclosure, rather like a family pew in church, was built as a mark of the town's gratitude.

And there they all were in it, awaiting the arrival. Lafayette's beautiful widow, Aimée, looked serene and fresh despite the heat in a fetching pale-gray ensemble with matching feathers in her bonnet and some fine pearls. My sister Teeny, my invaluable aide in matters of feminine fashion, told me this is what is known as half mourning. For the year immediately after Lafayette's death, when full mourning was obligatory, it was as if the Mother of Sorrows had consulted the fashion papers. She was a tender vision in black silk, delicate jet jewelry, and black Spanish lace. Teeny said she looked like an exquisite black butterfly.

Beside her elegant mother, Malvina Charbonneau Drumheller presented a stark contrast in her widow's weeds. She had worn deep mourning since her husband, Jacky Drumheller, was killed at Chickamauga twenty-one years ago. There is nothing half about Malvina's mourning. It is deliberate and painful. Her clothes are a rusty, faded black, her only ornament a large mourning brooch with a lock of Jacky's hair.

Among the boxes of papers and documents and pictures that people have donated to the paper's archives, I found a daguerreotype made at the time of Malvina's engagement. It shows a lovely young face framed by mischievous curls, trying to set itself in a soulful look, but failing in the attempt, betrayed by a radiant smile. Now she wore her graying hair severely parted down the middle and drawn into an unbecoming knot at the back. The brooch is tightly fastened at her collar.

Teeny says her appearance is calculated, her widowhood and grief are meant to be as conspicuous as possible, a living reproach, and suspects that Malvina's mother, who is so clever with clothes, has advised her how to achieve this effect. Malvina never forgave Jacky's mother, an insufferable woman from Kingsport, who persuaded her family to obtain a commission in the Confederate army for Jacky, and a prestigious assignment as an aide to General Bragg. Teeny said Jacky's mother had done it to separate her son from Malvina, that she was determined her son would marry a Kingsport girl.

Her actions failed to prevent his marriage to Malvina, but they sealed Jacky's death warrant. He died at Chickamauga Creek. There were thirty-four thousand casualties that day.

As I looked around, I noticed Mercy Merriman was in black as well. Teeny said she'd been sweet on one of her cousin Joshua Vann's friends from Washington College. There had been an understanding between them. He'd been killed in the Chickamauga bloodbath too.

After Mercy, I spotted other spinsters, other black gowns scattered through the crowd. I thought they were like a silent chorus in a Greek tragedy. So many young men dead, so many abandoned marriage beds and arms empty of children. Hecuba on the walls of burning Troy.

They are making a display of their grief for another girl.

I turned my attention back to the platform and the Charbonneaus. Lafayette's adopted brother, Daniel, and Lafayette's two sons stood behind Aimée and Malvina. In profile these young men very much resemble their uncle Daniel.

Has anyone else noticed?

It was a warm morning. Some of the older veterans were so red in the face from the heat and their tight old Confederate uniforms they looked ready to drop with apoplexy.

I pulled out the notebook and my pencil and was scribbling, "The floral tributes were many and beauteous, testifying to the taste and tireless handiwork of the Ladies Committee, whose fair hands did not stint the welcoming posy . . . ," when a train whistle in the distance made me stop. The crowd surged forward, craning their necks, and we all waited several breathless minutes while the train pulled into view and then slowed, coming to a halt too soon, so that the carriage bearing the ladies did not quite reach the place allocated in front of the band for the reception of the honored widow and that sacred maiden, her daughter.

Very slowly, as if considering its precious cargo, the train rolled forward again, then stopped.

For an expectant moment, nothing happened. I wrote, "The moment of anticipation was both joyous and respectful," but then the mayor stepped forward and cleared his throat, and the crowd fell silent. He straightened his waistcoat and patted the watch chain, and when he found it was still there, he took a deep breath and, gripping the handle of the carriage door, signaled to the band, slightly hidden from view by greenery, who at once struck up "Bonnie Blue Flag" with all their might.

Most, although not all, of the children waved small flags, the blue ones with a star in the middle that had been the unofficial flag of the Confederates. Their mothers had assembled them from scraps, and their fathers had fixed them to sticks. Much easier to stitch together than the "stars and bars," with its blue cross and thirteen stars.

The ones with the flags burst into song to join in on the chorus. "Hurrah! Hurrah! For Southern rights, hurrah! Hurrah for the Bonnie Blue Flag that bears a single star!"

My mother, it should be noted, refused to be present. I confess I found it uncomfortable to be there. I was far from wishing to honor the dead general's relict and daughter, who are now regarded as Vessels of the Lost Cause. No cause has ever been better lost, in my opinion. But needs must, I am a newspaperman now, and I must attend to events and write a good story.

The carriage door was thrown open, and the mayor whipped off his hat and bowed as low and gallantly as he could, only to realize it was a portly gentleman who had descended. The mayor straightened up and shook hands, trying to see over the man's shoulder.

I recollected we had been informed that the visitors' party would include a brother of Mrs. Calvert, who always traveled with her and his niece as their protector. I assumed this was he. The portly gentleman gave a dignified wave to the crowd and then turned with a flourish and held out his hand to the open carriage door. A lady's black buttoned boot appeared on the step, then a pale hand in a black buttoned sleeve reached imperiously for that of the gentleman waiting to receive it, followed by the whole lady, a stout matron in black bombazine and a hat with a black widow's veil attached.

There were no half measures in her mourning either.

This forbidding personage was Mrs. Augusta Calvert, relict of the great Confederate hero General Clovis Calvert, who died gallantly at Spotsylvania Courthouse, leading a charge against the enemy. Mrs.

Calvert was greeted with applause from the assembled throng. She vouchsafed a grim nod in acknowledgment.

But the appearance most eagerly awaited at the moment must have been that of General Calvert's interesting twenty-year-old daughter, Lorena Calvert. In addition to being the vessel of her father's sacred memory and the embodiment of the pure spirit of the cause, the young lady is said to be very pretty. Newspapers at other locations honored by a visit from the late general's family invariably refer to her as the Fair Visitor. No doubt she is both prim and vain.

She should follow her mother onto the platform any moment, and we shall judge for ourselves whether the adulation she has received so far is deserved.

We waited.

Where was she? Why did she not come forth? Surely not overcome by shyness and a delicate feminine reluctance to show herself in public. She ought to be used to it by now; she's been received and feted in every town between Baltimore and Natchez.

Long minutes are passing. Her mother is looking at the carriage doors as if she disapproves of them. Whither Miss Calvert?

I recalled what I had heard of the Fair Visitor's history. Born in Richmond, where her mother had repaired to her family home some months before. It was expected the general would summon his faithful wife when a convenient opportunity occurred for her to visit camp. But Miss Calvert was a babe of but three months when her father was wounded at Spotsylvania and a messenger came to Mrs. Calvert in the dead of night to bid her make haste with the child to her husband's side, as the worst was feared and the general longed for a glimpse of his only child.

Mrs. Calvert obeyed the summons, and she and the babe arrived in time for the general to bless his daughter and hold her in his arms briefly. He died just after handing her back to her mother and thus was the last mortal the general touched on earth. This fact accounts for the reverence and respect that greet Miss Lorena Calvert everywhere she goes.

I attempted to compose in my mind something suitably fawning for the paper, along the lines of "Miss Calvert has grown up the protecting shadow of her father's venerated memory and sheltered by her mother's protecting love. She is famed for her modest yet graceful acceptance of the tributes of veneration accorded to the daughter of one of the bravest and most illustrious heroes of the South. She stands before us an image of girlish purity, the embodiment of a noble cause, the living memorial to the fallen hero."

Sickening.

At Harvard my fellow students circulated a different story, claiming General Calvert had been shot by his own mutinous and exhausted men who wanted to go home, tired of fighting on half rations of cornmeal infested with weevils, reduced to using bayonets for lack of ammunition, felled like mown wheat to die where they lay or in filthy field hospitals, finally confused beyond endurance by conflicting orders from General Lee and General Longstreet, who could not agree whether the best strategy was to encircle or attack the Army of the Potomac.

Naturally I could include none of this in my report. Such information would cast a shadow over the arrival of our Fair Visitor, the most newsworthy event to take place in Grafton in two years, and agitate, upset, and infuriate the greater part of the *Messenger's* readers. Worst of all, the Confederate sensibilities of my typesetter, Reuben, would be mortally offended.

At Harvard, at my mother's particular wish, I read widely about the slave trade, the war, its causes and battles, the misery and destruction, death and ruin inflicted everywhere. I had read enough newspaper accounts of the battle at Spotsylvania and the general's indecision, if not incompetence, to sympathize with any of the poor beggars who took it into their heads to shoot him.

Though I do not speak of it, I am no more a friend to the cause or Southern rights than my mother is, and, thanks to my study of it, am wholly unable to regard it in any favorable light. I reminded myself I have chosen to be a newspaperman and am determined to make a success of the *Messenger*. My patrimony was invested in the undertaking. That will mean writing respectfully of this visit.

Where *is* Miss Calvert? Her mother has been conversing with the mayor and his wife for nearly ten minutes. This sun will broil everyone soon. The children have ceased waving their flags. Enthusiasm wanes.

Hark. A foot on the step, a hand reached forth. A ruffle could be seen. People shifted and craned their necks, the veterans stood to attention, Miss Calvert emerged on the train steps, and the mayor bowed and held out his hand. A slender form appeared, clad in pale blue. Bonnie Blue, Teeny said that particular shade is called, and told me Miss Calvert always wears it. The bonnet hid her face as she accepted the hand and descended. Cheering broke forth. A salute was fired, making her start and look up.

It must be conceded, she is rather pretty. Extraordinary, with such a mother. Her brown hair was gathered up in curls behind her neck, and a cameo brooch fastened a lace collar modestly at her throat. Her eyes were large, and for a moment, she surveyed the scene like a trapped animal until, nudged by her mother, she forced a smile. At her mother's side, she nodded her head to the left and right. A dragon and a swan. She raised her parasol, a lacy affair, against the sun. Mrs. Calvert said something from the side of her mouth, and Miss Calvert sighed and retracted her parasol.

Two boys were dressed in small Confederate uniforms. They each had a drum and, at a signal from the mayor, began to beat a march.

The veterans started stepping in place, and after a few minutes of banging, and a flourish with the drumsticks, the boys stepped forward, turned about-face, and led off in the direction of the hotel, where a welcoming collation waited. The veterans fell in behind the boys, and the mayor, momentarily uncertain whether he was meant to be marching as well, stepped in time lightly as he offered his arm to the widow

Calvert. The brother of Mrs. Calvert marched too, albeit with less certainty in his feet.

The stout widow Calvert had no intention of marching in time to drums. She gave both men a furious look as if to say, *Stop that prancing at once!* The mayor's feet were still. She took his arm and then her brother's and swept majestically forward, deigning not to look at the eager faces on either side as she passed with her entourage of the town dignitaries. Oh, the fathomless dignity of a general's relict!

The Charbonneaus followed, then the Marshalls.

But there was an oversight! Miss Calvert was left alone. Was she meant to follow without an escort? No one in the crowd seemed to have any idea what to do. The music continued. The children stared. Everyone stared. The Fair Visitor had been overlooked. She looked about her uncertainly, and I saw she was blushing with embarrassment. No, she was actually on the verge of tears. Having sisters, I could recognize the look.

I pushed forward quickly and offered my arm. "Miss Calvert, if you will allow me the honor of escorting you to the hotel."

She looked at me gratefully. I was right about the verge of tears; her large brown eyes were brimming.

"You may wish to raise your parasol, as the sun is very strong," I said as we walked slowly toward the hotel.

"Thank you! My mother thought it was wrong to obscure my face, but it is such a relief from the sun," she said with a sigh, and the lacy object unfurled again. She put her hand lightly on my arm.

There is always a curious sense of intimacy that comes from being half under a girl's parasol.

"We haven't been introduced," she murmured.

"Forgive me! I'm Ben Marshall, proprietor of the *Grafton Messenger*. My mother is er . . . one of the Ladies Committee in charge of the festivities." I thought mention of my mother might vouch for my respectability.

Though it is true my mother's skills at arranging handsome floral tributes made her an invaluable member of the Ladies Committee, she declined at first to take any part whatsoever in welcoming the relatives of a Southern general. She loathes what is often referred to as the sacred cause. She was a Quaker from an abolitionist family before she married my father. But she is rich, and she is prominent, and she is the mother of the proprietor of the newspaper, for whom she would walk over hot coals to promote his welfare. She arranged the flowers and pleaded indisposition.

She is also good at hiding her true sentiments behind the frigid mask of dignity—not altogether unlike Mrs. Calvert, now that I think of it—an expression that lends itself to misinterpretation, which is her object. My father died after returning from the war a broken man. He fought for the Union, though my parents disagreed on the necessity of war. She was devoted to him. But he is dead, and a widow is a widow. Some of the ladies believed her rigid demeanor hid a sense of shame for having a Unionist husband. For that too they honor her.

What is a woman without a sense of shame?

They mistake my dear mother in every particular.

"How interesting to our readers, to know I have had the honor of handing you to your chair at lunch," I said.

"My mother is so anxious to behave with the propriety expected of her that she is sometimes obliged to act without reference to . . . to me. Really, it is quite natural and understandable."

"Entirely understandable," I said. *The old dragon is jealous of her daughter, then.*

"My father's legacy must be guarded. The veterans everywhere hold him dear in their hearts, and Mother and I are but symbols of his devotion to the glorious cause."

"Mmm, very symbolic, to be sure."

"Sometimes the old men try to kiss my hand," she said. "I hate that!"

"What about the young ones?"

"My mother allows no young ones near me."

"I expect that tonight at the ball, Miss Calvert, there will be legions of young men fighting to dance with you, and it is very hard to dance with a partner at the other end of the room, particularly if it's a waltz. It will be a most delightful evening, the ball to be held in the open air, on the jetty. There are Chinese lanterns strung everywhere, ready for lighting, a stand has been built for the band, who, I hear, have been ordered to play till dawn. There is to be an elegant supper, and a special dance card bearing your name in gold has silk tassels and the names of almost every young man in town, with a few of the veterans' names thrown in for good measure."

She sighed. "It sounds delightful. Alas, my mother does not allow me to dance."

"For what reason? You seemed formed for dancing, Miss Calvert!"

"My mother objects to it most strenuously. She is adamant that my sacred waist not be encircled by impudent male arms. I am a mere vessel, Mr. Marshall. A vessel of Southern purity. A living monument to my father."

"Rather like a human sacrifice," I remarked. Then regretted it. This was impertinent, but really, a pretty girl not allowed to dance . . .

She slowed her steps. "Mr. Marshall, I would give twenty years of my life if I were allowed to attend a ball just once and not be obliged to sit on the sidelines with the old ladies and chaperones and watch the other girls whirling in time to the music and laughing and having fun while my attention is claimed by old men in smelly uniforms at whom I must smile. I dream of waltzing! I long, long, long to dance!"

Poor girl! So that's how it was. I thought for a minute. "You shall dance."

"How? My mother's eyesight is excellent. I can never avoid her notice."

"Let us consider . . . At what time does your mother retire?"

"We are always in our chamber by nine. Mamma takes a little tea, we say our prayers, and then she retires with her Bible until she falls asleep. But she often wakes in the night."

"Tea . . . hmm . . . Would you be willing to assist her slumbers a little?"

"What do you mean?"

"Laudanum, Miss Calvert. Most efficacious in assisting peaceful repose. Doctor Joshua Vann, the town physician, is a friend, and he would oblige me with a few drops in such a good cause. They could be put in her tea."

Her beautiful eyes opened wider. "Mr. Marshall! You don't propose I poison my mother! For shame!"

"I propose only this. That you retire as your mother wishes but put the drops in her tea and don't yourself undre—er . . . prepare to sleep. When she is sleeping soundly, go to the servants' stairs, which are at the back of the hotel. I'll be waiting at the bottom, and we can go to a place I know within hearing distance of the jetty, where we cannot be seen. It's a field where slaves once camped when they were marched south. We will put it to a happier purpose, and I will teach you to dance."

"I couldn't possibly!"

"Here is the hotel. Your mother would only enjoy a pleasant night's repose, and would be most unlikely to wake, if I am correct about the effects of laudanum."

"No, I couldn't . . ."

"Think of the waltz . . . Miss Calvert, where is your spirit?"

Then we entered the dining room, and Mrs. Calvert boomed, "Lorena, come here at once! Your seat is here!" She really was quite horrid and glowering.

"The waltz . . . ," I whispered.

"I will, Mr. Marshall! I will!"

"Ten o'clock."

Dr. Joshua provided the laudanum. I managed to conceal it in a posy of purloined flowers from the station. I gave a penny to one of the little girls to hand it to Miss Calvert as the assemblage was rising at the conclusion of lunch and many long speeches. Mrs. Calvert bestowed a sort of frosty grimace that I expect was meant to be a smile on my little messenger. Miss Calvert looked up and caught my eye. I bowed significantly, and she looked down at the nosegay and started suddenly. She must have seen the little brown bottle. She looked at me. I nodded.

Would she dare?

At eight the lanterns were lit, and the jetty was soon aswish with ball gowns as the music commenced, almost drowned by excited chatter and laughter as young men in evening coats rushed to sign their names on girls' dance cards. I saw Miss Calvert, in a different Bonnie Blue gown, sitting trapped between three deaf old ladies who shouted at each other across her. The widow Calvert and her brother repulsed every attempt by the young men to obtain an introduction and permission to dance with the Fair Visitor. At quarter to nine the widow Calvert stood and beckoned Lorena. Lorena submissively followed her.

At quarter past nine I was watching the servants' staircase when a maid carried a tea tray up to the Calverts' rooms.

At ten minutes to ten, the lamp in Mrs. Calvert's room dimmed. Then the window went black.

Fifteen minutes later, the door at the top of the stairs opened, and there was a pause as if someone was hovering, perhaps wondering if she really dared. Then there was a swish of silk and Lorena's quick footsteps on stairs. "Mamma is snoring!" She giggled nervously. I took her hand, and we crept past the trading post with its lights and the gay scene on the jetty. The field where the slaves used to rest was shielded by some low trees, but we heard the music clearly.

I turned her to face me and bowed. "Miss Calvert, may I have the honor of this dance?"

"What do I do?"

"Put your hand here on my shoulder, and I take your other hand like this. Then put my arm around you here . . . Now step with me for a moment in time to the music . . . one two three, one two three, now step back, now to the side, now forward . . . and again . . . Now we'll take a little turn . . ."

She was rather stiff at first, but little by little she relaxed and was soon following me as we waltzed round the field. The band played a mazurka next, and we tried that, and soon she was laughing too hard to dance. Next we did a polka. And then another waltz in the starlit field. And another and another.

There were faint signs of the dawn when we finally stopped. I didn't want to let go of her. "I fear we've missed the supper," I said.

"Mr. Marshall . . . Ben . . . thank you from the bottom of my heart! It was the most delightful thing I've ever experienced." Her hair had come loose, and curls tumbled over the shoulder of her modest ball dress. She had a string of pearls at her throat, and her eyes were shining, her cheeks flushed.

We had just danced to a stop, and she was still in my arms.

"You are the most beautiful creature I have ever seen," I said truthfully. We stared into each other's eyes, and I leaned forward to kiss her. She tried to draw back, and then she put her arms round my neck and kissed me with all her heart. I wanted to hold her there forever.

"You may think me fast but . . . thank you for that too!" she sighed, drawing away. "I will never forget this night, Ben, not as long as I live. Now I must go! Mamma mustn't see me still in my ball gown."

"Lorena . . . how shall I see you again? What could I do to find favor with your mother?"

Her happy smile died. "I fear we shan't meet again, Ben. We leave tomorrow. Mamma has determined I'm to marry a certain man and gives me no peace. I've resisted as long as I could, but he is rich and has agreed she will make her home with us. It is my duty to see that she is provided for—we have no money of our own."

"Lorena, what about your own heart?"

"My heart does not signify, Ben. Please say nothing more. I must not shirk my duty to my mother. I think she is not well, doctors are expensive, and we have no money. I must do the only thing I can."

We were both silent as I escorted her back to the hotel. At the bottom of the servants' stairs, she turned to me and entreated, "Ben, please, when you write your story for the newspaper, you won't mention dancing with me in the field, will you? It would cause me no end of trouble, and what I must do . . . I was almost reconciled before, but now it seems so hard. So hard." There were tears in her eyes again.

"I promise." I could scarcely speak.

She leaned forward and kissed me quickly on the cheek. "Thank you . . . I'll remember . . . until the day I die."

She gave a choked sob and flew away up the servants' stairs.

I watched the Calvert ladies depart the next day. Through the waving flags I saw her on the platform, waving graciously as the whistle blew and the train began to move. Her eyes searched the crowd and found mine and held them until the train disappeared.

I walked slowly back to my office and wrote four different accounts of the Calvert ladies' visit. I tore them all to shreds.

That night I drank most of a bottle of whiskey and wrote a fifth, which I published.

CHAPTER 41

PRISCILLA MARSHALL VANN

August 1899

It's been a busy time since Ben's death last spring. First there was the funeral, and the letters of condolence to answer, then his clothes and possessions to sort out and decide what his two boys wish to keep of their father's and what ought to be given away. But I can no longer put off a decision about the newspaper. I've been trying to decide whether I can do as he wished and continue the *Messenger* myself, at least until his two boys are finished at Harvard, or look for someone to buy it. Ben made a great success of the paper, and it is a daunting prospect for a woman to attempt it. But since my husband, Dr. Joshua Vann, died, I know that keeping busy is the only sure way to survive bereavement. My children are half-grown now—Sarah is fourteen and Evaline sixteen—and need me less than before.

"You can manage the paper, Teeny," Ben insisted when he was dying. "You'll see." The use of my old name made me cry. I miss him terribly. He was the best of brothers, and we were always close, even after he married Marietta. We understood each other perfectly. Some people said he might as well have been married to his newspaper. The *Messenger* was his life. Marietta, fortunately, understood this about him. She seemed to understand nearly everything. It seems cruel that she died of influenza so early in their marriage, especially as Marietta's older sister, who had once been engaged to Ben, also died before they could marry.

Ben had a vision for the *Messenger*, that it should be not just the instrument of news. He was very good at ferreting out old stories of the valley—such as the eagle man and the ghostly Indian child—and writing about what they meant, what they said about us in the valley. These were quite popular with the readers and made the paper a huge success.

I've been going through boxes and boxes of the stories, rereading long-forgotten ones as well as stories that he never actually published, usually because there was some thread left hanging.

I never appreciated before how much his best stories seemed to concentrate on the saddest aspects of the war—or what one old lady, Mrs. Preston Drumheller, always referred to as "the late unpleasantness." General Calvert's daughter, who once visited Grafton, was the subject of one such story. I believe the poor girl was hauled around like a zoo exhibit to enable funds for her mother to live on.

Ben had saved a clipping from a New Orleans paper that Miss Lorena Calvert's marriage to a rich industrialist in Louisiana took place at Christmas in 1885, and another from 1888 that the former Miss Lorena Calvert, General Calvert's daughter, died in childbirth. These clippings were in a file with a copy of a story he'd published on the occasion of a visit paid to Grafton by the widow of General Calvert and Miss Lorena several months before her marriage.

It was one of his finest, and we both owe a debt to our mother for her insistence on our northern education, which taught us classic Greek literature. Ben's story drew a parallel with the Greek story of Agamemnon, who sacrificed his daughter Iphigenia to ensure his success in the Trojan War, and the widows, sweethearts, daughters of anyone caught up in the conflict, like our aunt Catherine Stuart or Malvina Drumheller, who, together with their hopes, dreams, and love, were sacrificed to the Civil War.

Few people knew the story or understood the comparison as he intended. He all but described the blood dripping hot and reeking under the sacrificial altar, while people stopped him in the street to shake his hand and praise the piece as a paean to that will-o'-the-wisp, Pure Southern Womanhood.

There was a popular column in the paper devoted to notices of who in Grafton was coming and going and for what purpose. For many summers it was noted there that Miss Mercy Merriman and Mrs. Malvina Drumheller would visit Aunt Catherine, Mrs. Lawrence Stuart, in Lexington until the old ladies grew too infirm to travel, and then Aunt Catherine herself passed away. She always refused to move from the house where she and Lawrence had lived after their marriage. She never did find out what happened to him, whether he'd been killed or taken prisoner or died of typhoid. She must have hoped Uncle Lawrence would find his way back to her like our father found his way home, but he never did.

There was the obituary of our mother, Comfort, praising her as a shining example of devotion to her family, quoting the psalm about a virtuous woman and referring to Mama's abolitionist sentiments that she never compromised.

He wrote about horses and hunting dogs, hymns and dance tunes, Indian songs and the old carols people brought from England, which they still sing in the churches at Christmas, the old banjos and dulcimers and a very old fiddle still in the Vann family made by their Welsh ancestors.

One of the last pieces Ben wrote was about the hotel at Rehoboth Springs, and how it's changed since the Drumhellers first built it. It's becoming rather fashionable, a proper summer watering hole, on a par with Saratoga. Distinguished visitors are now numbered among the clientele. Last year a very rich family came down from Philadelphia in their private railway car, and another came from New York. Senators have graced its halls, and a foreign opera singer and her entourage spent some weeks at the end of an exhausting American tour last summer. It always amused Ben that there was an element of Marie Antoinette playing at being a milkmaid in the way these visitors come to enjoy rustic pursuits—hikes and dances and concerts and buggy rides up to Frog Mountain. Last September, a procession of motorcars carried a party of guests up there for the Blackberry Picnic.

"You must write about such things, the stuff of our lives here in Grafton," he insisted. He's wanted the paper to be a chronicle of this valley, so that when we, its inhabitants, die, a little of us is left behind to live in our stories. "That's what history is, Teeny. People's stories," he always said. "They'll make the *Messenger* outlive me. Say you'll take it over, Teeny. Promise."

I don't know whether I can do it, but he's left me no choice. I must try.

AUTHOR'S NOTE

I am a displaced native of both Virginia and Tennessee now living in what my English ancestors in America once regarded as the mother country, and it wasn't until I came to live on this side of the Atlantic that I saw American history from a different perspective. The longer I was away from the places where I grew up, the more clearly I saw them in my mind. Appalachian sunsets, in particular, remain an indelible memory. And the idea of a book—a trilogy—set in a fictional river valley somewhere between the mountains on the Tennessee/Virginia border began to take shape years ago. It was not unconnected to a lifelong fondness for history, a budding interest in genealogy, and a growing curiosity about my female ancestors. They'd confronted the challenge of the New World's wilderness—how had they managed to survive?

Their names and dates, discovered in family Bibles or census records or remembered by older relatives, begged intriguing questions about the world they lived in, how they might have seen it and their place in it, and the human stories behind the dry, basic facts. They were typical of women whose lives, actions, and courage were woven into the fabric of America yet whose stories rarely make it into the history books.

I began *The Valley*, the first book of the Valley Trilogy, with characters who experienced the New World of America from a European perspective, from an enslaved African perspective, and, finally, from the perspective of a "half-blood," the son of a European long hunter and Native American mother, a character who straddled the old world of America and its native peoples and the encroaching New World and the incomers from elsewhere. Each time I sat down at my desk to write about them, I saw a little more clearly the place that had been Sophia Grafton de Marechal's English inheritance, the fictional royal patent of Virginia land, somewhere between the Blue Ridge and the Appalachian Mountains; a great, winding river; wooded mountains rolling and fading into the distant horizon; the deer and bears and eagles; a great rock called the Old Man of the Mountain, standing guard above the Bowjay Valley.

A friend passed on a singularly apposite and encouraging quote from Victor Hugo at just the right moment, when I feared I had been overly ambitious: "A writer is a world trapped inside a person," Hugo wrote, neatly summing up my Bowjay Valley and its people.

I doubt people and their fundamental concerns have changed much during the course of human history, though the circumstances in which they live fluctuate and determine their actions and priorities. The women I wrote about were busy with the same things that occupy women in any period of history—matters of the heart, family concerns, children, birth, and death. The last two, childbirth and death, were often grimly and directly linked for a great many women. Throughout most of history, until relatively recent advances in maternity care, women's lives had an extra, precarious dimension. The Angel of Death lurked in the shadows at any wedding, hovered over pairings-off, was ever present in the corners of birthing rooms, ready to snatch mothers, wives, sisters, daughters, and their infants.

But my characters were also impacted and shaped by distant events beyond the Bowjay Valley: the institution of slavery and resistance to it, the Revolution, the Great Awakening and other religious movements, and of course the Civil War that left female casualties on both sides in its wake—widows, a Confederate general's daughter sacrificed to a lost cause, a rape victim, metaphorical sisters of Iphigenia.

I hope that a reader who completes all three volumes of this trilogy will perhaps be inspired to return to the first book for another look at how it all began, make the connections, and gain a fresh insight into the historical process. And as one of my characters says at the end of this book, "That's what history is. People's stories."

ACKNOWLEDGMENTS

As ever, I gratefully acknowledge a debt to the many people who ensured that my sometimes unwieldy manuscript became an actual book.

Enormous thanks are due to my agent, Jane Dystel of Dystel, Goderich & Bourret LLC, who is active in encouraging and forwarding the careers of the authors taken on by the agency. Her support at every turn is simply invaluable. Jane is unstintingly generous with her time, encouragement, and advice and is equally blessed with a rare sensitivity for knowing which, if any, of these would prove beneficial at the moment. I rely on her judgment and have been grateful for her sound, practical advice on many occasions. I am slightly in awe of her ability to instantly resolve any issue with tact and diplomacy, and I readily acknowledge her ability to temper my rashly optimistic approach to deadlines with a healthy dose of reality. I appreciate her unfailing support for me and my work more than I can say.

My thanks also to all the team at Dystel, Goderich & Bourret LLC who contribute to the smooth handling of my books and their associated concerns. In particular, I want to thank Miriam Goderich, who expertly vets my contracts and is generous with helpful editorial advice.

Yet again, I want to express my appreciation to the publishing team at Amazon and Lake Union. They are, one and all, wonderful to work with. First of all, huge thanks to Jodi Warshaw, my executive editor at Lake Union, for her unfailing support, engagement, availability, good humor, and what I can only describe as heroic reserves of patience and understanding of the writing process, given the time it took me to complete a very long manuscript.

It was a pleasure to work once again with developmental editor Charlotte Herscher, who has a finely tuned editorial sixth sense and possesses the ability to get straight to the heart of a book and transform it into a better version of itself. I know from experience I can trust her editorial judgment implicitly.

My thanks to copyeditor Laura Petrella, who, I also know from experience, has an eagle eye in the best possible way. She did a truly impressive job, letting no mistake or inconsistency past her.

I am grateful to Phyllis DeBlanche for her also eagle-eyed proofreading skills and for catching any last-minute "glitches."

To production manager Nicole Pomeroy and marketing managers Devan Hanna and Marlene Kelly, my thanks for supporting the book with your expertise and professionalism.

My deep appreciation to Rosanna Brockley, design director, and designer Shasti O'Leary Soudant for patiently bearing with my suggestions, which must have felt at times like backseat driving, and for searching for just the right image for the cover design until she found it. I am thrilled with the wonderful cover Shasti produced.

Finally I want to thank Gabriella Dumpit, author relations manager, for always being available, for being in touch, and for all she does to keep things running smoothly behind the scenes.

An author could not be more fortunate in having such an amazing team behind her books, but thanks are also due to my family, my biggest fans, my proudest and least critical supporters. My husband, Roger Low, ensures I have a quiet place to write and uninterrupted time in which to do it. He bears with late dinners and my distracted thinking and understands when I withdraw into my study to work in what I call peace and quiet and he calls "lockdown." His sense of humor never fails to buoy me up, and his calm in the face of domestic crisis is extraordinary. He makes everything seem possible. Our children and grandchildren and their partners and co-parents are a continuous, lively, and affectionate presence, who help me keep everything in perspective. The family is my rock, and everything I write, I write for them.

ABOUT THE AUTHOR

Photo © 2008 Nigel Sutton

Helen Bryan is a Virginia native who grew up in Tennessee. After graduating from Barnard College, she moved to England, where she studied law and was a barrister for ten years before devoting herself to writing full-time.

A member of the Inner Temple, Bryan is the author of five previous books: the World War II novel *War Brides*; the historical novel *The Sisterhood*; the biography *Martha Washington: First Lady of Liberty*, which won an Award of Merit from the Colonial Dames of America; and the legal handbook *Planning Applications and Appeals*. *The Mountain* is the second book in a trilogy, following *The Valley*, based on Bryan's childhood stories of ancestors who settled in Virginia and Maryland before Tennessee became a state.